THE MISTRESS MURDERS

The Perfect Poison Murders, Book 3
A Georgian Mystery

E.L. Johnson

ARE YOU SIGNED UP FOR DRAGONBLADE'S BLOG?

You'll get the latest news and information on exclusive giveaways, exclusive excerpts, coming releases, sales, free books, cover reveals and more.

Check out our complete list of authors, too!

No spam, no junk. That's a promise!

Sign Up Here

www.dragonbladepublishing.com

Dearest Reader;

Thank you for your support of a small press. At Dragonblade Publishing, we strive to bring you the highest quality Historical Romance from some of the best authors in the business. Without your support, there is no 'us', so we sincerely hope you adore these stories and find some new favorite authors along the way.

Happy Reading!

CEO, Dragonblade Publishing

Additional Dragonblade books by Author E.L. Johnson

The Perfect Poison Murders
The Strangled Servant (Book 1)
The Poisoned Clergyman (Book 2)
The Mistress Murders (Book 3)

CHAPTER ONE

Hertford, September 1806

IT ALL STARTED with a kiss, Poppy realized.

From the light touch of her lips on his, she had stood, wide-eyed as a deer when she had kissed him months ago. In response, he had stiffened, shocked at her unladylike forwardness, and stared as she blatantly confessed her feelings for him.

Constable Henry Dyngley. A man who had helped restore her reputation and good name, and encouraged her in crime solving. Since then she had ruined their friendship with a kiss. No matter how politely he responded, it was done, and she could not take it back.

But then weeks later he had called at the parsonage as she was getting ready for bed and had kissed her in the doorway, stunning her to the core. His kiss had stolen her breath away, and within a moment he had fled, like a dark specter in the night.

But that was months ago, and this was now. Summer had faded and wrinkled yellow leaves flew against the windows of the parsonage, reminding Poppy that within a matter of hours, she would be on her way to a new life.

On any other day, she would have gone through the routine of rising, dressing, and keeping her aunt company, reading her uncle's newspaper, walking with their maid, Betsey, into town to the farmers' market, or feeding the family's chickens in the yard behind the parsonage.

Instead, she now packed a bag for London, about to interview to be a companion for a lady she'd never met before in her life.

Thanks to a sudden whim of initiative, she had recently shown some very unladylike female independence. She had answered an advertisement in the paper, applying for the position of a lady's companion. Not that she had expected a response, but then it had come in the lady's own hand.

Dear Miss Morton,

I read your application with interest. I have been looking for a suitable lady's companion for some time and wonder if you would care to come to London for an interview? I would very much like to meet you. Please call on me on the afternoon of Thursday, September fourth, at two o'clock.

Best wishes,
Miss Beatrice Hayes

Poppy had re-read the letter a dozen times. She knew it by heart. Those polite words meant everything to her. The letter symbolized a change. It offered her the chance to stand on her own two feet, to make her own way in the world. It gave her the opportunity to search for her mother, whose identity had been hidden from her for years.

But most of all, it gave her the chance to get away from Constable Henry Dyngley, who had not spoken a word to her since their kiss months ago.

She had no business kissing him anyway. At the time, he had been engaged to another woman only to have her be proven a thief *and* a murderess. But despite all that, Poppy had kissed him, and he had kissed her back.

They had kissed. Properly kissed. Not just a polite peck on the cheek or a mistaken brush of the lips by accident. She still remembered the touch of his hands on her waist, the warmth of his lips on hers.

But then he had left, not saying a word. She had been excited, thrilled, and filled with delicious anticipation that made her aware of her own femininity as she walked through the parsonage's simple rooms, wondering when he might pay a call. But now, months later, she had not had a single social visit from him. Not even a note. As the days passed, she grew duller and eventually despaired of ever hearing from him again.

Never mind Dyngley. If all went well in London, she might be asked to stay. And better yet, be paid for her trouble. But all that was secondary to the true reason for her going: to find her mother.

For her entire life, Poppy's mother's circumstances had been a closely guarded secret. Having been told since she was a child that her mother was dead, Poppy had never given it a second thought, beyond wishing she could have known her. But an intruder at the parsonage months ago had ransacked her uncle's office, and in cleaning up his effects, Poppy and Constable Dyngley had come across her uncle's letters to her mother.

The discovery had shocked her: to find that her mother was alive and well, and was even exchanging regular correspondence with her uncle. She had stolen some of the letters and kept them hidden away in the writing desk in her room, where she read them each night before bed. Each night she memorized the swirling elegant script of her mother's handwriting and wondered why.

Why had her mother never written to her? Why had she never attempted to contact her? Didn't she want to know her own daughter? These questions plagued Poppy's mind relentlessly.

Through her own discreet inquiry, she had learned that her mother, Celeste Morton, was living in London as a mistress. Poppy didn't want to believe it. But she also refused to believe that her mother did not wish to know her. So now all that was left was to go to London and search for her. Then she would have answers.

But the weight of that decision fell like a heavy cloak that threatened to choke her. To leave her relatives, her home, Hertford, and everything she knew. To throw aside familiarity and comfort in search of something new made her stomach turn over with butterflies. Poppy's hands trembled as she folded a burgundy dress, now faded from washing. She fumbled it into a mishappen wad of clothing, dropped it on the floor, picked it up, and began to fold it again.

"Oh, give it here, you never were good at folding, Poppy." Her Aunt Rachel took it from her, folded the dress properly, and placed it in a bag.

Poppy stood by, watching her aunt work. Flinging some articles of clothing out of the bag and replacing them with others, Aunt Rachel's deft hands made short work of it.

"You'll never be the same once you go to London, my girl." Aunt Rachel declared, in turns both sour and sweet. "But then you must come back and tell me of the latest fashions."

That made Poppy smile.

Aunt Rachel tied her bag with a firm knot. "Why you are going, I do not know. It's not like you are in want of adventure."

Poppy glanced at her aunt, who stood with her hands on her hips, glaring at the offensive overnight bag.

"I..." Poppy started.

"Oh, never mind, I know why. Reginald thinks you want a little excitement in your life, but I know better. You're trying to get away from him, aren't you?"

Poppy glanced at her aunt.

"Don't give me those wide eyes, you know very well who I mean. Constable Henry Dyngley. But I don't see why. He spent all that time with you, looking into those thefts and the situation behind that clergyman's death." She sniffed, a sure sign of her disapproval. "But that's all done now. His fiancée was behind it all, and she's gone now."

"It's not like she's in jail, Aunt. She's on the run," Poppy pointed out.

"Exactly. And if she has any sense in that head of hers, she'll stay far away from here. But I don't see why you should leave, Poppy, especially when Constable Dyngley is single. He's a free man."

Poppy's shoulders slumped. "He is not, Aunt."

"What do you mean?" Aunt Rachel sat, the bed creaking beneath her weight.

"When we last spoke, he said he was not free to choose his own bride, however much he wanted to." She swallowed at the uncomfortable memory. So much hope had been dashed at those simple words. "He needs an heiress, Aunt. A woman with money. A handsome dowry. His family's estate needs it to survive."

"Well." Aunt Rachel took this into consideration. "I'm not one to speak my mind, but I dare say they would do better to sell the land. If they cannot afford such a living then there is no shame in selling. They could retrench and move somewhere else, like Hertford. Just think, we could be neighbors."

Poppy disagreed. From the way Henry had talked, it would be like losing a limb in battle for him to give up the family estate. He loved it and would do anything to keep it going, at the cost of having to be mercenary in choosing a wife. He had as good as intimated as much in their last meeting. He needed a rich woman, nothing else would do. He had no time to waste chasing after his own dreams, hopes, and desires when his family's estate was near ruin. But then they had kissed, and everything changed. The memory of it cast a shadow over her every thought of him.

"I don't think he would agree, Aunt. He loves the estate," Poppy said.

"Never mind him. Just as well you're off on a new adventure then, eh? Nothing to make the heart grow fonder than a bit of distance, I say. Heiress or not, he'll come running when he hears that you've gone to London. Mark my words, I wouldn't be surprised if he appeared where you were staying, just to pay his respects."

Poppy smiled at her relative. She loved her aunt dearly and wished her romantic fancies would come true, but Poppy had taken on some of her uncle's pragmatism and knew that she had been a burden to her relatives for some time.

She had already observed that she was gaining the reputation of a poor spinster and could not bear it. She had overheard more than one sly remark about her unmarried state and observed an increasing number of pitying looks from their neighbors. It was such a shame poor Poppy was unmarried, but, they whispered none too quietly, perhaps she would continue to do good works. Even their former houseguest, the young clergyman Mr. Ingleby, was on the cusp of becoming engaged to her former acquaintance, Jane, and was now off to take the living in the nearby village of Waterford.

"Aunt, if I have to see the ladies' pitying looks a moment longer, I shall scream." Poppy sat in her writing chair. She leaned against the hard wooden table and looked at her aunt fondly.

"Pitying looks, who has been doing that?" Her aunt's face was dark.

"Mrs. Sutton. And Mrs. Alleyn, especially now that Louisa is engaged to Dr. Wilson."

"Well, you know Mrs. Alleyn. She always was one to brag about her good fortune. Never you mind what she says, no one pays attention to her anyway. I, for one, feel for that fiancé of Louisa's. The good doctor was out of his mind, I think, in proposing to her. I rather thought he had taken a fancy to you, but I guess not."

Poppy gave an unladylike snort. The Alleyns had been very determined in their pursuit of the young town doctor, and merciless in throwing their eldest daughter, Louisa, in his path. They had once viewed Poppy as a rival to his affections, but that was no longer the case.

She liked the young doctor, to be sure, but felt no stirrings of passion within her at the thought of him.

Not like Dyngley.

"What do you even know about this person you are seeing? This Miss Hayes." Aunt Rachel frowned at the overnight bag again.

"She lives in London, and she is in want of a companion. I suspect she is a spinster."

"Who is a spinster?" Her uncle popped his head into the room.

"A Miss Beatrice Hayes, the woman Poppy is going to meet."

"Ah." His pleasant expression clouded. "Rachel, would you give us a minute? I wish to speak to Poppy alone."

Her aunt rose and left the room, closing the thin wooden door behind her.

Faced with her serious uncle, Poppy quietly gripped the hard wooden back of the chair for support. "Yes?"

He glanced at the door for a second before asking, "Is this really what you want to do, Poppy?"

"What do you mean?"

"There is no need for you to go. You may think that having been involved in two criminal investigations may have given you an air of unrefinement, but I would not let it trouble you."

"Uncle?" she asked.

He ran a hand through his thinning gray hair. "I overheard you and your aunt talking. I know that the other girls your age are getting engaged and that you must worry about how it looks. I can well understand the pressure you must face, approaching twenty and yet still with no husband. But I have come to tell you that life will undoubtedly throw the right young man in your path, and time will take its course. There is no need to run off to London to escape your peers."

Poppy's cheeks turned pink. "That is not why I am going."

He carried on as if she had not spoken, sitting on the bed. "I know you have not had the greatest fortune as of late, but I think you are too good to dwell on it."

He referred to what she privately called her murders. Twice now she had solved a murder in the town, and twice she had worked alongside Constable Henry Dyngley to find the culprit. While she did not relish the circumstances that had brought them together, she would not have changed the fact that they met. He was the one man who gave her hope. His encouragement made her feel valued for using her mind to ferret out the truth.

"Uncle, I go because I must make something of myself," she said. "I am already a burden on you and Aunt Rachel—"

"Nonsense," he cut her off. "Who put that idea in your head?"

"I want to work. I want to earn a wage. I want to be useful."

"Don't be ridiculous. Your aunt worked. I did not raise you only to see you worn out in a workhouse before you reach twenty." He pushed his round horn spectacles up on his nose. "Poppy, there is no need for you to work. Don't you have everything you could want, here?"

She smiled at him and felt the thin folds of her too-short dress. Her dresses were hand-me-downs, donated by well-meaning neighbors whose daughters had outgrown them. Just once, she would love to have a dress that was made just for her or a necklace that wasn't a loan. The only books, pens, and writing implements she owned came from her uncle and aunt as gifts. The only money she had to her name was the irregular pin money that her aunt or uncle gave her for the market, and she always brought it right back. She had never known independence before, and it beckoned to her like a flame.

She wanted to reach for it, even if it burned.

"I want a change, Uncle. I want to see something of life. I want to go outside Hertfordshire."

"Life? See something of life." He snorted and shook his head. "You are far too inexperienced in the ways of the world to know what it is you want."

"I want to be useful," she said.

"You are useful. We need you," he told her.

"You don't. Aunt Rachel has her friends, the neighbors, she has no want of company."

"And what about me?" he asked. "What am I to do without

you?"

She gave him a fond smile and knew she had won. "I want to do this, Uncle. Please."

He scratched his stomach idly. "Don't you understand that if you do become a companion, it is likely that you will spend your life in service to another woman? You will have to cater to her whims and fancies, even if they counter your own. You may disagree and have fights, and you will have to hold your tongue in order to keep your situation, or find yourself out on the street."

"I will hold my tongue," she said.

"And yet do you not also see that as a companion, your status as an eligible young woman will be diminished in the eyes of the world? Men will dismiss you as a servant, and not see you as a potential wife." He winced at the words.

Poppy was not to be deterred. "I wish to go. And there is no reason to say that the woman will invite me to stay, or if we will even get on. We might dislike each other on sight, you never know." She grinned.

Her uncle crossed his arms. "When she meets you, she is sure to like your company, as I do." He frowned. "I can see your mind is made up. But Poppy, I do not want you to feel you have to do this, in order to prove something. There is no reason for you to leave."

There was every reason. She wanted to prove herself and have an adventure, but she also wanted to track down her mother. Poppy knew that her uncle had accepted payment from her mother for her upkeep, but they had not discussed it.

She did not wish to, for she suspected that it would construct a wall between them she'd rather not build. They needed to address it, but she did not feel strong enough to have that battle yet. She had been taught that confrontation was unbecoming in a young woman, and to be avoided at all costs. But it irked her. It kept her up at night, knowing that the relatives she trusted benefitted from her mother's generosity while keeping her locked in a lie. Anger and resentment warred with a fondness for the only family she knew. What to do?

"Uncle, I…" she started.

There was a knock at the door.

"Come in," Uncle Reginald said.

Their petite blonde housemaid, Betsey, opened the door. "There's Mr. Ingleby downstairs."

"What does that man want?" Uncle Reginald rose from the bed. "Very well, I'll be down directly. What was it, Poppy? You were saying something."

"Nothing, Uncle. It can wait."

THE NEXT DAY her aunt dropped a handful of guineas into her small cloth reticule and handed it to her, saying, "Don't lose sight of this, whatever you do. And don't be afraid to come back home. You never know, the lady might have already hired someone for the position, or you might find she was just playing a joke. These grand ladies are always entertaining themselves at the expense of others."

Poppy climbed into their cart beside her uncle. They had recently bought a carriage secondhand from his patroness, Lady Cameron, but he felt the use of such trappings was a bit much for an ordinary parish clergyman, and so preferred to use the cart.

They waited in the middle of town until the Euston Flyer came roaring up the main road. In a cloud of dust, there was a sharp call for passengers, and the horses were changed, passengers disembarked, a bag of letters was thrown down and exchanged with another, trunks were tied to the top of the strong-looking carriage, and Poppy's uncle was paying the coachman and then he faced her, his countenance serious as he took her hand.

"Uncle," Poppy started.

"What is it?" he asked. "Are you having second thoughts?"

"No. Not at all. But I have been false with you." Her throat felt tight.

"What do you mean?" he asked.

"I am going to London not just to be a lady's companion."

"Aha. I knew it. You are looking to escape that young man. Poppy, let us turn around now and start for home. I will guide you on how to deal with men, and it is through no fault of your own that you may be feeling befuddled, but I assure you—"

"I am going to find my mother," she said in a rush, the breath rushing out of her.

His mouth dropped open. "Your mother is dead."

"She is not. I found your letters, the ones written between you. I know she is alive."

His face grew red. "Those were private correspondence and had nothing to do with you."

"They have everything to do with me. They concern me. She asks about me. Why did you lie to me for all these years?"

He was silent, his blue eyes watery.

"I am going to find her. I have a right to see my own mother."

"No. Do not do this. You don't know what you're saying," he said.

"You try to shelter me, but I am sick of it. The parsonage is like a prison."

"You call our home a prison? When we have clothed you and looked after you?" he asked.

"I will not be kept in the dark any longer. I'm not a child. I want to see her, and this is the only way I can think of to do it."

"You deceived me." His bushy gray eyebrows knit.

"I am sorry for it, Uncle, but you have deceived me as well, for years."

"You don't understand," he began.

"That my mother is a mistress? A prostitute? I learned that months ago."

He blanched. "Poppy, I... don't know what to say. Come home and we will discuss this."

"No. We could have talked about this before, years ago, but ever since I learned the truth I've been too afraid to bring it up.

Now it's too late. You've said enough. Now it's my time to speak to her, without you." She climbed into the carriage, her bag in her arms, and slammed the door shut.

He stood there like a lost soul as the carriage took off with a jolt. She looked out the window at his disappearing form, standing in the dust as the carriage took her away from him, Hertford, and the only life she had ever known.

CHAPTER TWO

POPPY BLINKED BACK tears at the thought of hurting her uncle, for she loved him so. But she didn't see any other way around it and couldn't hide the true reason for her going any longer. As the carriage rattled across bumpy dirt roads, the green fields of Hertfordshire slowly gave way to more developments as they passed by more towns and fewer villages. She slept a lot of the way, and taking her aunt's advice, she disembarked each time the carriage stopped to change horses to stretch her legs and use the privy. Even so, the twenty-mile journey took hours. By the time the carriage came to a stop at Euston, she felt bone tired and sore from sitting so long. Poppy disembarked with the other passengers and held up a gloved hand to shade her eyes from the setting sun.

Something brushed by her and she turned, only to hold up cut strings where her reticule used to be. A little boy scampered past.

"Oy, you! Stop!" She ran after him.

The youth glanced back, his ginger hair catching the afternoon sun like fire, and disappeared into the crowd.

"Stop!" Poppy hefted her overnight bag over her shoulder, and threw herself into the crowd of people, jostling and pushing. "Excuse me, excuse me," she said, stepping into one person's path and then another.

"Oy, what are you doing?" A young man stepped in her way.

"That boy there with the red hair, he stole my reticule." She looked past him but could not see, the boy was gone. "He has taken all my money." Her chin trembled.

"If you need money, I know how you can make more."

"No, I must get to Miss Hayes, or I shall be late, and I do not know how I shall get there," she said, close to tears. "He has all my money."

"Miss Hayes? Miss Beatrice Hayes?" he repeated.

"Yes, do you know her?" Poppy's voice was tight. She willed herself not to cry.

The young man turned and ran. Poppy took off after him, pushing through people and stepping into puddles and mud, her boots sinking into holes and twisting on the uneven cobblestone streets, which had been stamped and trodden on until worn and smooth. She shoved and pushed and slipped around sellers, sneaking around dallying men and women, until she came upon the man, holding a ginger-haired youth in the air.

The boy squawked and kicked, his little legs slashing at the air as the young man held him aloft, his bright hair flaming red in the sun. "Let me go!" he shouted.

"Not 'til you give back what you stole." The young man looked to see Poppy, her hair hanging messily from her bonnet and cheeks ruddy from the sudden run, as she gasped to catch her breath.

"Girl. Is this the boy?"

"He stole my reticule," Poppy said, clutching her overnight bag tightly to her back.

"Give it here," the man told the boy, who spat at him.

"Give it, Jack, or I'll wallop you 'til your backside is black and blue," the man said.

The boy snarled a curse and dropped the reticule into a pile of horse dung that sat below him.

Poppy's mouth dropped open and she raced to pick it up, fearful of any other enterprising young person who might take it.

If this was to be her introduction to London, she did not think she would stay long.

The boy jeered. The young man's face grew stormy as he glared and dropped the boy, who landed on the pile of manure. The boy groaned and rose, brushing off his seat. He cursed at them both.

The young man cuffed the boy at the back of the head. "Get off with you. Don't let me see you doing that again, or I'll tell your mother."

The boy ran off, and the young man approached Poppy. He offered her a handkerchief, and she used it to clean off the stinking remnants of the manure, wrinkling her nose. She offered it back to him and he shook his head. "Keep it."

For the first time, she looked at her rescuer. He was a handsome youth, perhaps around her own age, or nearer twenty-five, for he had a weathered look that did not come from manual labor or from the passing of the seasons. His appearance bespoke of hard living, but despite the coarseness of his skin, which bore one or two pockmarks, he had a handsome countenance with light brown curling hair, smooth curled sideburns, a light brown jacket, and darker trousers, with a stone-colored waistcoat and a loosened beige cravat. But it was his blue eyes that caught her attention, for they glittered with intelligence.

"Thank you," she said.

"It's no trouble. What's your connection to Miss Hayes, then? A pretty thing like you? She a friend of yours?" He looked her up and down. "You from the country?"

Poppy blushed, for she knew that she must appear different to the London ladies he was used to. "What gave it away?"

They shared a knowing smile. *Everything*, his look said. Her clothes, her way of walking, the torn and stained cloth reticule she clutched to her breast in her gloved hand, the unfamiliar feel of the ground beneath her feet that trembled at the thunderous horses' hooves striking the streets.

Wagons, carriages, and people everywhere flowed by them

like water. Onions, fruit, horse manure, and coal fires sent streams of smoke in the air.

She said, "I've just arrived from Hertford. I'm on my way to see Miss Hayes."

"What's your business with her?" He stroked his chin.

"I'm interviewing to be her companion."

His face broke into a smile. "Her companion? That's a new one. I didn't think she struggled to find companions unless she's tired of the man already."

Poppy's eyebrows knit in confusion. "What man?"

"Never mind. You'll see."

A large middle-aged woman, in a shawl and dirty mobcap beneath a bonnet, put a firm hand on Poppy's arm. "What's a poor dear like you doing alone? Come, if there's work you want, you just come with me, I need a maid to serve in my house—"

"Let her be, you old bawd, this one's spoken for," the young man said, yanking Poppy free of the woman's meaty hand.

Poppy caught a very unladylike grimace on the lady's face as she was forced to release Poppy's arm.

"Come girl, I'll call you a hackney," the young man said.

"Call me a what?" Poppy clutched her overnight bag and her reticule closer to her body.

He laughed. "I mean to call a carriage for you, to take you to Miss Hayes."

"Oh. Thank you."

He whistled loudly and threw an arm in the air, hustling her toward a black carriage that pulled off to the side, its wheels spattered with mud. He opened the door, pulled down the foot stand, and taking her hand, helped her up into the carriage.

The young man told the carriage driver directions, and he stood back.

"Wait," Poppy said, leaning out of the window. "How do you know where Miss Hayes lives? How did you know her name? And who are you?"

The man grinned. "You're an inquisitive one, aren't you? I

know Miss Hayes very well. You just tell her that Tom Harris sent you to her." He told the carriage driver, "Drive on."

The carriage took off, and Poppy was whisked back into her seat, gripping her small reticule and overnight bag. But as the carriage drove along, she set her things on the cushioned seat beside her and looked out the window, feeling very small.

The carriage rumbled through the winding London streets, past ramshackle buildings and courtyards with jostling crowds and noxious smells, along the outskirts of theaters and shops, until they reached a series of wide streets and clean paths, alongside manicured green spaces, gardens, some private and locked away behind fences, others open to the public where many a finely dressed person strolled.

Then all of a sudden it came to a stop. The driver tapped on the carriage roof. "We're here, miss."

Poppy took her reticule and slung her overnight bag over her shoulder. She disembarked and stepped down onto a clean cobblestone walkway. She looked around and said, "Oh, I must pay you."

"The gentleman already did." The driver flicked the reins and took off.

Poppy stuffed her reticule into her overnight back and stared at her surroundings. Here the air was cleaner, smelled sweeter, and she faced a series of tall stately buildings with modern architecture. She had less fear of being robbed here but was wary. She was to come to 56 Eaton Place, and as she gazed at the fine columns and clean walls, she looked up to see the numbers on the buildings. She faced 54, then 56. She came up to the front door and knocked.

It was opened a moment later by a housemaid with squinting eyes and a sour face, severely marred by the pox. The maid took one look at her and said, "Shove off."

"No, I have an appointment." Poppy fumbled in her reticule for the letter and fished it out. She held it out to the maid. "See, she invited me. This is Miss Hayes's residence, is it not?"

The maid screwed up her face. "You think I've got time to be reading letters? Gear off."

"Please, I'm supposed to be here. I have an interview," Poppy said. "Tom Harris sent me."

The maid's eyes narrowed. "He did, did he?" She shoved the letter back at Poppy. "We've no need for his girls and we're no charity."

"Fanny, what is it? Is someone here?" a woman's voice called.

The maidservant's gaze was sour. "Just a poor wretch, ma'am."

"Miss Hayes," Poppy called. "Miss Beatrice Hayes?"

"Yes?" A timid voice called back. "Move aside, Fanny."

The maidservant gave Poppy a glowering look and stepped back. She was replaced by a young woman in a silk chartreuse dress, with light blonde hair coiled in fashionable ringlets that trailed down her shoulders. "I am Miss Hayes. Who are you?"

Poppy held out the letter. "Poppy Morton. We wrote to one another a few weeks ago, about the advertisement?"

"Advertisement?" A wrinkle lined Miss Hayes's forehead. "What advertisement?"

"For a companion? To yourself, ma'am?"

Miss Hayes took a look at the letter. "Oh, of course! I had forgotten. Come in, come in. Fanny, make tea." She let Poppy enter, and led the way up a flight of narrow stairs.

Poppy followed Miss Hayes into a drawing room that bore an ornate yet thin worn carpet, small tables dotted around the room, a sofa boasting gray damask cushions, and two comfortable-looking chairs facing it. She noted the muted blue-green walls, devoid of portraits or works of art. The room was well lit from the sunlight coming in from the windows, and short stubby candles that sat in smart iron candle holders attached to the walls.

Beatrice took a seat on one of the damask-covered chairs and gestured to the sofa. "Please, sit. You must be tired after your journey. I must have placed that advert and completely forgotten about it, what a goose I am. Stephen will laugh at me, I am sure."

"Is that your brother?" Poppy asked, and sat, dropping her overnight bag and reticule on the floor by her feet.

"Stephen? Oh, no." Beatrice giggled. "He's nearer to a husband I suppose, but not quite. Nevertheless, we are very close. Could I see the letter again?"

Poppy handed it to her. Beatrice took it and read, nodding before she handed it back. "Yes, I remember now. I was feeling lonely, and Stephen thought perhaps a companion might cheer me while he was away. I am so glad you responded, although I am surprised you came."

"Why is that?"

"Well, I… No matter. In any case, let's sit down to business."

Poppy smiled, for they were already sat.

"Yes, well. Ah, here's tea. Thank you, Fanny." Beatrice smiled as the sour-faced maid set a tea tray down on an oval wooden table between them. Fanny shot Poppy a dirty look before leaving the room.

"Don't mind her, she's always sour about one thing or another. I would dismiss her but she's ever so good with the housekeeping and making sure no unsavory sorts bother me. Shall I pour?"

Poppy nodded as Beatrice attended to the silver tea service, pouring a cup of steaming black tea and handing it to her. Beatrice said, "So tell me about yourself."

"Um, I live in Hertfordshire, with my aunt and uncle. He is a clergyman, and—"

"You're a clergyman's niece?" Beatrice set down her bone china teacup.

"Yes. I can read and write, and I—"

"Are you a good walker? I love a long walk," Beatrice said.

"I am, but I'm a terrible baker." Poppy hedged a smile.

"Ha! I've never tried. Do you think the servants would let me try?"

"It's your household, isn't it?"

"It is, but they came with the apartment. I didn't choose

them, Stephen did." Beatrice rose and walked over to one of the narrow windows that overlooked the street and accompanying park. "And he is out there, watching me."

"Who? Stephen?" Poppy set down her cup and joined her at the window.

"No. My minder, Mr. Parks." Beatrice nodded toward a stocky man in nondescript clothes who stood by the park fence, facing the building. He smoked a pipe and watched the window.

"Why do you have a minder?" Poppy asked.

"Stephen says the man is there to have a care for my person, but really I think it is so that I don't get into trouble or entertain any male company that is not him."

"I don't understand. Why would you have a personal guard? Doesn't your husband trust you?"

"Stephen's not my husband. Although I rather wish he was. He's so handsome," Beatrice said, returning to her seat.

Poppy joined her and sipped her tea. "But then…if he's not your husband or your brother…"

"Oh, my, I thought you knew. Stephen's my gentleman. I'm his… I suppose you might say I'm his lady companion when he fancies some company." Beatrice blushed over her teacup.

Poppy's mouth dropped open. "You're a mistress."

CHAPTER THREE

"Oh," Poppy said, at a loss on what to do. Her would-be employer was a mistress. Not quite the grand lady or widow she had envisioned. She set her teacup back on the tea tray.

Beatrice grew alarmed. "Please don't go. I'm so lonely, I could use some regular company. It was my idea to advertise in the paper, not Stephen's. I have nothing to do all day but eat and get dressed or take a bath, and walk around. I have no company, and the only society I can have are the other ladies, but none of them like me and I'm always the butt of their japes..."

Poppy took another sip. The black tea was hot and after a long journey, her throat was parched. "I know how you feel."

"You do?" Beatrice looked at her.

Poppy nodded. "I've been sheltered from the world my whole life. I've never even been outside of Hertfordshire before. This is my first time in London, and within the first hour I got here, a boy tried to rob me. Thankfully Mr. Harris fetched my reticule back for me, otherwise, I would never have—"

"Mr. Harris? Do you mean Tom Harris?"

"Yes. Do you know him? He seemed to know you."

"Oh, we are close acquaintances. He's the one who introduced me to Stephen. You say Tom found you?"

"Purely by chance. He found the rascal and got my reticule

back for me. If he hadn't, I'd still be out there." Poppy glanced at the window. The former beams of afternoon light were now sinking, and soon enough they would be in darkness.

"You are lucky. And a clergyman's niece, my, you are respectable. Tell me, do you have any talents?"

"Talents?"

"Can you sing, draw, or dance? I love to dance."

"I like to dance, but I never learned music or drawing. My uncle never had the inclination and we spent our time doing other things, like visiting the sick, attending church."

"Oh. That all sounds very dull. I can see why you'd want to become a companion." Beatrice slapped a hand over her mouth. "I'm sorry. I've always been told I give my opinion more frankly than I should."

Poppy grinned. "I have an aunt like that. And you're right, visiting London is exciting. Back home we go to the assembly rooms for music concerts and dancing, but just being here is like a dream."

"What can you do?" Beatrice asked. "I mean, if you can't sing or play the pianoforte, or draw, what are your accomplishments?"

"Well…" Poppy paused in thought. "I can sew."

Beatrice's smile was apologetic. "I don't need a seamstress. I can sew as well as the next girl, and companions don't do that sort of work. If I need a dress mended, I have a maid for that."

"Oh." Poppy's gaze drifted toward her hands folded nicely in her lap. "Well… I can solve problems."

"What do you mean?"

Poppy told Beatrice of her murders, where she had made the acquaintance of Constable Dyngley and solved two cases. When she finished, Beatrice's eyes were wide. "Heavens above. Hertford must be a dangerous sort of place. And here I thought London and the big cities were bad."

"I love Hertford. It's not a bad place, it's just one or two people that can ruin a place, you know?"

"I do." Beatrice agreed. "I'm from the south of England, but once my pa was hanged for stealing, that did us in."

"What did you do?"

"My ma soon attracted the local butcher in town and remarried. But when he put his hands on me, I left and found my way to London. I could go back but... Mum would be ashamed if she knew what I was. Better not to."

"I see."

"So we're both alone, in a way. Although I bet I've not had nearly such exciting adventures as you." Beatrice set down her teacup and clapped her hands. "You must stay. At least the night. Please, will you? I feel like we are already friends and I feel safer just having you nearby."

"Safer? Oh, you mean without Stephen here."

"No, it's not that." The color drained from her face as she put her hands on her knees. They were rough-looking and reddened by hard work.

The girl might be wearing a finer dress than her and have her own London apartment, but Poppy suspected that life had not come easy to Miss Hayes. "What is it? Surely you're not afraid to be alone? Why, when you have the servants nearby?"

Beatrice sipped her tea, saw her hands tremble, and set the cup down again. "I'm being silly is all. I told Stephen about my troubles, but he wouldn't listen and now I'm so scared to go out, I was afraid you were the letter writer."

"Letter writer? What do you mean?" Poppy asked.

Beatrice rose and removed a handful of letters from a side table and handed them to her.

Poppy looked at the first one. In an elegant, scrawling hand, it read:

Don't go walking in the park today, the next walk might be your last.

> *Why not go to the street corner? It's where you belong.*
> *You're no lady. You never were and never will be.*
> *Don't bother telling the magistrate, he'll never believe a whore like you.*

"Goodness," Poppy said, reading one after another. "These are horrible. Who sent them?"

"I don't know." Beatrice returned them to the drawer in the side table. "But I'm scared to go anywhere. And I can't tell anyone. What would the servants think? They're not loyal, they don't even like me. They'll run at the first sign of trouble, I know it. And then it'll get back to Stephen that I've lost the servants and he'll throw me out and I'll be back on the streets again, and…" Her face flushed red, and her green eyes turned glassy.

"Hold on there, Miss Hayes."

"Beatrice, please."

"Beatrice, there's nothing to cry over. So you've received some nasty letters. Yes, they're horrible, but you're made of stronger stuff. Stephen wouldn't want to see you in tears," Poppy said.

"No, he wouldn't." Beatrice wiped her eyes on her silk sleeve. "I'm just so alone, and there's no one I can talk to, and now you'll leave me because of what I am, and—"

"I won't. I mean, I might. I can't promise I won't. But if I do, it won't be because of your situation."

"You won't?" Beatrice's eyes welled up again. "Whyever not?"

Poppy's heart went out to her. She could glimpse the odd hours spent alone with no company, no one to talk to but the servants, and even then they were not equals. Without a soul to talk to but her patron and no society to engage with except other mistresses, the empty hours would have pressed on Beatrice, suffocating her in the sense of the time being wasted and lost.

At that moment, Poppy realized that she might need Beatrice just as much as Beatrice needed her. They might not be kindred spirits, but they could form a friendship and keep each other company.

"I won't leave you," Poppy said, feeling warmth in her heart. She said a beat later, "My mum's supposedly a mistress. That's why I'm here."

"What?" Beatrice paused, a trail of clear snot running down her nose.

Poppy rummaged in her overnight bag and found the used handkerchief that Tom had given her. She passed it to Beatrice and said, "It's used, but it'll do in a pinch."

Beatrice took it and wiped her nose, then wrinkled. "It um, smells."

The girls laughed, and that broke the tension slightly. Beatrice hiccupped. "Tell me about your mother. What do you mean she's a mistress? She's like me?"

"My mother is a kept woman, I think. It's why I applied to you. I wanted to come to London to find her."

Beatrice's eyes grew wide. "She is? Who is she?"

"Celeste Morton?"

"I don't know a Celeste Morton. Celeste Grey I know. Could she be your mother?" She folded the used handkerchief and appraised Poppy. "I can see a resemblance. You're certainly as tall as her. But we don't move in the same circles. I don't know her very well. I've only met her twice. She won't remember me, I'm sure. But she was very kind."

Poppy's heart lifted. "That's all right."

"So we both have something we need. Will you stay?"

"Will you have me?"

Beatrice nodded, and over black tea and ginger biscuits, they hashed out the terms of Poppy's situation as Beatrice's companion. As Beatrice received an income from her patron, Stephen Farrars, a wealthy benefactor with funds to spare, they settled that Poppy would earn a wage each week, at a rate of up to twenty pounds per year.

It was more money than Poppy could have dreamed of, and she relished the chance to earn an allowance and not have to rely on her aunt and uncle for funds. It was the first step toward independence and excitement filled her, right down to her toes. She asked, "What will my duties be?"

"You'll be my companion, but not a lady's maid, so you

spend time with me at social events, entertain guests, but keep me company during the days and nights, except when Stephen visits." Beatrice added, "But you could have that time to yourself, and see London."

"Alone?" Her first introduction to the city so far had been less than welcoming.

"Well, you could always visit Tom. Although, maybe not. He's in Covent Garden, at the Shakespeare. It can be a rough sort of area if you're not careful. Or you could spend time with your mother."

"I don't know how to find her. I don't even know if she is the same person you speak of."

"I can contact her. I mean, I don't know where Miss Grey lives, but I know where she goes."

Poppy felt a wave of emotion pass through her. Was finding her mother as simple as making the right connections? Maybe.

"But first you must help me with these letters. They're frightful and I don't know what to do," Beatrice said.

The sour-faced maid, Fanny, entered the room. "You need to dress for dinner, Miss Hayes."

"Oh, that's right. Miss Morton, do excuse me," she paused. "Oh, I know, you shall come too."

"Is that wise, Miss Hayes?" Fanny asked.

"Of course it is. Miss Morton is to be my companion and she will accompany me in all things. Well, most things. I mean, maybe not the privy, or when Stephen comes, but in all others, I think it is best." She rose and gave Poppy's hand a little shake. "I knew this was a good idea. I'll introduce you to the others. That is if you have no objection?"

"The others?"

"Um, the other ladies of my, uh… My friends. You'll see."

Poppy glanced at her, butterflies in her stomach. "I should be glad to join you."

"Oh, good. Fanny, make up one of the rooms for Miss Morton, she'll be staying a while."

"For how long?" Fanny asked, giving Poppy a look belonging to an unwanted aunt.

Poppy glanced at the woman. It was an insolent question, and rude. The servant was short, thin, and hard, with an angular face badly scarred by the pox. She wore an apron over an old housedress that was too roomy for her thin frame, and her thin hair was pulled back into a severe bun.

"The night, at least," Poppy said.

"Yes. Let's see how it goes. You could always change your mind…" Beatrice's gaze drifted to the floor. "But I hope not."

Fanny sniffed and walked away, leaving the young women alone. Beatrice beamed at Poppy, "I know you'll like it here. I feel better already. Meet back in an hour, yes?"

Poppy nodded. Beatrice left her, and while Poppy waited for the maid to return, she sat back on the sofa and took in her surroundings. The sitting room was pleasant, but with its polished tables and dark furnishings, Poppy could see how it could feel oppressive.

"Don't get too comfortable. Beatrice is a good girl, but too trusting. If you're looking to take advantage of her, you can leave now." Fanny muttered behind her.

"I'm not. We've come to a business arrangement."

"Hah! The only arrangement she makes is from between her legs."

Poppy's mouth dropped open. "That is very rude."

"Not if it's the truth. Come on, your room's this way." Fanny started off, not waiting to see if Poppy followed.

Poppy followed her down a corridor, past two other rooms, to a room at the end of the hall. Fanny opened the door and said, "In here. Don't think I'll be fixing your hair or doing anything like that for you. I've got enough to worry about without a girl from the country giving me orders."

Poppy stared at the woman. "I can do very well for myself, thank you."

"We'll see about that." Fanny did not curtsy and left.

Poppy frowned and entered the room. It was small but clean, and had a lone window against the wall. There was a single bed, a cracked ceramic chamber pot beneath it, and a small table and water basin on a stand beside it. Poppy unpacked her small bag and reticule and closed the door behind her, sitting on the bed. It creaked far too easily and sagged in the middle. But she didn't care. This was different and less comfortable than what she was used to, but it was the start of a new beginning.

She removed her walking coat and bonnet and unpinned her hair. She had only brought three dresses and a nightgown to wear, but perhaps should have brought more clothes and toiletries with her. She wished she had been more sensible.

An hour later Poppy joined Beatrice in the sitting room and stood as she entered. "Oh, you're ready, excellent. I do love to be on time. I never am, and then Stephen gets so mad, but we make up for it." She giggled and called, "Nancy!"

A different maid, a more pleasant looking one, appeared. "Yes, ma'am?"

"Call us a hackney, would you?"

"Yes, miss." The maid bobbed a curtsy and left.

Minutes later Poppy was ensconced in the back of a carriage with Beatrice, who peered out the window. "I'm sure Mr. Parks will be following. He usually does."

Poppy observed a gold strand around Beatrice's neck that caught the light. "That's a pretty necklace."

"This? Stephen gave it to me." Beatrice traced her light fingers along the simple strand around her neck. "It's beautiful, isn't it?"

"It is. You must be lucky to have such a generous patron."

"I am. Although… I almost didn't wear it tonight." Beatrice's fingers drifted to her lap.

"Why?"

Beatrice chewed her lip. "Some of the jewelry I wear to these parties goes missing, sometimes. I don't know when it happens, or if I'm too drunk and misplace it, but the last time I lost a piece,

Stephen thought I sold it, and no amount of crying would persuade him I didn't."

"How odd. Do you know what happened?"

"No. But I have a suspicion," Beatrice said, her face serious.

"And what is that?" Poppy asked.

"Some of the girls are light-fingered, or they used to be. I wonder if perhaps…"

"One of them lifted your jewelry without you noticing," Poppy said.

"Yes, exactly. But how could I think such a thing when they are my friends? Is that not very bad of me?" Beatrice asked.

"I think if these ladies were truly your friends, they would not steal from you."

"No." Beatrice drew her little olive green cloak around her and adjusted her hair. Tonight she had it arranged in soft hanging curls around her neck, with the rest pinned up, dressed with a light green ribbon. "Oh, we're here."

They got out, paid the driver, and were admitted into an apartment building that boasted footmen, servants, and finer furnishings than Beatrice's home. "This belongs to Mollie Jones," Beatrice said, "her patron is Lord Aylesbury. He owns half of Essex if what she says is true."

"I see," Poppy said but cared little for the fine surroundings. She watched Beatrice wipe her hands on her cloak, fiddle with the cloak's strings as she tangled it in endeavoring to loosen them before handing it to a footman and adjusting the ribbon in her hair a third time.

"Are you quite well, Beatrice?"

"Me? Oh, I'm fine. Fine." Beatrice gave a tight smile and followed a footman up a grand staircase, and into a pleasant drawing room.

Warm candlelight lit up a large room, but on second thought, Poppy decided the room was decidedly uncomfortable. It had a scattering of settees and chairs, strategically placed around one main purple settee decorated in dark plum velvet. The walls bore a fine damask wallpaper, with deep violet curtains with gold tassels revealing the two large windows in the room. The final effect was gaudy, and Poppy found herself disliking the arrangement before she had even sat down.

As they entered the room, five pairs of eyes gazed at them. "Beatrice, we always encourage each other to bring guests, but I wonder at you sometimes. Who is this?" A bold voice said.

Beatrice turned pink and a red flush crawled up her neck. "Mollie, this is Miss…Miss.."

"Poppy Morton." Poppy curtsied slightly. "I am Miss Beatrice's companion."

Mouths dropped open.

"A companion? My, my, aren't we something? Come, let me have a look at you." The voice belonged to a woman who could only be the hostess, Miss Mollie Jones.

Poppy smiled thinly. "I apologize for interrupting your dinner. I hope it's not an inconvenience."

The woman waved a hand in the air. "Now we are to be six instead of five, that is to be an improvement."

Poppy was introduced to the women there. Mollie Jones, a redhead who wore a purple off-the-shoulder dress, was clearly the loudest and leader of the group. Justine Vane who wore blue, Penelope Smythe, a pretty brunette with an impish expression, and Harriet Sykes, who wore purple and gray. Each young woman looked lovely in her own way, but from their snide looks and thinly veiled barbs, Poppy understood why Beatrice felt uncomfortable in their company.

Justine brushed her rudely and said, "Sorry, need the necessary."

Beatrice shot her a look. She'd brushed by her hard, harder than was needed.

Penelope said, "Never mind Justine. She always did have a flair for the dramatic." She opened her arms for a hug and embraced Beatrice. "It's been so long since we've seen each other. Have you been hiding in a cave?"

Beatrice stiffened and gave a little laugh. "Not at all. And Penelope, we only saw each other last week."

Penelope released her from the hug. "Silly me, I'm so forgetful these days." She looked very pretty with long red hair coiled about her bosom, a set of heavy pink pearls around her neck, and a fetching pink off-the-shoulder dress.

Beatrice didn't help matters by being awkward. She moved to accept a glass of wine from a footman and tripped over her own skirts. She stumbled forward and landed on her hands and knees, spilling white wine on the carpet. "Oh, I'm so sorry," she said.

"God, you're clumsy. Now I remember why I never invite you to things. You waste more wine than you're worth and I end up spending a fortune on cleaning. Just sit down, Beatrice," Mollie said with disgust.

Poppy stood back as a footman offered Beatrice a handkerchief to wipe her dress clean, and another helped her up. "Thank you," she said shyly, her cheeks taking on a rosy bloom.

And there was her allure, Poppy observed. The sweet, shy, endearingly clumsy young woman. No single man stood a chance.

In contrast, the others were like medieval dragons of children's tales, Poppy decided, or serpents, all out to snap at each other. At the sight of Poppy's ordinary gray gown, Justine simpered, and Harriet hid a smile behind her fan.

Beatrice and Poppy sat by Mollie's right, on a striped lavender sofa. Mollie held up a monocle and peered at Poppy, taking in the sight of her wrinkled clothes. "You're not from around here."

"No, I am from Hertfordshire."

"Wearing country dresses I see. You have just arrived, I take it?"

"Yes, just this afternoon."

"That explains it. You will need one of us to show you to a proper modiste while you are in town. Justine, you can take her." She turned to Poppy. "She won't mind."

Justine opened and closed her mouth. "Of course," she mumbled.

At their knowing smiles, Poppy felt every inch a poor relation from the country. What was her plain gray linen dress compared to their rich silks and finery? She had no jewels to adorn her, and as they sat down to dinner, Poppy hazarded a glance at her companion and came to a realization.

"Beatrice," she said.

"Yes?"

"Your necklace is missing."

"Oh! Is it?" Beatrice's hand flew to her neck. Sure enough, the gold necklace was gone. "Maybe it came loose and fell down."

"What are you wittering on about?" Mollie asked.

"My necklace. I wore some jewelry here, but now I seem to have misplaced it," Beatrice said.

Mollie shook her head. "You are either the most forgetful or clumsiest person I know. You're always losing things."

"I didn't lose it," Beatrice said quickly. "I think someone here took it."

"You're just saying that to get attention," Penelope said.

"I believe her," Poppy said, "and I rode with her in the carriage. I saw it. She had a gold necklace on when she arrived."

"Well, I don't know. Who's to say what happens with these things? Maybe one of the servants took it," Penelope said.

"You're calling one of my servants a thief?" Mollie said.

"Should we call the watch?" Poppy asked.

The women laughed. Harriet said, "Not unless you fancy giving away your favors for free. They're more likely to find it, then sell it back to you for more than it's worth."

"They're not trustworthy," Poppy said.

"Oh, they are. For a price," Penelope said.

"What are we to do? None of us took it," Justine said.

"Judging from the look on Miss Morton's face, I'd say that's exactly what she was thinking," Harriet said.

"Miss Morton can find it. She solves problems like this," Beatrice said proudly.

"Problems? What sort of problems?" Mollie asked.

"Disappearances. Murders," Poppy said.

Beatrice added, "It's true. She's solved two murders already."

"What, since you arrived?" Mollie laughed.

"No, over the past year," Poppy said, turning pink. She didn't like the way this conversation was going.

"Who cares about all that? I want to know where Beatrice's jewelry is. Miss Morton, if you would be so kind, tell us who took it?" Harriet asked. "That's what you're thinking, isn't it, that one of us stole it."

Poppy thought aloud. "When we came in, we handed over our cloaks to the footmen, and came upstairs."

"You think one of the servants did it?" Mollie asked. "A fine way to repay my hospitality."

Poppy shook her head. "We came in here and were introduced…"

"Go on, I like this game," Mollie said.

"While we were talking, Miss Beatrice spilled her drink," Poppy said.

"Yes, we all saw," Justine smirked.

"If her necklace had a loose clasp, it should have fallen to the floor at that point, but it didn't."

Mollie and Harriet glanced at the bare floor.

"Which means?" Penelope asked.

"Which means it was already gone. Someone took it before she spilled her drink."

"Who?" Justine asked.

"Only one person had the opportunity. And only one person touched her this evening," Poppy said.

The girls looked at each other. "Who?"

"Shall we open our reticules?" Justine asked.

"Go on, do it. All of you," Mollie ordered.

The women complied, but the jewelry remained missing.

"Well, that was a waste of time," Mollie said.

"I'm not surprised. The person who stole Beatrice's jewelry is bolder than that," Poppy said.

"What makes you say that?" Harriet asked.

Poppy gazed at her. "What's a good piece of jewelry if you don't wear it?"

"Huh?" Justine asked. "I don't understand."

"She means that whoever stole the jewelry is wearing it."

"That's right. Eh, Penelope?" Poppy said.

Penelope turned red. "What, me? What are you looking at me for?"

"Penelope, could you lift your hair from your body for a moment?" Poppy asked.

Penelope shot her a dirty look and sniffed. "Anything you want from me, you'll have to pay for."

"Do it, Penelope," Mollie said, "I want to see."

"I won't. I don't have to do anything," Penelope pouted.

"You will if you want to stay here," Mollie said.

Penelope shot her a look. "I don't know this girl. She's just a companion. She's not even a companion, she's just a plain country girl and it's a stupid request."

"Miss Morton isn't stupid," Beatrice said.

"Go on, Penelope," Justine said. "You'll just prove her wrong. I believe you."

Penelope smirked. She slowly lifted her long red hair away from her chest, revealing an elegant pale neck that bore a set of pink pearls. "See? No gold necklace."

"Penelope, could you lift up your pearls, please?" Poppy asked.

"I don't have to listen to you."

"Justine?" Poppy asked.

Justine shrugged and approached Penelope, who backed away. "What is this? A questioning? I did what you asked."

"Penelope…" Justine paused, and slowly lifted the pearls from Penelope's neck. There beneath the thick strands lay a thin gold necklace, shining in the light.

"My necklace!" Beatrice said. "Give it back."

Penelope reddened. "I don't know what you're talking about. It's mine."

"Thief," Harriet said.

"Go on, give it back," Mollie said.

Penelope's eyes grew hard.

"Do it, Penelope, or I'll never invite you back here again," Mollie warned. "Besides, no one actually wears one necklace over another. If I didn't know you cared about fashion, I'd think you were mad."

"It's a new style." Penelope huffed.

Mollie waited, a bushy brown eyebrow raised.

Penelope looked at the others, then rolled her eyes and let out a long-suffering sigh. "I don't see what the big deal is." She tugged the gold necklace from her neck with a hard snap. "It's just a bit of fun. Beatrice doesn't mind. She would say if I'd hurt her feelings, wouldn't you?"

She held it out to Beatrice, who reached for it, only for Penelope to let it fall to the floor. "Silly me. So clumsy." Her smile was mean.

Beatrice turned pink as she reclaimed the stolen necklace from the floor.

Poppy locked eyes with Penelope. The brunette mistress's dark eyes were like chips of agate. Her smile made Poppy flinch.

Mollie clapped. "Bravo. I've not been so entertained in a while. You can stay, Miss Morton. If all companions are as diverting as you, I might find one for myself." She laughed. "Or steal her away from Beatrice. I'll make it worth your while." She waggled her eyebrows suggestively.

Poppy snorted.

"If you're quite done making a fuss over Beatrice's new companion," Harriet said, "I want to know about the new confectioner's shop over on Bond Street."

And so it went on. Over a dinner of roast pork and deliciously crunchy crackling with roast potatoes, the conversation shifted to the latest play at the theater, that season's fashions for dresses and bonnets, until…

"Has anyone seen Marie?" Harriet asked. "She was supposed to be here tonight, wasn't she?"

Mollie shrugged. "She was invited. But you know her. She's probably too busy washing her face again, or her hands. If she's not on her back, that is."

That earned a laugh around the dining table. Poppy looked to Beatrice who said, "Our little joke. But Marie is always very clean and takes her time to wash before and after company. And before and after meals, and even when she uses the necessary."

Mollie said, "Marie always was the cleanest whore in England." That got laughs from the others, including a cackle from Penelope.

"It doesn't sound very funny," Poppy said.

"It is if you know Marie. But enough about her. That was impressive, you know, your winkling out the truth about Penelope," Harriet said. "How did you know it was her?"

"She was the only one who touched Beatrice. So unless the necklace really did have a loose clasp and fall to the floor, or Beatrice did it herself…"

"Penelope was the only option," Harriet finished. "Smart. I like that."

"Thank you," Poppy said, "so is this what you do? Have dinners and parties together?"

Harriet's mouth quirked into a half-smile. "We spend lots of time together. When we're not entertaining our gentlemen, that is. Would you like to know who everyone is?"

"I've already been introduced," Poppy said.

Harriet gave her a coy smile. "That's not what I mean. You come from a farm, don't you?"

"Yes."

"Then you'll know what I mean when I say that we're like chickens in a henhouse. There's a pecking order to our little group."

"Oh?" Poppy asked, intrigued.

A footman came by and refilled their wine glasses with a red claret as Harriet leaned forward conspiratorially. "First, Penelope. She's a tradesman's daughter. She was seduced by a customer and he kept her in a flat near Covent Garden, but that only lasted for six weeks before he tired of her. She was back to living with her father and two sisters for a while."

"Does her family know of her situation?" Poppy wondered.

"Who do you think introduced her to the customer?" Harriet said, "I can see your expression, but it is the truth. She brings a tidy little income into the home, which more than makes up for the inconvenience of having a wayward daughter. Now if any customer wants to pay for a little extra service, her sisters refer them to her. Or did anyway. She mentioned tonight that she's got another man taking care of her, somewhere near Covent Garden."

"Goodness," Poppy said.

Harriet laughed. "Oh, Miss Morton, we're just getting started. I make it my business to know these things. But the evidence is there, all you have to do is look. Mollie herself was a painter's muse until he found another more to his liking."

Poppy looked. Upon closer inspection, she could see that Harriet was being uncharitable, but not far from the truth. Mollie wore a face full of makeup, with her eyelids dusted heavily with kohl. Her breasts sagged, even trussed up in stays pulled far too tight, and she bore an unsightly wrinkle between her eyebrows when she frowned, as she did now when she noticed Poppy and Harriet observing her. She smiled and hurriedly wiped her mouth with a napkin.

"You see that?" Harriet said, "She salivates."

"Perhaps she is still hungry."

"Perhaps she is taking mercury for the pox," Harriet said.

"Miss Morton, is dear Harriet feeding you lies about me? Something outrageous, perhaps? Your expression says it is quite horrid," Mollie said.

"Nothing you haven't fabricated yourself," Harriet said

sweetly.

Mollie laughed and patted the seat next to her. "Here, Miss Morton, let me look upon you. I would like to know the woman who has entranced our newest member into parting with her purse."

Poppy rose and came to stand beside Mollie, while the others chatted amongst themselves. There was little care for the common rules of etiquette here.

"Penelope, be a dear and move. I wish to talk to Poppy, and she is so tall it's like talking to a tree," Mollie said.

Penelope fixed her with a petulant look. "Why should I give up my seat? She is nothing to me."

"It is no trouble—" Poppy started, but Mollie held up a hand.

"Penelope, you will do it because I asked you to. You've already proven that you're light-fingered. Do you really need to show us that you are rude as well? What will our new friend think of us?"

"She's not my friend." Penelope left in a huff, knocking over her chair.

Poppy righted it when Mollie said, "Never mind her. She is just embarrassed to be caught. None of us knew about her little talent, although it would explain a few things."

Seeing Poppy's wary expression, Mollie patted her hand. "Let us take a turn about the room. There are some very dashing footmen over there who have been left alone for far too long."

Mollie linked Poppy's arm with hers and walked away from the table, strolling around the room. Poppy breathed in Mollie's perfume, a heady, floral scent, and coughed.

"Are you all right, Miss Morton?" Mollie asked.

"Yes, I'm fine. It is the air. I'm not used to London air."

"Of course, you're not. You're probably used to the smell of pig shit." Mollie laughed and took her past two footmen who stood in attendance. They were handsome enough, but Poppy ignored them, feeling uncomfortable when Mollie winked at one and grinned at another.

Mollie said, "So, I expect Harriet has been telling you all sorts of stories about us."

"A little, but only the most shocking things. I think she means to surprise me with tales of your exploits."

"Oh, joy. Do tell. Aside from insinuating I am old, what has she told you?" Mollie asked.

"Well… Did you really become seduced by a painter?" Poppy asked.

Mollie threw her head back and laughed. "Is that what she said? That is too good. No, not quite. But if that's the story, then I'll not tell you any different. Let me ask you a question. Did you really solve two murders?"

"I did, but not alone. I had help. I worked with a constable, you see, and—"

"I don't care about the particulars, only whether it is true."

"It is," Poppy said.

Mollie inclined her head. "You are a delight. Smart and refreshingly honest, but I wonder for how long. I shall tell the others what pleasant company you are."

"That is very kind," Poppy said.

"Not at all. It will stopper Harriet's wagging tongue for a bit, and make the others jealous. They'll question whether Beatrice has got the better of them."

"What do you mean?"

"It's simple. By introducing you into our little society as her companion, Beatrice has shown she has something the rest of us don't have."

"You make it sound like I'm a glove or a new hat," Poppy remarked dryly.

She continued as if Poppy hadn't spoken. "And you're smart and witty. You're not a silly fool like some of these girls, and I don't think you're out to get Beatrice's money, and that is a rare find. She has one-upped us, you see."

Poppy's face turned pink. "I am not a plaything."

"My dear, we are all playthings in the hands of men. The

question is whether you choose to accept it, or embrace it, as I do," Mollie said, patting her hair.

"But I am not."

"If you are not, then why else are you here? Do you know what the others are saying right now?"

"No."

Mollie steered her past the footmen, saying, "First you should know that my patron is Lord Aylesbury, the largest landowner in Essex. As a result, I am the leader of our little company. He is the highest-ranking out of all the patrons, and the wealthiest, so it's only natural that the girls rely on me for leadership. They would be lost without me."

"They're watching us," Poppy noted.

"Of course they are. The others are now no doubt wondering whether they can soon find a companion of their own to surpass Beatrice, or seek to steal you from her if they can."

Seeing Poppy's stern look, Mollie added, "You may not think you are a plaything, but in this company you are. What Beatrice means as a kindness, taking you on, the others will view as a ploy in our little game of one-upmanship. Don't be surprised if the next time we meet, one of the girls shows off a new pet, or fine coat, or a fashionable dress. We all compete with each other, you see. I'm telling you this for your own good, so you learn your place in our little society."

"You make it sound like I'm a piece of furniture."

"To some, you will be. But not everyone. You've already proved that by ferreting out our fair Penelope." A bit of drool trickled down the corner of Mollie's mouth, and she hastily unlinked her arm from Poppy's and dabbed it away with a perfumed handkerchief.

In the dim candlelight, Mollie looked older. Her eyes held no warmth or kindness, only bold-faced candor. What would her aunt make of Mollie, Poppy could only guess. At the thought of her aunt, Poppy felt a pang of homesickness in her chest.

"What are you thinking about?" Mollie asked.

"My aunt and uncle. I should write and tell them I am well."

"You're a very good sort of girl, aren't you?" Mollie said, "It's funny. I know we've never met, but I could swear I have seen you before. At the theater perhaps? You look so familiar."

"I must have one of those faces," Poppy said.

Mollie laughed. "You really are from the country. No one in their right mind would call themselves so common." She led Poppy over to the others, as more wine was brought in.

Justine was describing a scene from the play she was cast in at the Drury Royal. She said, "In the play, I'm playing Mary Antonet."

"Don't you mean Marie Antoinette? Queen of France?" Harriet asked.

"Yes, that's what I said. Now in the scene, I…" Justine went on.

As Poppy observed her strut and mince about, she doubted that the real Marie Antoinette had been quite so coy or giggling later in life.

Justine was in her element, and she strode among them like a peacock, wielding her fan, until she clutched her breast and said, "I cannot lie. Free my fellow aristocrats or cut off my head. I am willing to die for my beliefs, so help me, God!"

She broke into giggles. "And then I'm taken to the guillotine where my head is cut off. It won't happen for real, of course, it's just a melon they'll cut instead, and throw a dummy's head into the crowd." She grinned. "It's so exciting. Do say you'll all come to see me."

"And see your head cut off?" Mollie said. "We wouldn't miss it."

Justine blew a raspberry at her and made a rude hand gesture, earning a laugh from Mollie.

A footman entered the room and stood awkwardly. He looked ill at ease. "A letter, miss."

"For me? Bring it here," Mollie told him.

The man coughed delicately. "It is addressed to all of the

ladies present."

"What?" Mollie took the letter from the footman. She tore it open and began reading, then gave the man a look of disgust. "Is this a joke?"

"What is it, Mollie?" Harriet asked.

"This. Whoever sent it, it's in poor taste." Mollie held it out to her.

Harriet read it and turned pale. "Who sent this?"

The footman gave a minute shrug. "I do not know. One of the scullery maids said she found it by the back door of the kitchen."

"Thank you, you may go," Mollie waved him away. Once the man left, she beckoned the women over. "Read this."

Poppy stayed back as Harriet read aloud, *"To the mistresses, whores, and bawds here tonight. Soon all of you will be dead. You will each pay for your crimes. You cannot stop me."*

Justine let out a dramatic scream and fainted. Footmen hurried to her and lifted her to a sofa, where she quickly came to.

Beatrice glanced at Justine and said, "How horrible. Who would do something like this?"

"I don't know. But it was addressed to all of us," Mollie said.

Penelope snorted. "A likely story. It's probably Mollie trying to play a joke."

Mollie turned red. "I am not behind this. Why would I threaten people at my own party?"

Harriet smirked. "Aare you saying you'd do it at somebody else's?"

Mollie shot her a dirty look. "Be serious. This is no party trick. It's real."

"Well, I didn't do it," Penelope said. "What about her?" She turned and looked at Poppy.

"Me? I never met any of you before tonight. Why would I write a letter?" Poppy asked.

"It's true, we only met this afternoon. Miss Morton would have no reason to do it. She didn't even know where we were going," Beatrice said.

Penelope crossed her arms. "Well, I don't know. It's a stupid trick if you ask me. Someone's decided to play a little joke and scare everyone."

"But what if it's true?" Harriet asked.

"Don't tell me you believe it. I thought you were the sensible one," Penelope teased.

Harriet did not dignify that with an answer.

Poppy said, "Would someone have wanted to hurt you? Do you all have a common enemy?"

Justine fluffed her hair while Penelope snorted. "Don't be daft, of course we do. Everyone wants to be like us."

Poppy's eyebrows rose but she kept her mouth shut.

Beatrice said, "I don't know anyone who would want to write something like this. It's so mean. It's cruel."

"Stop that, you're just scaring yourself. You act so meek and innocent, but no one believes it," Penelope said.

Mollie cleared her throat. "That's it. I've had enough of these stupid party tricks. First Beatrice's missing necklace and now this. It's like out of a gothic novel. I'm done." She crossed the room and tossed the letter into the fire.

Poppy said, "Wait!"

Mollie froze. "What?"

Poppy watched as the letter curled and blackened into ash. "Nothing. I would have liked to see it, that's all."

Mollie shrugged. "It was just an ordinary letter."

AFTER THAT, THE women did not stay long, and the party broke up a short while later. As people were leaving, Harriet asked, "No one has seen Marie lately, have they?"

Heads shook. Penelope said, "Not for two days now, since we went to the races. She's probably with her man. Why?"

"We were supposed to go shopping today and she never came. And when I called at her apartments, no one was there," Harriet said.

"Maybe she has a new beau and she's hiding away with him," Mollie said with a smile.

"I doubt it." Harriet frowned.

The others began to leave. As Beatrice and Poppy stood at the entrance, waiting for footmen to bring their cloaks, Harriet came up to them. "I'm sorry to trouble you, but I think something might have happened to Marie. Will you two join me at Bow Street tomorrow? I'm going to report her missing to the magistrate but don't want to go alone."

"Why not?" Poppy asked.

Harriet and Beatrice exchanged a look. "To them, I am just a lowly whore, and they will either laugh at me or try to have it off with me," Harriet said, her eyes shadowed. "Will you come with me? I'm worried about Marie. She's my friend. It's not like her to miss our plans."

"Of course, we'll go," Poppy said, then stopped. "If that is acceptable to you, Miss Hayes."

"I wouldn't miss it for the world. This is the most exciting thing to happen to me in weeks," Beatrice said.

They agreed to meet the next morning at the Shakespeare Tavern, not far from Bow Street.

Once their cloaks had been fetched and they were stepping inside a hackney carriage, Beatrice shot Poppy a little look. "You're a special kind of person, aren't you?"

"I don't know what you mean. I'm just like you."

"No, things happen when you're around. Like Harriet asking you for help."

"I'm sure she was just being polite. She said herself, she didn't want to go alone," Poppy pointed out.

"It's more than that. She's never asked me to come out with her, not ever." Beatrice looked glumly out the carriage window. "Nothing ever happens to me. Since we've met, you've uncovered a thief, rescued my jewelry, and now we have plans to report Marie's disappearance. This is very exciting." Beatrice grinned. "Just wait until I tell Stephen."

"Will he approve of our going out?"

"As long as we are in each other's company, he won't mind. But I might not tell him the exact nature of our plans with Harriet. He does worry so about me." Beatrice smiled fondly.

"He sounds very attentive," Poppy said.

"Oh, he is. He's wonderful." Beatrice looked at her. "What about you? Do you have any beaus?"

"None at all," Poppy said, looking out the window. "Not even one."

CHAPTER FOUR

CONSTABLE HENRY DYNGLEY rode up to the parsonage in Hertford, enjoying the familiarity of the dirt path that led to the fine old building. As his horse's hooves trod the road, he felt like he was returning home, for the parsonage offered warmth and solace to all who entered its doors.

Small wildflowers dotted the walkway, their sweet blooms drinking in the last few days of the summer sun. He passed a growing tangle of wild pink roses reaching well over six feet in height. They did not boast such beautiful blooms as hothouse flowers, but they perfumed the air nicely and their sweet scent was undeniable.

He dismounted and tied the reins to the low-hanging branch of a large tree that sat close to the house. He looked up, eyeing the branch that extended to Miss Morton's window, remembering how some months ago he had suggested to Poppy that they meet in secret one evening to view a body. Unlike other women of his acquaintance, she had made no horrified reaction at his scandalous proposition and had agreed to meet him that night, unbeknownst to her guardians. She had climbed out of her window onto that very tree, before losing her footing and falling on him. He'd minded at the time but didn't care now, for she had proven what he had suspected since he had first met her: she had an enquiring mind worthy of any parish constable, and was incredibly smart.

Her talents were wasted on the socially acceptable ladylike pursuits of the day. Not only smart, she also had a way of thinking about things that lent itself to the nature of an investigation, which was why on that night, he had whisked her away to view a corpse.

He smiled at the memory. Not all young ladies would have been excited or thrilled at such an excursion, but Poppy had practically jumped at the chance. They had a friendship that passed beyond the boundaries of mere acquaintances or polite company, and he looked forward to spending more time with her.

But then she had recently revealed that she had feelings for him, and had even kissed him, shocking him to his core. He hadn't been prepared for it, except he had kissed her back once they had solved a mystery together. He felt a bit ashamed about his lewd behavior, for it was unbecoming of a young man from a good family.

Now as he faced the parsonage with its familiar brick walls, his resolve deserted him. What would he say to the girl he had often thought of but said nothing to? He had kissed her and left like a thief in the night, except he had stolen a kiss instead of a coin. *What a sorry excuse for a gentleman*, he thought. He wiped his hands on his trousers, surprised to find them sweaty.

From the humble stable nearby, the Greenes' horse peered out of its stall, watching. Dyngley paused and came over with his hand out to say a friendly hello.

The horse sniffed and licked his hand, but his attention took too long. A minute later, a window opened and a woman called, "Constable, you are very welcome to come inside... or do you find our stable more comfortable than my sitting room?"

Dyngley's mouth curled into a smile. However brusque Mrs. Greene sounded, he had grown to appreciate her forthright manner and decided opinions, even when they contradicted his own. When she spoke it was with conviction and he knew Poppy could not have grown up in better care.

He walked up to the parsonage and knocked on the door. He didn't know what to say to Miss Morton, all he knew was that he wanted to see her again. He wiped his hands on his trousers again and was admitted into the humble blue sitting room by the family's maid. He tugged at his stiffly tied cravat and stopped halfway into the room, stunned by the sight of just Mrs. Greene and beside her, an empty seat. Miss Morton was not there. Confused, he bowed to his hostess and said hello.

"Good afternoon, Constable, how good to see you again. Do sit down." Mrs. Greene, a ruddy-cheeked, stout clergyman's wife of middle years, adjusted her frilly white mobcap and gestured toward the hardback chair left out for visitors.

As he sat, she said, "I expect you're wanting to speak to Mr. Greene."

"Just paying a friendly call," he said.

"How kind of you. Reginald!" she called. "Constable Dyngley is here to see you."

Henry shifted in his chair. The seat looked hard as a rock, and was just as uncomfortable. "How are you, Mrs. Greene?"

"Oh very well, we are in fine health. Tolerable, I suppose. Shall I call for some tea?"

"No, that is not necessary—"

"Betsey! Bring in tea please!" Mrs. Greene's voice rang out.

Betsey's blonde head bobbed in the doorway. "Yes ma'am." She gave a polite curtsy and went to the kitchen.

Mr. Greene appeared in the doorway shortly thereafter. "Ah, Constable. Good to see you again. I hope nothing is amiss?"

"No, Mr. Greene. I was just paying a social call."

They exchanged pleasantries for a minute or two more before Mr. Greene said, "Well, you will have to excuse me, but I am called away this afternoon."

"Oh?"

"Nothing out of the ordinary. I would gladly sit with you, Constable, but I have a prior engagement with Mr. Ingleby, our new clergyman. He sent a note this morning saying he required my opinion on his latest sermon."

"Will you be back in time for dinner?" Aunt Rachel asked.

"I should say so. It's only in Waterford, so I won't be gone long. Constable." He bowed and left as Betsey swiftly removed around him, carrying in a tray with a pot of tea and two cups.

Once he had been served, Aunt Rachel said, "I expect you heard that Mr. Ingleby is soon to be engaged to Miss Jane Heyworth. They are practically wild for each other."

"Mrs. Greene," Henry began.

"Why even at the last dance, such behavior I have not seen in quite some time. Do you know, they danced two dances together and then after—"

"Mrs. Greene," Henry said.

"Once I would have thought another might do for him, but he's so madly in love with her, he doesn't see anybody else. I expect to read the announcement in the paper any day now."

"Mrs. Greene," Henry said firmly, "where is your niece?"

Mrs. Greene set her teacup down. "Poppy? Gone." She popped a ginger biscuit into her mouth.

"Gone? Gone where? She's not missing, is she?"

He had to wait for her to finish eating, but she chewed so dreadfully slowly, he could have quite cheerfully shaken her at that moment. Then she coughed, turned red, and gasped for air.

He slapped her back and she coughed, spitting the offending piece of biscuit out onto her lap. "Oh!" She coughed hard.

He pushed her teacup at her, and she took it, drinking and swallowing. She coughed again a few more times before she was able to speak. "Thank you, Constable."

"Are you all right?"

"Oh yes, thank you. So good of you to look after me," she said.

He waited a moment more as she collected herself and drank more tea.

"Mrs. Greene?" he asked.

"Yes?" She was the very picture of innocence. It was infuriating.

"Your niece. Where is she?"

"Gone." She picked up another ginger biscuit, then thought better of it and put it back. "She's gone to London."

"London?"

"Yes. Ginger biscuit?" She offered the plate to him.

"No, thank you. Is she visiting friends or family?"

"Who?"

Now she was toying with him. "Your niece."

"Oh. No, not exactly." She poured herself another cup of tea. "She applied to be a lady's companion."

"A companion? Whose idea was this?"

"Poppy's."

"And you let her go?" He stood up in his chair.

"Constable, sit down."

He sat.

She sipped her tea. "Poppy is a young woman with a smart head on her shoulders. She is very sensible."

"And she will be an easy mark for any ill-minded person who seeks to prey upon unsuspecting young women." His eyebrows knit together.

"What could I do? You know her as well as I. She can be headstrong, and the girl is in want of opportunity. You have done her a kindness, encouraging her and being her friend. But with no proposals of marriage and no prospects, Poppy must find other means to survive."

"Other means?" he repeated.

"Yes. Do you think that my husband will live forever? No. Once he is dead, I will be turned out before he is cold in his grave. The clergy has no use for widows, Constable. Of that I am sure."

"But they would not give away the living so soon," he said.

"Believe me, they would. There are many young clergymen in need of a community parish, and this is a beautiful setting. I would have to find somewhere else to live." She paled at the thought.

"And what of Poppy?" he asked.

"What about her? You take an eager interest in my niece, Constable, which I find it hard to approve of," she snapped.

He balked. "Whatever do you mean?"

"She is possessed of a fine, intelligent mind. But you have filled her head with ideas of solving crimes and catching murderers."

"She has done these things. She has been a wonderful help to me in the past," he said. "I just wish she had written to me of her plan to go. Did she not leave a note or letter?"

"None at all." She frowned at him. "I find it a bit much, Constable, this interest in her you have. I would not mind if I thought you had romantic designs on her—"

Henry stared. "Miss Morton is my friend."

"Oh, I know. But as you do not have any romantic interest in her, solving crime is not a suitable pastime for a young woman. She needs to be married, and soon before she gets any older."

"Miss Morton is not yet twenty, I believe."

"That is not the point. Poppy is young and headstrong and has already heard what some of the people in town are saying about her. Do you think it is any wonder she left when all she has for her troubles is an odd sort of friendship with a parish constable?"

He blinked. "Mrs. Greene, I—"

"You had your chance to court her, Constable, many a time. But you broke her heart when last summer you did not write, and then you came back with a young woman on your arm."

"That woman was my fiancée."

"You have fine taste in women. The girl was a thief. A murderer."

"I was blinded by her charms," he said.

"She tried to kill Poppy." Aunt Rachel set down her teacup and glared at him. "When I think of the hurt and wasted feelings you put my niece through… I wish to God you had never come back. Then at least she would have forgotten about you. If it weren't for you, she might now be on the point of marriage."

"With whom?" he asked, his heart thudding in his chest.

"Anyone. Anyone deserving who cared for her and did not mind her faults, her unladylike independence. Anyone but you."

He felt cut to the quick. "Mrs. Greene, if I have offended you in any way, I am—"

"Constable, I know you are a good and honest man. But did you not see the effect you had on my niece? Is it any wonder she left, when all that remains here for her is heartbreak and the derision of our neighbors?"

He breathed in through his nose. This was not how he had envisaged the visit to play out. "I came to pay my respects and call on Poppy. I wanted to visit and see how she was."

"She is fine."

"You've heard from her?" he asked.

"No, but I am sure she is very well."

"Where is she staying?"

"With her employer," Aunt Rachel said.

"Who is?"

"A lady of quality."

"Give me a name," he said.

"Why? So you can torment her again and chase off any suitors she might have? No, Constable, I will not do it." She rose and said, "Do excuse me, I have a touch of a headache and need to lie down. Betsey will see you out." She left him standing there.

A minute later, the maid, Betsey, came and brought him his hat. As she escorted him to the door, she opened it and whispered, "Constable."

He stopped.

"Miss Poppy is staying with a Miss Beatrice Hayes."

"Where?"

She shrugged her thin shoulders. "All I know is the name. But they miss her, even though they won't say so. Bring her back."

"I don't think Mrs. Greene wants to see me again," he said.

"Bring Miss Poppy back and they'll welcome you here again. Even if you break her heart." Betsey quietly shut the door in his face.

CHAPTER FIVE

CONSTABLE HENRY DYNGLEY rode back through town to the boarding house in Hertford where he was staying. He had not expected such a cold reception from Mrs. Greene, and he did not know what to think about her assertions regarding his treatment of Poppy. The girl was smart, independent, and headstrong. Everything he admired in a young woman. But she was poor, had not a penny to her name, and she had confided in him that her mother was a mistress.

Then it hit him as if he was struck by lightning.

That must be the reason she had left Hertford without a word. She had gone to find her mother and learn what she could about her past. If she meant to go under the guise of a companion, so be it.

But when he arrived at the boarding house and put his horse away in the stable, the owner, Mr. Higgins, came outside. "Constable, there's a man here to see you. He says he knows you."

"Where is he?"

Mr. Higgins jerked his thumb toward the house. "Sitting room. He wanted to wait in your room. I told him that mayhap he does know you, but I don't know *him* from Adam, and you haven't told me nuthin' about having visitors. Well, he didn't like that one bit. But I told him that's the way I run things, so he can either wait for you in the sitting room or outside. So in the sitting room, he is."

"Did he give you a name?"

Mr. Higgins scratched his chin. "That's the funny thing. The man said he's your brother, and that he's the son of a baronet. Does that mean he's a lord?"

"No. His father is a baronet. He's just a self-entitled prat."

"Well, he's drunk a bottle of wine already. Who's going to pay for that?"

"He will, I expect. Thank you, Mr. Higgins." He entered the drawing room.

There holding court sat a man he'd known for years, who raised a glass of wine in greeting. "Henry, you're here. Finally."

"Hello, John."

John stood and clapped him on the shoulder. "Glad you've come. It's been dull without you. Now there's something I must discuss with you—"

"Will you be needing more to drink, sir?" A middle-aged man appeared at John's shoulder and bowed at the sight of them. "Mr. Dyngley."

"Robert," Henry said with surprise. "You're here."

"Of course, he's here. I can't very well leave and not take my valet along. Speaking of, I brought yours, too. He seemed a bit lonely, and I knew you would need him with you."

"Geoffrey is here?"

"Oh yes. If I'm not mistaken, he's upstairs mending your shirts."

Henry removed his hat and ran a hand through his hair. "Is he?"

"I've never seen him happier. Now I must talk to you." John drank more wine.

Mr. Higgins stood in the doorway, openly listening while two other men sat nearby had put down their papers, watching.

"Shall we go out?" Henry asked. "I've longed to show you the Crosskeys. It's my favorite pub in Hertford."

John's face lit up in a smile. "Lead on, old man, you don't have to tell me twice. Robert, fetch my things. And tell Geoffrey we're leaving." He turned to Henry. "I don't suppose they do a good meal? I haven't eaten in hours."

ONCE SAFELY ENSCONCED in a wooden alcove in the Crosskeys, tankards of ale in hand, with their valets drinking nearby, John glanced at Henry. "Nice sort of town, this. I can see why you're fond of it." He winked at a passing barmaid.

"John, why are you here?" Henry asked.

"What? Why so serious? Can't a man visit his younger brother?" John flashed him a cheeky grin.

That willful smile made Henry want to shake him. He loved his older brother dearly, but John never took anything seriously. Much to the disappointment of their parents, who attempted to straighten him out by arranging a marriage between him and Petunia, a severe woman who had less personality than a stick. But she had appeared fetching with an angular face and jet-black hair in her portraits, so John had agreed to the match before ever meeting her.

Big mistake. She was everything John was not. Stone-faced, rigid in her deportment, frigid in her demeanor, she moved with a stiff grace and acted with decorum, but had no warmth or depth of feeling. With a wife like that, Henry couldn't blame his older brother for wanting an escape. Their parents' attempt to knock some sense into him by pairing their eldest son with a stern woman had failed on an epic scale.

"It's a long way to come just to see me," Henry said.

"It's not so far a distance. Besides, I needed to talk to you." John said.

"What is it?" Henry gripped his tankard. He needed the drink.

"The fact is, I'm in a spot of bother. You see, the last time I was in London I met this girl…"

"Oh, no." Henry rolled his eyes.

"None of that now, Henry. I get enough grief from our father. I don't need it from you too."

Henry nodded. "Go on. You met a girl."

"Justine," he said with a sigh. "She is performing in a delightful little play at the Theatre Royal. Well, when I saw her I was struck by Cupid."

"An actress," Henry muttered and drank. "Cupid."

"Yes, quite. She is so beautiful. So full of life, and laughter, and good cheer."

"Uh-huh."

"And then I got married to Petunia. Justine didn't like that, not at all. But when I set her up in my townhouse, she didn't mind—"

Henry sputtered. "Your townhouse? You mean the *family's* townhouse on Park Street?"

"What is wrong with that?" John asked.

Henry slapped his hand on the table. "It's not your townhouse, it's the family's."

"It is Father's and someday it will be mine, once I inherit the title. He always encourages us to use it when we are in Town, so I don't see the problem."

"It's not your house to give. You can't just set up guests in there," Henry said.

"Justine is not a guest, she is my lady," John told him.

"She's your mistress."

"What a rude thing to say. She is my lady. My female companion."

"Do not use that term with me," Henry growled, "I've heard enough of companions for one day."

"Honestly, Henry, what has gotten into you? You've gotten so uptight lately, you're almost as bad as Father," John said.

"And what does Petunia think of this?" Henry asked.

"Well, that's just it. She didn't know until Justine wrote a letter and Petunia read it—"

Henry stared. "John, tell me you're not still seeing Justine."

"Course I am. I'm not going to let a silly thing like marriage get in the way of my love and happiness. Especially when it's just a marriage of convenience to a bluestocking like Petunia."

"What did she say?"

"Petunia? She demanded I dismiss the girl without a reference. Then she asked if we might go on holiday to Bath." John looked down at his tankard. "You'd think she would have an issue with me sleeping with another woman, but she wasn't bothered at all."

Henry's mouth dropped open. "And the girl. You still have her at the townhouse?"

"Is that all you can think about? Yes, she's still there. Where else would she stay?" John asked.

"Wherever she did before," Henry grunted.

"Now that's not very charitable, you should have seen the place she was in before. In a bad part of Town and not very nice at all. At least in my townhouse she is safe," John said.

"Our townhouse," Henry said, drinking more. He drained his cup and beckoned a barmaid over to refill it. When she did, he said, "Leave the pitcher."

"You're drinking more often than you used to," John said.

"You're giving me a reason to," Henry replied.

"So will you help me or not?"

"Help you do what?" Henry asked.

"Well it's just... I've run out of funds. Between keeping Justine in comfort and paying off Father's debts, plus now that Petunia has caught wind of our relationship... I need to let Justine know that our time together has to end, at least for now. Until I can see her again. But not in my townhouse."

"Good luck," Henry said.

"That's why I need you to go and tell her for me."

"What?" Henry said, earning startled looks from nearby patrons. Nearby, he saw John's valet wince and finish his ale.

"Keep your voice down," John told him.

"I must not have heard you right. I thought you said you wanted me to go and tell your mistress it's over."

"That's right," John said.

Henry drank again. "And you see nothing wrong with this request?"

"Well, I won't have the heart to tell her no. And besides, you cut such a forbidding figure, you can use your serious constable ways to tell her to clear out. She'll listen to a constable more than she ever would me."

Henry frowned. "Why not tell her yourself?"

"Petunia doesn't trust me. Wants me to stay away. She doesn't even know I'm gone, to be honest. She thinks I'm running errands in town."

"Won't she notice your disappearance at dinner?"

"I didn't say which town." John grinned, pleased with himself.

"So what are you doing in Hertford? You came all this way to tell me this. You couldn't have sent a letter?"

"There wasn't time. Please, I'm asking you as a brother. Won't you do this for me?" John asked.

"No. Absolutely not. This is your mess, John. You clean it up," Henry said.

John's expression was sad, as he traced his finger around one of the rings many tankards of ale had stained into the wooden table. "I thought you might say that."

Henry leaned back in his seat, crossing his arms over his chest. "Good. Then we're decided."

"I'm afraid you have to go, Henry," John said.

"And why is that?" A seed of dread grew in Henry's stomach.

"Because I gave the girl your name."

Henry almost fell off his chair. "You did what?" he shouted.

"I told her I was you. You are me. Don't be so dramatic, Henry," John said.

"Why in God's green earth would you do that?"

"Couldn't very well give her my real name, now could I? Me? Son of a baronet? Keep a girl on the side? I have my good name to think about."

"And what about mine?" Henry uttered. His hands shook. He

tried to control them and put them on his knees.

"Henry, I'm married. What would Petunia think? She may be stiffer than a maypole, but she loves me dearly. Finding out the mistress is mine would break her heart."

"Wait a minute. Let me state the facts clearly. You've taken up with an actress and set her up in our townhouse."

"Yes."

"And the girl wrote a letter and Petunia found it."

"Yes."

"But now you tell me that you gave the girl my name, so she thinks I am you."

"Correct."

"And presumably, Petunia your wife thinks the letter the girl wrote is addressed to me, so she thinks I'm leading a girl on, in our family's townhouse."

"Oh. I suppose so," John said thoughtfully, "rather, yes."

Henry could have cheerfully slugged his brother at that moment. He reached for the pitcher with shaking hands, only to find it empty. "More ale," he called out.

John said, "Now you grasp the situation. But it doesn't have to go on, once you go and break it off with Justine. I'd do it by letter, but Justine is very passionate; it's one of the things I like about her. Did I ever tell you how we met?"

"John, what about her? Why not do it by letter?"

"Well it's just that she's so emotional, she last told me that if I ever broke it off, she'd track me down to the ends of the earth and set wild dogs on me. So I waited until she fell asleep and left."

Henry's face was grim.

"Tut tut, Henry. Don't go getting any ideas. It's just… You know how these actresses are."

"I'm afraid I don't," Henry said coldly.

"Well they say one thing and it's all drama. But Justine, she's the type that actually *would* track a man down and show up on his doorstep. So that's why I need you."

"To save your sorry skin and my reputation."

"Not just us, the whole family. Can you imagine what would happen if Father or Petunia found out? It would be the end of me."

"And I am supposed to just go along with this," Henry seethed. "What am I to tell her when we meet?"

"That you are me. You can pretend to be the heir and I'm your bumbling younger brother with not a penny to his name."

"You've got the bumbling part right."

"Steady on, old man. So what do you say, Henry? Will you do it?"

Henry glared at his older brother. "If I do this—"

John's face lit up.

"If, and I mean if, then you have to do something for me."

"Anything. Name it."

"Come clean to Petunia. And Father."

"Anything but that. I can't. I won't."

"Then you've got a mistress in our family's townhouse to look after. What should I tell Father when he next comes to London and wants to stay there?"

"That we're having improvements done and it's currently unlivable."

"He'll want to see it, inspect the improvements for himself."

"Then I'll create a storm, or take him away to the theater—"

Henry laughed. "Enough theater. Not even you can change the weather. John, you have to come clean. It's not fair to me, and you cannot keep lying to Father, Justine, and Petunia forever. They will find out."

John ran a hand through his dusky blond hair. "I know. It's just… It was so much easier being you. No worries, nothing to be concerned with. Will you do it, Henry? For me?"

Henry welcomed the interruption of a barmaid with another pitcher of ale. Once he had drained another tankard, he glanced over to where their valets were quietly drinking, not so subtly listening to every word they said.

"Geoffrey," Henry said.

"Sir?" Geoffrey turned, ever attentive.

"Ready the horses. We leave in the morning." Henry ignored the look of delight on Geoffrey's face and drank more as he saw relief come over his brother's features.

London did have its attractions. He wanted to see Poppy again, and they might run into each other in London. He wanted to talk to her, to make things right with her. He wanted to know how she was faring as a lady's companion, and how she was getting on with her search for her mother.

A part of him wanted to know what she thought of their kiss, and why she had left without a word or even a note to him. But he looked at his brother's hopeful face and thought again. John needed him, and blood was thicker than whatever passing fancy he might have.

Let Poppy get into whatever scrapes she fancied. In London awaited a girl whose heart needed breaking.

CHAPTER SIX

POPPY SPENT THE day with Beatrice. They had a nice luncheon, walked around the park, were chased indoors by the rain, and at tea, they met Beatrice's gentleman. Stephen Farrars was a middle-aged man with money that he had invested well, and he liked keeping track of things that belonged to him. Poppy had expected to meet a young man with money to burn, but instead, she found Stephen to be of an average height, balding, and running to fat. He hid it well beneath fine clothes tailored to him, but there was no hiding a portly middle, or the rosy cheeks that bespoke of a love of wine.

Beatrice doted on his every word, and while he was a bit surprised to find she had engaged Poppy as a companion, he didn't disapprove. He took one look at her and said, "You will no doubt keep my Beatrice out of mischief."

"That is the plan."

"Tell me about yourself," he said. It was more of a command.

Poppy did but kept her remarks fixed on life as a clergyman's niece, who spent her time watching over the chickens and doing good works in the neighborhood. She pointedly did not mention the crimes she had solved in the past, for she suspected that Stephen took a less liberal view of life that did not extend to female investigators.

After a meal of roast partridge, peas, potatoes, and wine at a fashionable hour, Stephen took Beatrice out to the theater while Poppy settled down for a quiet evening with a book.

WHEN THEY RETURNED that night some hours later, Beatrice flew into the sitting room in a flood of tears.

Poppy, half asleep, jumped as Beatrice hurried into the room. "Beatrice, what's wrong?"

"It's him, Poppy, it's Stephen," she cried and plonked herself down on the sofa beside Poppy. She pointed as Stephen entered the room with a frown. "He's leaving me."

Stephen's red face grew stormy. "I am not leaving you, I am just going to be absent for a while. I'll still be in the city."

"With your wife," Beatrice accused. She wiped away angry tears.

"I have to. Ann has been at me for weeks and I had to placate her. She doesn't understand why I spend so much time in London." His face quirked for a moment as he appraised Beatrice's sorry state, and Poppy could see him mentally reevaluating his situation. Why leave a wife who made excessive demands of him, only to put up with another woman who did the same thing?

Poppy swallowed. She had to act fast or her time as a companion would be of short duration, and then she would never find her mother. "Please, Mr. Farrars, let me talk to Miss Hayes. She's just upset."

"I can see that. Maybe you can talk some sense into her."

Beatrice sniffed loudly and blew her nose on a silken handkerchief.

His expression grew harried, and he ran a hand through his thinning hair. "Beatrice, I leave in the morning. I expect you to see me off and say goodbye properly. It will be the last time I will be around for a few weeks."

Beatrice stopped crying. "Where will you go?"

"To my family's house in the city. You know how it is. While my wife is in town we cannot be seen together. You know that."

Beatrice rose from her seat and closed the distance between them. She tucked the handkerchief away in a sleeve and took his larger hands in hers. She gazed up into his eyes.

Poppy began to see the spell Beatrice cast on him.

He reached out and stroked Beatrice's chin, and touched one of her blonde ringlets that had gone astray. His stony expression softened.

"I wish you weren't going. You won't stay away long, will you?" she asked.

He raised one of her hands and kissed it. "No. Not very long."

Beatrice pursed her lips and gave him a coy smile. "There is a new cloak I would like to show you. Would you come see it?" She winked at Poppy as she took his hand and shyly led her lover away to the bedroom, all tears forgotten.

So that was how it was done, Poppy realized. As she spent more time in the company of mistresses, she began to understand that each woman had her own particular talent, her own personal spell of charm, manner, and behavior that she cast to bewitch a man. Poppy wondered if she would ever have one herself, or if that lay solely in the sphere of mistresses' tricks.

But, she thought with a bittersweet smile, it's not like she had anyone to cast it on, even if she did have her own particular charms to employ. For the man she would have chosen did not even call to say goodbye.

On Saturday, Stephen asked to see Poppy alone. Beatrice shut the door of the sitting room, sealing them inside. Poppy stood by quietly and observed him. He sat in a comfortable chair, a smoking pipe in one hand, a newspaper in the other.

"You wished to speak to me, sir?" Poppy asked.

"I wish to discuss your situation here," he said.

"My situation?"

"You're a smart sort of girl, aren't you? You're not just out to drink yourself silly and read ladies' magazines." He held up his London paper.

"No."

"I am happy to pay you to stay on as Beatrice's companion. She should have come to me first, of course, but I think she thought she might be wasting my money. The fact is, this is the first smart thing she's done in ages, and with you by her side, I daresay you'll keep her out of trouble."

Poppy smiled at that.

"My man, Mr. Parks—"

A man stepped out of the shadows and Poppy flinched; she hadn't known he was there. He took one look at Stephen and bowed. He loomed out of the darkness. He'd seen her flinch and smirked.

"As I was saying, my man, Mr. Parks, is here to look after Beatrice's person. He will be present at all of your excursions together and report back to me. I trust that is acceptable to you?"

"Forgive me, but why the need for such security?"

"Has Beatrice told you about the letters she has received?"

"Yes."

"What she doesn't know is that she has only seen a handful. The truth is that I have intercepted more, and hidden them away so as not to alarm her."

Poppy blinked. "May I see them?"

"That's a bit irregular. Why would you want that?" Mr. Parks asked.

"Call it my womanly curiosity," Poppy said with a slight smile. "If Beatrice is being threatened, I want to know what we are up against."

"That's none of your concern," Mr. Parks said. "What kind of woman wants to see some nasty letters?"

"A curious one," Poppy said.

"A sensible one," Stephen said at the same time. He set aside his pipe and newspaper and opened a small portfolio that sat at his feet. He removed a few sheets of paper, handing them to her. They were written in an elegant hand. One read:

Watch out or I'll cut off your pretty head.

*You can't suck a **** with no tongue*
You won't be so pretty without a skull
Leave him or I'll cut out your heart

Poppy handed the letters back in disgust. "These are horrible."

"Yes, they are. But it's why I've hired Mr. Parks to look out for her. Now with you both here, I am confident Beatrice will be safe."

Poppy ignored Mr. Parks's sour expression. "Have you gone to the local magistrate about this?"

"My local magistrate is a drunk. I'm better off catching this man myself. But I wonder… My wife, Ann, won't be happy if she catches me with these. May I leave them in your care?"

"No proper wife would find them," Mr. Parks said.

That earned him a dirty look from Stephen. "My wife has a nervous disposition and fears the worst. She has gone through my things before, and I'd rather not give her more reason to suspect me."

Mr. Parks grunted and was silent.

"Now, one last thing," Stephen said, "your salary. I am happy to pay you for your trouble. Would seven and a half shillings a week be sufficient?"

Poppy nodded. "Thank you, that is very kind."

"It is not kindness or charity, Miss Morton, it is business." He paid her two weeks' wages, which she accepted gratefully.

Then he motioned for her to go, replacing the letters back in his folder. She curtsied, then turned back. "Mr. Farrars, why didn't you do what the letters said and end your relationship with Beatrice?"

Stephen looked up from his newspaper. "Because she is mine. She belongs to me. And no one tells me what to do, especially with the people I care for. It makes me cherish her all the more." He returned to his paper, and their audience was at an end.

As she turned to go, he added, "We will keep you here on a

trial basis, Miss Morton. And when I return from my trip, if you are still to Beatrice's liking, we will discuss the possibility of extending your stay."

"Thank you," she said and silently quit the room. As she walked back down the corridor, she was stopped by a hand on her arm. She whirled around. "Mr. Parks."

"I don't know what you think you're doing, but Miss Hayes don't need you sticking your nose where it don't belong."

"I'm only trying to look out for her."

"That's my job. You telling me a woman could protect her?" His hand gripped her arm so hard it hurt.

She glared into his beady eyes, finding only darkness there. Nothing she could say would convince him. "Of course not. But if there is a threat to Miss Hayes, I want to know about it, so I can protect her as best I can." She looked pointedly at his hand on her arm.

He released her, smirking at the bright red mark his grip had left on her bare skin. "I'm her protector. Don't you forget it." He stalked away.

She stared after him and stood still, then once he had disappeared, let out a breath and rubbed her sore arm. He might be a problem.

Once she was back in her own room, Beatrice was there waiting for her and wanted to know all the details. She was delighted to hear of the arrangement. "That's perfect. I was thinking about it. He will go away and miss me so much, he will be mad about me and will have to keep you on." She clasped Poppy's hands and shook them excitedly.

THE NEXT DAY Stephen left, which suited Beatrice and Poppy very well. They walked in the park, fed the ducks, and had a late luncheon, just in time to meet Harriet at the Shakespeare's Head pub. Harriet sat inside nursing a cup of ale and waved at them across the pub. "Hello there." She rose and curtsied. "I'm so glad you came. I was worried you'd forget."

"You shouldn't do this alone," Poppy said.

"Thank you." Harriet downed her cup of ale. "Shall we go?"

But when they reported Marie's disappearance, the magistrate and his men were less than impressed.

"You want us to go looking for one of your girls, when she's probably spreading her legs around the corner or flat on her back in some man's bed." The magistrate laughed, earning smirks and jeers from the men. "She's probably drunk out of her mind."

Another said, "She's probably just lying there."

To which another answered, "Not if she's any good."

"The girl's likely earning her way. You don't worry your pretty little head about it, she'll come home sore but happy." The magistrate grinned.

"Marie has been missing for three days. Won't you look for her?" Beatrice asked.

"How much you willing to pay?" One of the men asked.

Beatrice backed up, right into a man standing behind her. She jumped and said, "Oh excuse me."

"What's your trouble?" he asked, a dirty grin on his face.

"She's not paying you sixpence, now get a move on," Mr. Parks loomed beside Poppy and glared at the men.

At the sign of his imposing figure, the mood in the room changed. The men shifted and the air grew tense as Poppy realized the men were quietly spoiling for a fight.

The silence was broken by a cheeky whistle singing a tune outside. The door to the building opened and a voice behind Poppy said, "There you are. Getting into trouble already, are we?"

Poppy turned. "Mr. Harris."

Tom gave her a cheeky smile and winked.

"Tom Harris, I should have known. These girls with you?" The magistrate asked.

Poppy opened her mouth to speak when Tom stepped on her foot. "Course they are, they're not causing any trouble, are they?"

Poppy shot him an annoyed look and he grinned at her. She

made to speak again, and he stepped harder on her foot. She shut her mouth and fixed him with a glare.

The men relaxed and Poppy released a breath she hadn't realized she'd been holding.

"No trouble. Get 'em out of here. I got enough to be worrying about without bawds running wild," the magistrate said.

Tom laughed along with the rest of the men and put a hand on the small of Poppy's back. She tensed. "There now, go on," he said loudly. Then he whispered to her, "I'll handle this."

The ladies left, followed by Mr. Parks. Poppy was the last to go when she heard Tom say, "The bawds are right, one of my girls is missing. Marie. Brown hair, buxom, beauty mark on her left cheek. Nice country girl."

"With nice country manners?" one of the men asked.

"The nicest. Very welcoming. I'd hate to see anything bad happen to her."

"Aye, well, we're busy men."

There was the sound of a clink of coins as Poppy heard money being exchanged. She stepped outside just as Tom said, "There's more where that came from if you find the girl."

Poppy stepped into the midday sunshine and never felt better. The air was not so sweet as in Hertford, but it felt good to be outside and away from the oppressive warmth of the room, and the leering looks of the men. She could well understand why the ladies distrusted the magistrate's men.

Tom came out a moment later and dusted off his hands. "Well, that's taken care of. Not bad if I do say so myself—"

"How could you say that?" Poppy asked, her face pinched.

"Say what?" Tom asked.

"Insinuate that I am one of them. Those men thought you were my pimp. I was fine on my own."

He laughed. "Is that what troubles you? Girl, this is a man's world. To them, you're nothing but a girl off the street. I just saved you."

Her face was mutinous.

"You could say thank you, or are they not taught manners out in the country?"

He grinned as she stepped close to him. "I am not one of your girls."

"You mean you're better than us?" Harriet turned from five feet away.

Beatrice approached them. "What's happening?"

"Your companion," Harriet said, "thinks she's better than us, just because we earn our living on our backs."

"I never said that," Poppy said. She looked to Tom for help, but he crossed his arms, his mouth firmly shut.

Poppy turned to Harriet. "I never said that. I would never."

"But you did. That's what has got you so angry. That the men thought you were a whore, like us."

Her uncle's warning was ringing true in her ears. She was already being judged by the company she kept.

"Poppy, is that true?" Beatrice asked.

"She's a worse judge than those louts inside. At least they make no pretense at what they feel. A whore is a whore, isn't that right, Miss Morton?" Harriet's voice dripped with scorn.

"Hold on Harriet, you're being a bit harsh," Tom said.

"I didn't mean anything by it. Just that I'm not like you," Poppy said.

"You've made that abundantly clear. I wonder how you are able to stand being a companion to us when you can't stand our company. Or did you just mean to use Beatrice for her money, like a leech?"

Poppy was silent. "That's not what I meant at all."

"I don't know why you trust this girl, Miss Hayes. She's nothing but trouble," Mr. Parks said, stepping out of the building.

Beatrice's face dissolved into unhappiness. "I think I'd like to go home."

"All right, we'll go," Poppy said.

"No, not together. I need a walk. With my own society. Poppy, you can find your own way back."

"Come on, Beatrice," Harriet said, leading her away.

Mr. Parks shot Poppy a look. "Maybe your stay won't be that long after all." He walked after them.

Poppy stood there, forlorn.

"Now you've done it," Tom said at her shoulder. "You couldn't keep your mouth shut, could you? They may be mistresses, but they have feelings, you know. They're sensitive, especially about their trade."

"I didn't mean—"

"Oh, I know what you meant. And whether you see it or not, I did save you in there. Those men wouldn't have listened to a word you said. Why were you down here anyway? You don't know Marie."

"Harriet asked us to come with her to report her disappearance. She knew it was unlikely the magistrate's men would listen, but she wanted to try."

"And you came with her. A fat lot of good you've done," he told her.

Poppy turned to him, hurt and angry. "I know." She looked away. "What if Miss Hayes throws me out?"

"I wouldn't blame her if she did," Tom said. Seeing her face, he added, "But Beatrice isn't like that. She's a good girl, like you. She's a little too trusting, but she'll forgive an honest mistake, and there's not one of us who hasn't talked out of turn after a few drinks. Go to her tonight and make your peace, and she'll take you back."

"You think so?"

He nodded. "I'd bet on it. Speaking of which, you owe me for paying for Marie."

"What? I don't owe you a cent."

He grinned. "And you owe me for that carriage ride to Beatrice's apartment. Those don't run cheap, you know. Carriages don't just pay for themselves."

His joking tone was lost on her. "I don't have any coin on me," she said.

"I know how you can make some." His face was sly, and seeing her horrified reaction, he laughed. "Only teasing. If anyone owes me, it's Harriet for dragging you both down to the magistrate's in the first place. If I hadn't been there…"

"You were watching us?" Poppy asked.

"Three pretty girls alone in this part of Town? Course I was. And I wasn't the only one. You're just lucky it was me and not some toff. At least Mr. Parks was around. Doesn't say much, but he looks handy in a fight."

Poppy felt a flutter in her chest. He had included her in the description of pretty girls. No one had really told her that before, aside from her own family.

Trying hard not to smile, she said, "What do you mean, toff?"

Tom scratched at the small day's growth on his chin. "You know, one of those wealthy sods who hasn't worked a day in his life. He comes to Town with his purse overflowing and heads straight for the taverns, the seedier the better. They're too stuck up and think they can get away with treating us like dirt. And they can, as long as they pay for it."

"These men sound awful," Poppy said.

"They are. But with their lofty manners and fine clothes, the girls are too poor, hungry, or lovestruck to say no. I keep an eye on all my girls as best I can, but…" He shrugged.

"That is very good of you," Poppy told him.

"Not just good. It's business." He tapped his head. "I can't quote from Seneca, but I can tell you the names, looks, and where to find the best one hundred girls in the city."

Poppy's mouth dropped open. "You're not serious. You're exaggerating."

He shook his head. "Swear I'm not. Although the number's closer to two hundred now."

"I don't believe you."

"You won't have to. A writer came to my uncle a few years back, asking for his knowledge of London whores. They wrote a book together. Next time you're at a bookseller's pick up a copy of *Harris' List.*"

"I couldn't do that. Not if it's indecent," Poppy said.

He laughed. "You'll be good for Beatrice, all right. Fine, I'll get you a copy. Then you'll owe me. That knowledge doesn't come cheap you know."

"I will be able to pay you, just as soon as I return to the apartment. I'll get my wages," Poppy said.

"Forget it, I'm not interested in your money."

"But what about the carriage ride? On my first day in London?"

"It was my welcome gift. Come on, I'll walk you home."

As THEY STROLLED along the riverbank on the Strand, Tom asked her, "You remind me of someone. Like I've seen you before somewhere, but I can't say who or where."

"I just have one of those faces," Poppy said.

"No, you don't." He stopped and looked at her. "Your face is unique. I think if I saw it anywhere, I'd remember it. That's why it bothers me, not knowing."

She started walking again and he kept pace with her. "Miss Morton," he began. "Why did you really come to London?"

"I told you, to interview to be Miss Hayes's companion."

"But a girl like you..." He shook his head. "It just doesn't make sense. You come from a good family, you've got genteel manners, you're smart... What are you running away from?"

"Nothing." She answered too quickly, and his interest latched on like a cat to a mouse.

"The man you're running away from. Who is he?" Tom asked.

"He? He is no one. There is no one. I'm not running away from anything."

"What is it? An uncle or cousin who tried to touch you? A neighbor, perhaps?"

"No," she said firmly.

He would not let up. "Did some jealous matrons run you out

of town and threaten you if you ever came near their husbands again?" He grinned.

She smirked. "Now you are teasing me."

"I tease everyone."

"And do they always tell you what you want to know?"

"Usually." He flashed her a winning smile. "Tell me, Miss Morton."

"Tell you what? I have nothing to tell."

"Anything."

She looked into his eyes and found them earnest. If his expression were to be believed, here was a man who genuinely wanted to know about her and what she thought. He was a willing listener, which was hard to find in any social stratum. So she told him. She shared how in the past she had solved not one but two murders, and then she stopped.

"What?" he asked.

"You're not laughing. People tend to laugh at me when I tell them that."

"Why?"

"Because they think it is rude for a young woman to be telling tales, or if they think I am telling the truth, then it is unladylike to be solving a murder. They think I am sticking my nose in a man's business, and it is wrong."

"Do you think that?" he asked.

She paused. "I think if it solves a murder and brings a killer to justice, then it doesn't matter if I put a few noses out of joint."

"And you think I would laugh at you for this?" he asked.

"Well no, but maybe."

"There you go again, Miss Morton, assuming that people are all alike. I'm different from the other people you've met. I'm unique. And you're leaving something out of your story. Something or someone important, I can tell."

She gave a tiny sigh and glanced at her shoes, then said, "Well…"

"You didn't solve these crimes alone, did you?" he asked.

"No one would have believed me if I'd had. But no, there was a constable."

She told him of Dyngley, and how in the pursuit of finding a killer, they had become friends. It was easier to talk about him with a stranger.

"And you two are just friends?" Tom asked.

"Yes. He is the second son of a baronet and I'm a companion. But maybe I'm not even that after what I said. I didn't mean to hurt them, I just..."

He glanced at her.

"They have their trade and I have mine, and I don't want to be mistaken," she began.

"For a whore," he said.

"Yes, exactly. Is that so wrong?" She met his eyes, and they were kind.

"No one in their right mind could mistake you for that, Poppy," he said, "You're too polite and genteel. Too genuine. Innocent. You're too... wholesome."

"You say that like it's a bad thing," she pointed out.

"It's not, it's just a rarity to find those real qualities in a woman in our sphere, that's all. But, many young women with the clap also make it their business to seem sweet and wholesome like you, so it could all be a ruse." He grinned.

She rolled her eyes. "So you're unique and I'm a rarity," she said, "What an odd pair we make."

"I rather like the sound of that," he said, "but aside from rarities and uniqueness, even those of us like Marie who strive for cleanliness, it's like the men can always tell. Like a hidden spot or a stain that's on the girls, they can't hide the fact that they're whores. Even Marie, who bathes constantly."

"What is she like? She must be popular to have so many people looking for her."

He smiled. "She's one of the nicer ones. And she never gets sick, she's as healthy as a horse. And unlike some girls I could mention, she's never caught the clap, or the pox, or the French disease."

Poppy blinked. What accomplishments indeed. "I like her already. What does she look like, again?"

"Brown hair, like a nut brown, like yours. Wide eyes and a beauty mark on her left cheek."

Poppy pointed to something white floating among the reeds. "What's that? Some rags?"

"I don't know." Tom followed her gaze and together, they walked down a set of stone steps to a safe riverbank, where the white object drifted. As they came closer, Poppy's boot slipped on wet grass and she fell in.

Cold murky water enveloped her, and she cried out, river water filling her mouth. She clawed at the weeds and grasped for purchase, lifting her head above the water. Her feet struck the sandy bottom and she bobbed, spitting and coughing. She turned to grab at the floating rags when her gloved hands touched the floating object, and it floated closer, bobbing up to her face.

Poppy realized then that the object was no object at all, but a dark-haired woman, her body bloated and pale, with eyes wide and glassy in death, and a beauty mark on her left cheek. The very water stank with her bloated corpse smell and as Poppy touched her, her hand was swallowed up by black water.

Poppy screamed, "It's Marie!

CHAPTER SEVEN

"OH MY GOD!" Poppy said, sinking into the River Thames. Cold water filled her vision as she slipped and swallowed river water. She bobbed to the surface, coughed, and sputtered, her boots slipping on the unsteady bottom as she launched herself backward. Her gloved hands felt cold and heavy, powerless against the cold current.

Tom cursed and lunged into the water. "Take my hand!" He reached out to her.

Poppy praised her lucky stars for her long legs that could touch the river bottom, for the current could have easily swallowed a shorter girl. As her body's warmth deserted her, she knew she had to get out. The water was shockingly cold. She already began to lose feeling in her hands and her gloves felt like deadweights dragging her down. She reached for Tom, and he clawed at her hand and tugged, pulling her through the water.

His grip was strong as he tugged her gloved hand, dragging her toward him. She spat out river water and coughed as he pulled them both free of the water and up onto the riverbank. He released her as she fell to her knees, coughing. She looked up at him, as he dragged the bobbing body out of the water and onto the shore not far away from them.

"Thank you," she said, "is that? Is it…"

"It's Marie. I recognize her," he said, his voice tight. "My

God. What was she doing?"

Poppy looked at him and shivered. "We need to fetch a constable. They'll know what to do."

"This isn't the countryside, Miss Morton."

"A member of the watch, then. Someone must come," she said.

"Yes. I'll go. Can you stay with her? If it's not too much trouble." Tom glanced at the white form and looked away, repressing a shudder. His eyes landed on Poppy and only when his gaze wandered up did she realize she was soaked through. She pulled her walking coat tighter around her, even though it was soddened. "Go, I'll be fine here."

"I won't be gone long." He took off, even though he was wet to the waist.

Poppy took that opportunity to examine the body. It was a young woman, with brown hair, almost black. It had floated like gossamer or silk in the water and was now plastered across a white face. She couldn't have been more than twenty or twenty-five at most, but it was hard to tell from her glassy eyes that stared straight ahead, her dead-fish white skin, and her mouth that hung open in a mute plea. The girl's body lay only partially on the pebbly bank, the tide making her booted feet waver and bob against some weeds. Marie's dress was pale and dirty, and her cheek bore a slight beauty mark like Tom had described.

What Poppy couldn't tell was how the girl had died. At first glance, she bore no cut or gaping wound, no bloody clothes or sign of injury. Presumably, she had drowned. Could it have been an accident? Could Marie have tripped and fallen in and not knowing how to swim, drowned? Being September, a few of the days were still warm, but it was rather too chilly to go swimming. Even then, Marie wore a white patterned walking dress and a dirty tangled coat. Could it have been foul play?

Poppy didn't know. She needed to speak to someone who had known Marie.

She was joined a short while later by Tom, two men of the

watch, a parish constable, and two boys with a cart. Poppy stood back as the men took charge and bore Marie's body away.

Tom sagged against the stone wall and rested his hands against his thighs. "I can't get over it. Marie, gone. I'd just seen her a few days ago. Hard to believe she's…" He swallowed.

"Were you close to her?" Poppy asked.

"Not that close. I knew her, but I wasn't her lover if that's what you're asking."

Poppy shook her head. "Could she have tripped and fallen?"

"Maybe. But if she fell, would there be marks on her somewhere? Scratches or bruises? Cuts maybe."

"Maybe, but if she was in the water for a long time, the blood would have washed away," Poppy said.

Tom scratched his chin. "That'd explain why there was no blood when I fished her out. She could have been there for days." He turned pale.

Poppy's expression softened. "When was the last time you saw her?"

"Me? No more than two to three days ago."

"I need to speak to Harriet. She too noticed that Marie was gone. They had plans to go out together and she became worried when Marie didn't show up."

Tom gazed at the ground where Marie had been taken from the riverbank.

"Tom, would you accompany me back to Beatrice's apartments? I don't know the way yet," Poppy said.

"Course." He walked along, eyes on the ground. "I'll speak with her patron. See if he knows anything about this."

"What about her family?" Poppy asked.

"She didn't have any, or if she did, she never said." Tom brought Poppy back in good time and rapped on the door.

It was opened by Fanny, who upon seeing Poppy, said, "She doesn't want to see you. Clear off."

"Oh get stuffed, you old hag," Tom said and pushed his way in. "Miss Hayes," he called, "Miss Hayes."

Beatrice's head appeared over the top of the stairwell. "Tom, what is it?"

"We've come to tell you the news. Tell your guard dog to let us in."

"Oh, Fanny, do let them in."

The sour-faced maid shot Poppy a baleful look and stepped aside as Poppy went in. She felt unwanted and small. What had she done to offend the woman? Aside from being rude to her mistress. Poppy wondered as she followed Tom upstairs, ignoring the feel of Fanny's glower that pricked between her shoulder blades.

Poppy found Beatrice and Harriet in the parlor together, sitting on one of the sofas. At their arrival, Poppy earned a severe look from Harriet. "What is she doing here? And what happened to your clothes? You're soaked through."

"We fell in the Thames. But never mind that," Tom said, "Marie's dead."

"What?" The blood drained from Harriet's face. "No."

"She can't be," Beatrice said. "We had plans to see her. You must be mistaken."

"We're not. We found her," Tom said.

"Where?" Harriet asked.

"By the river. She'd drowned."

"That makes no sense. Could she even swim? What was she doing in the water at this time of year? It's too cold for a swim," Harriet said.

"She might have slipped and fallen in. But it's her, Harriet. I saw her with my own eyes," Tom said.

"I just don't understand. What she was she doing there?" Beatrice asked.

"Maybe her gentleman came to visit," Poppy said.

"Perhaps. But even so… Now what do we do?" Harriet asked.

"The constables already know, they've taken her away," Tom said.

"To be laid in a pauper's grave, no doubt." Harriet's face was twisted.

"Oh Miss Morton, I'm scared," Beatrice took her hand. "What if something foul happened to her?"

"You've been listening to Miss Morton's stories too much," Harriet said with a frown. "Surely it was likely an accident."

"But what if it wasn't?" Beatrice asked.

"Accident or not, I want to know. Where is she now? I want to see her," Harriet said.

"Miss Sykes, you do not. She is… it's not a pretty sight."

"I don't care. I want to see my friend. I want to see Marie," Harriet said.

Tom looked at her. "You won't like it. Besides, seeing a body is no place for a woman. They wouldn't let you in."

Tears rolled down Harriet's cheeks. "It's not fair. She was my friend." She walked away from them, over to a set of windows. She held her arms close to her chest, hugging herself as she looked outside. Beatrice dropped Poppy's hand and went to her.

Tom turned to Poppy and said quietly, "I'm sorry our walk was disturbed. Might we walk again sometime?"

"I would like that."

"Good," he said with a ghost of a smile.

Once Tom had ushered Harriet away, Beatrice sank into one of the fine chairs in the room, caring little if she appeared ladylike or not. "Miss Morton, I—"

"I'm sorry." Poppy interrupted. "I should never have been so rude about your profession. You are a lady and… I never meant to offend you."

Beatrice's mouth crinkled into a gentle smile. "I know." She blinked and wiped away a tear. "It did hurt, you know. But I don't care. I am more than a mistress and you are more than a companion. Please don't go. Harriet said I should dismiss you."

Poppy tensed.

"But I don't want to. I'm scared, Miss Morton."

"I'm sorry about Marie," Poppy said.

"What do we do?" Beatrice asked.

"There's not a lot we can do. The magistrates have her body, so they will handle it."

"But what about…" Beatrice paused.

"What?"

"It's just… When I saw her last, Marie wasn't herself. She was nervous about something. She seemed scared. She kept giving each of us the oddest looks and jumped at little things. I've never seen her so anxious before."

"Did she say why?"

"No. Not to me anyway. But she is usually so bright and warm and confident. Could we investigate a little?" Beatrice asked.

"What for? The parish magistrates declared it an accident."

"But what if it wasn't? I'd want to be sure. And I know Harriet does too, even if she pretends not to."

A funny feeling grew in Poppy's chest as if Beatrice knew something she did not. "What do you propose?"

"What would you normally do for a situation like this?" Beatrice asked.

"I'd speak to her family, her friends, anyone that knew her and see if she had any enemies."

"I can answer that. Marie was an orphan. She grew up in the streets. But she didn't have any enemies, she wouldn't hurt a fly," Beatrice said.

"Miss Hayes, what makes you think her death was suspicious? For all we know, she slipped and fell, or she might have tried to swim and went too far out. It happens. The current is strong." Poppy glanced down at her semi-dry clothes.

"What happened to you?"

"We were walking along the Thames when I spotted her in the water. I didn't recognize her at first and so went closer to see, then fell in. Tom fished me out, which is why we're both wet."

Beatrice's eyebrows rose as she noted Poppy's damp walking coat and sodden dress underneath. "I see." She gave a little sigh. "Marie never swam. I don't think she could swim. Even when we had little bathing parties on Bermondsey Beach, she never went in. Trust me when I say that Marie drowning *is* suspicious. She may have been clean to a fault, but she would never go in the river, or the ocean."

"All right. In that case, we'll need to speak to the others. Harriet for sure. Maybe she'll know why Marie was scared or what she was nervous about. And we'll have to visit her lodgings to see if there are any clues she left behind."

Poppy left Beatrice to return to her room and dry off. In that moment, she wished Dyngley was there. He would know what to do. She felt that she had experience and skills she could bring to winkle out whether Marie's death was suspicious or not, but she'd feel better if he were there with her. She let out a little sigh. He didn't even know she was gone. What would he think of her now?

CHAPTER EIGHT

A T THAT MOMENT, Constable Henry Dyngley rode in one of
the Dyngley family carriages with his older brother John
and their valets, Robert and Geoffrey, along with a footman up
top and a driver, making the journey to London. As they stopped
at the Bell Inn in Highbury to eat a meal and change horses,
Henry wrote a letter to their father, Sir Edmund Dyngley,
explaining that they were on their way to London to close up the
townhouse and settle some outstanding debts. Then unbeknownst to John, Henry penned a letter to John's wife, Petunia.
He asked that she forgive John's sudden disappearance, as it was
in haste to save him from some unfortunate circumstances, and
passed on John's love for her. Then he sealed it and sent it on the
dispatch to Essex, while John ate, drank, and flirted with the
barmaids.

They couldn't leave too soon, Henry decided, judging from
the amorous looks John was giving *and* receiving in return. Henry
practically dragged his brother away from the inn, much to the
relief of the innkeeper, whose daughters John had been admiring.

Now safely on the way to London, Henry would have liked
to settle back and let the jostling of the carriage lull him to sleep.
Instead, he asked to see the letter from Justine, interrupting John
mid-sentence. John pulled it from his pocket and handed it to
him.

"What do you want to see that for?" John asked.

"If you are courting a young woman in my name, I wish to know what you have been saying." Henry unfolded the letter. It smelled faintly of a woman's perfume, like crushed violets. It read:

Dearest Henry, I miss you so much. When will you come back to town? I—

Henry read its contents, folded it up, and returned it to John. The letter held nothing of consequence, and it felt wrong somehow to be reading a letter for his brother, even if it was addressed to him.

He could have cuffed John at that moment for causing such trouble. Thank God none of their family or friends knew. And if Poppy knew… it didn't bear thinking about. She would never forgive him for courting another woman so soon after his engagement had ended, and to take a mistress while stealing kisses from her was even worse. It was not to be borne.

He shook his head and would have said something harsh to John, but refused to do that in front of the valets. A mix of servant and friend, their valets were good men but in Henry's mind, like attracted like, and while he felt Geoffrey was trustworthy, John's manservant Robert was not. With his wagging tongue, it was a wonder that all the servants did not know of their predicament already.

HENRY JOLTED AWAKE hours later.

"Where are we?" John asked sleepily.

"London," Henry said. He knew it to be true from the sound of the horses' hooves on the road. Their footfalls were no longer the thudding and pounding against country dirt roads, but instead had been replaced with the sharp clatter of tough hooves striking cobblestones, and the scent of smoke, rotting fruit, blood from the butcher's, and horse dung pervaded the carriage.

"What a stink," John said, holding a perfumed handkerchief to his nose.

The Dyngley carriage pulled slowly through busy streets, crowded with people. Men, women, tradesmen, and shopkeepers all jostled for position as the carriage moved at a slow pace. The smell of dung and refuse grew stronger as they moved at a snail's pace past human traffic, moving along Fleet Street and then up along the back of St Paul's, as it took the street past Bloomsbury and the British Museum. By the time it finally pulled up outside the family's townhouse in Park Street, John was the first to bound out of the carriage. He stepped out and put a hand on the door as Henry disembarked. "What is it, John?" he asked.

"Well, I just realized, um, the townhouse probably isn't ready for visitors yet."

"You have a woman living here. I'd say it's been visited fairly frequently."

John shot Henry a look. "What I mean to say is, let's give Geoffrey and Robert time to set up the place and freshen it up a bit first. I don't know about you, but I'm parched and could use a drink, and a chance to stretch my legs. What say you to a quick drink before we go in?"

Henry shrugged. One drink couldn't hurt.

But one pint of ale led to another, and Henry found himself hours later, past pleasantly intoxicated and now approaching fairly drunk, with John singing at the top of his lungs in a pub that bore a sign of the king. It had crossed his mind that distracting him might have been John's plan all along, but he didn't mind. John would have to face the problem he'd created soon enough. One more day wouldn't make a difference.

But then a woman strolled by on the arm of an older gentleman and Henry's mouth dropped open.

"Henry, what is it?" John stopped his warbling to ask.

"Who was that?" Henry sputtered.

The man had looked ordinary enough, tall, silver hair fading to white at the temples, with a sturdy physique and long fingers like a piano player's. He wore a form-fitting dark coat, trim dark breeches, and had his hair tied back in a queue. But on his arm stood a statuesque lady of quality. She stood of an equal height, with light brown hair and dancing eyes, a mouth that half quirked in a private joke, and pale skin worthy of a milkmaid. She gave John an amused look and whispered something to her companion. The man laughed and escorted her upstairs, as Dyngley stared in disbelief.

"Henry old man, what's the matter? You look like you've seen a ghost."

"I think I have. Who is that?"

"Him? That's only Lord Blackwood. He owns Blackwood Manor, in Somerset."

"And his lady?"

"So that's what caught your eye. Stop staring, fool. She's taken. That's the Grace."

"The Grace?" Henry repeated.

"That's what they call her. Cause she's so charming and witty, like one of the three graces, out of Greek mythology. She can charm the angriest man and soothe the meanest temper. She's smart. I wouldn't try for her, Henry, she's out of your depth. And if you don't mind my saying so, she's a bit old for you. She's nearer fifty but doesn't look it."

"What's her real name?"

"Does it matter? Why the sudden interest? If it's girls you want, we'll go to Covent Garden. I'll introduce you to my man Tom, who can find any young lady you like for your pleasure. I'm glad to see you enjoying yourself, Henry. If only I'd known that all it took was a few drinks to get you to…"

Henry ignored the drone of his brother's voice until it faded into a faraway buzz. If he was not mistaken, he had just seen Poppy's mother.

THE NEXT DAY was not to be a pleasant one for Henry, for he woke up in a bed he did not recognize. Sunlight streamed through his window, blinding him, and he'd awoken with a splitting headache. He grunted, belched, and winced. His breath tasted foul, like sour ale. Still fully dressed in the clothes he wore last night, he stumbled out of bed, splashed some water on his face from the blue and white ceramic basin on the side table, and used the chamber pot. Then he stripped and dressed in a fresh set of trousers, clean shirt, and cravat. Once fully clothed, he stumbled down the shadowy corridors of the townhouse before tugging on a clean coat and making for the nearest coffeehouse.

Fortunately, he did not have to travel far. One thing he liked about London was that taverns, inns, and coffeehouses were in good supply, and even if the city was too full of people for his liking, they were prime places for gossip. He walked a little distance and spotted a coffeehouse on the corner of Portman Street, not far from Portman Square. Inside, the room was full of men and the air was rich with the heady smell of fresh coffee. Henry ordered a cup and sat at a lone table, drinking the harsh brown liquid, almost black. He closed his eyes and inhaled the heady scent as he ignored the crowd of men and waited to come back to life.

In a short time, he did and listened as men discussed the news of the day. Which plays were good, which establishments offered good gambling, which taverns did not, where could one find loose women and the latest outcome of the horses at the races. Then something caught his attention. One man said, "I heard they fished the girl's body out of the Thames yesterday. Sorry thing when a girl kills herself."

Dyngley's ears perked up.

"But it's just a whore. Whores die every day. If it's not the pox or the clap, then it's only a matter of time before the girl meets with an accident or the wrong man. What does one dead whore matter?"

Henry listened through the fog of his drink-addled brain.

"She was a mistress. Just wait 'til her man finds out she's gone and drowned herself. You know how these lords are about their girls. See them as part of the family, almost."

"The best part," the other man jibed.

"Shut your mouths, you two," a young voice cut through their chatter. "Marie Watkins was a good girl. Didn't deserve what happened to her."

Henry drank more coffee as the two men mumbled what could have been an apology and found an excuse to leave shortly thereafter. The young man smirked and helped himself to their empty seats. "Serves them right," he muttered.

Dyngley waited a moment, then raised his head. "Who was the lady?"

The young man started and looked at him. He was a youth of about twenty-five, with unruly light brown hair and a polite expression, with ice blue eyes that narrowed at the sight of Henry's clothes. His skin was tanned from being outdoors, and his face had a pockmark or two. But his curled hair and sideburns gave him a youthful appearance, as well as his cheap looking light brown jacket and beige trousers, with a loosely tied cravat.

With seconds the youth had taken the measure of Dyngley, from his dark hair that was mussed from a fitful drunken sleep, and the day's fuzz on his chin, to the hastily tied cravat and jacket that needed straightening on his form. But Henry didn't care for any of that. He met the young man's eyes and waited.

"Who wants to know?"

"I do. I'm with the constabulary."

Two men instantly moved back their chairs and left. The young man watched them go with a smirk. "But you're not from around here. You have no jurisdiction."

Henry's mouth firmed into a tight line. "Who was the lady? The one who died."

"Why do you care? A whore's a whore, isn't that right?"

"You are confusing me with the other men. Was it Miss Beatrice Hayes?"

The young man's expression grew pinched. "How do you know her?"

"My friend. She works as a companion to Miss Hayes. I think."

Recognition sparked in the young man's eyes.

"You do know who I am talking about. You are acquainted with Miss Morton?"

"You mean Poppy?"

Henry bristled at the man's familiar use of her name.

The young man leaned back in his chair and helped himself to a leftover cup of coffee. "Yeah, I know her. Who are you?"

"Constable Henry Dyngley."

"You're Dyngley?" The young man took a closer look at him, memorizing his features. There was again the look of recognition, but his expression held some thought that Henry did not like.

"I am. Who are you?" Henry asked.

"Everyone knows me. I'm Tom Harris." He scratched his chin.

Henry's brother's mention of the man made his mouth curl in distaste. His voice held a note of scorn. "I've heard of you."

Tom brushed imaginary lint off his jacket sleeves. "I'd be offended if you didn't. But I know about you, too, Constable. And from a lady known to us both." His grin was cocky.

Henry was up out of the chair and looming over the man before Tom could speak. His hands curled into fists, and he used every ounce of self-control not to shake the man senseless. "Where is she?" Henry demanded. "Where is Miss Morton?"

"Oh, she's fine. Doesn't need any help from you. She's off being a good little companion," Tom said, leaning back in his chair.

"Tell me where she is. Her aunt and uncle are worried about her."

"Sent you to bring her home, did they? Am I right? Aye, well, good luck to you. Trouble follows that one."

"How do you know her?" Henry asked.

"She the companion to Miss Hayes, who happens to be a good friend of mine. Although if Poppy didn't tell you that, I wonder how good friends you two really are," Tom said with a slow smile. "Sit down, Constable, half the coffee shop is wondering if you'll break my head in two."

Henry wasn't opposed to the idea. "Don't give me a reason. Where can I find this friend?"

"In her house."

"You're toying with me. What kind of woman is she, this Miss Hayes? Is she a spinster?"

Tom laughed aloud at that.

Henry reddened. "All I have is a name. She's not on any peerage lists I've seen. Is she a lady of quality?"

Tom chortled. "I'll tell her that, she loves to laugh. Beatrice in the peerage? She'll be in stitches."

"She is no lady, then." Henry sat down.

"She's someone's lady all right. She can be yours too, for a price." Tom winked.

Henry's jaw dropped. "You mean Miss Hayes is…"

"She's kept in style by a certain gentleman."

"My God. You mean Miss Morton is a companion to a whore."

"Where's your sense of civility?" Tom asked. "I thought you toffs were all about having good manners to a fault."

"I am not a toff," Henry said.

Tom laughed again. "That's just what a toff would say. Miss Morton never said you were funny. Go on, tell me another. I love a good joke."

"Miss Morton talked about me?" Henry leaned forward in his seat.

Tom grunted and drank his coffee. His expression darkened. "What's your relationship with her then anyway?"

"I beg your pardon?" Henry asked.

Tom's blue eyes were serious. "Do you have an understanding?"

"Our relationship is no concern of yours."

"Oh, but it is. My friend Miss Hayes has enough to worry

about without a parish constable running around, stirring up trouble."

"I assure you, I have no intention of involving myself in your affairs," Henry said stiffly.

"Then why are you in London?" Tom asked.

"Personal reasons."

"Uh-huh. Well, mind your business don't keep you too long. London's got enough constables without adding one more from the country."

They exchanged a hard look.

Tom grinned and finished his coffee. He rose and said, "Enjoy your stay in London, Constable. May it be of short duration." He sauntered out, whistling a catchy tune.

Henry let out a breath he'd not known he was holding. "Jesus, Poppy, where are you?"

CHAPTER NINE

AT THAT MOMENT, Poppy was chatting over breakfast with Beatrice and Harriet.

Over cold ham and toast, Harriet said, "I don't know but something has to be done. Marie was my friend. She wouldn't have gone swimming, she didn't know how to swim."

"But what can we do? The magistrates have her body," Beatrice said.

"Are we certain that that's how she died? By drowning?" Harriet asked.

Both young women looked at Poppy. "You're very quiet, Miss Morton," Harriet said. "What do you make of all this?"

"There is no reason to believe Marie did not drown," Poppy said.

"Except we know she was no swimmer," Harriet pointed out.

"Could Marie have been meeting someone? A lover or her gentleman perhaps? Did she have any enemies?" Poppy asked.

"Besides us, you mean?" A ghost of a smile drifted across Harriet's pretty features. "No."

"Why would you be her enemies? I thought you were all friends," Poppy said.

"We are, to a point." Harriet looked at Beatrice. "But the fact is, we are all in a funny sort of situation. We're higher than the bawds on the street corner and have some freedom. But to many, we're just a higher class of whore, and of course, are unacceptable to all good society. We belong to a unique little club, and only have each other for company."

Poppy thought that sounded rather miserable. "Would any of your group want to hurt Marie?"

"Hurt? No. Humiliate, embarrass, or take advantage of? Absolutely," Harriet said with a frown. "When we aren't putting each other down, we are inviting each other to parties, to show off our latest gowns or jewels—"

"And flaunt our wealth," Beatrice added, "and to make the next move to one-up everyone else."

Harriet shot Beatrice a look. "If we wanted to *hurt* Marie, we'd call her dirty or tell her she smelled. She's such a stickler for cleanliness and washing all the time. All that water couldn't have been good for her. But none of us would actually hurt her."

Beatrice coughed delicately and mumbled, "Except Frances."

"Who's Frances?" Poppy asked.

"Nobody. It's ancient history." Harriet shot Beatrice a dirty look.

"What is?"

Harriet shook her head and glared at them both. "Oh, hell. I can tell from Beatrice's face that she is going to tell you anyway, so I might as well. I knew her longer, so at least I can tell you the facts. But not here. Let us go outside if we are going to air our dirty linens."

Once suitably attired in walking cloaks, gloves, and hats, the women followed Beatrice's lead and set out on a walk, followed not so subtly by Mr. Parks.

Once they had begun walking on a smooth path through a green park, Harriet began, "Frances Landry was a whore."

Poppy blinked.

"She was a mistress like us. A kept woman. Wealthy, too."

"Her patron was a lord, wasn't he?" Beatrice asked.

"Yes, although I'll not say who. He was very rich and kept her in style. In our little rankings, she was closest in wealth to Mollie, but they weren't friends," Harriet said, "bitter enemies, more like."

"That's right, I remember seeing her once at dinner," Beatrice said. "She and Mollie seemed close, but after a few drinks I've never seen two women go at it like that. They acted like… like…"

"Whores? You can say it, it won't offend me. They acted no better than the streets they came from. I recall that night too, for it was the last time any of us saw Frances."

"What do you mean? What happened to her?" Poppy asked.

"There's something you need to understand. Even among our little group, we have rules. Like… regimens to live by, vows we abide by and obey. But even with us, there is a cardinal rule," Harriet said, "you can tease, insult, even steal from your patron all your like. But Frances did the one thing we dare not do."

"What?" Poppy asked.

Harriet glanced at Beatrice. "Frances cheated on her patron with another man."

Poppy's eyebrows rose.

"You might not think it so great a matter. We are whores, after all. But to our gentlemen, it is a very grave issue."

"Almost a sin," Beatrice said.

"Yes. Our gentlemen already pay for our favors, and they don't take kindly to any of us bestowing our company on any other men, especially for free."

"I see. So what happened?" Poppy asked.

"The last night we saw Frances, Mollie was teasing her for having such an old patron and um…" She made a rude gesture with her fingers to show a drooping index finger. Beatrice giggled.

"I'm sorry?" Poppy said.

"You're rather chaste, aren't you?" Harriet rolled her eyes and explained, "Most older gentlemen are not so quick to become aroused as young men. They are still virile and enthusiastic, but can require a bit more coaxing." She grinned and said, "Too much alcohol and it can happen. In any case…" She smirked at Poppy's blushes. "Mollie was teasing, and Frances had drunk one too many. She rose to the bait and told us all that she didn't have to worry about that, anymore, as his son was serving her needs very well and was most satisfactory in that area."

"Oh." Poppy clapped a hand to her mouth.

"Yes. Mollie laughed and they kept talking as if nothing was the matter, but the next day Frances's patron found out and he kicked her out without a penny. She had nothing. She was back on the street that same night, or at least that's what I heard."

"Could she not have found another patron?" Poppy asked.

"No one would have her. No one wanted to cross the earl and no man wanted his castoffs. It would be unseemly. We never saw her again," Harriet said.

"Did none of you try to help her?" Poppy asked.

"Of course, we would have, but none of us could find her. It was like she disappeared."

Beatrice said, "I heard a rumor that she got the pox."

"Small wonder she'd want to hide away if she caught that. A mistress lives by her beauty and if not that, then her wit and charm, as well as her talents in the bedchamber. To be so diseased and disfigured…"

"It would leave her starving on the streets. No one would want her then," Beatrice said. "I also heard she's in Newgate prison for stealing."

Mr. Parks called Beatrice, and she went over to speak with him.

Harriet watched them and sniffed, "To anyone, Frances would just be a whore, her body on sale for a halfpenny. And that is why we were so offended at your words to Tom earlier. We hold ourselves to a higher standard than the dirty bawds you find on a street corner, even if it may seem laughable to some."

"I'm sorry," Poppy said, "I didn't realize."

"Now you do. Do you still feel that way, Miss Morton?"

Poppy's mind felt somewhat unchanged, but she knew she had to make peace. Her uncle's warning about the company she kept rang in her ears. "No. I'm sorry I offended you."

Harriet looked slightly mollified. "I accept your apology. But words, as fine as they are, and however earnestly said, are often meaningless. So I suggest you try a bit harder to prove your worth as a companion to Miss Hayes. She may forgive you, but trust is another matter." She gave Poppy a hard look. "I don't think you are a bad person, Miss Morton, just naive in the ways of the world. I would take care to choose your words a bit more carefully around the society you move in. You wouldn't want to end up on the street."

"Is that a threat?"

"Call it a friendly warning," Harriet said as Beatrice rejoined them.

"Look who I found," Beatrice said, "Mr. Harris."

Tom bowed to the group, his light brown hair looking slightly disheveled. "I was just passing and saw you lot enter the park. I was thinking, what if Marie's apartments had some clue as to how she died?"

"A clue?" Harriet repeated.

"Yes. Anything she had on her person would have washed away in the Thames, but what if one of her servants saw something amiss? They might not even know their mistress is dead."

"What about her patron?" Poppy asked. "Shouldn't he be told?"

"He should be if he hasn't heard already. It was all the conversation in the coffee shop this morning." Tom gave Poppy an odd look. "He might have been the one who did it, for all we know."

"We'll need to speak to him anyway. Surely he would want to know the particulars."

"I wouldn't. To find out my mistress is dead? That would be enough for me." Tom shuddered.

"I know where he drinks," Beatrice said. "He's often at the King's Head around midday."

"I know that place, it's where a lot of the toffs drink." Tom glanced at Poppy again.

Beatrice said, "I can find him there, I'm sure of it."

"You shouldn't go alone," Harriet pointed out.

"It's settled, then. Miss Morton and I will visit Marie's apartments while you two talk to her patron," Tom said.

"What should we say?" Harriet asked.

"Tell him she died. An unfortunate accident. And watch him for his reaction. See if he acts sad or surprised," Poppy said.

"Of course, he'll be surprised. She's dead," Harriet said.

"But if he already knows, then he might act suspiciously."

Beatrice gave Poppy a knowing look and the group parted ways.

Tom hired a hackney carriage and soon they were on their way to another part of London. Poppy instantly looked out the window to her left, eyeing the grand buildings, the people walking, and even the boys who cleaned up horse droppings from the street. There was so much of London she didn't know and hadn't seen, it was a wonder to her how anyone could come to know it all.

"Penny for your thoughts," Tom said.

"Why did you wish to separate from Harriet and Beatrice? We could have gone with them. I'm sure they would have appreciated your presence. There was no need to split up our party."

"Perhaps I wished to be alone with you," he said with a flirtatious smile.

She stiffened. She had knowingly entered into a carriage with a young man, alone, without an escort. It was highly questionable and if she were at home in Hertford, no doubt she would have gotten an earful from her aunt and uncle. It was inappropriate, unthinking, and immoral behavior. She had unconsciously compromised herself and now relied on Tom's gentlemanly nature not to speak of it. She also realized she hadn't been to church in some time.

"What day is it?"

"Saturday, why?"

"Thank goodness. I can still make it to church tomorrow."

Tom snorted. "I should have known that's what you were worried about. Not whether we are on the hunt for a murderer, but whether you have church tomorrow."

"It's a valid concern."

"Once a clergyman's daughter, always a clergyman's daughter." He grinned.

"I'm a clergyman's niece, thank you very much."

"And what does that signify?"

"That perhaps I'm not so holy as I seem. Maybe I'm more worldly than you think. I might surprise you."

That made his eyebrows rise and he laughed. "Of that, I have no doubt."

"Tom, be serious."

He grinned at her. "In truth, I did not want Beatrice and Harriet to see Marie's apartments, just in case someone did mean her harm."

"You think we will find a bloody scene?" Poppy asked.

"Possibly. I don't know. But I don't need two silly girls screaming, fainting, and spreading false rumors across the city."

"Tom, really. We are not all like that," Poppy said.

"Miss Morton, you may not be. But for many women, you are the exception, not the rule. These girls may hold themselves to a higher station amongst whores, but they exchange gossip like we do pleasantries."

"But don't we want to know what really happened if Marie did fall into harm's way?"

"No. Do you think I want rumors flying around town that my girls are dying off? I'd lose half my customers overnight. It's bad for business."

She stared at him. "I had no idea you could be so cold. A woman died, Tom."

"I know. My reaction is not for want of feeling, it is my being practical. Word like that gets around and suddenly the toffs go elsewhere. We all have to earn a living somehow, Miss Morton. This is mine and theirs. And yours."

"Mine?"

"Yes. You think Beatrice will want to keep a companion when girls randomly start dying after you've come to Town?"

"No one's died except Marie, and I had nothing to do with that," Poppy said.

"I know that, and I mean to keep it that way."

She realized his true purpose. "By keeping an eye on me?"

"No one will suspect you as long as you're with me. Everyone knows me," he said with a cocky smile.

"But you're a pimp."

"That word is offensive. A procurer of talent, you might say. And you're a companion, to a mistress I might add. At most, people will think I'm trying to persuade you to a different line of work."

"You wouldn't dare." Her body tensed.

He grinned and looked pointedly at her face, small chest, and thin body. "You would pull in a pretty price to the right bidder. I know some lords who would relish the idea of deflowering a young clergyman's daughter. Oh, forgive me, a clergyman's niece."

"I have no interest in that life."

"You say that now, but there are fortunes to be made."

She shot him a dirty look.

"I'm just saying." He flashed her a boyish smile.

The carriage pulled to a stop and out they went, with Tom taking her hand to help her down. From the outside, Marie's apartments stood outside the center of town, and while they weren't in the most fashionable district, the area was respectable.

"It's middling, this. Not quite the *ton,* but not bad either," Tom told her.

At Tom's knock, the door opened and a maid in a clean uniform greeted them. She recognized Tom and said, "Miss Watkins is not at home, Mr. Harris. She's not been home for a few days now."

Tom exchanged a look with Poppy. "May we come in? We need to speak with you."

"With me? Why?"

"It's about your mistress."

Once inside, Tom said bluntly, "Girl, your mistress is dead."

The maid stood stock still, her mouth open. "What? You must be mistaken. My mistress, I saw her two days ago. I don't believe you. Tom, if this is a joke, it's in poor taste."

Tom shook his head and spoke to the maid quietly as she struggled to keep her composure. The maid wiped away a tear and said, "What's your business here, then?"

"This girl is working with me. We want to find out if anyone meant Marie harm," Tom said.

"No, no one. When did she die?"

"The magistrates found her body this morning by the river. It looks like an accident."

The maid led them into a small sitting room, at a loss for what to do. As Tom and Poppy sat on a small sofa for visitors, the maid fretted, wringing her hands.

"Did Marie keep any irregular company? I mean instead of her normal society. Did she seem distressed?" Tom asked.

The maid sat down across from them in a smart chair with a sad pouf and thought. "I don't know. Maybe. I'm not sure. When I saw her last, she was going out for a walk. She was meeting someone."

"Did she say who?" Tom asked.

"No. But I know she didn't like him," the maid said.

"Why is that?"

"When she's meeting her gentleman or her friends, she takes her time in putting herself together in front of her looking glass. But this person she didn't like at all, I'd say. She dressed and walked out in a rush, without a care for how she looked."

"Maybe she was late for an appointment," Poppy said.

The maid glanced at her as if noticing her for the first time.

"Perhaps."

"I hate to ask, but can we have a look at Marie's rooms?" Tom asked.

"Beg your pardon?"

"Her things. It's untoward, I know, but her personal effects might hold some clue as to what befell her."

"I don't know…" the maid hedged.

Tom flirted, "A pretty girl like you? Your mistress was right to hire you, I'd trust you with me life." When that earned him a smile, he added, "Don't worry, we won't disturb anything. We'll be as silent as the grave."

The maid paled as Poppy shot Tom a look.

"Sorry," he said, "slip of the tongue."

They were shown into Marie's private bedchamber and parlor, both of which were scrupulously clean. Upon entry, Poppy took a moment to appraise her surroundings.

Marie's looking glass sat framed in an iron stand on a dressing table, surrounded by perfume bottles and cosmetics. However, upon closer scrutiny, this was no haphazard array of items, for it soon became clear that these were arranged in an orderly fashion, and each had its own proper place on the table. At a glance, Poppy observed that this arrangement spoke of a very organized mind. It came as no surprise to Poppy to learn that Marie had been one for cleanliness, although it did make her wonder at Marie's choice of profession.

Even the girl's writing desk was clear of papers, and as Poppy glanced at the orderly piles on the desk, she could see they were clearly organized into invitations to social outings, especially parties by Mollie, or theater tickets. Poppy flicked through the piles of paper but found nothing out of the ordinary.

Then she spied something unusual.

There, peeking from within a tiny drawer, sat a bit of paper sticking out. Poppy looked closer and tugged at the drawer, but the bit of paper made it stuck. Poppy tugged harder and spied a bit of ribbon caught in the drawer as well. She pulled and the drawer came free, as did the piece of paper that had first caught her attention. She picked it up. It read:

You are the dirtiest whore in London.

Poppy dropped it, seeing it sail to the floor.

Tom asked, "What is it, Miss Morton? Are you all right?"

"Yes, I'm fine. Just a slight headache." She turned to the maid. "Could I trouble you for a drink?"

"Of course, miss." She bobbed a curtsy and left.

Tom came to Poppy's side and picked up the letter from the floor. "You don't have a headache, do you?"

She shook her head and put the letter in his hands. "Marie was receiving nasty letters too. Just like Beatrice."

He breathed in and read its contents. "This could be anyone. Just someone's little joke. I'm sure you've learned by now that those mistresses will play all sorts of tricks on each other for a laugh."

Poppy scanned the drawer's contents, finding more letters tied up in a ribbon. She untied it and read another: **You will never wash away your sin. A whore is a whore no matter how clean her hands are.**

And another: **You can't wash your hands of me. I see you for the dirty hussy you are.**

Your hands might be clean but you're still just a dirty slut. Go back to the street corner where you belong.

You must see reason. Why are you destroying a marriage? You are ruining people's lives with your wantonness.

And then one at the very top of the pile: **Meet me at the riverbank along the Strand at midnight or I'll tell everyone your dirty secret.**

"This is interesting," Poppy said.

"What is it?" Tom asked, taking the papers from her. He read through them one by one. "These are disgusting. No wonder Marie was out of sorts."

"They are vile, but look at them. They're written on expensive clean paper. This sort of stuff isn't cheap." She looked at the paper and turned it over. "Are there many stationers in Town?"

Tom snorted. "Only all over Fleet Street. Why?"

"I wonder if we could find out who owns this paper. If it's nicer quality, there'll be fewer people who have it," Poppy said.

"You think it's a person of quality who did this?" he asked.

"Why not? Not everyone can read or write," she pointed out. "And look, this one was at the top of the pile and looks relatively new, whereas the others appear older. I think this must have been the last letter Marie received." The words came from her lips and her blood ran cold. She hastily put the letter back on top of the pile and tied them together with the ribbon.

Once the maid returned, Poppy asked, "Did your mistress say anything about her letters, do you know how she got these?" She gestured to the pile.

"What do they say? Are they from an admirer?" the maid asked.

"No. How does she get the post? Do you deliver it to her?" Tom asked.

The maid scratched her head. "It gets delivered, I suppose. She don't like them though. I seen her throw some papers into the fire before when she didn't think anyone was watching. Are you sure they're not from her gentleman? She told me she had an admirer."

"She did?"

"Aye, about a month ago. She was getting letters and I asked if they were from her gentleman, but she said no. But she looked so unhappy, I asked her what was wrong." The maid looked at Tom and Poppy and blushed. "I know it's not my place, but she seemed so troubled. She said they were from an admirer she didn't like but she didn't want her gentleman to know. 'He gets so jealous,' she told me, 'Lucy, don't say anything about these to Mr. Hollingsworth. I will deal with this,' and that was that. More letters came and she looked frightful unhappy, but I didn't see her entertain anyone but her gentleman, and any letters she got from her admirer, she tossed into the fire." Lucy paled. "You don't think it was this admirer who done it, do you? Some jealous man?"

"We don't know," Tom said. "Where is her gentleman, Mr. Hollingsworth? We'll have to speak to him too."

"Last I heard he was gone on a trip to the West Indies, a month ago. She don't expect him back for months." Lucy sat, her face pinched in anger. "I hope you find whoever did this. Miss Watkins had her ways, but she wasn't a bad woman to work for. Not half so bad as some I could tell you about."

"Thank you, Lucy," Tom said and led Poppy outside.

Poppy noted that he had snuck the letters for Marie inside his coat. "Give me those," she said.

"Why?"

"Because they are evidence, and I want to see if they bear any resemblance to the nasty letters Miss Hayes received."

"Very well. But Miss Morton, I don't like this. Someone meant to hurt Marie. If Beatrice received the same letters…" he began.

"Then maybe they are after her too," Poppy finished. "Could it be a coincidence or a prank?"

"Pretty nasty prank if you ask me. I'll ask around and see if I can find anything else about Marie's rude admirer." He called her a hackney carriage and sent her back to Miss Hayes's apartments.

But when Poppy arrived, Beatrice and Harriet were waiting for her. "Miss Morton!"

"How did it go?" Poppy joined the pair in Beatrice's sitting room and sat as the girls poured her a cup of black tea.

"We went to the pub, but her gentleman wasn't there, and when we found him upstairs at Macklin's, he was saying how his trip to the West Indies was delayed. He didn't know us at first but then we asked for a private visit, and then we told him."

"What did he say?"

"He thought we were pulling a joke on him. But when he saw we were serious, he almost fell over," Harriet said.

"I watched his face," Beatrice said, "He was very sad. I don't think he knew, or that he hurt her. He was too unhinged when we told him."

"Unless he's a very good actor," Harriet said and looked at Poppy. "I don't like this."

Poppy laid down the letters she and Tom had removed from Marie's apartments. "Look at these." She untied the ribbon and spread the letters across the table.

"My word," Harriet said, picking up one after another. "Who wrote these?"

"We don't know. But that one," Poppy said, tapping one, "that was at the top of the pile. You can see it looks newer than the others. I think it was the last one Marie received before her accident."

Harriet picked it up and read aloud, "'Meet me at the riverbank along the Strand at midnight or I'll tell everyone your dirty secret.'" She repressed a shudder. "I was closer to Marie than anyone. She didn't have any dirty secrets. She was an open book."

Beatrice looked at Poppy and Harriet. "I've been receiving letters too. Like those."

Harriet glanced at her. "You have?"

"Yes. It's partly why I wanted Miss Morton here, to help me and find out who is behind this. If the letter writer hurt Marie, what if they come after me?"

"I won't let anything happen to you," Mr. Parks said, entering the room.

The girls jumped. "Mr. Parks, I didn't see you," Beatrice said.

Mr. Parks grunted and turned pink. "This came in the post for you." He extended a letter to her.

Beatrice tentatively reached for it, then hesitated. Harriet took it and opened it, heaving a sigh of relief. "It's just an invitation. Penelope is hosting a little party and invites us to join her at the races. Won't that be fun?"

From the dirty look Mr. Parks gave her, Poppy wasn't so sure.

CHAPTER TEN

T HAT MONDAY WAS warm and the sun was shining as Poppy, Beatrice and Harriet took a carriage together to Epsom Downs. There the crowds were thick with well-dressed ladies and dapper-looking men, all placing bets, drinking, eating, and just generally having a pleasant time. Harriet accepted drinks from a passing footman and pointed out, "Look, there's Penelope. No doubt she's already placing bets on the horses."

"Which does she think will win, I wonder?" Beatrice asked.

"It doesn't matter. She doesn't know the first thing about horses and doesn't care. She just loves to play the odds, so she'll take whatever bet is available. Just don't let her gentleman know." Harriet smiled.

"Isn't that rather dangerous?" Poppy asked. She'd been raised to believe that all gambling was sinful.

"Only if you don't have a steady income," Harriet said.

"Or a gentleman with deep pockets." Beatrice added, "Are you going to bet on a horse, Miss Morton?"

"I'm not sure," Poppy said.

"She probably thinks it's too naughty to place a bet," Mollie joked, joining them. "You religious families are all the same. Dull, quiet, and too afraid of your own shadow to do anything so wild as betting on a horse."

Poppy frowned at Mollie. "I am no such thing."

"Oh really? Prove it."

"Mollie…" Beatrice started.

"I wasn't addressing you. I was asking Miss Morton, here, if she was too scared to place a bet. Or is it that you aren't paying her anything? Is that it, Miss Morton?"

Poppy's face turned red enough to match Beatrice's. "That is not the case."

"Hah," Mollie smirked, taking the arm of an approaching middle-aged gentleman and fawning over him. She shot Poppy a self-satisfied look and strolled away.

Poppy stared after her, feeling a seed of dislike burrow into her mind. Why Mollie needed to be so rude was beyond her, but she did not like her one bit. With society like hers, who needed enemies?

"Don't listen to her, Miss Morton, she just likes to make trouble," Beatrice said.

Harriet agreed, "It's true. You should ignore her. She has a talent for finding out everyone's weak spots and then toying with them. If you ignore her, she'll find someone else to torment."

"It sounds like what she needs is to be taken down a peg or two," Poppy said.

"Well, when you decide to do that, let me know and I'll back you. She deserves it," Harriet said.

"Never mind Mollie, she's always rude or sore at something. Miss Morton, are you going to place a bet?" Beatrice asked. "I will if you will."

Poppy smiled at her. It was a tricky thing, to navigate the waters between paid companion and friend. "All right. One bet won't hurt, I think."

Poppy began to enjoy herself, as the day was pleasant and she was happy to be outside in the fresh air. She used a small amount of her wages to buy a ticket to bet on a horse, called Blueblack on account of its mane, which was so black it almost looked blue. Poppy joined Beatrice and Harriet in the stands, when Harriet pointed out, "Look, there's Penelope."

Penelope stood near the front, drinking one glass of liquid and then another. "If she's not careful, she'll need the privy soon at the rate she's going," Harriet said.

"And she'll be drunk," Beatrice added.

"You really think so?" Poppy asked.

"Depends on what she's drinking, but I'd say so. Penelope likes to have a good time."

A gunshot cracked through the air and then the ground trembled as the pack of horses flew down the race path.

The crowd surged ahead and cheered, and the air was a cacophony of sound. Poppy could barely hear herself when she saw Penelope walking toward the stands in a daze, making a beeline for the front.

An icy shiver went through Poppy. "What is she doing?"

Beatrice asked loudly, "Sorry?"

"Look at Penelope."

"What? Oh, don't worry, she's probably drunk," Beatrice said.

"She's acting strange." Poppy began to rise as Penelope wandered perilously close and stumbled and fell, landing on her hands and knees, directly in the path of the oncoming horses. Her pink striped dress lay flat around her body, and her head lolled to one side. Poppy's heart rose in her throat. Penelope was going to die.

A scream cut through the noise and Poppy lunged out of her seat, climbing around and walking in front of cheering people. "Penelope!" she cried, trying to make her way through the crowd. But with the thundering sound of the horses incoming, she would be too late.

CHAPTER ELEVEN

P OPPY WATCHED IN horror as Penelope lay almost unconscious on the path of the racecourse, the horses turning around a bend as they fast approached. It would be only moments before their hooves trampled her.

"Help!" she cried, "Somebody help!" Poppy called out.

But just as people glanced up out of their seats to stare at her, a woman dodged around the crowd of people and dashed to the front, pulling Penelope away, just as the racehorses thundered past.

People stood up, whooped and cheered, clapping and drinking, giving Poppy the chance to dash around them. Poppy ran out of the seats before she knew what she was doing and hurried down to the front fences, where a small crowd had formed around Penelope and her rescuer.

As Poppy reached them, she found Penelope sitting on the grass, holding a hand up shading her eyes from the sun. She squinted and said, "What's going on? What's happened?"

"You had a close call," one man said. "You should be grateful this lady spotted your mishap in time. She saved your life."

Penelope blinked in surprise, gagged, clapped a hand over her mouth, her eyes wide, and vomited into the grass.

The onlookers uttered sounds of disgust. "She's foxed. Too much to drink," one man said.

"What kind of lady does that?"

"You answered your own question, mate," another told him.

The crowd dispersed, leaving just Poppy, Penelope, and her rescuer. Poppy helped Penelope sit up as the lady offered a handkerchief to Penelope, who accepted it and wiped her mouth.

"That was a very smart thing you did," Poppy said to the stranger, as Penelope retched on the grass.

Penelope's rescuer was short, with a round face and straight dark hair. She wore a fetching gray bonnet and smart gray and white striped dress and light gray gloves. She had a doll-like prettiness, with sharp dark eyes and a small mouth. She spared a pitying look for Penelope before answering. "Thank you. I saw the young lady wander out and thought she might be in some distress. I never imagined she would be drunk."

Penelope sat up and wiped her mouth, looking sweaty and pale. "I don't understand. I've never felt so sick. I only had two drinks."

"Maybe two is too much," said Mollie, as Beatrice and Harriet joined them. "You never could handle your drink."

Penelope squinted up at her and threw up again, earning a smirk from Mollie, who soon left.

Poppy picked up the glass of spilled wine and sniffed its contents. It smelled sickly sweet, and she wrinkled her nose. "This wine smells odd." She held it out to the lady.

The lady took it and gave a delicate sniff. "It does. How strange. Do you think someone put something in this young woman's drink?"

Beatrice said, "Penelope wouldn't have gotten so topsy turvy from two glasses of wine, surely."

Penelope used the handkerchief to wipe her mouth again. "Hullo, Beatrice." She hiccupped.

"She's right," Harriet took the glass from the lady and sniffed it. "This is very odd, and it's different from the wine they've been serving here. Where did you get this, Penelope?"

Penelope's eyes narrowed. "Just from a servant. A nobody."

"Are you feeling all right?" Poppy asked.

"Well enough. My stomach feels like it's been punched, and my head is killing me. Could someone fetch me a drink?"

"Don't you think you've had enough?" Harriet asked.

"I need something to clear my throat. Water would do, or lemonade. All I can taste is bile. Could someone get me a drink please?" Penelope asked.

Beatrice hurried to fetch a drink while Harriet helped lift Penelope to her feet.

"Well, I can see the poor girl is in safe hands." The strange lady moved to leave when Penelope said, "Wait." She reached behind her and said, "You dropped this." She held out a shining bracelet that glittered in the sun.

The strange woman's eyes widened. "My word, I didn't even know it had fallen off. How clumsy of me. Thank you, this was an expensive piece from my husband. I would have missed it very much." She took the bracelet with pleasure and place it back on her wrist.

Penelope looked forlorn as Harriet and Poppy exchanged a glance. Penelope was up to her old thieving tricks again. "It was no trouble," Penelope mumbled.

"I wonder, would you like to come for tea tomorrow? I know so few ladies in London, it would be nice to make your acquaintance properly and see how you're getting on. If your health permits it, of course."

Penelope brightened at this and bobbed her head meekly. "Jolly good."

The woman blinked and smiled pleasantly. She fished out a calling card from her reticule and handed it to Penelope. "Do call on me tomorrow afternoon." She curtsied and left.

Once they were out of earshot, Harriet said, "Penelope, what happened? You almost died."

Beatrice reappeared and handed Penelope a cup of lemonade, which was gratefully accepted. Penelope said, "Honestly, I don't know. One minute I'd taken a drink from a servant, and then a queer sort of feeling came over me, and a horrible old creature told me I was going to hell. She was so vile I left, but then I found this in my reticule." She gestured to a stained reticule.

Poppy took the reticule and pulled out a note.

It read: ***Trying your luck? No race will save you from prison, especially when I tell your little secret.***

Poppy shuddered. "What a horrible note. May we keep this?"

Penelope said, "Take it. I don't want it. It's vile. I felt horrible enough already. I felt so strange, like I'd drunk an entire barrel of wine. So I went in search of fresh air, but then the sun was so hot and it was hard to see what was going on, the earth kept moving. I landed here, as you see me."

"It sounds to me like your drink was altered," Poppy said, as Harriet scanned the note.

"Why? Who would do such a thing?" Penelope asked.

"Who was the servant?" Harriet asked.

"I've never seen her before. When she was rude I laughed and gave her a tip on a horse. Told her if she won then maybe she could purchase some cosmetics for her face. Or a mask. Maybe a veil." Penelope snickered.

"Why?" Beatrice asked.

"She was ugly."

"That's no reason for rudeness," Poppy said.

Penelope rolled her eyes. "You don't understand. The old woman had pox scars all over her face. She was a miserable creature, mean, too. Anyway, did my horse win? Was it Bright Star?"

Harriet checked the winning horse walking by. "No, it was Midnight's Folly."

Penelope grimaced, all thoughts of rude servants forgotten. "What rotten luck."

That afternoon Poppy, Beatrice, and Harriet asked the footmen circulating around if they had seen an older female servant with pockmark scars on her face, but no one had. It was like the person had disappeared.

"Maybe it was a ghost," Beatrice said.

"Don't be ridiculous," Harriet told her, "ghosts don't exist."

"Says you. I've been to church at midnight for Christmas and I'm sure I saw a ghost walking around," Beatrice said.

Harriet snorted.

"So, what do we know?" Penelope was targeted by someone. She received a note. "Let's see it again," Poppy said.

Harriet handed it over. Poppy read it and said, "Let's head back. We'll need to compare it to the others."

"Could it have been a random mad person?" Beatrice asked.

Harriet shook her head.

Poppy said, "It accuses Penelope of gambling and debts. Does she have debts?"

Harriet and Beatrice exchanged a look.

"What?" Poppy asked.

Beatrice gave a little nod. "She does. It's why she takes things, or so I've heard." She shot a look at Harriet.

"It's true," Harriet confirmed. "Some girls in our profession do help themselves from their patrons' effects from time to time, and the men look the other way. They know we depend on them. But I didn't think Penelope's taste for gambling was so widely known." She took the letter from Poppy and read it again. "What are you thinking?"

Poppy said, "That either a maid heard a rumor and tried to make some quick coin by threatening Penelope or doctoring her drink, or..."

Harriet and Beatrice waited. "Or?" Beatrice prompted.

"Or the maid knew her. It's someone of Penelope's acquaintance. They know each other."

CHAPTER TWELVE

A T THE RACETRACK at Epsom Downs, Henry and John took in the sights. They drank lemonade, placed bets, won some, lost some, and generally spent a pleasant afternoon in each other's company. Henry was ready to leave when John said, "What a view. Look, Henry."

"What is it? The horses have already raced."

"Don't be daft, I don't care about the horses. Look at the women. Just think, maybe I'll see Justine today," he said hopefully.

Henry fixed his older brother with a frown. Earlier, they had found a note meant for John but addressed to him, which had bid them to meet Justine at the races that afternoon.

John could not wait and dragged Henry along too, with their manservants. It wasn't that they needed the extra company, Henry thought John just liked having them around. As if being the eldest son of a baronet was not enough, his older brother liked having a small entourage too.

Henry shot his brother a dirty look.

"You're still mad about Justine's invitation, aren't you? It's not my fault you can't enjoy a day out at the races. You didn't have to come."

"It is your fault we are in this mess in the first place. You gave her my name. You dragged me into it. How could you do that?"

Henry asked.

"Well, I couldn't very well give her mine. At least you are single, no one will blink an eye if you take up a mistress."

"Only all good society," Henry muttered.

"And since when have you cared about what society thinks? There is no young lady you share an understanding with, or a girl who has taken your fancy, is there?"

"Of course not," Henry said.

"Then I fail to see the problem. I have done you a favor, dear brother. To many, you are a spoilsport and dull to be around. Thanks to me, you now have a bit of notoriety, which is much more exciting." John grinned, pleased with himself.

Henry could have struck him. He cursed and wandered off to get a drink. He could sense his manservant, Geoffrey, at his heels but held up a hand to forestall him. At a shake of his head, Geoffrey stopped in his tracks. Henry knew his manservant was loyal to a fault, and even if Henry told him to stay away, Geoffrey would not be too far behind. But not right now. Henry wanted a moment alone to himself, to think.

He joined a crowd of people who were chatting before a bar serving drinks when a husky feminine voice said, "You will be waiting a while if it's a lemonade you're after."

The voice sounded silky and seductive. Henry turned around and started. "You," he said.

The owner of the voice looked at him askance and fluttered her fan like a lazy butterfly, but her wide eyes betrayed her. "Me."

"I've seen you before. At the tavern. With a gentleman."

She was older than him, at least forty. Her skin was pale, and she stood tall and slim. Her light gray eyes surveyed him with curiosity. "I'm sure I don't know what you mean."

"I've seen you. You remind me of a young woman I know well."

She began to grow bored, he could tell. She glanced away and fanned herself when he played his only hand. "Are you acquaint-ed with a Miss Poppy Morton?"

The lady froze for a second, and her gray eyes pierced him, as steely as any hawk's. "I'm afraid not. Do excuse me." She would have slipped away when Henry grabbed her elbow.

"You are Celeste Morton, are you not?" he asked.

She sidled up to him until they stood very close, yet he could barely hear her hard murmur, "You seem to have mistaken me for someone else." She looked pointedly at his hand on her arm until he removed it. She took a step back as her gentleman friend approached holding two glasses of lemonade. He had a head full of silver hair, turning white at the temples, and wore an expensive-looking slate gray suit jacket and matching waistcoat.

"There you are, Celeste. Not waiting too long, I hope."

"Not at all, I was just about to search for you." She took a glass and sipped the tart liquid delicately, while taking her friend's free arm.

Henry looked at her and her gentleman, who picked up on the slight tension between them. "Is this man bothering you?" the man asked her.

"No. He said I reminded him of someone, but he was mistaken. He was just leaving," she said.

"Who might you be?" the gentleman asked.

"Henry Dyngley. I'm a constable of Hertford parish."

"I see." The well-dressed man nodded, extended his arm to the lady, and escorted her away.

Henry stood watching when Geoffrey said at his elbow, "You want I should follow them?"

"Yes. See what you can find out about them."

He watched as the lady strolled away with her gentleman, Geoffrey close behind them. A short while later, Geoffrey returned with a personal calling card and a sour expression. "She bid me give this to you. Said to call on her tomorrow at the proper hour." He handed Henry the card.

"What's got you annoyed?"

"She knew I was with you, somehow. Looked at me with a smile on her face as if she was laughing at me."

"How did she know you were my man?" Henry asked.

Geoffrey shrugged. "She just knew."

Henry read the card, which bore in very flowery script,

Celeste Grey

Orchard Street adjoining Portman Square

Henry blinked. It was in a fashionable part of town. Nothing too ostentatious and not so middling as to be frequented by families who made their living in trade, but respectable. For a mistress, it was a lofty height indeed.

He pocketed the card and rejoined his brother. They were just about to place bets on a new race when a young female voice cried out, "Dyngley!"

Henry and John turned toward the sound. There stood a young woman, dressed in a fetching rose and white striped dress and smart hat. She bounded up to John and seemed about to throw her arms around him, then appeared to remember they were in polite company and stopped herself in time. "My Lord Dyngley."

John's face lit up with pleasure. "Justine."

She gushed, "It's ever so good to see you again. I have missed our talks." She met his gaze with an impish giggle and bowed low, low enough to offer the gentleman an enticing peek at her cleavage.

Henry looked away while John observed openly, his smile growing wider. "Miss Vane, the pleasure is all mine. I have longed for your company but alas, business outside of town has kept me away, longer than I anticipated."

Justine giggled and rose from her curtsy, and noticed Henry staring at her. "Who is this? A cousin of yours? He looks quite like you, but so serious." She gave Henry a warm smile.

"This is my brother," John said, "John."

Henry shot him a dirty look. "I fear, madam, that my brother has played a trick on you."

Justine's happy expression crumpled. "What do you mean? What trick?"

"I mean that—" Henry stared at a sight in the distance, his mouth open.

John stepped in front of his brother, stepping on his foot. "Don't listen to him, pet, he's just teasing. My brother is a consummate actor, aren't you, John?"

"John… look." Henry pointed past him.

"What?" John asked.

"There." Henry stepped around his brother.

"I don't see anything," John said.

"Hey, wait a minute. He called you John. Is that a joke? Is John a middle name?"

"No," Henry said.

"Well, then which one of you is Henry?" Justine asked.

"I am," both brothers said, and looked at each other.

John pulled Justine into a passionate embrace and held her close. "I don't want anything to come between us."

Justine lifted her face to his, her expression full of happiness. She stood up on her tiptoes for a kiss, and pouted when Henry said, "Don't look now, John, but…"

"Not now, Henry, I'm busy," John said.

"John, look," Henry said.

"What?" John looked up. "Oh no."

"What is it darling?" Justine took his arm possessively.

A familiar sight came into view, with a face like a thundercloud.

Justine asked, "Do you know that woman? She looks frightful mad."

"That's not just any woman," Henry told her, "that is Mrs. Petunia Dyngley."

"Oh, is she a relative of yours?"

"Worse," John muttered, as he tugged at his collar. "My wife."

Chapter Thirteen

Seeing the woman bearing down on them like a ship, John gave the newcomer a grin. "Hello, Petunia, how good to see you. I didn't know you were coming to the races today. Whatever are you doing here?"

The woman was fearsome indeed. Her coiled jet-black hair was arranged artfully atop her head, and her angular face was tight with fury. At the sight of John and Justine arm in arm, her lips thinned in distaste. "I could ask the same of you. It was a funny thing, you go missing and then I receive a letter saying utter hogwash. So of course I had to come. I can see you've been entertaining yourself." She cast daggers at Justine, who clasped John's arm more tightly.

"I'm Miss Vane. Who are you?" Justine asked.

"The wife of the man whose arm you're holding," Petunia snapped.

"Your wife?" Justine dropped John's arm like a hot coal. "I didn't know you were married, Henry."

"Henry? What lies has he been telling you?" Petunia asked, her glare intensifying. "That man is John Dyngley, heir to the baronetcy at Faulkbourne Manor." To John, she asked, "Have you been deceiving this poor girl?"

John turned to Henry. "You wrote to her?"

"Someone had to. She deserved to know," Henry said.

"Wait a minute, hold on. Would someone please tell me what is going on?" Justine asked. "I came here and ran into Henry, but now his brother says *he* is Henry and that is John. Who is the real Henry?"

"I am," the brothers said, and Henry glared at John, who turned red.

John cleared his throat and said, "Miss Vane, that is to say, I may have been mistaken with the names and introductions, you see. A man in his cups will say anything you know, it's easy to get muddled up with who is whom, and what…"

Petunia gave a harsh laugh. "I see how it is. You came here on false pretenses to lure young, innocent girls to your bed, deceiving them into thinking you are your eligible brother. For shame, John."

John turned redder and shot her a dirty look. "It's not as bad as all that, really."

"Keep telling yourself that, John." Petunia said and turned to Justine. She snapped, "You. Girl. Did you know that my husband was married?"

"No." Justine shook her head.

"Well, that is one thing at least. Leave us." She turned her back on Justine without a second thought. "John, I am tired and wish to speak with you in private. Kindly escort me home."

"No." A meek voice piped up.

Petunia slowly turned around. "Excuse me?"

"I said no," Justine said in a shaky voice. "He's not going anywhere with you."

John stared at her in surprise, his mouth hanging open. "Justine?"

"Close your mouth, John, you'll catch flies. You're coming home with me," Petunia said.

"No. John, Henry, whoever he is, I don't care. He came to me for a reason. I'm not leaving him." Justine grabbed John's arm.

Petunia's face turned puce. "You insolent girl. Don't you understand? Whatever relationship you think you had with my husband is over. Go back to wherever it is you came from."

A tear ran down Justine's face. "So it's like that, is it? You dismiss me like I'm nothing. Well, let me tell you when a man comes to me begging for it like Henry—"

"John," John interrupted.

"John," Justine shot him a look. "Then it means he's bored or unhappy at home. Looking at you, I can see why he came running to me."

Petunia stood stiffer than a rapier. If she could have struck down Justine with a gaze, she would have done. Instead, she hissed, "Girl. You do yourself no credit to insult your betters. I had given you the benefit of the doubt, but now you are just being silly. Go on, now. Go." She made a shooing motion with her hands like she would clear off a mangy dog.

"Petunia, really, there's no need for rudeness," John said.

"I am not the one who is being rude. You are the one who started all this. John, send the girl away, and let's be off. I want to return home as soon as possible."

There was a sniffle behind her. Petunia turned to see a teary Justine, who said, "I can't. I've nowhere to go."

"What do you mean? Go back to whatever hovel you came from," Petunia said.

"I can't."

"Why not?"

Justine looked at John, who coughed and turned pink. "Um, you see, I was on my way to London to close up the family townhouse and um…" He nodded toward Justine, who beamed at him.

Petunia's mouth dropped open. "No. John. Tell me no. Say it's not true."

"What, buttercup?" he said.

"Tell me you have not been having this girl in our townhouse. In our bed." She blinked hard.

John looked at Petunia and then Justine, then his eyes rolled back, and he crumpled into a heap.

Henry stared.

"What's happened?" Petunia asked.

"John!" Justine said.

Both women knelt at John's side. Petunia shot Justine a dirty look. "It must be the heat. He's fainted. Fetch some water."

"I'm not leaving him," Justine said.

Petunia rolled her eyes. "Henry, will you?"

Henry sent off Robert, John's valet, immediately, while he shuffled the women aside. "Let me see him."

He leaned down with Geoffrey and put his head to John's chest. It rose and fell, and he could hear the dull rhythm of John's steady heartbeat.

"Will he be all right?" Justine asked.

"He's alive," Henry said.

"Oh thank goodness," Petunia said.

John's eyes fluttered and Henry got a glimpse of his brother, looking so heavy-lidded, he appeared to be asleep. "What he needs is air."

Geoffrey and Henry helped sit John up, and he slowly awakened, blinking. "What happened? Lord, it's hot."

"You fainted," Petunia said sourly.

"I did? Oh." John gratefully accepted a glass of lemonade from Robert, who returned with a doctor.

The man introduced himself as Dr. Cuthbert and surveyed John closely. "Just a touch of the sun, I expect," he said a moment later. "It's good you had your wife and daughter nearby. I'm sure they'll look after you properly."

Petunia smirked while Justine pouted. John colored and said, "Yes, well. Thank you, doctor."

Justine stood by patiently as he quietly nursed his glass of lemonade.

Petunia said, "We are going home." She waited for John to stand and turned to Justine. "I understand that my husband installed you in our townhouse."

Justine stood close to her, her lips pursed. "Yes, he did."

"Be a dear and clear out your things."

"What? But I live there," Justine said.

Petunia sniffed. "My dear girl, it was never your home. You should have known it was only temporary. Now we have need of it."

"But—"

"I am taking *my husband* out to dinner for a fortifying meal. I expect we will be out until quite late. I trust you will do me the courtesy of not being there when we return."

"But where am I to go? I have no other lodgings," Justine said.

For a moment, Petunia's expression softened, and it looked as though she might take pity on the poor girl. But seeing Justine's proprietary hand on John's shoulder riled her. "That is not my problem." At Justine's shocked expression, she hissed, "For who knows how long, my husband has committed adultery with *you*. He has been wasting his time, instead of spending time with his family and doing his duty. Be grateful I do not call the watch."

Justine stood, open-mouthed, as Petunia dragged John away in the direction of the carriages.

"But where will I go? I have nowhere to stay," Justine said.

Henry asked, "Do you have any friends or acquaintances you can stay with?"

"What do you care? You're just like them," she said.

"I am not my brother." Seeing her mutinous glance, he said, "We have not been properly introduced. My name is Henry Dyngley. I am a constable and before two days ago, I had no idea of your existence, nor your relationship with my brother, John."

"But I sent you letters…" she started, her hand drifting to her mouth.

"They were for my brother. He's played you false."

Justine lowered her hand. Her small hands became fists by her sides. "He's played us all for fools, then," she said gravely. "I have a friend, Beatrice. She might let me stay with her a while."

Henry blinked. "That wouldn't happen to be Miss Beatrice

Hayes, by any chance, would it?"

"Yes, why? Do you know her?" she asked.

"I don't. But a friend of mine does, I think. Has Miss Hayes recently hired a companion?"

"Yes, some tall girl. Peony or something," Justine giggled.

Henry's heart lifted. "Do you mean Miss Poppy Morton?"

"I think that's it. Is she your friend?" Justine asked.

"She is. Do you know where they are staying? I should like to visit her."

Justine looked at him askance. "I do, but I don't know if I should tell you. We've only just met. How do I know you are trustworthy?"

His family's unkindness toward her had no doubt influenced her mind against him.

"I am a constable."

"You're not a London constable. Besides, I've heard enough lies from the Dyngleys for one day. No, I'll find my own way." She turned and disappeared into the crowd.

"Wait," he said, going after her. He soon overtook her, touched her sleeve and she turned around, a small knife in her hand. "What you want?" Her accent was harsh, and not so pretty, then.

He swallowed. "Please, I mean you no harm. I only want to ask after Miss Morton. Would you tell her where I am staying and ask if I may call on her?"

Justine looked at him closely, as if taking the time to memorize his face, and take the measure of him at the same time. "I might."

"Thank you. You can send me a note at the Dyngley townhouse."

"Can't." She shook her head.

"Why not?"

"Can't write. I never learned."

CHAPTER FOURTEEN

A FTER A LONG carriage ride back to London, Poppy and Beatrice were visited by Justine, who came with trunks of clothes, theater scripts, and her personal effects. Poppy had never seen quite so many accessories or cosmetics, but as Justine was an actress, no doubt she used them for her performances. Justine was in a foul mood and after she stowed her belongings into one of the spare rooms, she helped herself to a bottle of wine and plonked herself down on the settee in the main room.

"What happened?" Poppy asked.

"Her gentleman's cast her off," Beatrice said quietly. "It happens sometimes."

Justine hiccupped. "Thank you, Beatrice. You're a true friend. Not like that Mollie."

"What do you mean?"

"I saw her at the races, her and that man of hers. I told her my situation and asked her to put me up for a day or two. D'you know what she did?"

"What?" Poppy asked.

"She laughed in my face, right in front of her gentleman. She stuck her nose up in the air and said, 'I can't help you if you can't help yourself. It's not my fault you can't keep a man. If you can't convince him to look after you, why should I?'"

"She didn't," Beatrice said.

"She did. Said she wasn't in the business of charity, and I should learn to sort out my own problems." Justine threw a hand across her forehead dramatically and laid herself across the settee with a big sigh, holding the wine bottle close.

"Oh Justine," Beatrice said, "I'm sorry."

Justine wiped away a tear. "And what really gets me is that horrible woman, acting as if she were his owner or something. Just because they're married...." She sniffed. "It's not your fault anyways, Beatrice. It's that woman, Petunia. And Henry, or John. Whoever he is. I hate the Dyngleys, all of them!" She cried in a fresh bout of tears.

Poppy froze. She blinked and passed Justine a clean handkerchief. "Did you say the Dyngleys?"

Justine's eyes grew guarded. "Yes, I did. Do you know them?"

"I know one of them. Constable Henry Dyngley is my friend."

"Well, he's no friend of mine, not after the way he's treated me. He and his whole blasted family of his. He threw me out on the street. Or his brother did. And his wife."

"What do you mean?"

"My Henry, he romances me for months. Sets me up in his lodgings in town and then kicks me out, as soon as his wife and brother show up. Men." Justine screwed her face up as if she wanted to spit on the floor, then thought better of it.

Poppy felt crestfallen. "Your Henry," she repeated.

"Not anymore. He was never mine to begin with. But he never told me he was married."

Poppy sat on a chair, grateful for its support. "How long has he been married?"

"Not long. I doubt he'll stay that way either. Not if he's already seducing a girl like me." Justine sniffed.

Poppy felt a flash of anger. She was mad at Henry for not telling her he was married. She was annoyed at Justine for romancing the man she had fancied for months and even kissed. But most of all, she was angry with herself, for believing in him at all. She had kissed a man and didn't even know he was married. How great a fool she had been. It was no wonder he did not speak to her after that.

Their kiss had clearly meant nothing, for he had been getting more than that elsewhere and from a girl much more practiced than her. She could have crawled under a rock at that moment, she felt so embarrassed, angry, and hurt. She had been a fool, throwing herself at a man who wasn't just married to another woman, but who was entertaining a mistress on the side. How naive could she be?

Beatrice watched Poppy's face carefully. "You say he is a friend of yours, Miss Morton?"

"Yes. But I did not know he was married," Poppy said.

"That makes two of us." Justine sulked. "Oh. Come to think of it, he did ask about you. His brother, I mean."

"He did? What did he say?" Poppy asked.

Beatrice looked at her curiously. Justine shot her a wary glance and sat up. "Only that he wished to pay a call. I've his address if you want it."

"No, I'm all right. It would be Henry I'd want to speak to, not his brother." Poppy felt her face warm and she stood up. "Do excuse me." She quietly exited the room.

Justine said to Beatrice, "Looks like I'm not the only girl crossed in love."

Poppy went to her bed chamber and shut the door, just in time for the first tears to fall. Dyngley, married. Henry, with a mistress. And cavorting around London all this time. And she had kissed him. She felt like a fool. To think, she had basically thrown herself at him at their last meeting, and he had pulled away. No doubt out of politeness because he had a wife. And a mistress. How could this be the same Henry Dyngley she knew so well? Perhaps the man she thought she knew had only been an illusion and not the man of her dreams after all.

He had a whole other life outside of the one he led in Hertfordshire. She threw herself on her bed and wept silent, bitter tears. What a fool she had been.

And his brother wished to pay a call, probably to let her down easy and tell her the honest truth, that Henry was married, and that she was a fool.

SOON ENOUGH SUNDAY arrived, which meant church. Poppy donned her Sunday best, which compared to the fine fashionable ladies walking around London, wasn't so fashionable at all. But at that moment she didn't care, for she felt that God didn't judge her for what she wore, even if her walking gown was a hand-me-down and her bonnet was four years old. She slipped quietly out of Beatrice's lodgings and over to the nearest church.

St. Botolph's church was an old building. Pleasant enough with stark white walls outside a steeple and a fenced inner courtyard, with a small number of gravestones out in front, dotting the green on either side of the path that led to the church doors. It was in a nice area and Poppy spotted people dressed in their fine Sunday clothes walk up to the entrance and enter the church. She joined the queue and instantly felt a wave of homesickness for her aunt and uncle.

She loved them dearly but relished her independence. But now, back with the familiar sights and sounds of wooden pews, the stale lingering scent of incense in the air and fresh flowers, the drafty creaks of wooden beams, dusty books, and the sound of restless parishioners taking their seats in the wooden pews, Poppy began to feel at home.

As a clergyman's niece, she was used to taking pride of place at the front, but this time she stayed toward the back of the church. She was joined in her pew by two others and stood with the congregation as the service began.

The rector, an older man of senior years, droned on about the merits of women obeying their husbands and how that obedience would lead to a happy home and was the key to a happy marriage.

Poppy heard a quiet sniff and looked around, but did not see anyone she knew. She somehow doubted the merit of the man's sermon. For what if the man she was sworn to obey was a drunken lout who administered discipline with his fists, or had a wandering eye? Or worse, had an affair and took up a mistress? Henry's comely face appeared in her thoughts, and she scowled. She did not want to think of him. Not anymore.

She turned and met the gaze of a woman a few rows over who looked familiar. Then she realized, it was the woman who had saved Penelope from being trampled on by the racehorses. Her eyes widened in recognition, and the woman offered a polite smile. Poppy returned the smile and faced forward. What a coincidence. The woman must live locally.

Once the service ended, Poppy stepped out into the sun and met the woman, who said, "Good morning. Forgive me, but I recognize you," she said, "we met yesterday, at the races."

"Yes, ma'am," Poppy said, "I was there when you rescued the young woman."

"Oh, that's it, of course. Such an eventful day. Although I wouldn't say I rescued her, she just became indisposed," the woman said, spots of color rising in her cheeks.

What an odd way to brush off saving someone's life. Poppy said, "It was very brave of you."

"That's very kind. What did you say your name was? Forgive me, I'm terrible with names."

"Poppy Morton." Poppy curtsied.

"Ah yes, of course. I am Mrs. Ann Farrars. So good to meet you, it is a pleasure." The lady inclined her head.

They were interrupted by a loud voice arguing, "—Well then, you have no business preaching what you do not know. You have no right to say what a woman should and should not do. How do you know what makes a happy marriage? Have you ever been in one?"

Poppy and Mrs. Farrars turned to see the cause of the commotion, as two people stepped outside of the church. The clergyman's pallid expression suffused with red, and his ears turned pink. Tufts of gray hair stuck out over his ears as he said, "Madam, my sermons speak the truth. If you find my sermon so troubling, perhaps it is you who should make a closer inspection of what makes a happy marriage."

The lady, a tall, proud woman with a hawkish nose, angular features, and jet-black hair, scoffed and said, "What are you trying to say?"

"Only that instead of critiquing my sermon, you might attend to your husband. I do not see him here today. Why is that?"

Now it was the lady's turn to turn red. Her hazel eyes were like sharpened daggers as she said, "I will have you know, my husband is a good God-fearing man. We got into town late last night and I let him sleep. Or would you prefer he snore during your sermon? Tell me, rector, what makes a happy marriage, a husband in bed asleep, or awake and disagreeable early Sunday morning? Do instruct me, for I should greatly like to know."

The rector's mouth quivered as if he'd eaten a lemon, and he walked off, his black cassock flapping behind him. He ignored the other parishioners who stood by watching the spectacle.

"Hah! Serves him right," the argumentative woman declared. Seeing Poppy and Mrs. Farrars looking at her, she approached them and said, "That man is a buffoon. He had no business dictating to me how to have a good and happy marriage. No woman will have him, he's as innocent as Eve."

Poppy coughed. "Forgive me, madam, but I don't think Eve was supposed to be all that innocent. I rather thought it was her in the garden of Eden who tempted Adam."

"She was made of his backbone, was she not? Seems to me she has all the backbone, and he doesn't. At any rate, it falls to us women to bring the strength where men do not. Although, I'm not surprised there's no mention of that in the Bible." She gave Poppy a steely-eyed gaze. "Who are you?"

"Miss Poppy Morton." Poppy curtsied, and said, "May I introduce Mrs. Ann Farrars?"

The women stood there, assessing each other silently. Poppy

stood feeling awkward.

"I think the rector does not like to be disagreed with," Mrs. Farrars said.

"That is of no consequence to me," the hawk-nosed woman said bluntly.

Poppy added, "Most rectors don't. At least those I've met."

That earned her a curious look. "And do you have occasion to meet many clergymen, girl?" the hawk-nosed woman asked.

Poppy shrugged. "My uncle is a clergyman. He sometimes entertains fellow rectors and curates at the parsonage in Hertford, or we have them come look after Sunday services if he is ill or called away. But I have never met one who did not think he was right in most things," she said with a smile.

The hawk-nosed woman said, "Hertford, you say? How strange you should mention it. My husband went there the other day, to visit his brother. Now they are in London causing all sorts of mischief."

"Who are they? Perhaps I know them," Poppy said.

The woman looked her up and down, taking in her ordinary clothes. "I doubt it, unless you have had a run-in with the law. His name is Henry Dyngley. I am Mrs. Petunia Dyngley."

A sliver of ice stabbed Poppy's heart. Not only was the news that Henry was married true, but she was now making small talk with his wife. As if the day could get any worse. He had gotten married so quickly. How could he have fallen for such a fearsome creature? She was older, too, at least thirty-five or more. But now the woman was looking at her expectantly.

"I am acquainted with the constable. I consider him a friend. He once helped me clear my name of being suspected of murder."

Petunia looked unimpressed, but Ann looked upon her with interest. "And what are you doing in town, Miss Morton?"

"I'm a lady's companion."

"Who is that? She must be grand indeed to hire a vicar's niece."

"Miss Beatrice Hayes."

Neither woman knew her but that suited Poppy very well. She curtsied and said, "I should get back. It was a pleasure to meet you both." She left in a hurry, leaving the two staring after her.

Poppy felt an unhappy lump in her throat and felt glad of the shade of her bonnet. Her face was heated, but not from the midday sun. She felt like such an idiot. It was a cruel twist of fate that the day after she learned Henry was married, she met his wife. It still struck her as odd that he had married such a dominating woman, but nothing surprised her at this point. The man she thought she knew was only a figment of her imagination. She had never thought her trip to London would be so eventful, or so heartbreaking.

She swallowed and kept walking. Just because the man she had spent so many wasted months admiring was nothing more than a friend, did not mean she had to cry her eyes out and mope about like a lovesick girl. She was better than that. She had to be.

She walked along the Strand, where she paid the entry fee, and entered Somerset House, to see the Royal Academy.

As she entered the Exhibition Room and viewed the fine gallery of paintings, she quickly became diverted. Having the time to herself was a luxury, and she could find no better use for it than looking at art.

But her thoughts were messy. Who could possibly be sending those poisonous letters to the mistresses and why? Why would anyone want to harass a bunch of mistresses? What could they possibly have to gain? That was what confused her the most, there was no sense behind it.

She stood admiring a landscape when a voice said by her ear, "Let me guess. You are thinking how dull Beatrice is as an employer, and are wondering how to remove yourself from your unhappy situation. I can well understand it, for she is as meek as a church mouse and has less sense."

Poppy turned around. "Good afternoon, Miss Jones."

"Miss Morton." Mollie inclined her head grandly as if she was a duchess. "And just what do you do here, away from your mistress?"

"I—"

"Never mind, I already know. No doubt Beatrice has chased you out so that she might spend time with her gentleman, is that it?"

"No, I was just—"

"She's not spending time with him? And you here alone? That is strange. Did you two have a falling out?" Mollie asked.

"Not at all. I simply—"

"Well, do not trouble yourself. Beatrice is a good enough girl but has little sense in that pretty head of hers. If you worked for me, I would never kick you out of your home, or leave you alone with nothing to do, especially when I have dresses that need washing. You will tell me if she mistreats you?"

"I… That is, Miss Hayes is a very kind woman." Seeing she was making no headway in changing Mollie's mind, she asked, "What are you doing here?"

"Me? I always like to view the gallery and take in the sights, and the men." She winked. "London has so much to offer, it is endlessly diverting. Don't forget what I said. I would treat you well, and I can see we share the same interests already. You'd never be bored with me. Not to mention I'd pay you handsomely, too." Mollie flashed her a self-assured smile and walked away, approaching an older gentleman and taking his arm with a predatory air.

Poppy breathed a sigh of relief to see her go. Aside from the fact that she had barely been able to get a word in, she couldn't shake the feeling that Mollie was out to cause trouble and found amusement in tormenting others. Stirring the pot, as her aunt would say. Poppy had no doubt that if she was so unlucky as to find herself in Mollie's employ, she would be very badly treated, and poorly paid. Of that she was certain.

Poppy stood looking at a painting when she bumped into a

person. "Oh, I'm sorry," she said, turning.

It was Petunia Dyngley. She said, "Oh, hello, Miss Morton. What a surprise. I did not expect to see you here."

Mrs. Farrars joined them. "Miss Morton, how pleasant to see you again. Do you come here often?"

Poppy smiled at her. "I have never seen an art gallery before. This is my first time."

"And how are you finding it?"

"Beautiful. Such skill. Seeing the works of these masters, it is no wonder that drawing and painting are considered the accomplishments of the day," Poppy said.

"They are impressive, but I wager some young women would show equal skill if given the opportunity," Petunia muttered.

"I would like to see that," Poppy said.

"What of yourself, Miss Morton?" Mrs. Farrars asked. "Are you skilled with a paintbrush?"

Poppy shook her head, feeling her cheeks warm. "No, I never learned. My aunt and uncle never had the inclination and felt any spare income was better used to feed the poor or support the church. Buying bread for the hungry was much more valued in their home." She smiled.

Petunia's gaze flickered over her with interest. "Certainly charitable, but rather lacking in accomplishment. I was taught to draw when I was ten. What about you, Miss Farrars?"

"Twelve. But I was never a proficient. I showed much more promise at the pianoforte. Pray, Miss Morton, who was that young woman you were speaking to? She looked... like an original person."

Poppy nodded. "That was Miss Mollie Jones. She was asking how I was enjoying being a lady's companion."

"Ah. I would recommend you choose your acquaintances more carefully, dear girl. You may have had a wholesome upbringing in Hertfordshire, but not all the company you keep were so fortunate, I fear," Petunia said.

"I beg your pardon?" Poppy asked.

"I happen to know on good authority—"

"Whose?" Mrs. Farrars asked.

"My own." Petunia shot her a look. "I saw for myself, that women is not so original as distasteful. She is a boil upon society. When I was looking for my husband who was out running errands, I happened to look inside a tavern or two, for he was late in coming home. On my journey, I saw that young lady on the arm of a gentleman and thought nothing of it. But later I saw her again at a different tavern, with a different man. What do you make of that, Miss Morton?" Petunia looked down her hawk nose at her.

"Who was the man?" Mrs. Farrars asked.

"Never mind who, it matters not," Petunia said. "Miss Morton?"

Poppy shrugged.

"I can tell you. That woman is no lady at all, she is an adventuress, a good for nothing. A kept woman," Petunia said with such venom, that Poppy stepped back.

"My goodness," Mrs. Farrars said.

"You are wise to be guarded, Miss Morton. For I too was surprised to see you talking with her. You are lucky it was only us two who saw you conversing, and not ladies of the *ton*." Petunia whipped out a fan and began fanning herself violently.

"Oh?" Poppy asked.

"Yes indeed. For if more ladies of quality saw you speaking with that woman, the doors to all good society would be closed to you," Mrs. Farrars said.

"What? For having a conversation?" Poppy asked.

"You do not want to be seen talking to the wrong people. Not when there are people of good society walking about." Petunia added, "Pray, what did she ask you?"

Poppy was at a loss for what to say.

"Never mind, the girl is unremarkable. And so she would be. No doubt you find yourself stricken at the thought of exchanging words with such a woman," Petunia said.

Poppy cleared her throat. If she did not speak and make herself known, she might inadvertently perjure herself or give rise to false rumors.

Poppy felt her face turn red. "Mrs. Dyngley, Mrs. Farrars, I am acquainted with that woman. You are right, she is a kept woman. But we are not on friendly terms." She took a deep breath. "I assure you, I do not value the connection."

Ann stared, and Petunia harrumphed. "Nor should you. Nor should anyone for that matter. But how are you acquainted with her?" Petunia asked.

Poppy turned pink. "She is connected with my employer. They move in the same circles in society."

"Goodness. And your employer is aware of that girl's occupation?" Ann asked, a hand pressed to her chest.

The girl in question was likely on the latter side of thirty. "Yes, she is," Poppy said.

"My word. How singular. Tell me, is your mistress a dilettante, or does she run a salon for intellectuals and artists? Bluestockings and radicals? Perhaps she amuses herself to circulate with all members of society."

Poppy blushed harder. "I wish that were the case, but unfortunately not. I would not mislead you, but my employer is…" she swallowed.

"Yes, Miss Morton?" Mrs. Farrars asked quietly.

"Tell us, girl," Petunia demanded.

Poppy took a breath. "My employer is also a kept woman, like Miss Jones, and is of such value to her gentleman that they have engaged me to be her companion." She looked them dead in the eye. A second later she wished she hadn't.

Petunia's mouth dropped open. Ann stood there, shocked, her eyes wide. "But that means… that is to say you are…"

"A mistress's companion," Poppy said.

"My word. Oh, my goodness," Mrs. Farrars babbled, "to knowingly associate yourself with such persons of low birth and dubious reputation…" She shook her head.

Petunia turned puce, her eyes narrowed, and she drew herself up to her full height. "For a well-bred girl, you show an alarming lack of common sense." She attempted to look down on Poppy but failed, for Poppy stood as tall as she. Instead Petunia satisfied herself with an indignant sniff. She met Poppy's eyes and walked past her, offering no parting words or farewell curtsy. Ann hurried after her, glancing back once.

Poppy breathed inward and realized this was the cut direct. She might as well be a statue, for all that Petunia was concerned. This was a first-class snub, and so much emotion was expressed in such a look, a blank look that wasn't sneering or scornful, but gazed through her as if she didn't exist.

As their heeled shoes echoed on the stone floors, Poppy was grateful, for no one was there to see her cry.

CHAPTER FIFTEEN

THE REST OF the day, Poppy didn't know what to do. She felt despondent and wandered home. Beatrice greeted her with a smile and relayed that Justine had gone to the playhouse, to rehearse for their new play. Poppy listened to this news with a wan smile.

"Miss Morton, are you unwell? You look pale," Beatrice said.

"I'm fine, just a touch of the sun, I think," Poppy said.

Beatrice glanced at the windows, where the skies were decidedly overcast, then urged Poppy to sit down. "What shall we do today? More detecting?"

Poppy smiled at her employer. She cared, but her heart was full. Regret, embarrassment, and shame all warred within her.

What could she do? She had taken up her employment knowing full well her mistress's occupation. Did it make any difference to her whether Beatrice was a grand lady or a man's mistress? A little. But they had to survive somehow, and if that was the profession Beatrice had fallen upon, Poppy felt it would be cruel to judge her, for she had felt a modicum of that judgment herself, from Petunia Dyngley and Ann Farrars. To that end, she decided to make the best of a bad day and take action. There must be something she could do.

"I wonder how Penelope is getting on after her tumble yesterday," Poppy said.

"I thought that too. But how lucky, for her to be rescued by that lady, and to be invited to tea afterward. nothing like that ever happens to me." Beatrice pouted.

Poppy grinned. "Shall we go out for tea? There must be a tea shop somewhere nearby."

"Oh yes. A wonderful idea. Perhaps there might be sweets too. I should like to try a pastry or a tart."

"That's settled then, let's go." Once suitably attired for going out, they walked together, followed by Mr. Parks, and stopped by the first tea shop and confectioners they found. The Ice and Lemon was a little shop on a street corner that sold candied fruits, marzipan, and other sweets. Once the young women had taken a table and were nibbling on delicate pieces of marzipan with small cups of fortifying tea, Beatrice asked, "Are you all right, Miss Morton?"

"Yes, of course. Why wouldn't I be?"

"Well, it's just… What with Justine coming by yesterday and mentioning how her gentleman was your friend, I thought you might be struck by the news." Beatrice watched her closely.

Poppy swallowed a mouthful of marzipan and reached for her teacup. "It's true, I was surprised. I think he is not the man I knew. The way he has acted is certainly different from how I would have described him."

"Men always have secrets. Our object is to ignore their petty trifles and keep them entertained. They've got wives for all the other bits of life."

"You wouldn't want to be a wife, then?" Poppy asked.

"Lord, no. I'd get fat, be stuck with the children, and then wonder where my man was all the time. I'd expect him to dally with a girl like me on the side, just to escape. No, I'm happy as I am. And Stephen is too. Isn't he, Mr. Parks?" she said, looking over Poppy's shoulder.

Mr. Parks joined them and touched his hat. "No one could be bored with you, Miss Hayes," he said gravely.

Beatrice laughed. "He always makes me laugh. Thank you,

Bertram."

He nodded and took up a place not far away to keep an eye on them.

"Bertram?" Poppy questioned.

"Yes. He told me one night when he was drunk. What a name. Can you imagine if we were a couple? Bertram and Beatrice?" She laughed.

"Is he always so serious?" Poppy asked.

"Always. Stephen found him in prison and agreed to take him on as a manservant, but he was a bit too rough for anything other than minding me."

"Don't you find it a bit intrusive on your privacy?"

Beatrice shrugged and gave her a sunny smile. "I don't mind. If he's around then I know I'm safe, and when he's not there, Stephen is. It's a blessing, really."

"How so?"

Beatrice's smile faded. "Being alone on the streets of London, or anywhere, is not a safe place for a woman. It can be dangerous. That's why I'm so grateful to Stephen for putting me up. And it's why Justine is so heartbroken to suffer at the hands of the Dyngles. Or Dingleys, or whatever their surname is." Seeing Poppy's look, she said, "I know he is your friend, but he's treated Justine abominably. She wouldn't mind if he's married or not—"

Poppy uttered a sound of indignation.

"But to kick her out of their lodgings like that, without any warning? Shameful behavior. And I daresay his treatment of you has been poor as well. For what kind of a man goes around befriending women, seducing women, and then hides the fact that he has a wife at home?"

"What man indeed," Poppy said, looking out the window.

LATER THAT AFTERNOON at Beatrice's lodgings, the pair were joined by Harriet, who appeared despondent. After exchanging pleasantries, Poppy asked, "I wanted to ask about Marie. What will happen to her body? She had a little money, but now, who will bury her?"

"What about her gentleman?" Beatrice asked. "Surely he will pay for her funeral."

"We can ask him, but I doubt he'll want much to do with it," Harriet said.

"What do you mean?" Poppy asked.

"Marie was clean and pretty enough when she lived, but no man wants to be burdened with a dead whore," Harriet said bitterly. "Now that she's dead, her gentleman has got other things to spend his money on. It wouldn't surprise me if he gave no money for her funeral at all."

Poppy's mouth dropped open. "How callous."

"It's practical. Marie was a pauper. She's no use to anyone now that she's dead." Harriet wiped away a tear.

"What should we do?" Beatrice asked.

"We could ask at the church if they'll bury her," Poppy said.

"No church will hold a service for her, don't fool yourself," Harriet said, "but... There's always Cross Bones."

"What's that?" Poppy asked.

"It's a burial ground. For whores, paupers, ne'er-do-wells, anyone who can't pay for a proper funeral or is like us."

As a trio, they went down to the magistrate and enquired where Marie's body was. They learned she was one of a few dead collected to be buried at Cross Bones and was likely already underground. Harriet's face fell. "So soon?"

One of the magistrate's men looked at her. "Bodies carry infection. Can't leave 'em out or they'll carry the plague."

Harriet nodded, and after a quiet request from Beatrice, Mr. Parks hired a carriage to take them to Cross Bones. In a short amount of time, the carriage crossed the river into Southwark and took the girls to the entrance. Harriet fretted, "We don't even have flowers."

"That's easy enough." Beatrice walked a little way on and found a girl selling flowers. The girl was young, about ten, but her eyes were old as if she had seen too much of life already, and none of it pretty. Beatrice returned with a small bouquet of drooping wildflowers and handed it to Harriet.

"Thanks." Harriet eyed a cart that was carrying bodies and stopped before an open grave. But at the heady scent in the air that was downwind from the cart, she gagged. "Oh God, the smell." She held the flowers up to her nose.

It was true. In the late afternoon, the smell of decayed flesh drifted in the air, and Beatrice gave a little shudder. Mr. Parks stood by, a watchful guardian. Poppy and Beatrice stood still and resolute as Harriet marched up to the cart driver and started talking to him.

Poppy joined her, braving the increasing smell that assailed her nostrils. She frowned and looked down at the mass grave. The smell was overpowering, and she pinched her nose.

Beatrice stood by as Harriet muttered, "I don't think I can do this."

"Toss the flowers in; she'll know you're thinking of her," Poppy said.

"I don't know what to say." Harriet looked at the grave, tears falling down her cheeks. "You're a clergyman's daughter, can you say a few words?"

Poppy smiled. She didn't have the heart to correct Harriet that she was a clergyman's niece, not daughter, but it made no difference. She had, however, attended a few funeral services in her time.

She said a little prayer, fully aware of the cart driver lugging the bodies of the recently deceased off the cart not ten feet away and dropping them into the pit. The mundane, ordinary sound of the man lifting stiff lifeless bodies like they were fallen tree branches and tossing them to smack onto a pile wasn't just indecent, it was grotesque. Despite the light stains of quicklime on the inside of the pit, the stench was almost unbearable, and the sight of so many men, women, and children lying there like cordwood made Poppy's stomach turn. She swallowed and tried not to gag at the smell, or at the small clouds of black flies that hovered over the pit, feasting on the dead flesh. It was an indelicate affair, and Poppy felt faintly ridiculous. But she also knew that it mattered to Harriet.

Once Poppy had finished reciting a prayer, Harriet tossed the wildflowers into the grave and said, holding her nose, "I don't even know if she's in there. She didn't even get a proper funeral."

"She knows you're thinking of her. That's something."

"Is it? Does it matter when she's considered worthless to the people who knew her? To her gentleman? To her servants? It pains me to think that this is the fate for all of us in this trade. To be so unloved, unwanted, to end up as so much dirt. I am done. Let's go, I don't want to stay here any longer than I have to."

Poppy nodded and together, the three of them walked away from the mass grave.

CHAPTER SIXTEEN

Henry rose late and waited until the proper sociable hour. He had dressed in a slate blue overcoat, a light waistcoat, and dark trousers, with his white cravat loosely tied. He clapped his hat on and was preparing to leave when Petunia walked into the townhouse with another woman.

"Oh, Henry, you're here. Tell me you've not just woken up," Petunia said, removing her hat and its blue feathers that whipped from side to side like a fierce dog's tail.

"Not at all, I've been awake for hours. Hello." Henry removed his hat and bowed to the newcomer.

"Oh, let me introduce my friend, Mrs. Ann Farrars. Mrs. Farrars, my brother-in-law, Henry."

Once they had bowed and curtsied, Ann asked, "Is it true, sir, that you are a magistrate?"

Petunia snorted while Henry smiled. "No, ma'am, just a town constable. Nothing so grand as that."

"Of London?"

"No, Hertford, in Hertfordshire." He doffed his hat and began to pass them when Petunia said, "I've heard enough of Hertfordshire for today. Who knew a young girl like that would be so well-bred and yet show such a disturbing lack of common sense?"

Henry turned around. "Mrs. Dyngley?"

His sister-in-law was removing her gloves. "And to think, she a clergyman's daughter. I've never seen the like before. I have a good mind to write to her father."

"I agree," Ann said, watching Henry.

"Petunia," Henry said.

"Yes, what is it, Henry?" Petunia glanced at him. Her hazel eyes were fearsome.

"Who is it you're talking about?"

"Nobody. Just a girl we met at church."

"From Hertfordshire?"

"Yes. Oh, she claimed an acquaintance with this family. But I highly doubt it, unless, of course, she's another one of John's *acquaintances*." But by the tone of the last word, she made it clear what she thought of that.

"What's her name?" he asked.

"Peony? Persephone? No, it was…"

"Poppy? Miss Poppy Morton?"

"Yes, that's it. Do you know the girl?"

"She is a friend of mine. You say you met her?"

"Yes, at church today, and again at the Royal Academy this afternoon. Although I must say, Henry, you do choose strange friends. Did you know she is a companion?" Petunia asked.

"Yes, I had heard that."

"But to a kept woman? An adventuress?"

Henry stopped. He looked hard at Petunia, who returned the look.

"A mistress," Ann confirmed.

Henry swallowed. "Is she? I had heard a rumor of that nature."

"It's no rumor, we heard it from her directly. She was in the company of other wild girls when I saw her. I don't mind telling you, I warned her she should not be seen with such rude women as they would reflect badly upon her, but she told me cheeky as anything that she was not only acquainted with the women, but she worked for one of them as well."

The air went out of Henry's sails, so to speak.

"Did you know about this, Henry?"

He let out a breath. *So it was true. To hear it from a stranger in a coffeeshop was one thing but to hear his fear confirmed by Petunia was quite another. Poppy, a mistress's companion. Knowingly working for a prostitute. A whore. What was she thinking? Was she out of her mind?*

"Where is she?"

"We met her at the Royal Academy, at Somerset House. Why?"

Henry frowned and pulled on his gloves. "I need to speak with her. She may be in some trouble."

"I hope not. Henry, are you sure you should seek her out? You cannot condone this kind of willful behavior." Petunia said, "Ann, wouldn't you agree?"

Ann swallowed, "It does suggest a certain want of propriety."

Henry frowned. "I knew she was applying to be a companion but did not know for whom. I assumed it was for a lonely widow or a spinster."

"Hah! If only. What will you do now?"

"I shall speak to her about her situation," Henry said.

"And then will you write to her father?" Petunia asked.

"She has an aunt and uncle as her guardians. I shall write to them," he said.

"I am surprised they allowed her to do this at all," Petunia huffed.

"I think they assumed it would be a short-term visit to London. I gather they assumed that once she learned of the particulars of being a companion, she would find the lifestyle less appealing and return home."

"We can only hope."

Henry bowed to them both and left, his mind all a flutter. Poppy, companion to a mistress. He had to find her before she damaged her reputation further.

Dyngley walked, but his thoughts were scattered like an upturned deck of cards. He did not like this business of Poppy's; what did she think she was doing? By taking up a position as a companion to an unworthy woman, and putting herself in a subservient role to a stranger, she unknowingly entered into a sphere inappropriate for young ladies. Worse, she accepted their society and the consequences thereof upon herself. Doors would be closed to her, and naught but the cheapest of establishments would welcome her entry.

He grimaced and then he realized, the answer lay with her mother. Celeste Morton, or Grey, as she chose to be called. She would know what to do.

He fished out the calling card Celeste had given him. Orchard Street, adjoining Portman Square. In no time at all, he approached the street, knocked on the door, and presented his card to a well-dressed footman. He was admitted and shown into a comfortable parlor. Its furnishings were not at the height of fashion but were clean, charming, and bespoke of an easy comfort without pretension. He met his hostess and bowed.

She received him as befitting her nickname, with grace. "Constable Dyngley," she said with a low feminine voice.

If Poppy was tall, her mother was statuesque. There was no mistaking the resemblance, for as she curtsied with ease and bid him sit, he felt more and more assured he was looking at Poppy's mother.

Today she wore a dress of deep purple silk, trimmed with white linen at the bodice. Her figure was like Poppy's; long, thin and fragile like a bird's. She rang for tea and as a servant brought in a tray and set down the tea things, Celeste waited for the servant to leave.

Henry spoke first. "Mrs. Morton, I—"

She held up a hand. "That is not my name. My surname is Grey."

"But we have a connection, you see..." He stopped.

She poured him a cup of green tea. "Why don't you tell me of yourself, Constable."

He began to tell her of Hertford, and of how he became a county constable. It was purely gradual when he began talking of

Poppy, her family, and how she had been instrumental in helping him solve a few local crimes. When he first started talking of her, Celeste sat still and guarded, politely drinking her tea. But as Henry told her more stories of the mysteries they had solved together, her face lit up with pride, and she offered him a warm smile.

"It is a pleasure to hear of a young woman doing so well. It sounds like she has a good head on her shoulders," she said.

"You would think so," he began, "but an alarming report has come to my ears, and for that, I could use your help."

"Me? Whatever for?"

He drank his tea, surveying her over his teacup. *How would this woman take the news? What if he had been mistaken and was telling all this to a stranger? What if it was not Poppy's mother at all?* "This friend of mine, Miss Morton, has recently taken up a position as a companion."

"Oh? I am surprised her aunt and uncle allowed her to do so."

"I suspect they thought nothing would come of it, or that she would find the lifestyle trying and return home."

"From what you tell me, this friend of yours sounds independent and headstrong. Two traits not generally admired in a woman of today," Celeste said evenly.

"They are by me," Henry said.

Celeste gave him a curious look, and he cleared his throat. "She has come to London, not just for the purpose of earning a wage, that is just the guise under which she operates. In truth, she has come to find her mother, whom she was told is a kept woman."

Celeste froze. A second passed, then she delicately sipped her tea. "I see."

"If I had known what she was about, I would have tried to stop her. Or at least see that she was appropriately chaperoned."

"But what is the harm in her searching? If she is a companion, she is always in polite company. However kind, there is no need for your involvement."

"She is the companion of a mistress."

Celeste stopped, holding her teacup in midair. She set it down on the table. "And just who might that be?"

"Miss Beatrice Hayes."

Celeste gave him a blank look.

"You see, an actress was living at my townhouse—"

Her eyes grew wide. "You show an eager interest in this young companion, but then cite a connection to an actress? What do you hope to achieve, Constable? To unburden yourself of one mistress only to gain another?" Her eyes were steely.

"No, not at all. Miss Morton is my friend. My only concern is for her health and wellbeing."

Choose your next words carefully, her look said.

He swallowed. "The actress is an acquaintance of my brother, John. She learned of John's circumstances, and—"

"His prior relationship with his wife, you mean," Celeste said, "I hear things, Constable. Some even turn out to be true. It has reached my ears that your family threw the girl out on the street, without a penny to live on and just the clothes on her back. Have any of you tried to see if she is even still alive?"

Henry blushed. "No, but I—"

She snorted, an indelicate sound.

"She informed me she would stay with Miss Hayes, who is the employer of my friend, Miss Morton."

"Go on."

"You know that with Miss Morton attaching herself to dubious society, it will damage her reputation and put her in the way of those who are unscrupulous. Low-born women will think her one of their own and attempt to cheat her, or men will seek to seduce her."

"Why do you care what happens to this young woman?" Her look was intense.

"She is a friend of mine," he said. "I care for my friends."

"Your concern outweighs that of a mere friend. I have many friends, but none save one who would care so much for me. Do you two share an understanding?" she asked.

"Certainly not. She is just an innocent young woman who I do not wish to see come to harm." He looked away.

"What are your intentions toward her, should you find her?" She sipped her tea.

"I will turn her mind from this course of action and return her home to her aunt and uncle."

"And if she refuses to go?"

He had not thought of that. "I will deal with that when we come to it. She is a sensible girl, she will see reason."

"She is lucky to have a friend like you."

"I am lucky to have her," he said.

She flashed him a small knowing smile. Warm but uninviting, it suggested he was the butt of a private joke.

He said, "Miss Morton is an innocent, sweet girl. She knows not the consequence of her actions."

"And what is that to me?"

"I thought that as her mother, you might—"

"Let me stop you there, Constable." Her warm gaze vanished. "I decided to meet you because you piqued my curiosity at the races, and I wondered why a man like yourself would seek an audience with me. But it is clear that you are under a misapprehension about me and this young friend of yours."

"But I thought—"

"I have sympathy for this young woman, but she has no connection to me. I appreciate your concern, but I have no children and have never met this Miss Morton you speak of. If indeed she is in trouble, then I suggest you find and advise her against this course of action."

"I do not know where she might be. I was hoping that you could tell me where Miss Hayes lives."

"That I cannot help you with. I'm afraid you have gone on a wasted errand, Constable." She rose.

"But your daughter—" he began.

"I have no daughter," she snapped. "I have no husband, nor

any children. Any suggestions otherwise I would consider impertinent and rude. Do me the courtesy of refraining from mentioning that in the future, for it is untrue."

He got to his feet. "I have offended you."

"You have not. I simply do not appreciate false assertions about my life from a man I have just met. You understand."

He inclined his head.

"I regret to cut our conversation short, but I too have calls to make. My maid will show you out."

He bowed and turned to leave.

"Constable Dyngley," she spoke, causing him to turn. "If it is in fact this girl and her mistress that you seek, why not try the theater? If they are housing that actress of yours, no doubt they will want to see her perform."

"Excellent idea, madam."

She gave a small curtsy and watched as he left.

As he walked out, there were two things he was certain of. Firstly, Celeste Grey was definitely Poppy's mother. It was like looking at a taller, wealthier model of her, but in her mid-forties. The resemblance was remarkable. And second, he needed to find Poppy before it was too late. He hadn't a second to lose.

CHAPTER SEVENTEEN

T HE FOLLOWING MORNING at breakfast, Poppy stared at a piece of toast on her plate when Beatrice confronted her. "You seem in low spirits today, Miss Morton. Are you disturbed by our visit to Cross Bones yesterday?"

Poppy shook her head. "No."

"Then what is it? You're not homesick, are you?"

"No."

"Well, I too am feeling dull today. Stephen has written to say he is still in town with his wife, so he cannot see me in good conscience."

Poppy glanced at Beatrice. "Do you not feel…"

"What?"

"That it is wrong, somehow, to have a relationship with Stephen?"

"Why? Because he is married?" Beatrice poured herself a cup of tea.

Poppy nodded.

"Not at all. It is more of a transaction. He comes to me for company…"

"And pays you for the privilege."

"Exactly! I like that." She shot Poppy a sideways glance. "You don't judge me for this, do you?"

Poppy ate a bite of toast. She hadn't really given much weight to it, as she knew that men kept mistresses whether they were married or not. It just hurt to know that Henry was one of them.

"No, I don't. It's how you survive. But what about Stephen's wife?"

Beatrice shrugged. "I never did anything to hurt her. For all I know she dislikes the marriage bed and is frigid. Stephen comes to me for comfort, he goes to her for everything else. If I turned him away, I would find another gentleman."

"What about a different profession? Surely there is a trade you could learn."

Beatrice's smile hardened. "I could I suppose. And be as good-natured as you are, and go to church on Sundays, but... I do not wish to. I like my life. We cannot all be well-bred clergymen's relations like yourself. Thanks to Stephen's generosity, I have a roof over my head and fine dresses to wear. He pays for my upkeep and yours, in case you forgot."

Poppy reddened. "I'm sorry. I meant no offense."

"None taken. But it's worth remembering that even if you do not approve of my lifestyle choices, it is what pays for your supper, and the toast you are eating now." Beatrice pointed out.

Poppy swallowed, feeling the toast sink in her stomach like a dead weight. It tasted wrong in her mouth, but why? Could she not reconcile herself to her situation? She did disapprove of Beatrice's lifestyle but what was it that disturbed her so?

"I wonder if it is not my choice of profession that concerns you, but rather the knowledge that Justine was your friend's paramour. Is that what troubles you?"

Poppy looked up from her plate. Beatrice's eyes were kind. "You did not know, did you?"

"No. I knew he had been engaged before but to a different woman. To learn that he has gotten married in such a short time, and has carried on with Justine, it feels dishonest."

"To them or to you?"

"To everyone involved. If a man is unhappy in his marriage then perhaps he does find solace in another woman's company, but this is unlike him. The man I know is honest, decent, incredibly smart, and kind. We are friends. If he were to do this, I am sure I would know of it."

Beatrice munched on a piece of toast. "I know. But men do what they will, and we are to go with the flow or leave, but never rock the boat."

Poppy's eyebrows rose.

"I told you, I'm from down Bristol way. I've been on ships before."

Poppy smiled.

"What you need is some diversion. I know, let us call on Penelope today. I found out from Harriet where her new lodgings are. She has no doubt taken tea with her rescuer and with any luck, hasn't stolen any of the woman's jewelry."

Poppy grinned.

AFTER BREAKFAST THEY dressed for social calls, meaning they were suitably attired in walking coats, boots, long dresses, and bonnets to match. Beatrice wore a fetching yellow bonnet with a deep orange ribbon, to match her pale-yellow walking coat, while Poppy wore the same faded overcoat and bonnet she had arrived in. They walked a few streets down, not far from Covent Garden. The area was noisy and full of people, but Beatrice steered Poppy away from the side alleys, child gangs, and men of a dubious appearance.

Once outside Penelope's building, Beatrice and Poppy knocked, waited, and knocked again. There was still no answer. A worrisome feeling filled Poppy.

Beatrice smiled brightly at her. "Maybe she's entertaining her gentleman."

"Is there any way to tell?"

"Not especially. But it's odd, normally her maid would answer it." They knocked again, but no answer.

"This is strange. Could something be wrong?"

"Perhaps she is out. Her maid could be cleaning and cannot

hear us knocking," Beatrice said.

Poppy looked around. It was a busy main street, but they were off the main road. Poppy started to wonder what to do when Beatrice said, "Look, there's Tom. Let's ask him. Tom!" she called.

Tom caught sight of them across the street and waved, then crossed the road. "Hello, you two. Paying a call to Penelope, eh?" He gave Poppy a warm smile.

"Yes, although no one seems to be in. Have you spoken to her lately?" Beatrice asked.

"No. Isn't her maid in? Someone should answer," he said.

"No one is answering," Poppy said.

"That's odd." He looked up at the windows and called, "Hello there!"

Still no response.

Poppy noticed that they were standing on the top of a small set of steps, bordered by a thin iron railing on the right. Beyond it about ten feet below was a lower set of stairs for tradesmen. She leaned over the railing and wobbled slightly on her feet.

"Hey there, don't go falling." Tom instantly grasped her waist and pulled her back. His hands were warm as he held her steady.

"Thank you." She looked beyond and noticed that the door was open. "Look at that."

"What?" Tom released her and stood by to see. "That's odd."

"What is it?" Beatrice asked.

"The tradesman's entrance is open."

Poppy moved around him and started walking down the steps.

"Hold on, Miss Morton, it could be dangerous," Tom said.

"An open door?"

His smile disappeared. "You shouldn't go down there. It's trespassing."

"We can at least ask the housekeeper where Penelope is. Surely that's allowed."

"I don't like it," he said, rubbing his chin. Seeing her resolute expression, he said, "All right, let me go first." He passed her and walked down the steps and inside. "Hello?"

Poppy and Beatrice followed him. The inside led to a small kitchen that had an air of abandonment. A bit of bread dough lay on the table, ignored. It had been left long enough to grow a hard crust from its exposure to air. A dying fire was in the hearth, but it was small and left untended.

As the wind passed into the kitchen from the open door behind them, a sense of stillness was present, and Poppy felt something was wrong. "Where would Penelope be? It looks like her servants just left."

"She'd be upstairs, in her bedchamber I expect," Beatrice said.

"I don't like this," Tom said. "Why are there no servants around?"

"There doesn't seem to be anyone around," Poppy said. "Does she have many servants?"

"Not so many. A housekeeper, cook, and lady's maid and then a man to do odd jobs," Beatrice said.

Together the three of them crept up the stairs to the ground level of the house. They stood like awkward guests in a foyer, which held a dining room to the left, and a small parlor to the right.

"I'll look upstairs," Tom said, "Beatrice, you take the dining room. Miss Morton, the parlor is yours."

Poppy nodded and called out, "Miss Penelope!"

She watched Tom walk up the stairs. The rooms themselves were dark aside from the bit of sunlight let in from the open curtains. Beatrice disappeared into the dining room and Poppy stepped into the parlor. At first sight, she saw nothing out of the ordinary and went upstairs.

She found Tom in the upstairs bedroom but there was no one present. He stood in front of a small vanity table, strewn with cosmetics. "Tom," she said.

He turned around. "I found this. Look." He handed a small card to her.

She took it and realized it was the calling card of Mrs. Ann Farrars. "I remember, she gave this to Penelope at the races the other day. She invited Penelope to take tea with her."

"Look at this." He stepped aside.

There on the table beneath a bottle of perfume and some makeup pots were a few letters. Poppy picked up one. It read: *You are a curse upon men.*

Another read: *You could have any man. Why not leave husbands alone?*

"So she's been getting notes too."

"It looks that way. Where do you think she could have gone? It's odd that not even the servants are here. It gives me an odd feeling," he said.

"I agree."

There was a knock at the door. Poppy and Tom looked at each other.

The knock came again.

"I suppose we should answer it," Poppy said. She took the card and went downstairs, just as Beatrice was opening the door. She said, "Hello?"

A large middle-aged man with graying hair and a dark red waistcoat filled the doorway. "Who are you? Are you Miss Penelope Smythe?"

"No. We are looking for her. Why?"

The man took in the sight of Poppy and Tom coming down the stairs. "I'm Jon Wilkes. Member of the watch for London. A maid has come in saying her mistress Miss Smythe is gone, and that she's a fine lady. What are you lot doing 'ere?"

Poppy and Tom exchanged a look. Tom said, "We too were looking for Miss Smythe. We found the kitchen door open downstairs and thought something had gone amiss, so were searching for her."

The man looked at Tom. "I recognize you. You work at the Shakespeare's Head, don't you?"

Tom nodded. "Tom Harris, Head Waiter." He puffed up

with pride.

"Aye, I know. You fetched that girl Mary Louise for my friend Michael."

"A fine girl. I trust your friend enjoyed her company," he said with a smile.

The man's polite expression disappeared. "She gave him the clap. Come along, you're all coming with me."

Tom's face fell. "But sir, surely these two young women can return home. They came out of concern for Miss Smythe."

"I don't care. I don't like the idea of coming to the girl's lodging and finding you here nosing around. What's to say you didn't harm her yourself?"

"Now see here—" Poppy said when Tom cut her off. "I assure you, they know nothing." He stepped hard on Poppy's foot.

She shot him a glance. "It's true, Mr. Wilkes. We don't know what happened to her."

The man looked suspiciously at her and was silent for a moment, then said, "All right. I've got enough to deal with. Mr. Harris, come along. Can't imagine either of you know anything useful."

Poppy's mouth dropped open.

Tom shot her an apologetic look. "Go home, Miss Morton."

"No."

"Oh, so you want to join your friend?" Mr. Wilkes's face pulled into a hard sneer.

"No, we do not. We'll go home as you said. Come on, Miss Morton." Beatrice took her arm.

"Very well." He motioned for Tom to precede him and waited for the women to follow them outside of the building.

The maid stood outside. She said, "I was that worried," in a Cornish accent.

"Do you know these women?" Mr. Wilkes asked.

"I know her, that Miss Hayes. She's an acquaintance of Miss Smythe's," the girl said. "Don't know the other girl, although I see Mr. Harris now and again."

"When did your mistress go missing?" Tom asked, "We've just been looking for her. Thought something was wrong when we saw the kitchen door open."

"Oh, I must've left it open by mistake. I'm always leaving doors open and getting told off for it," the girl said.

"Very well. Mr. Harris, you're with me. Girls, don't let me see you here again." Mr. Wilkes walked away.

Poppy and Beatrice watched as Tom accompanied the man. Beatrice gripped Poppy's arm.

"We should go after him," Poppy said.

"No, we shouldn't. Tom told us to go home. It's safer for us."

"But what about Tom? He needs our help."

Beatrice shook her head. "He's better off without us. He can charm his way out of anything. We'll just make it worse for him."

Poppy shot her a look. "I wish we could help him."

"The best thing we can do is leave him be. He won't want us in the way. But why did Tom not want us to say anything?" Beatrice asked.

"Probably so as not to incriminate ourselves," Poppy said.

"What does that mean?"

"So as not to get ourselves in any trouble."

"Oh."

They walked on and passed the local church. Poppy said, "Miss Hayes if you don't mind, I'll just step inside and say a quick prayer."

"As you like." Beatrice shrugged.

"Would you like to join me?"

"I'm all right. I'll see you at home." Beatrice spotted Mr. Parks across the road, watching. "I can always call on Harriet if I want company."

They parted ways and Poppy went inside. She had missed the latest service but didn't care, for the church was calm and quiet. It felt peaceful, and despite rarely feeling inclined to spend much time in a church at home, here she felt a connection. As if by sitting quietly in a pew, she felt her home roots again.

She sat quietly and thought on what she knew, when a polite voice said behind her, "Miss Morton."

Poppy turned around. "Mrs. Farrars." She blushed. Mrs. Farrars looked very smart in a light purple silk gown trimmed with white linen panels, beneath a long gray walking coat that looked cheap at first, then based on the frills and fripperies of cloth, Poppy assumed was expensive. Her brown hair was coiled atop her head prettily, beneath a fetching bonnet with a thick gray ribbon.

Poppy refused to meet her eyes. She felt like a coward, but no doubt the woman would soon skewer her with a well-thought-out insult. She rose from the pew. "Excuse me, I was just leaving."

"No, please, don't go. I saw you go in and wanted to speak with you."

Poppy stopped.

Ann sat in the pew behind her. "I wanted to apologize for the other day. Please, sit."

Poppy's eyes widened and she sat down.

Ann looked down at her lap and folded her hands primly. "You took us by surprise when we saw you conversing with that woman in the Royal Academy. Companions are common enough, but to find one who is in the employ of a kept woman is… an oddity."

"That's all right, I understand."

"No, it's not all right. Our behavior was unpardonable. Mrs. Dyngley was overly harsh to you, and I was taken aback by the discovery. I did not know how to act and I'm afraid I followed Mrs. Dyngley's response, when I should have stayed." She took a breath and said quietly, "I think it is very daring and brave for a young woman to strike out on her own and seek employment. I was not able to do that, but I appreciate that for some, this may be the only option. While I cannot condone your choice of employer, I hope it keeps you in good stead." She met Poppy's eyes and her gaze was kind, if prim. Her dark brown eyes seemed encouraging.

Poppy said, "To be fair, I did not know my mistress's profession when I came to London. But... I find we are not so dissimilar."

"Miss Morton, there is no reason to compare yourself to a wanton harlot like that. If any of us had known your circumstances we would have written to your family and taken you in."

Poppy smiled. "I only compare myself in regard to her, that we both find ourselves in need of employment. I have learned I must not be so judgmental of these women's profession, it is what keeps a roof over my head."

"But do you truly need to work? I understand your relations are in the clergy. Some livings do very well. What made you leave? Was your own home an unhappy place? I understand you are from Hertfordshire."

"No. I was very happy. I..." Poppy sighed. "The truth is I am twenty, unmarried, and I am not a great beauty. The closest thing I had to a romantic relationship was with Constable Dyngley and..."

"And you found out he is married and has a mistress. Mrs. Dyngley told me," Ann said.

"Yes."

"That must have been hard to bear."

"I couldn't stand it. It's why I left Hertford in the first place. Do you have any idea how horrid it is to be standing alone at assemblies, overlooked by dance partners, while the women go around dancing and talking about you like you're a leper? I had been accused of murder once, and Constable Dyngley helped prove my innocence. For a time the gossip stopped, but then he left, and it all started up again."

"That does indeed sound horrid, but rather a lofty reason for a girl to go adventuring in London unaccompanied."

"I have my reasons," Poppy said, uncomfortable with saying more. She quickly changed the subject. "Did you meet with Miss Smythe?"

"Who?"

"Miss Penelope Smythe. The girl who fell at the races, who you helped. You invited her to tea," Poppy said.

"Oh yes, I did. But she never showed up. It was very odd. Why?"

"I think something has happened to her."

"Oh dear. That's worrisome. Especially a pretty young woman like that. I hope she is all right," Ann said.

"Me too."

"I say, it sounds to me like what you need is a bit of diversion. I am new to London, but I hear the theater is very entertaining. Why not go to a performance?" Ann said.

"That is a good idea. I will."

"Good. I hear the play *Marie Antoinette* is being played at the Theatre Royal. Perhaps I might see you there."

"That would be nice," Poppy said.

They parted ways. As they walked out, Poppy said, "Thank you for understanding, Mrs. Farrars."

"Nonsense. Anyone can see you are a sweet, innocent girl who is trying to find her way in the world. Would that I had had the same chance."

Poppy cocked her head. "Oh?"

"Never mind. I hope to see you at the theater. Good afternoon, Miss Morton."

As Poppy left the church in the company of Mrs. Farrars, she realized something. One, Justine would have a full house at her next performance. But second, had Mrs. Farrars lied about meeting Penelope?

CHAPTER EIGHTEEN

POPPY RETURNED HOME to find Beatrice in the parlor, saying, "Oh Poppy, it is very exciting. We have tickets to see Justine in her play, *Marie Antoinette!*" She held up a pair of two paper tickets. "I've secured a box for us both. Isn't that wonderful?"

"I've just been hearing about that."

"We must go. It is tomorrow night. Do you have anything suitable to wear?"

Poppy looked down at her dress. It was plain, simple, and ordinary, just like how she felt. It might as well have been a reflection of her person, so dull it was.

"Never mind. I'll loan you one of my gowns," Beatrice said with a smile.

Poppy smiled back at her kindness but felt a pinch of embarrassment at not having her own gown to wear. As much as she appreciated Beatrice's charity, Beatrice was also definitely shorter than her. She would look odd, if not indecent, with her ankles exposed. "That is very kind of you, but I am fine as I am."

"Nonsense, you'll look ridiculous in a day dress. Besides, I have a gown the modiste sent over that is too long for me. I have yet to send it back for alterations, so you can wear it and no one will know."

Poppy wasn't so sure, but Beatrice was adamant. "I can't very well be seen in finery and have my companion look like a pauper."

Poppy blushed briefly. She did not feel her clothes were of such poor quality, but she knew Beatrice was trying to be generous. "Um…"

Beatrice surveyed her thoughtfully. "And then we'll have to arrange your hair and touch up your complexion. You're not averse to wearing a bit of rouge, are you?"

"Pardon?"

All too soon Poppy stood in her room, gazing at a dress that lay folded in a modiste's box. It was a fetching blue and white dress, which bore white satin cap sleeves with blue muslin panels draped from the bosom to the floor. It was very pretty. Beatrice took it out and held it up. "This will look very nice on you, I dare say."

Poppy had never touched satin before. She gently took it from Beatrice and held it up against her to judge the length. "It seems long enough."

"There. Perfect. You can wear it for tonight. It will be good because then I can see how it drapes or whether I want to have the design altered. Oh, do you have evening gloves?"

"Um… Not with me," Poppy said, feeling warm.

"Never mind. You'll borrow a pair of mine. And we'll send up Nancy to do your hair. I bet you'll look stunning." Beatrice rubbed her hands together, looking over Poppy's coiled bun at the nape of her neck. "I can't wait."

THE FOLLOWING EVENING, Poppy was visited by Beatrice and Nancy, who fussed, combed out, and then pinned up her hair again, while Beatrice came in with an armful of pots and began dabbing at Poppy's cheeks and lips.

"What are you doing?" Poppy asked.

"Stop! Don't lick your lips. Not until we are at the theater, and you have a glass of wine."

"Why?"

"I don't want the lip cream to come off, silly."

Poppy purposely faced away from the looking glass in her room, and instead sat quietly while Beatrice hummed and supervised the maid attending Poppy's hair. Once they were done, Poppy slipped off her day clothes and gratefully accepted the maid's help in putting on the borrowed evening dress. It felt light and airy, and reached down to the ground.

"Oh, you look lovely. You need a necklace though," Beatrice said, looking at Poppy's chest.

"No, I couldn't. Isn't this a bit..." Poppy touched her collarbone.

"What?"

"Too low?"

Beatrice laughed. "That is the style, Miss Morton."

"It can't be. I feel like I'm on display. A shop window has more modesty."

"A shop window will not be escorting me to a play. I have a reputation to uphold and so do you."

Poppy turned around and looked at her reflection in the mirror. She stood tall and had her hair out of her face, but the bodice at her dress was low cut and showed her assets off to a startling degree. She blushed and turned away. "I'll need a shawl."

"Oh and gloves, of course. I have a white shawl and I'll fetch those gloves for you." Beatrice disappeared.

A rude voice said, "Don't see why you're getting all dressed up like a tart."

Poppy turned. There in the doorway to her room stood Fanny. Her face was partially obscured by her mobcap pulled low, but her mouth was twisted into a sneer, and her cheeks were marred by pockmark scars.

Poppy sniffed. "Go away."

The maid sneered. "You just watch your step. London's no place for a girl like you."

"And what is that supposed to mean?"

"You just listen to what I said." Fanny disappeared as Beatrice re-entered with a pretty white shawl and long gloves.

"Poppy, what is it? Are you unwell?"

"The maid was rude."

"Who? Nancy?"

"No, the other one. Fanny. Her face…" Poppy gestured to her cheeks. "She was rude."

"Well never mind her, she's only a servant. She's probably just afraid you'll take a dislike to her and kick her out on the street." She approached and handed Poppy the shawl and gloves. "There now. You look lovely, if I do say so myself."

Poppy smiled. "It's so kind of you, Miss Hayes. Truly."

"Call me Beatrice, please. We are so formal all our lives, a little informality between friends never hurt anyone."

"Beatrice, it's too much, really."

"Not at all. Although maybe I shouldn't have dressed you so well. I don't want you to receive any gentleman callers yourself!" Beatrice joked.

Poppy's eyes widened for a moment, then she smiled. "Somehow I doubt that will happen."

Poppy sat in the parlor as Beatrice dressed and eventually emerged dressed in a pretty white satin gown trimmed with small seed pearls at the low scooped neckline. Her golden hair was up in an elegant updo, and her elbow-length gloves looked pearly white and satin.

She said, "Ready to go?"

Poppy nodded and they had a servant call a carriage for them.

They climbed in and with their reticules, shawls, and carefully arranged in the carriage, they set off for Drury Lane. The carriage was bumpy and jostled unevenly against the city streets, the horse's hooves clattering against the road.

The carriage pulled up along the front of Brydges Street, and Poppy's mouth dropped open. The outside of the theater was very grand. It bore many round openings for each entrance, and Poppy and Beatrice walked closely together as they entered a crowd of people moving toward the entrance. The building itself was stone and rose high up into the sky. Atop the building was a turret and above that, a statue. Poppy felt very grand to be attending such a place.

Inside was a crush of people. Poppy and Beatrice clasped hands so as not to lose each other, and Beatrice led Poppy through like a river of bodies as they moved by men and women, some dressed finer than they, others dressed more humbly. Smells of perfume, men's cologne, scent, and body odor filled Poppy's nose. The scents of wine, tobacco, and unwashed bodies filled the air, along with the smoky hints from sputtering candles that burned through cheap tallow candles. The air was hot, Poppy felt overly warm and certain that her hair would soon slump out of its fine arrangement, but she didn't mind. The inside of the theater was beautiful.

As Beatrice and Poppy climbed the first of four staircases that led up to the higher levels, they turned, passed through a set of doors and a corridor entered Beatrice's box, and took their seats, along with two drinks from a passing footman. The box held two empty seats behind them.

"Beatrice, I wonder, where is Mr. Parks?" Poppy asked.

"Oh, I'm sure he's around somewhere. I got him a ticket too, but he said he had errands to run for Stephen. He said he'd join us later," Beatrice said.

After a short time where Poppy leaned forward and observed that they were one box of many that aligned the half-circle of seats around the stage. "My goodness, there must be hundreds of people here."

"Oh yes. It's an amazing theater, isn't it? Much better than any I've seen," Beatrice agreed.

As Poppy looked around, she observed the people in the nearby boxes and saw, much to her dismay, the glaring gaze of Petunia Dyngley a few boxes away. The woman's gaze was fierce, and as soon as they locked eyes she gave an indignant sniff and turned away.

"Who is that woman?" Beatrice asked. "She does not seem to like you very much."

"That is Mrs. Dyngley," Poppy said, "the wife of my friend."

"Oh. I see. The one who threw out Justine." Beatrice looked at her thoughtfully. "She's not very pretty, is she? More handsome than anything, especially with that hawk nose of hers."

Poppy winced. Then a voice distracted her. "Is this seat taken?"

She looked and Tom entered their box, dressed in a suit. "Hullo, you two." He winked at Poppy.

"Tom, I didn't know you were coming," Beatrice said.

"I thought I'd take in a show. Saw you two going up the stairs and thought I'd drop in. Got yourself a box, eh? Very nice." He looked around appreciatively. "Must've cost you a couple of shillings."

"Where are you sitting?" Poppy asked.

"Here, if you'll let me." He grinned.

Beatrice shrugged. "I don't mind. Mr. Parks should come by soon enough."

"And where's your gentleman today, Beatrice?" Tom asked.

"Off with his wife. Mr. Parks delivered a message earlier, he wrote to say he had to spend time with her." She rolled her eyes and looked appreciatively at Poppy. "At least I am not alone."

"You're not alone at all, look there. Mollie's looking mad as a hornet." Tom pointed past Poppy's ear.

They looked. There was Mollie sitting in her own box, with a gentleman, but looking quite put out, as she was in a box lower than them, just slightly above the crowd standing in the pit facing the stage. She glared at them and then looked away, fanning herself. She wore a dark purple dress that clung to her like silk, with a large feather stuck in the back of her hair.

"I wonder what bird she killed for that feather. It looks like an ostrich." Tom laughed.

Poppy smiled and glanced at Tom take a seat behind her, just as the lights began to dim and the noise in the large theater began to quiet.

The play began, and Poppy was enthralled. If she didn't know better, she wouldn't have recognized Justine, for she was dressed in fine clothes with a noble circlet for a crown and a blonde wig.

Poppy became entranced by the music, the jokes, and the charm as the young hapless Marie Antoinette, played by Justine, was married off to King Louis XVI and ushered into a new household. Perhaps it was English sentiment influencing the play, but it portrayed Marie in a very poor light, making her abuse lower-class people and throw away food to her dogs while her subjects starved in the streets.

When the lights came on for the intermission, Poppy sighed with disappointment.

"How are you liking the play, Miss Morton?" Tom asked.

"Very much," she said as a footman entered their private theater box.

"Is there a Miss Morton here?"

"Yes, I am she." Poppy stood.

The man bowed. "A Miss Justine Vane wishes to speak with you backstage. If you would follow me?"

"Me? Why would she want to see me? We hardly know each other," Poppy said.

"This is odd. I'll go with you," Tom said.

"And me. She's my friend. I'm coming too," Beatrice added.

The footman looked as though he might object, then shrugged. "This way." He led the three of them down a back set of stairs, down a corridor or two, through an entryway that led backstage. The man took them past actors, stagehands, footmen, servants; it was like a series of ants, Poppy reflected, each with their own different purpose. She followed the man and then saw him knock on the door of a small dressing room. It was opened and Poppy went in to find Justine in tears.

Poppy said, "Miss Vane, what is the matter?"

Justine sat on a chair, her blonde wig askew. She wore a robe for modesty and her eyes were rimmed with dark heavy kohl. But her tears had carved black lines through her stage makeup, and she looked very sorrowful indeed. She wiped away tears and said,

"This. I got a letter."

"What of it, it's probably some admirer," Tom said with a smile. He came up and put his arm around her, but she shook him off.

"I'm serious," she said, wiping her nose on her sleeve. "Look." She picked up a letter that lay amidst pots of cosmetics, sticks of kohl, a standing mirror, a handheld mirror, and clothes strewn about the room.

Poppy took the letter and read aloud: *"Give up your gentleman tonight or heads will roll."*

"What does that mean?" Beatrice asked.

"I don't know," Poppy said.

"I do. In the second act, my character, Marie, is taken and killed." Justine let out a tearful sniff and hugged her arms to her chest. "I'm too young to die."

"Nothing is going to happen to you," Tom said, patting her arm.

"I don't know what to think. I didn't think anyone could get in my room, but then when I came back here for the interval, there it was, sitting there on my seat." Her pretty face crumpled into tears. "Someone's going to try and kill me. I'm sure of it. But why? I haven't done anything wrong."

"Maybe it's someone playing a nasty joke," Tom said.

"Or perhaps it's an angry wife. Read it again, it talks about giving up your gentleman. Who else would want that but his wife?" Poppy asked.

"Or his children," Beatrice said.

"My gentleman doesn't have any children. And we haven't talked since... you know." She glanced at Poppy. "Why would she do this?"

"Who?" Tom asked.

"That woman. Petunia Dyngley. His wife. She hates me. Why would she do this?" Justine asked.

"To frighten you, no doubt," Tom said. "Those Dyngleys are all the same. Think they can treat anyone beneath them like trash."

"Tom," Poppy said.

He ignored her. "She clearly sees her husband still has feelings for you and wants him to give up the connection. If he can't be moved, she'll try to scare you into leaving him."

"But I already did. He kicked me out on the day of the races. I've been staying with Beatrice ever since," Justine said.

"How can you tell her that?" Beatrice asked.

"I know. I can go to their box and tell her it's over. Poppy, you'll come, won't you?" Justine asked.

Poppy tensed. The last thing she wanted was to see Henry and Petunia, together. It shook her to the core.

Tom said, "I know the Dyngleys. I'll go and tell that wife of his to leave you alone. It's not right, them thinking they can toy with you like this."

Justine wiped her eyes. "You're right, Tom." She peered in the small mirror on her dressing table. "Oh, I look a fright. Go, there's only a few minutes left. I'll see you out there. Tom, you'll come back when it's over and escort me home? I'd feel better if you were with me."

"We'll all come," Beatrice said.

Poppy nodded.

"I'll take this." Tom slipped the letter into his jacket. "Don't worry, Justine. We'll sort this."

Together they wandered back through the maze of entrances and corridors, but Poppy tripped and fell, landing hard on her knee. She picked herself up to find a gentleman walking by. "Mr. Parks?" she said, "What are you doing backstage?"

"Looking for Miss Hayes. Have you seen her?"

"You just missed her. She…" Poppy looked around. She'd lost them already. "She went back to our box, the sixth on the second floor. You can't miss it."

He began walking and Poppy said, "She went back that way." She pointed toward the exit.

"I'm going to find the privy. Can't imagine you'd want to

come along." He sneered. He left her without a word, and Poppy stood and dusted herself off. She soon joined Beatrice to reclaim their seats, while Tom peeled away to find the Dyngleys' box. Once inside their theater box, Beatrice asked, "Are you all right, Poppy?"

"I'm fine."

"It's all right if you're not, you know. You don't need to pretend with me."

Poppy looked at her.

"I could see you didn't want to confront the Dyngleys over this," Beatrice said.

Poppy shook her head. "No. Petunia Dyngley is… not a kind person. I would rather not have another run-in with her." She felt cowardly as she gripped the stiff wooden railing of their box, all that protected them from falling to the ground below. "No. I will go. They do not know Mr. Harris and will likely refuse to hear a word he says. Me at least I can claim an acquaintance with them."

"Are they really so horrid? You make them sound cruel," Beatrice said.

"Not all of them are." Poppy's hands trembled and her heart fluttered in her chest as she followed the path Tom had taken. She passed by Mr. Parks approaching Beatrice's box and took relief from the knowledge that at least Beatrice was being looked after.

She heard the sounds of a commotion and hurried as she found Tom arguing with a footman. "I have a right to speak to them. Tell them I know what they are about. I have a—"

Poppy came and put a hand on his arm, cutting him off midsentence. She addressed the footman, "Excuse me, might I speak with Mrs. Dyngley, please?"

The footman gave her a hard look. "Who are you?"

"Miss Poppy Morton. I am acquainted with Mrs. Dyngley."

The footman turned and disappeared into the box. A moment later he reappeared. "Mrs. Dyngley does not wish to speak with you."

Poppy's face broke into a smile. Of course, she should have known. "That is unfortunate. Please do tell her that we have the letter she wrote, and wish to speak with her about it. Otherwise, we could always go to the magistrate, but I suspect she would rather avoid a scandal."

"What scandal do you speak of? Who are you to cause such trouble?" A strong hand gripped her arm like iron and swung her around.

She came face to face with… "Henry."

"Poppy." Constable Henry Dyngley's face froze, and his hand relaxed on her arm. "What are you doing here?"

Her heart leaped in her chest. How could she tell him what she feared? There was so much she wanted to say, and no time at all, nor privacy to speak a single word of how she felt. "I…."

"We've got a letter here from Mrs. Dyngley to Justine Vane, threatening her." Tom's voice was harsh as he pulled the letter from his jacket and held it up.

"What is this?" Henry released Poppy, took the letter, and read it. "Anyone could have written this."

"That's just the sort of callous thing I thought you'd say. Don't you toffs know you can't toy with people? That girl is in tears because of your wife," Tom said.

"My wife?" Henry's eyes widened and his face grew red. "You have no idea of what you are speaking of. Go away."

"No," Tom said, stepping closer.

"I will have the footmen escort you from the premises. Miss Morton, I am sorry you have to see this, but I assure you—"

Tom shoved Henry back, hard enough to make him topple. Henry flew back, falling to his feet.

"Tom, no!" Poppy said, going after him.

"That's it. You've caused enough trouble." The footman motioned to a colleague and two of them grabbed Tom tight by the arms. Tom snorted and cared little as he glared back at Henry.

Poppy kneeled by the constable's side. "Constable, are you all right?"

"I'm fine," Henry growled, pushing her hands away. "You know that man?"

"Yes."

"How disappointing," he said.

"Miss Morton and I are very well acquainted," Tom said.

"Come on." One of the footmen said as he and his fellow prepared to take Tom out.

"Wait." Henry's voice was commanding. "I would speak with him."

Poppy spied the constable giving Tom a dreadful glare as he got to his feet. He picked the letter off the floor and said, "How came you by this letter?"

"Justine found it in her dressing room. She knows it's from Mrs. Dyngley."

"What makes you say that?" Henry asked.

Tom almost spat at him. Instead, he saw Poppy's face and stopped himself. He said, "The letter tells Justine to give up her gentleman. Everyone knows she only had one man like that in her life." He shot an apologetic look at Poppy.

Poppy swallowed. She must not lose her composure. Not here, not now.

"It is true, Constable. The girl is afeared for her life," she said.

"I can see why. The letter is horrid. But Mrs. Dyngley did not write this letter," Henry said.

"How do you know that?" Tom asked.

Henry gave him a withering glance. "Because she has been in my company all evening, and before that, in the company of others. She has had no time to write a letter, or to go wandering about the theater unescorted."

"She could have paid a servant to deliver it," Tom said.

"She would not. Mrs. Dyngley is an honorable woman. She would never do such a thing."

"For heaven's sake, what is all that racket?" Petunia Dyngley stepped out of the nearest curtain and laid eyes on Poppy. "Oh, it's you. Henry, what is this about?"

"Do you know anything about a letter?" Tom asked.

Henry moved to hold the letter away, but Petunia plucked it from his grasp. "What is this? Oh my." She handed it back to Henry. "What is this to me? Who would write such a thing?"

"We thought you did," Poppy said.

The look Petunia gave her would have quelled a fox in its tracks. "I was not addressing you. Why would I write a letter?"

"It was sent to Justine, the actress who—"

"I know who she is. Have you stopped to think that maybe the young harlot was not just seducing one man, but had more at her beck and call? I only praise God that my husband escaped her clutches." She looked proud of herself for saying that.

"So you wrote no letter?" Poppy asked.

"To an actress? Certainly not. I have had no time and frankly, have not thought of the girl since we met a few days ago." She turned to Henry. "Henry, have you seen John? He disappeared during the interval to fetch me some punch and he hasn't returned. Find him for me, would you?"

"He's probably off finding a new bit of fluff," Tom said.

Petunia's gaze snapped to Tom. "I cannot abide rudeness." She peered at him. "Are we acquainted? You look familiar."

Tom grinned and winked at her. "We could be."

Petunia ignored him and returned to the safety of her theater box.

Henry said, "Take him away."

Poppy watched Tom glare at Henry and shrug off the footmen. "All right, enough. I'm leaving. I'm gone. I'll not trouble your master again." With a final look at Poppy, he left.

Once Tom and the footmen had gone, Henry let out a little sigh and turned to Poppy. "Are you all right?"

"Me? I'm fine. What about you?"

He took her hands in his. "I am well. I…" Henry looked down at Poppy and her heart rose. "There is much to say. May I call on you?"

Poppy opened her mouth to speak when…

"Henry? Have you found John?" Petunia's voice came out.

Poppy shut her mouth like a trap. "I do not think it appropriate."

Henry dropped her hands. "From what I can tell, you are a poor judge of that."

"I beg your pardon?" Poppy stepped back.

"You. Consorting with kept women and mistresses. What are you about, Poppy? This is not some scheme of yours to find your mother, is it? For I already have."

"What? You found her?" Poppy's mouth dropped open.

"Yes. She was not so hard to find." He frowned at her. "She is… Never mind."

"Where is she? Where can I find her? You spoke to her?"

"I did." He held his breath. "What are you doing here? Let me return you to your party."

Poppy sniffed. "I would rather we part here. I would hate to inconvenience you or disturb your sensibilities."

"What do you mean? Oh. Your party…"

"I am here with my employer, her guardian and we had just run into Mr. Harris."

"You should stay away from that man. He's a dangerous fool."

"He is open and honest with me, which is more than I can say for you, Constable," Poppy said.

"What on earth are you talking about? I have been honest with you," he said.

"Have you? And when in all the months of our friendship, did you plan to mention that you were married? Or had a mistress?"

"What nonsense are you talking about?" he asked.

"It's not nonsense if it's true."

"Poppy is this about…"

Her laugh was bitter. "The fact that I kissed you? A married man? You could have done me the courtesy of telling me I was mistaken, instead of letting me think I had wronged you in some way. Here I thought you disapproved of my behavior or were repulsed. Instead, I find you already have your hands full of women." She turned. "What was I thinking? I have been such a fool."

"I am the fool," he said. "You are a young woman, innocent of the ways of the world. Is that why you came to London? To see a bit of society outside of Hertford?"

"Yes. And to find my mother. Tell me, where did you find her?"

"In London. May I call on you?"

"Um. It wouldn't be proper. I live with my employer and her gentleman…"

Henry's face clouded. "I see. I walk by the Rose and Crown on Park Street most mornings. They are near a coffeehouse. Would you meet me there tomorrow morning?"

"I must go."

"I will wait for you," he said.

Poppy fled back to the box, her heart fluttering in her chest. She arrived just in time to see the curtain open on the stage.

All was well as Poppy took her seat beside Beatrice, who was flanked by Mr. Parks. The man shot her a dirty look as Beatrice said, "Where were you? Did you speak with Mrs. Dyngley?"

"I did."

"And did she write the letter? Did you confront her?"

"Ahem." Mr. Parks cleared his throat.

"I did," Poppy whispered.

"Well?"

"I'll tell you later." Poppy glanced back at Mr. Parks.

"Where is Tom?" Beatrice whispered.

"He was escorted out by footmen. He got into a fight and—"
Mr. Parks coughed loudly.

Poppy and Beatrice exchanged a glance. "He's fine. I'll tell you once it's over."

Poppy sat back and folded her hands in her lap, but could not calm down. She had seen him again, the man she had dwelled on for many months now. Constable Henry Dyngley. Her friend, her comrade in solving crime, and the man whose strong chin and dark eyes had haunted her dreams. He was here, at the theater, in London. What were the odds they would be here together, attending the same play?

But then, of course. Justine was his mistress. Of course, he would have come to see her perform.

Poppy's shoulders slumped in disappointment. She sat quietly, watching the events of the play unfold, even though she paid little attention to it.

She watched Justine cross the stage, flanked by two prison guards amidst a jeering crowd. Her character was stripped of her crown, and her great royal robes until she wore naught but her plain shift, which gained many oohs and appreciative whistles from the audience. She cried out to the judge, "I am innocent, so let me live! All my wrongdoing I have done for my people. They are my people, and I am not afraid to die for their love."

This was met with boos and jeers, and she climbed the parapet and looked up, in the direction of the boxes and the people sitting there, watching. She cried, "If you shall not give me justice, then I give the good people of France my head." She laid down on the chopping block.

Poppy stared at the guillotine's blade that glinted in the light, and her heart stopped. "Oh my God."

"What is it?" Beatrice asked.

"It's—No!"

She stood up in her seat, frozen with horror as the black-hooded executioner pulled the cord. The blade went crashing down smooth as silk and lopped Justine's pretty head off.

There was silence, then a lone scream cleaved the air as her head rolled and blood poured onto the stage.

CHAPTER NINETEEN

N O ONE STAYED after that bloody display. The play was in an uproar. Actors screamed and fled the stage. Women screamed and fainted dead away, some pointed and laughed it was just a joke, men cried out, bellowed, and called for help. Some fought, others fought to get out, to get away. In seconds, it was bedlam.

Beatrice said, "Poppy? Did that? Did she?"

Mr. Parks stood with a hand on Beatrice's arm, his face grave. "We're leaving. Now."

She looked at him. "Yes. No, wait, I want to see."

"There's nothing for you there. The magistrate and his men will be all over it."

"But Justine… she was my friend. I want to know what happened," Beatrice said.

"She's dead, Miss Hayes. Your pretty friend is gone."

Beatrice's face grew pale. "Poppy, you'll go, won't you?"

Poppy nodded. "I'll meet you back at the house."

"Good." Beatrice allowed Mr. Parks to steer her away and into the crowd.

Poppy followed and turned away from the people, moving toward them. She tried to recall the route Tom took to go backstage but it wasn't hard, people were milling about, trying to get away.

Poppy found and pushed her way to the front, where she found a group gathered at the stage. Blood had pooled on the floor and in the dim candlelight, looked almost black. She could make out the large guillotine contraption, complete with a long platform and a horrible wooden top that no longer bore a blade. The heeled shoes of Justine's body stuck out on the platform, lying prone. The sight of the heeled shoes chilled her. Justine was dead, in the worst way possible. Poppy realized then that she had failed her. They all had. Justine's fears had come to light, and now it was far too late. Any dislike she felt for Justine died in that moment as she realized the girl had died alone, afraid, and in front of hundreds of people. What a way to go.

She entered the fray of men circled around the body and found a familiar sight. "Constable Dyngley."

"You shouldn't be here." Henry frowned at her.

"I knew the girl," she said.

"So did I." His displeasure intensified.

She bristled at him. It was bad enough that the girl was dead, but did he have to rub it in her face that she was his mistress? It was arrogant and insufferable.

"All right, what's all this, then?" A man with an impressive gray mustache climbed onto the stage, dressed in a cheap evening suit. "Lucky I was here, eh? Here I was, sitting in the crowd when a bloke says to me, 'Francis, you're a magistrate, aren't ye?' And I says 'yes' and he says you'd best go see what that there body is all about, and so here I am." He looked around the small group of people with a smile. When they offered no reaction, he coughed, stroked his mustache, and said, "I'll get to the bottom of this. Looks like a case of a stage prop gone wrong. Accidents happen, eh?"

Poppy cleared her throat. "Forgive me, sir, but I think it was no accident."

He rounded on her. "This is no place for a lady. Who are you?"

Poppy swallowed. "Miss Poppy Morton. I knew the actress."

"You an actress too?" He eyed her cleavage appreciatively.

A growl emerged from Dyngley's throat.

Poppy ignored him and met the magistrate's eye. "No. But I knew her and before the second act started, she was scared. She had a letter—"

"What letter?"

"During the interval, she asked to see me and my friends, and when we found her, she was afeared for her life. She had received a nasty letter, threatening her."

"What did it say?" the magistrate asked.

"Never mind that," Henry cut in. "Magistrate, I am Constable Henry Dyngley, and I—"

"My God! Is that Justine?" A young man pushed into the circle surrounding the body.

"Not now, John," Henry said.

John peered over his brother's shoulder and turned pale. "Oh my God. Justine."

"Who is this?" The magistrate asked.

"My brother, John." Henry shot John a dirty look.

"Is he a constable too?"

"No," Henry said, as John answered, "Certainly not." Henry shot John a look of annoyance.

"But I knew the poor girl. She was an acquaintance of mine. She was very dear to me." John's face fell and he clapped a hand to his heart.

"Yes, well. What's all this about a letter?" the magistrate asked Poppy.

"It demanded she give up her gentleman or heads would roll." She shuddered.

"Her gentleman? She was somebody's whore?"

"I say, have a care, sir," John said.

The magistrate shot John a knowing look. "And where is the letter now?"

"I have it," Henry said.

"Why have you got it?"

"She brought it to me." He shot Poppy a look as if to say, *keep your mouth shut.*

"I see. Give me the letter."

Henry reached into his suit jacket and handed it to him. The magistrate read it and stuffed it into his pocket. He turned to a man who stood beside him, looking visibly uncomfortable. "You're the manager here. What do you know about this? Did you know the guillotine had a real blade?"

"No, no, not at all. It's just that the guard is missing."

"What do you mean?" Poppy asked.

The man shot her a look. "When we built the contraption, there was a dull blade attached to it, to look real. But when the actors practiced using it, they got too nervous, so we had a carpenter install a wooden guard to catch the blade." He removed a handkerchief from his pocket and wiped his sweaty forehead. "I don't know how it happened. It couldn't have happened. It doesn't make sense."

"You mean the guard would have caught the blade as it descended, so it would look like it was about to cut off her head but didn't," Poppy said.

"Yes, exactly." The man paled at the sight of Justine's body lying prone on the platform and cringed. "This is a nightmare. We'll be ruined. Completely ruined."

"Who could have done this?" John asked.

"Whoever wanted to see her dead, I imagine," the magistrate muttered.

"But no one would want to hurt Justine, she wouldn't hurt a fly. She was a sweet girl," the manager said.

"Let's talk to the executioner. Bring him here," the magistrate said.

The manager brought forward a big, hulking man dressed in black. His face was wet with tears. He babbled, "I don't know what happened. One minute she was smiling at me, and I pulled the cord, and then she was gone and..." He saw her head, a bloodied mass of hair, lying on the stage. "Oh God. I'm going to be sick." He turned and ran from the stage. The sounds of gagging and vomiting filled the air.

The magistrate's nose wrinkled in distaste.

Henry told Poppy, "This is no place for a lady. You should go home."

"Not when her friend has asked me to help," Poppy said.

"What can you do? You're just a woman," the magistrate said.

"I'll have you know that this dead girl was just a woman, and no thanks to your men, she is dead." Petunia's clipped tones cut through the chatter. She marched onto the stage like a steamer ship, and Poppy beheld the older woman's fury.

"You are doing nothing about this girl's death, are you?" she demanded.

The magistrate, a tall fellow with an impressive gray mustache, rubbed his chin and said, "Who are you?"

"Mrs. Dyngley, of Essex. I was acquainted with that young girl, and she deserves to be treated properly. I demand you start a search into her death," Petunia said.

"She's dead. We don't need any search," the magistrate said, sidling up to her.

John rushed up. "Petunia, darling, what are you doing here?"

"I should ask the same of you. Where were you? You disappeared during the interval."

"All right, that's it. The lot of you, clear off. We've got enough to deal with here without you people sticking your noses in where they don't belong. Clear off," the magistrate said.

"I would be happy to help investigate this crime," Henry said.

"Who says it's a crime? Maybe the executioner was careless."

"The manager himself said the guard was removed, and the girl received a nasty letter during the production. This was no accident," Henry said.

The magistrate frowned.

"And considering she is not the first woman of low repute to be killed recently, I'd say you have a problem, sir."

"This isn't your jurisdiction, son. What good would a village constable do me? I have men. This was an accident, plain and simple."

"But what if it wasn't?" Poppy said, "Justine was afraid. She wanted Tom to escort her straight home after the performance, she was so scared that someone might try to hurt her."

"But if the letter said to give up her gentleman, who would want her to do that?" the magistrate asked. "That's likely why she was killed."

Poppy glanced at Petunia, whom she expected to turn red. Instead her face staid cool and resolute.

"Constable Henry Dyngley will help you find whoever did this. He is renowned in Essex and Hertfordshire for solving murders. No doubt your men will find themselves at a loss for a crime such as this," Petunia said. Her tone allowed no argument.

The magistrate blinked. "And why should I let him in on my investigation?"

Petunia sniffed as if it were obvious. "Because it is clear that whoever killed the poor girl was a person of genteel society, and not someone of the lower classes. Poor people do not write letters, they have someone else do it for them. You are looking for a person of the gentry. Someone of good family and breed-ing."

"So?"

"Your men could not possibly enter into those circles."

"I am the magistrate. We can speak to whomever we want," he said.

"But will they speak to you? I doubt you would be admitted into any of their houses. You will knock and they will watch you from their windows as their servants tell you they are not at home."

The magistrate glared at her. "This is my town. I can speak to whoever, whenever I want. Don't matter to me if they're high born or low."

Petunia's smile was frosty. "And that is precisely why you

need the constable's help. He can find out whoever did this in no time."

"Mrs. Dyngley…" Henry began.

"He's that good, eh?"

"Better. Leave it with him. He'll solve it in no time."

"Mrs. Dyngley," Henry said.

"All right. You've got one week. Any longer than that and I'm arresting you," the magistrate told Petunia.

"Me? What for?" she demanded.

"Interfering."

"I say, my good man, my wife has nothing to do with this, nothing at all," John said, rallying forth.

"Your wife?" Poppy said.

John looked at her, then at Petunia. "Yes."

Petunia's face softened, when John decided at that moment to say, "I say, is that blood?"

Then his eyes rolled into the back of his head as he fainted dead away, landing in a heap beside the guillotine on the stage.

"Oh, John. Not again," Petunia said. She whipped a small bottle of smelling salts from her reticule and held them under his nose. In moments, his eyes fluttered and he came to life.

"Justine…" he mumbled.

Petunia shot him a hard look and glanced at Henry. "He's of no use to anyone like this. Help me take him home."

Henry knelt and helped John to his feet. He shot a look at the magistrate, "Leave it with me. I will solve this."

"Of that, I've no doubt. Otherwise, I'm closing this case."

The magistrate and Henry exchanged details of where to find each other in Town, before Henry helped Petunia escort John away.

Poppy observed as the magistrate called for men to come and take Justine's body away. The men, pale at the sight, removed Justine's corpse from the platform, whilst another man carefully wrapped her bloodied head and took it away. All that remained was the large guillotine and a pool of blood on the stage. In the candlelight, it looked almost black.

She began to make her way toward the exit when she spotted Tom waiting for her outside. "Tom," she said.

"Miss Morton." He bowed. "Didn't see you leave so I thought I'd wait. Where's Justine? Is she free or is she surrounded by a crowd of admirers?"

Poppy swallowed. "Neither."

Tom chatted amiably. "If she has decided to forgo my company, she could at least have sent an errand boy to tell me, rather than keep me here waiting outside in the cold. Oh, I saw that friend of yours leave with that lady friend of his."

"Yes," Poppy said, "Tom—"

"Shall I escort you home?" He offered an arm to her. "I'll call you a hackney. It would be my pleasure." He raised an arm and whistled as one approached.

"Tom."

He looked at her. "Are you all right? You seem out of sorts."

"Justine is dead."

"What?" He froze.

"It is just like the letter said. That heads would roll…" She shivered and he came close and put his arms around her, holding her for warmth. She didn't know who needed the touch more, him or her. It would have felt so comforting to lean in and let him hold her close, to breathe in his manly scent and feel that everything would be all right.

But it wasn't. Justine was dead.

In another instance she would have found the feeling of Tom's arms around her inviting, but her mind was too disconcerted to appreciate the gesture. Besides, it was overly forward. She stepped back from his embrace. "Tom…" She shook her head.

"Tell me what happened." He let his hands drop.

"It was in the second act. Justine was Marie Antoinette and there was a guillotine on stage and…" She swallowed.

He muttered a curse. "I can't believe this. Someone killed her.

She was right. Someone really was after her."

"Did you not believe her?" she asked.

"I didn't know what to think." He hailed the approaching hackney carriage and said, "Poppy, I don't like this. Allow me to escort you home. I couldn't bear it if…"

The carriage pulled up alongside them. "I will be fine, Tom."

"Where is Justine now? I should go to her."

"The magistrate's men have already taken her body away. There's nothing for you to do here."

"Except find out who did this and drown them in the Thames," he said darkly.

Poppy stared at him. "Don't talk like that. Not after Marie."

He colored. "Of course. Travel home safe, Miss Morton. I'll see you tomorrow." He opened the door for her.

She told the driver the street name, climbed in, and closed the door behind her.

CHAPTER TWENTY

THE NEXT DAY Poppy woke early and strolled down Park Street, where she spied the Rose and Crown pub. She did not want to venture into a pub alone, but as she approached, a man's voice called, "Miss Morton."

Her heart lifted at the sound. "Constable."

Like a man out of her dreams, he strode toward her wearing a smart grey suit and shined shoes. He bowed to her. "There is much to say. Would you promenade with me around the park?"

She swallowed the lump in her throat. "Would it be appropriate?"

"That is why I have asked my brother John and his wife to join us. I believe you two are acquainted."

She looked past his shoulder. "Mrs. Dyngley."

Petunia surveyed her severely. "Good morning." She gave a brief incline of her head.

John was much more forthcoming. He offered her a warm smile and said, "A pleasure to meet you, Miss Morton. It is a fine day out. Shall we all promenade together?"

Poppy nodded and followed them toward the nearest park.

Petunia walked beside her. "When I heard that Henry was going to speak to you, I knew we had to come. You may have made mistakes in your judgment, but I am an excellent judge of character, and I will not have him compromise you by something so innocent as walking around unescorted."

Poppy blushed. "Thank you."

"It is like Mrs. Farrars said, 'Miss Morton is a good girl, who is alone in Town. We must look after her.'"

"That is very kind," Poppy said.

"It is the truth. Now, tell me the facts. You knew that actress?"

"Yes." Poppy relayed what had happened at the theater.

"That is disturbing," Petunia said. "I, of course, wrote no letter. I didn't need to. We met at the races and after sending the girl away, we never saw her again. Isn't that right, John?"

"Yes, absolutely," John agreed, looking away.

"The question is, who would have done such a thing?" Petunia wondered.

"The likely suspect is yourself, Mrs. Dyngley. But if you didn't write the letter, then... I do not know. But I believe whoever killed Justine knew her. It was the same with Penelope at the races."

"What do you mean?"

Poppy explained, "For weeks now, some of the women in my acquaintance have been receiving nasty letters from an unknown person, calling them horrible names and demanding they give up their way of life."

"What way is this?" John asked.

Poppy looked at him briefly before blushing at the ground. "Begging your pardon, sir, but they are all mistresses."

"Oh, I see. How interesting," John said.

Petunia shot him a dirty look. "Pray, continue."

"On the night of the theater, during the interval, my friends and I were called to Justine's dressing room. She was frightened, for she had received another letter, threatening to kill her. You all know what happened after that."

"Yes. The poor girl. The question is who would have done that and why? Do you know if she was seeing any other gentlemen?" Petunia asked.

"Not to my knowledge. She seemed rather cut up about Mr. Dyngley," Poppy said.

"A tragedy," John said, before shutting his mouth at a sharp look from Petunia. "But what can we do?"

"Nothing. I will investigate this. Miss Morton has helped me in the past, she will assist me," Henry said.

"Over my dead body," Petunia said, then paled at the remark. "She will not go alone in your company. I will not see her ruined over a paltry investigation of a dead whore."

"Mrs. Dyngley…" Henry began, "there is no need for you to get involved."

"I will help," John said. "He's absolutely right, Petunia, there is no need for you to involve yourself in this matter. Henry and I will solve it and bring the miscreant to justice before teatime. You should return to Essex."

Petunia laughed at him. "Don't be ridiculous. I'm not going anywhere without you. Do you really think me so docile or slow-witted as to go meekly home while my husband goes gallivanting around London? I did not come all this way just to be sent home again."

"My dear, but there is a crime to be solved. Henry needs my help."

Henry grunted.

Petunia laughed, a harsh sound. "I'm not leaving without you."

"Well, I'm not leaving Henry," John said.

"Then I'm not leaving either."

"You can be incredibly frustrating, do you know that?" he told her.

"It is one of my many charms," she said sweetly.

John threw his hands in the air. "See what I have to deal with?" He walked away.

Petunia frowned and hurried after him.

That left Poppy and Henry alone. Henry was the first to speak. "Poppy, I…"

"She is not your wife. Petunia."

"No."

"I thought she was," Poppy said.

"She is not. She is married to my brother, John."

"All this time I thought you were married," she said.

He blinked. "You did?"

"And when I met Justine, I thought… She was your mistress."

Henry's mouth dropped open. "That is what you thought of me? My God, that explains it. But how could you think that? I thought we were friends, Miss Morton. How could you arrive at such a low estimation of my character?"

"What was I supposed to think? We kiss and then you disappear from Hertford, and then when I come to London I encounter a woman who claims to have been your mistress for months, and then I meet Mrs. Dyngley." Her voice shook. "Please, tell me how I was mistaken. I should greatly like to hear it."

He glared at her, meeting her steely-eyed gaze in return. "Would I have treated you so poorly?"

"You tell me. I thought we were friends."

He ran a hand through his dark hair. "We are. That is…" He let out a sigh. "I did not know what to do, or what to think. When you did not write to me, I wondered if you had decided we were not so close after all…"

"Me write to you? Typically it is the gentleman who writes first, is it not?"

"I had thought that if you truly wished to relay your thoughts on the matter you would have written, or paid a call—" he said.

"Call on you?" she repeated. "Oh yes, because that is the precise thing a lady wants to do when she acts forward and the man does not kiss her back, to visit him and receive more humiliation. Do you have any idea of the embarrassment I felt when you did not kiss me in return, or say a single word after? You ran off into the night. I assumed you did not wish to renew the sentiments that were so troubling. And when you did not visit, my family thought I had offended you in some way. Meanwhile, the other young women of my acquaintance are coming out and becoming engaged, while I receive the pitying looks of the matrons in town."

"You are above them, and you know it," he said.

"Do I? What am I supposed to think, when the only man who I had romantic feelings for and kissed, ignored me?"

He had the grace to blush. "I went to the parsonage to see you. To talk to you."

Her eyebrows rose.

"Instead your uncle was gone on an errand and your aunt nearly choked to death on a biscuit. She misses you, Poppy."

Her eyes widened. "Is she all right?"

"She is fine. Your aunt is in the bloom of health."

Poppy relaxed.

He continued, "When I visited, your aunt accused me of paying too much attention to you, and of inspiring false hopes in her niece. I didn't know what to do, so I went home. But there I found my brother."

"John," she said.

"Precisely. He came unannounced. He had fled our family home in Essex and left his wife, Petunia, there in the company of my father, who has been unwell. When I enquired as to the nature of his visit, he pressed me to join him in London, to clear out our family townhouse and eventually sell it. I had no wish nor desire to leave Hertford, for everything I treasure was there." He met her eyes. "I refused. He is the heir, it is his business to close it up if that is what is necessary. But he demanded I come too."

"Why?"

"Because he encountered some difficulty he needed my help with. I learned that for some time now, he has kept the company of a young lady and was so bold as to set her up in our family townhouse."

Poppy's eyes widened. "Justine."

"Exactly. I know not how long he has carried on this dalliance, I only know that rather than get himself in trouble, he gave her my name, and told her he was me. The problem came, of course, when he left her alone for too long and she wrote to me, thinking I was him, at our home in Essex."

They walked on. The flowers bloomed and the manicured green grass was pleasant, the air was refreshing and cool in the morning sun, but Poppy felt none of it.

"Mrs. Dyngley intercepted the message and was furious, as you might imagine. John left. But when we arrived in London, I discovered that the girl was still present and that John wanted me to end their relationship for him. I refused, and instead wrote to Mrs. Dyngley to come here."

"You wrote to her?"

"It seemed like the only way to make John see sense. He must see he cannot go around toying with women." He kicked a small bit of turf and sent it flying ahead.

"Why are you angry?"

"I am angry with him, not with you." He walked on. "John is the heir, but he cares little for what that means or the responsibilities it entails, especially with our father being unwell. He relies on us more and John's future is assured. Mine is not. As the second son, my good name is everything. To have it spread about that I am entertaining a mistress and set her up in our family home in London…" His gloved hand curled into a fist. "It does not bear thinking about. At least John has a wife who cares for him."

"I thought she was your wife."

"She's not."

"Then you are…"

"Unmarried. I have never had, nor will I ever have a mistress." He met her eyes. "Poppy, I would not blame you for being displeased with me, but, it was never my intention to mislead you."

"There you are, Miss Morton." Petunia joined them, dragging

her husband by the arm. "We have decided. The four of us are going to solve this crime."

"Petunia, surely we all have better things to do than this. I have to close down our townhouse and get you home…" John started.

"Nonsense. Miss Morton, tell us your thoughts. You said these girls were receiving horrid letters."

"Yes. It's true. Shortly after I arrived in Town, I learned from my employer that an acquaintance of hers had gone missing. A friend and I found her body floating in the Thames."

"My goodness." Petunia pulled out a fan and fanned herself.

"It's true. We learned that she had received rude notes from a mysterious person and that my employer had as well. On the day we visited the races, we found that Miss Penelope Smythe, another acquaintance of ours, had been drugged and received a note as well, threatening her person. Shortly after that, our friend Harriet disappeared and now with Justine dead…"

Henry looked at her. "Someone is writing poisonous letters to mistresses and then killing them."

"Yes. If you can investigate the actors at the theater, I will speak to the women of my employer's social circle and learn what I can," Poppy said.

"Me too," Petunia said.

Heads turned to her.

She said, "I'm sure you all think me unpracticed in the methods of detection, but I assure you, I can very well inveigle the truth out of anyone. I will speak to the ladies of my acquaintance and see what they know about these mistresses."

"Would they know anything?" Poppy asked.

"A wife always knows, my dear. Even when we wished we didn't," Petunia said, glancing at John.

CHAPTER TWENTY-ONE

T HAT DAY POPPY sent out invitations. At the appropriate social hour, the visitors came, and in a short time, Poppy and Beatrice sat in the parlor drinking tea with Harriet. Mollie arrived later in a cloud of perfume. The floral scent was strong and made Poppy cough, but she cared little for it and instead inhaled heavily from her tea.

The conversation began with many asking about Justine, and the missing Penelope. "Run off to avoid her creditors, I'd wager," Mollie said.

"I don't know. It's strange," Harriet said. "Who would want to hurt her? Either of them?"

"The same person who sent them both letters," Beatrice said.

"What letters?" Mollie asked.

"Ahem," Poppy cleared her throat.

The group looked at her.

She said, "The reason we've called you all here today is to discuss the present situation, and share what we know."

"What situation?" Mollie asked.

"You cannot be so blind, Mollie. The fact that someone is going around killing mistresses," Harriet said.

Mollie shot her a dark look. "No one is killing me."

"Give them time, I'm sure any self-respecting toff who got the clap would have a bone to pick with you," Harriet grinned.

"Now hold on just a minute," Mollie rose, pointing her finger. "What on God's green earth are you talking about?"

Poppy said, "All of you have been receiving nasty letters from a strange person, have you not?"

"Yes," Beatrice said.

"Me too," Harriet added.

Poppy continued, "And we know that before their deaths, Justine and Marie received the same sort of horrible letter. When we went to call on Penelope, her lodgings were abandoned, and we found similar letters amongst her correspondence."

"Let me see," Mollie said.

Poppy took out the small sheaf of letters she had collected and spread them on the table. "These came to Marie, these were for Penelope, and these for Beatrice. The magistrate has the one sent to Justine. It was delivered to her the night of her death, in her dressing room at the theater."

"Lord, you make it all sound so dramatic. Maybe you should pursue the stage," Mollie purred.

"What about you, Mollie? Have you received letters too?"

Mollie glanced at them on the table, reading. "Of course I haven't. No one would dare toy with me. My gentleman is Lord Aylesbury."

"Why didn't you tell us?" Harriet asked. "We've all been frightened over these notes."

Mollie scoffed. "And say what, that I hadn't received a letter? Forgive me for not keeping you all abreast of my correspondence. I have more important things to do with my time."

Harriet shot her a dirty look.

Mollie said, "Don't be silly. Someone is clearly having a little joke with all of you."

"Bit far for a joke," Beatrice said.

Mollie narrowed her eyes at Beatrice, then Poppy. "I notice that you haven't received any letters, Miss Morton. However this did all start to happen when you arrived. What have you to say on that score?"

Poppy snorted. "I had never met any of you until that first night. Why would I go to the trouble of harassing you all?"

"I can think of a few reasons. You're a clergyman's daughter, are you not? No doubt you are judging all of us for our wanton lifestyles and want to scare us into a life of goodness."

Poppy glanced at her. "If that is what you think, I wonder why you came at all."

Mollie glared at her. "I can think of another reason. Something more telling. Beatrice, your mistress. She's often the butt of our little jokes. She's too weak and cowardly to speak up for herself, but you work for her. It would be an easy thing for you to instruct her to write such mean things to all of us. And like the good girl she is, she would do it. There you have it, girls, Miss Morton's the one behind it." She smirked and crossed her arms beneath her chest.

"There's just one issue," Poppy said.

"What's that?"

"The letters are not written in my hand."

"Nor in mine," Beatrice added.

"How are we to believe that? Either of you could have altered your handwriting to be different," Mollie said.

"There's also the fact that we all started receiving the letters before Miss Morton met any of us," Harriet pointed out.

Mollie sulked. "I still say she's at fault."

"Mollie, you shouldn't insult Miss Morton like that. She's innocent, just like the rest of us," Beatrice said, her voice high-pitched.

"Oh no, and what are you going to do? Quail like a little rabbit? Come off it, Beatrice, I'll say what I want to who I want. If you don't like it…" Mollie shrugged.

"You can leave," Beatrice stood.

"Don't mind if I do. I have better things to do than muddle over who's sending who letters. And your tea is cold." Mollie walked away without a curtsy or goodbye.

Once the door to the parlor closed behind her, Beatrice let

out a little sigh. "Well."

"That was very good of you, Miss Hayes," Poppy said. "Thank you."

Beatrice beamed with pride. "It was nothing."

Harriet looked glumly at the letters. "We're no closer to solving this. And Justine is dead. What will become of her body?"

"I would guess the same fate as Marie," Poppy said.

"You mean the paupers' graveyard, in those pits. Justine deserved better than that. She was a silly thing, but she was nice enough." Harriet frowned.

There was a knock at the door and the sour-faced maid, Fanny, led in Tom, who bowed to the group. "Ladies. I hope I'm not interrupting."

"Please, sit down, Tom. Join us. We would be glad of your opinion," Beatrice said, gesturing to an empty spot on the sofa beside Poppy.

He needed no further urging and happily took the spot, his knee brushing Poppy's. She subtly moved her knee away a fraction, but from the way he tensed, she could see he had noticed.

Tom sat straight in the seat and allowed Beatrice to pour him a cup of tea, then glanced at the letters. "Is it a council of war you're having?"

"Sort of. We called the rest of our little circle here, but Mollie got fed up and left," Beatrice said.

"That explains why she was looking so annoyed on her way out. I passed her as she was leaving."

"It's strange though," Poppy said, "that she hasn't received any nasty letters while the rest of you have."

"You don't think Mollie is behind this, do you?" Beatrice asked.

"I wouldn't put it past her. You heard her, she likes to be seen as most important out of all of us," Harriet said.

"Surely if she were behind it, she would make sure to send some letters to herself, to avoid suspicion. Otherwise, it would be obvious," Tom said.

Together they looked at the letters. They were all written in the same hand, on the same fine paper. "Tom, could you visit the stationers on Fleet Street and see who might have bought this paper? If we could narrow down who bought it, maybe that would give us a clue," Poppy said.

"It's a good idea, but there are loads. Still... One of them might recognize the paper. I'll take some of these with me." He picked up a few of the letters.

Harriet stood. "I'll take my leave. I don't want to be out after dark."

Poppy rose. Tom asked, "Where are you going?"

"To church."

"I'll join you," he said.

"I never thought you were religious, Tom," Beatrice teased.

"I'm not. But I'm heading that way anyway. Shall we?" He rose and offered his arm to Poppy.

She looked at him askance but had no other option but to take it or be rude.

As she donned her bonnet and walking coat at the entrance of the building, he said, "I hope you don't mind my joining you."

"Not at all. I'll be glad of the company."

"Good," he said.

They exited the house and began walking. She knew the route to church so was only slightly surprised that he kept pace with her.

"Miss Morton," he started.

"Yes?"

"I was wondering. You're a genteel sort of girl."

"That's kind of you to say."

He rubbed the side of his face. It needed a shave. "It's true, though, isn't it?"

"I don't really know. I've been brought up well, but since arriving here, I don't seem to fit in anywhere and people seem to either dismiss my manners as being from the country or treat me like a child, as if being aged nineteen is far too innocent."

"You're not alone. Most people think me a rough sort of man, due to my occupation."

She shot him a look of disapproval. She too thought him a rather common, low-born man, but he had shown her kindness and helped her upon her arrival in Town, and she was grateful for that. "What of it?"

"What if I told you I was not? That I too, had claims of gentility?"

Her face broke into a smile. "Then I wonder why you ignore the trappings of your background in pursuit of a more colorful career."

He winked and said, "I wanted to make my own way. My aunt was determined to have me as a draper. Can you see me as that? Selling cloth all day?"

"Better that than women."

His expression sobered. "It's not so bad, you know. These girls need money to survive and have made the choice to sell their services. Some even enjoy it. I just introduce them to the right sort of man."

"I'm not sure what society makes of your matchmaking schemes, Mr. Harris."

"Call me Tom, please," he said.

"Very well. Tom, if you do come from a more elevated background, why do you not return to it? Surely you could study law or medicine?"

"I get sick at the sight of blood and have fallen afoul of the law often enough, I have no wish to make it my profession," he said.

"What about the army or the navy?"

"And spend my days on a ship with a few hundred men fighting the French, with nary a woman in sight? God help me," he joked.

"What about the clergy? You are persuasive."

"Glad you think so." He winked, then said, "But spinning

sermons at a sleepy congregation sounds duller than watching grass grow. Forgive me, I know your uncle is a clergyman. But I would sooner have a faster way of life than looking forward to preaching on Sundays. Miss Morton, during your time in London I have felt we have become friends of a sort. Would you agree?"

"I suppose so. You have been very kind to me," she agreed.

"Yes, well. I feel I can talk to you. More than the other girls."

She smiled at him.

"I wonder, are you attending the Thorpes' assembly on Tuesday next?"

"I have never met them. I can't imagine we would receive an invitation." In fact, since she had arrived and taken up her post as a companion, they had received few invitations to dine or socialize anywhere. She was used to dining with her neighbors, but here, she didn't even know who they were. It was odd.

"They are friends of Beatrice's gentleman and a few others. I would be surprised if you did not receive such an invitation," he said. "If you are to attend, may I have the first dance?"

She blinked at him. Tom wanted to dance with her? "Of course, it would be a pleasure."

"Grand. I'll see you there." He kissed her hand and shot her a sunny smile before dashing off.

She watched him go. What had gotten into him?

AT CHURCH, SHE went inside and sat down in one of the pews. The reverend was nowhere to be seen, so she thought she would wait. She knelt down in prayer and let her mind wander. It had been a week since she had last attended church, but it felt like it had been months. She bowed her head. Before she knew it, she was feeling so tired and overwhelmed, that she drifted to sleep and laid down on the pew. It was sometime later that she heard the voices.

"Did anyone see you?"

"No, not that it matters. No one ever sees me. Not anymore." The voice sounded bitter.

"Be sure to keep it that way."

"Having second thoughts? It's too late for that now, Mrs. F. You're as much a killer as I am," a voice sneered.

Poppy's eyes flew open. She laid sideways on the lengthy inside of a wooden pew. She dared not move. Had the person really insinuated murder?

"It's not my fault. You said she was the slut seducing my husband."

"I did."

A sigh of relief. "Then it's over. Our business is at an end."

"Not so fast, Mrs. F. It's over when I say it's over. We ain't done yet." The voice was harsh.

"What do you mean?"

"The actress was a whore, but not the one stealing your husband away, oh no."

"You tricked me. You told me this was the last one. You said if I wrote the note, then it would scare her and that would be the end of it," the voice carried. "Instead I watch the poor girl get beheaded on stage. I nearly fainted from sheer fright. I never thought you'd actually kill the girl."

"Did the *heads will roll* not give it away? For a smart woman you're remarkably dumb."

"No more. I won't do it. No more letters, no more notes. I won't get involved."

"You already are, Mrs. F. And if you get any bright ideas about turning me in, I'll give your name to the authorities. That'll make the newspapers. 'Society woman kills whores for pleasure.'"

"If I had known you would be like this, I would have left you in prison."

A coarse laugh. "Don't you want to know which one of those girls is spreading her legs for your husband?"

Silence.

"Do you trust him? You're a good Christian woman. You trust in the Lord, so why not your husband too? I'm sure he'll never pick up any nasty disease or give you the clap, of course not. But then, of course, if he did, he'd blame it on you, you see. Men always do. They're never the ones at fault, you see, even when they know it. Oh no, you'll be the one branded as an adulteress, mark my words."

Suddenly there was a creak and a voice said, "Did you hear that?"

"It's nothing. Just an old church."

"If my husband finds out…"

"He won't do nothing. And as long as you keep your mouth shut, he'll never know," the harsh voice said.

"Why don't you just tell me who it is and be done with it? This relentless charade of yours is useless. I refuse to be a part of it. I have half a mind to go to the constable now." A nearby pew creaked as a person stood.

"Sit down," the voice snapped. "Need I remind you of what's at stake here? If you don't help me, I won't help you. Unless you're happier not knowing."

"I've been miserable since the day you got out of prison. I'd rather go to jail than this."

"You say that now, but prison is no place for a lady. The men would love to make your better acquaintance in the dark. Again and again. They don't care much for fancy manners or your clothes. They'll rip those off you right quick."

"Stop it. I don't want to hear this."

"Just saying. If you turn me in, that's what awaits you. And the men don't take no for an answer. Your husband won't like being married to a murderer, so he'll be the one to lock you in and turn the key. No uppity manners will help you then."

"I'm leaving. I've had enough of this." The pew creaked again.

"Fine. But this time, there's another chance for you make this right. I heard there's a ball coming up at the Thorpes'."

"I know. We are to attend."

"What if I told you that his mistress will be there?"

"Who? Who is she? Please, you must tell me now. I've done your dirty work."

"Nuh-uh. Not until you write me another note."

A sigh. "Very well. What would you have it say? Why can I not meet her? Perhaps she will see reason if we were to talk."

"She only sees two things: your husband's member and his money. She won't give up either just because you bump into each other at an assembly. Do you really want to be pitied by a whore?"

"I feel like I could go no lower. My husband already ignores me, I could hardly be lesser in his estimation."

"Then write me a note, and no one'll be the wiser."

The people left after that. Poppy waited, then rested there a few minutes more before she sat up. The voices sounded familiar. But who were they? And who was Mrs. F? Either way, she knew these were the people behind the nasty letters, and she knew when they were going to strike next. She might not know who they were, but she would be on her guard.

CHAPTER TWENTY-TWO

THE NEXT EVENING, Poppy dressed up. She wore the same long dress she had worn to the theater, for she had nothing nicer to wear. It was long and touched the ground, with layers of light blue dyed material that seemed to float around her. Poppy had taken it in around the chest and waist, so it fitted her tall, skinny form better, and with the kind administrations of Beatrice and her maid, she looked very well indeed. Her mouse brown hair was pinned up in a solid bun and Beatrice had loaned her a blue ribbon to style it. Complete with a shawl and the borrowed pair of evening gloves, Poppy was ready for the ball.

She joined Beatrice at the entrance, who wore a light pink gown with little cap sleeves adorned with ribbons around the bodice and hem. Along with a strand of pink pearls around her neck and elbow-length white gloves, Beatrice presented a very pretty picture.

Accompanied by the stony-faced Mr. Parks, they took a carriage to the Thorpes' house, a rather nondescript townhouse that looked just the same as its neighboring buildings, bearing the same brown brick face with white trim and many windows. But inside it was very grand, with wide open corridors, long tables boasting fruits, meats, and nibbles, and many a footman circulating with drinks. The inside was lit with hundreds of candles and upon their entry, they joined a mad crush of people.

Poppy picked up a dance card and wore it on her wrist, and remembered to write in the first dance for Tom. She had no sooner written it when she and Beatrice were met by others.

"Miss Hayes, Miss Morton," Tom greeted them.

"Tom," Beatrice said. "You look so different."

He flashed her a warm smile and looked at Poppy, eyeing her long blue dress. He bowed and said, "The dancing is just starting, and Miss Morton, you promised me the first dance. May I?" he held out a hand.

Poppy blushed and took his hand, feeling Beatrice's eyes on her.

Tom glided her in a dance, and it was pleasant to be in a society where she could move freely and not have to worry about the townspeople's pitying or watchful looks. That was one of the joys about living in London, she realized, the ability to reinvent yourself and wear whatever face and persona you chose. And with everyone too focused on themselves to care or notice her, she could enjoy herself, the dance, and her partner in the moment.

But the pleasure ended all too soon, as Tom rubbed his thumb against her gloved hand and said, "I've wanted to dance with you for days now, Miss Morton."

Poppy laughed at him.

He looked affronted. "I'm serious."

She tried not to laugh. "I'm sure you were truly keen to risk having your feet stepped on."

He grinned and eyed her shoes. "With that getup, I'll take my chances." he stepped with her in time and said quietly, "I need to tell you something. About our little investigation."

"What is it?"

"I went to Fleet Street and asked around. That paper you found from the letters, it's not so common as you might think."

"No?"

He shook his head and moved with her in the dance. "Only two shopkeepers on the street sell that type. It's expensive, so not many people buy it. But they couldn't remember who their buyers were or wouldn't tell me, even when I offered to pay."

"Then we're no closer to knowing who wrote the letters."

"Dunno about that. We know it was likely a woman who wrote them. Some wife who found out about her husband's piece of fluff and wants to tell her off. What about that Mrs. Dyngley? She's a rude woman and I could see her doing that," he said.

"Could you? I think she's more of a type to confront the mistress and scare her off."

"That there constable has his hands full with her, that's for sure. It's no wonder he was cheating on her."

"Ahem," a voice sounded behind her as the dance ended.

She turned to see. "Constable Dyngley."

He looked very handsome in a dark suit and cleverly tied white cravat, with his dark hair tousled just so. But he was frowning at her dancing partner.

"Constable," Tom said.

"Mr. Harris," Constable Dyngley acknowledged. To Poppy he said, "Might I have the next dance?"

"I—"

"Sorry, mate, we agreed to dance the first two dances together. The girl promised. You understand." Tom tugged her hand away from Dyngley's and pulled her into the set for the next dance.

"Tom, what are you doing? You know we don't have any such promise," Poppy said.

"I know, but you don't mind, do you? I like dancing with you. You're not so bad on your feet. And besides, I don't like you around him."

"Why not? He's my friend," she said.

"I don't like the way he looks at you. He watches you like you're a prize to be had, or a problem he cannot fix. Either way, I don't like it."

"You're wrong. Besides, we haven't seen each other for some time now. He is probably interested to catch up."

"I doubt that," he said darkly. "Why do you refuse to think badly of him?"

"Why are you determined to do so? What do you have against him?"

He muttered, "I have my reasons."

The music started and the dance began. This one was a quadrille and in the set of four dancers, they moved quickly, and had to be light on their feet. Poppy mentally thanked her aunt for drilling the steps into her, and for the many opportunities she had to learn these dances back in Hertfordshire.

"Poppy," Tom began. "I've been meaning to ask you something."

"And what's that?" Poppy asked as she spun into the pairing of a different partner. She glimpsed Tom's annoyed face for a moment until she was spun out again and back to holding his hand. He gripped hers tightly and said, "I wonder if I might call on you."

"You call on us often. Why?"

"No, not like that. I mean socially. Just to call on you."

Poppy stared at him a moment, uncomprehending. He wanted to call on her. Just her. Why?

Then it dawned on her. He liked her. He fancied her?

This was most confusing.

"Tom," she started, "I don't really have time to entertain gentleman callers. I have too much to do with being a companion to Miss Hayes, and looking into these letters—"

He gripped her hand and pulled her close to him, out of the dance. "Poppy, I… care about you. You're different from the other girls. You don't belong in this world."

The other dancers frowned, and Poppy felt a small red flush drift up her neck. She could feel their disapproval from where she stood. "Tom, I—"

"Is this fellow bothering you, Miss Morton?" Constable Dyngley interrupted them, looming beside them. He shot a dark look at Tom. "Unhand the lady, Mr. Harris."

Tom sneered at him. "Oh well, let's all bow down to the aristocrat in the room, all hail Constable Dyngley, reigning constable of Hertfordshire and beyond! I bet the criminals are shivering in their boots at the sight of you."

"Tom—" Poppy started.

"That's enough. Say what you like about me, but do not disturb this young woman. Let go of her," Henry said.

"We were having a private conversation. Not that it's any of your business."

"Anything that concerns the welfare of Miss Morton *is* my business," Henry said.

Tom laughed, a harsh sound. "Sounds to me like you don't exactly have her best interests at heart. Why else would she have run to London? Seems to me she was looking to get away from you."

"Tom," Poppy snapped.

The men looked at her.

"I don't know what you're on about, but stop this," she said.

Tom jabbed Henry in the shoulder. "See? She doesn't want anything to do with you."

"Don't touch me," Henry warned.

"Oh no? What are you going to do about it?" Tom reached for Henry's cravat and Henry slapped his hand away. Tom shoved him, and Henry fell back a few steps.

"Tom!" Poppy said. "Stop this!"

Tom ignored her and went for him. Henry saw him coming and warded off his punch, and gave him an uppercut that sent him back. Tom grinned, wiping a spot of blood from the corner of his mouth. "You'll pay for that." He lunged at Henry, who sidestepped him.

Tom fell on his face and glared up at him.

Henry said, "Perhaps you had best remove yourself from the festivities. It's not the right sort of place for you."

Tom scowled and got to his feet. "I will, once I wipe that smug look off your face."

Poppy had had enough. "No."

Tom and Henry ignored her. Tom rushed at Henry and Poppy slipped between them, just in time for Tom to grab her. He froze and tried to catch his balance, but failed and grabbed hold of her shoulder. Together they slipped and fell to the floor, and the music stopped, people stared. At least one woman gasped.

Poppy sat on the floor, dazed. She'd landed hard. Her bottom ached and her hands felt painful from where she fell.

Henry knelt by her. "Are you all right?"

"I'm fine. Will you two stop fighting?"

Henry looked at Tom, who said, "Poppy, I'm so sorry. Oh, no." He looked at her arm.

"What is it?" She looked at her left arm and there, her delicate cap sleeve had been torn in the scuffle. It hung forlornly like a wilted flower. "Oh."

"You will pay for that," Henry said.

"Oh really?" Tom snarled.

"Both of you, enough." Poppy rose to her feet, refusing the help of either gentleman. "I don't know what's gotten into you, but I'm sick of it. Go fight outside if you must."

"But Miss Morton…" Constable Dyngley said.

Two men came forward, dressed in livery. They put hands on Tom, and he said, "All right, all right, I'm going." He shot Poppy a sorrowful look as he was escorted out.

Henry approached her. "There is not much I can do to hide it. Allow me to give you my suit jacket." He began taking it off.

"No, no, I'm fine, really," Poppy said, stepping back. Her face flushed pink from all the people watching.

He said, "Please, Poppy, allow me."

"Sir, I am sure you have many good intentions, but unless you happen to have a needle and thread on your person, you will be of little use to the girl. Let me take her," a husky voice said.

Poppy turned around. There stood a woman an inch or so taller than her, with the same mouse brown hair, wide eyes, pert nose, and angular chin. Except while Poppy's appearance was rather humble, *this* woman's appearance spoke of riches. Her hair was coiled in a high bun with pretty brown ringlets hanging down around her shoulders, her skin was pale and fetching, her mouth was like it had been kissed by a red rose. The dress she wore was long and clung to her body simply, but it was elegantly made. As Poppy made eye contact with the stranger, it struck her.

Poppy said, "Mother?"

CHAPTER TWENTY-THREE

THE WOMAN BLINKED, then entwined Poppy's arm with hers. "Come, you must walk with me. Someone needs to tend to that sleeve of yours." She began walking with purposeful, brisk steps, and Poppy was quick to obey.

The statuesque woman led her away from the crowds of people who quickly resumed their places on the dance floor and began a reel, and it was all Poppy could do not to become overwhelmed by the crush. The woman held her hand tight within hers and did not let go, so Poppy was led through crowds of men and women and followed her rescuer out of the ballroom, then upstairs through a foyer, up into one of the upstairs rooms.

A servant was walking by, and the woman stopped them. "Bring a needle and thread, quickly. This girl's sleeve has been damaged. We'll be in… here." The woman sent off the maid with a stern look and quickly opened the door. It was the inside of a parlor, well-lit with candles. There was no fire in the hearth, but Poppy didn't mind. It was a relief to be out of the hot room and away from all the people.

"Who are you?" she asked.

The woman closed the door and turned around, offering Poppy a quick and graceful curtsy. "Celeste Grey, at your service. You are Miss Poppy Morton, if I am not mistaken."

Poppy curtsied, feeling awkward. She looked at the woman,

greedily drinking in the sight of her. "Are you, really? Are we…"

The older woman smiled. "You live with your aunt and uncle in Hertfordshire, I believe. At the parsonage in Hertford."

"Yes. They raised me since I was a child."

"Did you ever ask of your mother? Did you think of her?"

"Only every day. I thought of her every moment. But they told me she had died, and after a while, I stopped asking."

Celeste's pretty face darkened. "Did they?"

"It wasn't until I found a book in the main room, that had a family tree written in it, with the name of my mother as Celeste Morton, and I saw it crossed out, did I start to wonder again. I had an acquaintance look for her. She had connections in Town. But what she said, I could hardly believe."

Celeste's mouth smiled briefly. A brief flutter of the eyes. "No doubt you heard that she was dead, or worse. That she was living in sin as a whore." She said it nastily. "No doubt your uncle persuaded you through a lifetime of religious teaching that such lifestyles are wrong, and any woman pursuing such a life was to be pitied and scorned."

Poppy looked at her. For a woman so remarkably beautiful and wealthy, it was as if she had removed a layer of makeup or lowered a luscious silken fan, and revealed a face more vulnerable than Poppy could imagine.

"If that were the case, then why would I come to London? Why would I take up a position as a companion to a gentleman's mistress?"

"You had no way of knowing the girl was a kept woman. It's not something a woman normally mentions in her correspond-ence."

"True. But I stayed on."

"No doubt you needed the money," Celeste pointed out.

"I could have gone home. My uncle and aunt would have welcomed me back and I'd never have to mention or go to London ever again." Poppy stepped toward the woman, who leaned back against the door. "I came for one reason, and one reason only. To find you."

Celeste's mouth dropped open in a little *o* of surprise. Her eyes quickly became wet and glassy, and she blinked back tears.

"Are you my mother?" Poppy asked. "Because I think you are."

CELESTE GREY LOOKED at the face of this young woman before her, who appeared almost like a mirror image of her younger self. The girl waited for an answer. She deserved one. But the words that Celeste had wanted to say felt trapped behind the confines of her tongue. Celeste dared not answer, she dared not speak. At that moment, she hadn't the words. They had become lodged in her throat, along with all the depths of feeling she had pushed aside and overlooked, all the motherly concern she had tamped down over the years because it was too painful to speak of.

But now the source of her pain and joy stood before her and she could not ignore it. She swallowed and came toward the girl. She stood woodenly, at a loss on what to do. "For so long I have played a part, as successfully as any actress on the stage, and I know my part well. I am the mistress of Lord Blackwood of Blackwood Manor, and I know my place. I am called 'the Grace' by some and ignored by others, but I wield my wit, charm, and beauty, as skillfully as a duelist, and yet… Almost twenty years ago, I bore a child out of wedlock to my patron and gave it up, to my sister and her clergyman husband in Hertford."

Poppy breathed in, her chest tight.

Celeste looked at Poppy. "I have not been prepared for this meeting. I doubted I would ever meet my daughter, much less encounter her at a ball." But now the girl had gone and declared her thoughts, and Celeste didn't have the heart to lie to her. Not to Poppy, her daughter. Celeste could see the resemblance instantly, from her head to her toes. There was no mistaking the connection. Anyone could see it from a mile away. This was her daughter, her kith and kin.

Celeste took a breath and slowly opened her arms a fraction.

Poppy sailed into them without a second thought, and Celeste grasped her and held her close, almost crushing the girl in her arms.

To Poppy, the older woman smelled of roses. Expensive rose water perfumed her hair and there was a touch of rose scent along her neck. The woman's skin was chilly and pale, and her chest and heavy jeweled necklace were cold against Poppy's bare skin as they embraced. Poppy didn't stop the tears from falling down her cheeks.

To Celeste, the young girl before her smelled sweet, like a warm summer's day. As she closed her eyes and embraced the girl she had never known for more than a fortnight, she breathed in her scent. She took in all she could of Poppy's plain hair that had tendrils pulled free from the dancing, her gown that was long and pretty enough, but her ears, neck, and arms, painfully in need of jewels. Not to mention the girl's complexion. Like hers, it was pale and sweet, as delicate as any milkmaid's, but her countenance was so plain. The girl still had a girlish sweetness to her cheeks, but she looked and moved like an ordinary duckling before it became a swan. If she took anything after her mother, the girl would be pretty indeed. She had observed the girl amidst the dancing and saw her stuck in the altercation between the two men. Damn that constable for his cheek and assertions. Any mystique or distance she might have wished to keep between them was gone. There was no help for it now.

"Poppy," Celeste breathed into the girl's hair. "I am… glad to finally meet you in person." Her cheeks were wet, and she stepped back, breaking off the embrace. She felt wooden, like a marionette puppet on strings that required the touch of a master to decide where to go and what to say next.

"May I call you Mother?"

"Oh. My. Um. I… That is…" Celeste didn't know what to do.

What to say. It all felt terribly awkward. She had never imagined she would ever meet Poppy in reality, and so now that she faced her child, she felt struck at the enormity of the situation, and distressed at her own inability to speak her mind.

"I can not if you'd rather," Poppy said, taking a step back, and biting her lip as she looked at the floor. "If you'd rather not acknowledge me, I understand."

"No, no dear girl. it's not that. It's just…" It was exactly that. Celeste had her reputation to think about, and Poppy's.

What would Lord Blackwood say if he discovered he had begotten a child on her, and she had never told him? He would not care to meet the daughter whom he never knew existed for twenty years. And he might well dismiss her for lying to him. Hugh loved children, he loved his family. But he kept those two worlds apart, and with good reason. Their relationship was of a curious nature, for he had his wife and family, but he desperately sought out the comfort and solace Celeste offered him time and again. It was why she became comfortable with herself, with being alone. In return for her upkeep and being installed in fine apartments with all the servants, clothes, jewels, and entertainments she could want, she would forsake all other men and be only loyal to him. It was the price to pay for her life in wealth and comfort, but she chose it knowing the cost.

There was a knock at the door and the maidservant entered, with a needle and thread. "I can mend that sleeve of yours, miss," she said.

That was the interruption Celeste needed to clear her thoughts. "Yes, very good. Come in." She stepped aside as the maidservant entered and went to Poppy's side.

"If you'll sit, miss, that would be easier," the maid said, for she stood a head shorter than Poppy.

"Of course." Poppy moved to a nearby chair and looked at Celeste, who stood by, watching. They waited in silence until the maid finished and left, closing the door behind her.

"When I saw you, there were two young men fighting over

you," Celeste murmured.

"It was nothing. Just two friends who got the wrong idea, I think. It's like they lost control of their senses. I can't imagine what would make them act like that."

"Can you not?"

Poppy looked at her mother. "No."

"You are a pretty girl, Poppy. Is it any wonder that you have men literally fighting over you?"

"That's not it at all. Constable Dyngley is a friend and Tom…" She shrugged. "I think they don't like each other. Tom has been somewhat rude toward the Dyngleys, but I think he has a bit of a chip on his shoulder when it comes to the aristocracy."

"I see. And what will you do now?" Celeste asked. "Your Tom has been escorted out, and the constable is no doubt waiting for you. Which will you choose?"

"We are just friends. There is no decision to make."

Celeste smiled. The girl was young and naive. She would enjoy looking after her. "There is much to be said. Where are you staying?"

"With Miss Beatrice Hayes, at 56 Eaton Place."

"I know it. I will call on you tomorrow. If that is acceptable to you?"

Poppy nodded. "You are the reason I came to London."

Celeste smiled and was rewarded with an identical smile in return. "You've found me."

"We've found each other," said Poppy.

"What will you do now? I will spend time with you and write to you when you return to Hertford, for there is no need for you to stay in Town. Now that we are finally introduced, there is nothing to keep us apart."

"But my uncle…" Poppy started.

"I will deal with him when the time comes. For now, won't you return home? Surely you realize the disadvantaged situation you have placed yourself in, by attaching yourself to a mistress."

Poppy blinked at her. "Do you speak of my employer, or

yourself?"

"Both. Your connection with me is not your fault, only an instance of birth. But by choosing to ally yourself with Miss Hayes, you must understand what that means for your reputation."

"Do you think I care for that?" Poppy asked, heat coming to her face.

"You should," Celeste said.

"I came here to find you. Becoming Miss Hayes's companion was a matter of course. She gave me room and board and a position while I sought you out."

"And now you have. So now you can give Miss Hayes your excuses and return to Hertfordshire. There is no shame in that. She will understand."

"But I do not want to," Poppy said.

"Why not?"

Poppy frowned at her shoes. "Miss Hayes and her friends have all been receiving rude letters."

Celeste waved an airy hand. "That is of no import."

"But what has happened afterward is. All of them have been receiving letters and within a few weeks, one of them dies. They are being killed by this letter writer," Poppy said. "Beatrice—I mean, Miss Hayes, she is frightened out of her wits."

"And yet she overcame her fear to attend a ball," Celeste mused.

"She was terrified when I came to her, and it is only through our companionship that she is moving around in society. Well, she has me and Mr. Parks, a guardian sent to watch over her by her gentleman. But I think—"

"You think very highly of yourself," Celeste said.

Poppy stared at her. "I speak the truth. But I would not leave Miss Hayes's employ, not now. She has been receiving these letters too and I think she would feel worse if I were to leave her."

"But this has nothing to do with you. And worse, you are in a dangerous situation. Why won't you leave?"

"She is my friend," Poppy said. "I will not abandon her."

Celeste let out a noisy breath. "Enough of this. I cannot see why a daughter of mine would refuse to see reason. Let us return to the ballroom so I might see you dance. You have been trained in the dances?"

Poppy nodded.

"Then let us return to the party. Tomorrow I will visit you and we will talk properly. But I do not like this, Poppy. I do not like it at all."

Poppy smiled at that.

"Why are you smiling? I'm perfectly serious."

"You said my name. *My mum* said my name." Poppy beamed.

They returned to the ballroom together but did not stay in each other's company for long. Poppy accepted Henry's immediate offer of a dance, and as he whirled her around on the dance floor, she hardly noticed his attention. A few weeks ago, even an hour ago, she would have been thrilled from head to toe to be dancing with him. She would have relished each and every moment later when she was alone before bed; she would replay their dance movements and his every look and phrase in her mind as she drifted off to sleep. But now her mind was full of another, and it took all her composure not to look beyond the dancing couples in her set and run to her mother's side.

"You seem distracted," Henry said.

"I suppose I am. A lot has happened tonight."

"I am glad your sleeve was mended."

"Me too."

"And the lady who escorted you away, did she make herself known to you?" he asked.

Poppy looked at him. "She did. She is my mother."

He smiled with relief. "I am glad you found each other." He cleared his throat and said, "I must be honest. I saw her days ago, when I first arrived in London."

"You did? But why didn't you—"

He took her hand and moved her in the dance. "I didn't know where to find you, and I wasn't sure myself if it was her. I saw her at the races and tried to talk to her, but she was occupied with her gentleman at the time. I called on her another day, but she did not admit to being your mother. When I pressed the subject, she bid me leave."

"She does not know you," Poppy said.

"That I understood. Has she… I mean, I don't know how you must be feeling right now. You must be overwhelmed with the emotion of it all. Are you sure you wish to dance?"

She smiled and took pleasure in executing another dance step in formation with the other couples. "Yes, for she asked to see me dance." She beamed, and could not stop smiling, even when it hurt her cheeks.

He laughed. "Then I shall do my utmost to allow you to show off your dancing skills."

Together they moved as a seamless couple and danced, just for the sheer pleasure of it.

As the dance ended, he bowed to her and she looked around, but her mother was gone.

Poppy begged off another dance with Henry and wondered if she was truly in her right mind to do so. She went to find Beatrice, who had just finished dancing a set with Mr. Parks, surprisingly enough, and now stood by chatting gaily with a few gentlemen. She looked around the assembly for a certain person as Poppy entered her social circle.

Beatrice beamed at them all and said, "If you will excuse me, sirs, my companion is here." She took Poppy's arm and began to walk away. "I saw you in the middle of that fight with Tom and that other gentleman. He's handsome, isn't he? Did you know him? What were they fighting about?"

Poppy whispered, "Miss Hayes, I have found her. My mother. She's here."

"She is? My word. Where? I should like to meet her properly. This is wonderful!"

"Well, she was. I don't see her now. But we met, and she's going to call on me tomorrow."

Beatrice shook her hands with joy. "This is excellent. We shall stay at home all day and wait for her to call. I'll ask the maids to prepare some iced buns just for her. Come, let us leave while we still are in our right minds. Any more wine and I'm liable to start flirting, and that gets me into no small amount of trouble."

They left and under the watchful eye of Mr. Parks, hailed a carriage home. Beatrice chatted the entire ride back, and as they entered the apartments, Poppy bid Beatrice good night and walked into her room.

While the room was dark and the curtains open, she could see easily from the lights outside. London was a busy place. Gone were the sounds of the birds singing and the wind whispering through the trees. The sweet music of the countryside had been replaced with a cacophony of urban sounds, from the distant clattering of horses' hooves as they drove carriages down the busy streets, to the noise of men and women drinking, laughing, talking, arguing into the night. Dogs howled, and amidst it all, Poppy looked out the window, her chest filled with happiness.

She had met her mother. Her mum. What a sweet thing to be able to say. But as she removed her cloak and laid it on the back of a chair, she spotted something on her pillow.

She strode over to the bed and picked it up. But she could not read it, for the room was too dark. She took a flint and lit the candle on the nightstand beside her bed, and in the dim flame's sputtering light, she saw a poorly drawn caricature of a woman lying down, and a few inches away, her head.

The note read:

Go home or lose your head.

CHAPTER TWENTY-FOUR

T HE NEXT DAY Poppy and Beatrice barely had time to break their fast and put on morning dress before they were besieged with visitors. Poppy entertained Harriet while Beatrice finished dressing.

Harriet said, "Have you heard at all about Penelope? Any word as to where she's gone?"

"Nothing. Have you heard from Tom? He was at a ball last night, but he got into a fight and was taken out."

Harriet's eyebrows rose. "Indeed? How did he manage that? He never fights."

Poppy blushed. "He and my friend the constable had a disagreement."

"Over what?" Seeing Poppy's discomfort, Harriet added, "Well, never mind. I'm sure Tom is fine and suffering from wounded pride, which he sorely deserves. I meant to ask you, have you and Beatrice had any luck investigating these crimes, or the letters?"

Beatrice joined them, just as the sour-faced Fanny announced, "You've got some visitors. Dyngleys." She glared at them all and left.

"So rude," Poppy mumbled, as Harriet said, "She looks familiar somehow. Strange."

In walked Henry, John, and Petunia. Poppy rose to her feet,

shocked to see them all here, in Beatrice's parlor. Beatrice was equally surprised. "Miss Morton?"

Poppy said, "Allow me to introduce you. Miss Hayes, this is Constable Dyngley, Mr. Dyngley, and his wife, Mrs. Dyngley." To the group, she said, "This is my employer, Miss Hayes, and her friend, Miss Sykes."

The men bowed, and Petunia surveyed the ladies there with a sniff of her hawk nose. Her jet-black hair was pulled back severely in a bun worthy of any self-respecting school matron.

Beatrice said politely, "Won't you sit down? I'll ring for tea."

"It is too early for tea," Petunia informed her.

Beatrice colored and said nothing, then gestured for the others to find seats. Petunia took the round curved seat at one end of the short table, while Beatrice sat across from her. Poppy sat beside Harriet on the sofa, while Henry and John sat across from them in two chairs. John looked at Harriet and Beatrice with an eager interest, Poppy noticed.

Beatrice was just about to open her mouth when Petunia said, "You are probably wondering why we have all come. I assure you, I do not wish to trespass upon your hospitality any more than necessary, but it seems that matters have taken a turn which must be addressed."

"Oh?"

"Yes. You were acquainted with the dead girl, were you not?" Petunia asked. "The actress."

Harriet blanched. "If you mean Miss Justine Vane, then yes. We all were."

Petunia pierced Harriet with a stern gaze. "Very well. It strikes me that we all must come to a decision together."

"A decision?" Beatrice said.

"On what to do about this sorry business. Forgive me, but are you aware of the matter? Perhaps we might just speak with your companion and not trouble you with the details," Petunia said.

Poppy felt Beatrice's ire from five feet away. Beatrice was small but mighty and had a fire in her when pushed too far.

"What concerns Miss Vane also concerns me. Perhaps you might inform me of the details of your visit. It would be no trouble." Her voice was steely. "And I will have tea. Even if it is unfashionable."

Poppy cleared her throat. "Let us lay out the facts. As we know it, a few ladies of our acquaintance have received nasty letters from a hateful admirer. We do not know who this person is, but they are cruel. In at least a few instances, the letters contain death threats, and have been followed by attacks on their persons."

"Go on," Constable Dyngley said.

"We know the first was Miss Marie Watkins, who Mr. Harris and I found in the Thames. Then we saw our acquaintance Miss Penelope Smythe at the races, who was drugged and was almost trampled by the horses."

"Do you really think that was an attack, or was the girl just in her cups?" Petunia asked. "I have asked the ladies of my acquaintance and they all think the girl was drunk. All this nasty letter business they believe is nothing but a bit of nonsense to divert silly girls from their dull lives."

Harriet protested. "I knew Penelope well. She liked her drink, but she did not drink to excess. You can't, in our profession. It's not a safe practice."

"She is a wanton woman. Who's to say she didn't run at the horses to draw attention to herself?" Petunia said.

Harriet uttered, "Because Penelope would never do such a thing. She didn't care about being the center of attention, she only liked the horse races. She admitted to us later that someone had been horrid to her, and her drink tasted funny."

Petunia crossed her arms beneath her chest and looked at Poppy.

Harriet added, "Justine was the one of our little circle who most liked attention."

"Yes, and we all saw how that turned out," Petunia said.

"Mrs. Dyngley," Poppy said.

"What? I'm only speaking what we already know."

"Petunia, dear," John started.

She frowned at him and turned to Beatrice. "Very well. I will join you for tea."

"As will I," John said, flashing Beatrice a winsome smile. "A grand idea."

Beatrice walked to a corner of the room and tugged a little bell pull. Within moments a young maid arrived and was asked to bring up tea.

Poppy said, "So we know that Marie was first. Mr. Harris and I found nasty letters in her apartment, including one inviting her to meet. We think it was the last one she received."

"So someone is writing letters to various women of ill repute and then killing them," Petunia said.

Harriet made a noise of protest in her throat but said nothing. The maid returned with tea and left as Beatrice poured cups of tea for everyone present.

Poppy continued, "After her there was Penelope. Thankfully Mrs. Farrars was present to help her, and I think she invited Penelope to call on her the next day."

"Ann? Ann invite a kept woman to her home? Poppycock. What nonsense is this you've heard?" Petunia asked.

Beatrice squeaked and turned her attention to her tea, which almost slopped over the side of her cup.

"I was present at the time, and she did indeed invite the girl over. I think she was doing it out of kindness, and concern for Penelope's health," Poppy said. "She didn't know the girl's occupation at the time she invited her. But it was odd, we didn't hear from Penelope after that. When Mr. Harris and I called on her, her apartment was empty, and the servants didn't know where she had gone."

"Perhaps she went off to a gambling hell or a brothel to seek some work," Petunia said.

"That is it." Beatrice set her cup of tea on the wooden table and stood. "Mrs. Dyngley, I appreciate you are a woman of genteel birth and good breeding. But you are a guest in my home, and you are insulting my friends. I would ask that you please keep a civil tongue, or if you cannot, then please leave." Her voice shook, but her body was steadfast as she locked eyes with Petunia.

"Well. I never," Petunia said, looking around. "John? Aren't you going to say something?"

"Er, what?" John looked up from his tea, and his gaze lingered on Beatrice's chest. "Yes, dear?"

Petunia groaned. Henry said, "Mrs. Dyngley, perhaps you would be more comfortable outside in the park."

"Me alone? Unescorted? I would be an attraction for footpads, no doubt."

Poppy tried to restrain herself from smiling at the idea of the hapless footpad who dared lay a finger on Mrs. Dyngley. The poor man would need a drink after the attempt.

Seeing the group was against her, Petunia heaved a loud sigh. "Very well. Go on."

Poppy looked at Henry, standing there in a gray suit jacket, light silken cream waistcoat, dark breeches, and shiny black hessian boots. His dark brown hair was ruffled from wearing a hat, and he looked at her. She raised her eyebrows, surprised that no one suggested Mrs. Dyngley offer an apology to Beatrice and Harriet, but the look Henry gave her said that there would be none coming. She had best make do with Petunia's silence.

Poppy sipped her tea and said, "After that, it gets a bit muddled. Penelope as far as we know is missing. No one has seen her for days. I spoke with Mrs. Farrars, and she said Penelope came for a visit and left. She did not seem unwell or out of sorts."

"Hah," Petunia said, then stopped at the dirty looks she received. "Hmmm."

"We attended the theater the other night, Miss Hayes and I. Mr. Harris joined us and at the interval, we three were called backstage, at Justine's request. She had received a nasty letter threatening her, and she was afeared for her life. Mr. Harris did his best to calm her down and promised to escort her back to our lodgings after the performance, so she wouldn't be alone."

Petunia stiffened. She looked at John and then focused on her tea.

"It was then that we met Constable Dyngley and Mrs. Dyngley. Mr. Harris was asked to leave, and we returned to our seats. Then during the second act, Justine was killed."

There was silence as the others took this information in. Having tea helped.

Poppy said, "What seems most likely is that the person who wished to harm Justine slipped the note into her room while she was on stage acting, and then during the interval, slipped backstage and removed the guard section of the guillotine device so that she would be killed. During the interval, lots of people would be moving around the theater so there would be no one the wiser if someone wandered around at that time. Then once they finished, they could return to their seat."

Harriet paled. "This person wanted to kill Justine. To go to such trouble... Why? She was a sweet girl. A bit annoying at times, but she would never go out of her way to hurt anyone."

Petunia sniffed loudly. The others looked at her. "You speak well of this girl, but conveniently forget that she seduced my husband and knew very well what she was doing. She was not blameless. She sought out a life of sin and..." She clamped her mouth shut. "I'm just saying, she wasn't completely innocent in all this."

John looked at Poppy. "Miss Vane was a nice girl. She didn't know I had a wife when we met. Not until the day of the races."

"That still does not excuse her behavior. Even after she learned of John's marital status, she was keen to bestow him with her smiles and charms, in the hope he would take her up again. And she had been living in our townhouse." Petunia shuddered with the indignity of it all.

"So we need to figure out who would have wanted to hurt Justine, and why," Poppy said.

"Well, it's obvious. The wife of Justine's gentleman would have wanted to get rid of her," Harriet pointed out.

Petunia turned to her. "If you wish to accuse me of murder, I ask that you do me the courtesy of addressing me, rather than make snide remarks."

"Fine. I think you're a suspect. We know you disliked her," Harriet said.

"Of course I did. Do you really think I would befriend the girl who seduced my husband?" Petunia looked around. "I would be a suspect, yes. But I didn't move from our family's theater box from the moment we arrived, except to see what the commotion was about during the interval. But then I returned. Henry and the servants can speak for me, I didn't move from that spot."

"It's true, she didn't," Henry said. Beside him, John quietly sipped his tea.

"Where were you, Mr. Dyngley, during the interval?" Harriet asked.

"Me?" John blinked. "I was… Occupied."

"With what?" Harried asked.

"Miss, there is no need to question my husband. He was with me during the performance and is above suspicion," Petunia said.

John smiled pleasantly and returned his attention to his tea. Harriet frowned.

"Who else could have wanted Justine dead?" Poppy asked, "Did she have any enemies? Some of the actors, maybe?"

Harriet shrugged. Beatrice gave her a blank look.

"I will go and speak to the stage manager, and see if any of the actors saw something. Perhaps one of them can tell us something useful," Henry said.

Harriet stood. "I will go seek out Mr. Harris and see if he has heard anything about Penelope. It's not like her to disappear."

"You seem less concerned for her than for Marie," Poppy noted.

Harriet gave her an even look. "Marie was my friend. Penelope… was a gambler and a thief. If she went into hiding, it's likely she had a good reason. Perhaps avoiding debt collectors or…"

"Or a murderer," Beatrice said.

Poppy said, "I wonder if it was an actress. Or a maid. Or a society woman."

"You're speaking in riddles, Miss Morton," Henry said.

She looked at him. "I was in church the other day and I happened to fall asleep. I woke and overheard a conversation between two people, discussing the letters. The very ones sent to the mistresses."

"Are you certain?"

"Yes. The voices seemed familiar somehow as if I'd heard them before. But I couldn't look up to see who without giving myself away."

"Why didn't you?" Petunia asked.

"They were talking about killing people. I didn't want to attract their attention," Poppy said. "They were talking about the letters, and one of them had been in prison. It was odd."

"I'll visit the prisons in town to see about who was recently released. They'll know which men are around," Henry said.

"That was the other funny thing," Poppy said, "they were both women."

At that moment the parlor doors opened and the sour-faced maid said, "There's a clergyman and his wife here to see you."

"Me? What for?" Beatrice asked.

"Not you. Her." Fanny jerked a thumb at Poppy.

In strode Poppy's uncle, Mr. Greene, and his wife, her Aunt Rachel.

Poppy's mouth dropped open.

Mr. Greene's face was red and dark as a storm cloud, whereas Aunt Rachel looked around the room pleasantly. Catching sight of Poppy, she said, "Oh Poppy! At last, we found you." She crossed the room and not a second after Poppy set down her teacup, enveloped her in an embrace.

Poppy looked over her aunt's shoulder to see her uncle standing stiffly at the room's entrance, disapproval scrawled on his features. His mouth withered at the sight of her.

Aunt Rachel released Poppy from her arms. "How I've missed you."

"I've missed you, too."

"Do introduce me to your friends."

Poppy hastily made introductions. Henry instantly vacated his seat and offered it to Mrs. Greene, who sat down with a quiet poof.

Mr. Greene said, "I should like to speak to my niece alone, please. Is there somewhere we could go?"

"We were just leaving," Petunia said, setting her teacup on the table and rising to her feet.

Mr. Greene turned to Henry. "I might normally be surprised to find you here, but now I am glad of it. How long did you know my niece was in Town?"

"Only a few days. It took some time to find her."

"How did you find out where I was staying?" Poppy asked, keenly aware of the restrained anger of her uncle.

Petunia said, "Oh, that was my doing. I invited them."

❦

CHAPTER TWENTY-FIVE

"Y OU?" POPPY SAID. She could hardly believe it.

Petunia sniffed. "It is unseemly for a good clergy-man's girl to attach herself to a wanton woman for money. I did what any concerned woman would do and wrote to your relations immediately."

Poppy's mouth dropped open again.

"You should thank me. Who knows what trouble you could have gotten into before they arrived? You may not see it now, but I did the right thing. Come, John." Petunia took her husband's arm and led him away.

Harriet curtsied to Beatrice and followed, leaving just Poppy, Beatrice, Henry, and Poppy's aunt and uncle in the room.

"Well, this is a pretty sort of room. Very comfortable looking. And such fine furnishings. Not at all like I expected," Aunt Rachel said.

Beatrice looked at her hopefully. "I'm so glad you like it. I have no mind for decoration, so I was grateful when Stephen purchased furniture and set me up here."

"Stephen?" Mr. Greene asked.

"My—"

"Benefactor," Poppy said. Beatrice blushed.

"I see," Mr. Greene said. Unlike his wife, he did not take notice of the room's furnishings. He frowned at Poppy. "We need to talk."

"Why have you come to London?" Poppy asked.

"To bring you home. Back to Hertford, where you belong," he said.

"I belong here. I'm doing well here," she told him.

"Nonsense. You've had your adventure, I see that now. Now be sensible and pack your things. We can be back in Hertford by tomorrow morning if we get a carriage in the next hour," he said.

Poppy looked at him. "No."

"No?" Aunt Rachel repeated. "What do you mean, no? We have come all this way. Do you have any idea how uncomfortable those carriage seats are? I'll have sores for weeks on my backside—"

"I know, and I'm sorry for your trouble. But I am happy here. I mean to stay," Poppy said.

"What for?"

"I am a companion. I earn a wage."

"Which you have no business doing," her uncle interjected.

"And I have a degree of independence, which I never had before."

"You're out of our house, that's what you mean," he said.

"No, it's not that. I feel at liberty to make my own decisions, to act as I choose—"

"With a mistress as a role model?"

Beatrice paled and looked down at her teacup.

Aunt Rachel saw her reaction and said, "Reginald, really."

He glanced at Beatrice. "I am sorry if my words offend, but I speak the truth. I refuse to hide behind social niceties when the facts are laid bare before us. Poppy, I am disappointed in you. You deceived us."

Poppy stared at him. "I told you of my plan. You knew I was coming to London to interview as a companion, and my reason why." She looked around and saw she held the attention of the room. "Everyone in this room knows the real reason why I came—to find my mother."

Aunt Rachel tensed. Beatrice fetched an empty teacup and poured her a cup of tea.

"Thank you, dear," Aunt Rachel said, taking the cup in her hands.

"How can you speak so plainly about—?" Mr. Greene said. "I have done my best to raise you as a good and proper girl, but I can see I was too lax in my instruction. For a smart girl, you show a serious lack of common sense. Have you any idea the trouble you've landed yourself in?"

"What do you mean?"

He ticked the reasons off on his fingers. "You ignored us, Poppy. You never wrote to us, to let us know how you were getting on. For all we knew you could have been accosted and lying in a ditch somewhere. Second, you lied to us about your situation. How did you think we would react upon learning that our very own niece had offered herself as a companion to a prostitute?"

Beatrice gasped. Aunt Rachel politely sipped her tea. Poppy glared at her uncle.

"But that is not the worst of it. No, that you kept your true reason from me, for wanting to leave Hertford and the comfort of our home. What you said to me that day when you left was insulting. Have you no thoughts for the feelings of others? The entire town has been wondering if we drove you away through animosity or neglect. Instead, I find you gallivanting about London in mixed company, without an escort, which I never would have even learned of had not Mrs. Dyngley taken it upon herself to write to me, out of concern for your safety." he seethed.

Poppy's eyes narrowed. "Uncle, I…" She bowed her head. "I am sorry. I never meant to distress or alarm you."

"No thanks to that woman," he barely acknowledged Beatrice with a glance. Beatrice withered under his distant gaze.

"I have been working for her, but also to help. She and the other girls are being targeted by a cruel letter writer, who is stalking them and trying to kill them," Poppy said.

"And just what business is that of yours? You should report it to the magistrate, or the local constable here, and leave them to their jobs. Detecting is not a woman's province, Poppy. You belong in the home or at church, like the good girl we raised you to be."

"Sir," Henry said, standing by. "What Miss Morton says is true. Her employer and acquaintances are being targeted by a killer."

"All the more reason to remove my niece from this den of iniquity and see her returned home, where she belongs," Uncle Reginald said.

Poppy glared at him. "But Uncle, there is good I can do here. I am helping."

"How? By having tea and attending dances?"

"By staying by Miss Hayes's side for her protection. She needs my help. The girls all do."

Her uncle surveyed her severely, his bushy eyebrows knitted into a firm line. "You claim you are doing good works by helping these unfortunate women?"

"Of a sort, yes. But it is not charity. It is because I want to."

"Oh, please let her stay, Mr. Greene," Beatrice interrupted. "I'm ever so scared the man will come after me next, and I'm that frightened of going out, even to take a walk in the park. 'Til Miss Morton came, I barely went out at all. Now I feel safe with her around. She's ever so smart. As smart as any man, I dare say." Beatrice looked up at Mr. Greene through her eyelashes.

Poppy observed Beatrice in her sweet, innocent act and wondered if it ever worked.

But at that moment she didn't care, for the doors to the parlor opened, and in walked...

"Mother," Poppy said.

"Daughter," Celeste Grey entered the room and stopped, instantly the center of attention. She surveyed the room and declared, "Ah, Mr. Greene, Mrs. Greene. Constable. How good to see you all again." She nodded hello to Poppy and Beatrice.

"You," Mr. Greene scowled. "What are you doing here?"

"I have come to pay a visit to my daughter. What are you doing here? If I'd known you were in Town, I would have offered an invitation to dine." She smirked at his increasingly red face. "Well, to my sister, at least."

"Hello Celeste," Aunt Rachel said.

"Rachel." Celeste offered a polite incline of her head.

Aunt Rachel set down her teacup and rose to embrace her sister. They gave each other a warm hug and then stood by each other as Mr. Greene fumed quietly.

"I heard some of what you were saying and as her mother, I say Poppy can go gallivanting if she wants. She is a good, sweet girl and she is too smart to land herself in any real trouble."

"That is precisely where you are wrong. Just a year ago she fought a girl at an assembly and ended up a murder suspect. You have no idea of the trouble she can get into."

"And whose fault is that? If you had let me see her on occasion instead of forcing me to abide by your stupid agreement, I would have been there to guide and advise her. Instead—"

"Oh yes," Mr. Greene's laugh was harsh. "Because you yourself have shown such great intelligence in your life choices. Madam, no sooner had you dropped your babe at our doorstep did I decide you were the last person I should ever wish her to spend time with. You are a harlot. A highly paid one no doubt, but a whore all the same."

Celeste looked as if she had been struck.

"Uncle," Poppy said, "stop this. She is my mother and we have found each other finally and I want to spend time with her. I want to help these women. I want—"

"I do not care what you want. You are coming home with us, now. Pack your bag," he said.

"She will do as she pleases, Reginald," Celeste said.

"Under your authority? Please. All any judicial court has to do is look at you and they'll send you packing. She will stay with us, in Hertford, where she belongs."

"Uncle, please." Poppy bowed her head. She had caused enough trouble to suit her for a year. "I am sorry for the trouble and inconvenience I have caused—"

"Inconvenience? Your actions have caused us more than an inconvenience. You risk ruining your good name and throwing our entire family into disrepute. Has that ever occurred to you?" He seethed and stepped toward her. "You are not a child any longer and for that, I will spare you a beating. You have never had cause to vex me so before. But by God, Poppy, you will come to know the consequences of your actions."

"Sir." Henry moved in his path.

"Get out of my way. Remove yourself, Constable, you have no jurisdiction here. This is a family matter," Mr. Greene said.

"The wellbeing of Miss Morton concerns me, as she is as close a friend to me as there ever was."

"Do not make me repeat myself, Constable. You may inspire loyalty in the ladies, but not with me. Your involvement in my family's affairs is impertinent and unwanted," Mr. Greene said.

"It is you who should step aside, Reginald," Celeste said. "Lay one finger on my daughter and I'll make you regret it."

Poppy glanced at her mother with a warmth that filled her, but felt too distraught to speak.

"I have no wish to cross paths with a whore," Mr. Greene sneered.

Aunt Rachel put two fingers between her teeth and whistled, a high-pitched sound that shocked them all into silence. She said, "You are all acting like children. I've heard enough of this bickering. Celeste, do sit down. My neck aches from looking up at you."

Mr. Greene sneered as Celeste stood, unmoved.

"Reginald, there are some very pretty flowers in the park across the way. Perhaps you might go tour the grounds."

"I have no wish to." He sniffed.

Aunt Rachel's pleasant face turned cross. "Then find some

other diversion. But for goodness's sake, leave me to speak with our niece. You too, Constable."

The men looked at her. Aunt Rachel put her hands on her hips, and said, "I will not move from this spot until you both are gone. This is a conversation for ladies and ladies only." Seeing Mr. Greene's mutinous face, she added, "And before you go on making a nasty remark that not all of us are ladies present, I'll remind you that our hostess has been kinder and more obliging to us strangers who invaded her home than you have shown many unfortunate souls in the past year. Now begone and let us talk amongst ourselves."

"I do not think that is wise," he started.

"I did not ask your opinion," she said archly, earning a bemused smile from Celeste.

"If you think I will submit to such poor treatment, you are mistaken," he told her.

"And I did not come all this way just to be silenced. Give us an hour and return. You might visit the confectioner's shop two streets away."

He wished to protest but paused at her hard expression. He straightened his collar, cleared his throat, and said, "Very well." He turned and quit the room.

Constable Dyngley bowed to them all and left shortly thereafter.

Once the ladies heard the parlor doors open and close, Aunt Rachel sank back onto her seat and said, "Now then, what's happened, Poppy?"

Celeste joined Poppy on the sofa and helped herself to a biscuit. Beatrice smiled at Aunt Rachel as Poppy began.

She told her story of how she came to London and met Beatrice, and how they first learned about the letter writer, then their adventures at the races and the theater. She omitted the parts of being insulted by Petunia and Mrs. Farrars at Somerset House, for she had no wish to relive them and did not wish to cause a fuss. During this explanation, Beatrice rang for more tea and a fresh plate of biscuits. Once properly seen to, Poppy finished, "And that's why I wish to stay. There is more I can do here, more good I can accomplish by helping others, than resuming my duties back home. And I've just found my mother. I don't wish to leave now."

Celeste smiled at her and blinked hard. Aunt Rachel observed them both and said, "Reginald will be cross with me."

"He's always cross about something," Celeste said.

At a look from Rachel, Celeste looked at her lap. "Sorry."

Aunt Rachel looked at Beatrice, then Poppy. "If you were a young girl I would agree with your uncle and take you back to Hertfordshire this very moment. But you are not. You are a young woman, and you have your own decisions to make. I can see you are of some use here, even if your choices do seem questionable at times."

"Is it really so very bad, my being a companion?" Poppy asked.

Beatrice chose that moment to excuse herself. Once she left the room, Aunt Rachel said, "Not at all. For any young woman of good birth and good family, it is not necessary. But I know you have been unhappy in Hertford as of late. Your uncle thinks we can all be good Christians and devote ourselves to our neighbors and good works, but we are individuals too, with our own hopes and wants. You have made a place for yourself here, and all on your own. While I cannot openly approve of your choice of employer…" She looked Poppy in the eye. "I am proud of you."

"You are?"

"Yes. You have gone out and sought employment, rather than be a burden to us. You would never be a burden, you know. But I know you have also longed to know your mother, and I would not step between you now. I never approved of Reginald's decision to keep you both apart, and I won't stand in your way now."

"Thank you, Aunt." Poppy smiled at her. "You don't mind if I stay in London for a time?"

"I do not mind, although I wish you had better escorts. But Miss Hayes seems like a nice enough girl."

"What will you tell Uncle? I know it won't be long before people hear about the company I keep. What will you tell the townspeople?"

"Let me deal with your uncle. My dear, I don't imagine they will hear anything of it. Your uncle and I simply won't tell them. We shall share that you are working as a companion to a lady, and you are doing good works in London. That will be the end of it." She looked down. "Poppy, do you mean to stay here forever? You don't have to work to survive. I think that is what concerns your uncle most, although he will not say so. Your choosing to work when you do not need to. I can well understand the desire to earn a wage and be independent, but I think he views your newfound independence as a dislike of his home and way of life. To choose such company on top of that... He found Mrs. Dyngley's letter most distressing."

Poppy's face fell. "I never meant for that to happen. I would never dream of insulting him so."

"You'd best find a way to apologize, then, for his feelings are sorely hurt. He feels like you have rejected him, and he cannot accept it. He cannot be happy with the loss of you, and that stings, especially when you did not write."

Poppy bowed her head. "I am sorry, Aunt."

"I will look after her," Celeste said. "She can stay and be a companion to Miss Hayes for as long as she likes, as far as I'm concerned."

"But what about your gentleman? Will you tell him about Poppy?" Aunt Rachel asked.

Celeste bit her lip, a gesture that Poppy found oddly endearing. "I have not spoken to my gentleman about my child. He does not know, and I didn't tell him, for fear he would end our relationship." She looked at Poppy.

"And now?" Rachel asked.

"I will..." She stopped. "You both have been so brave. I will take some of your courage and when the time is right, I will tell him."

Poppy breathed in, her chest feeling tight.

Celeste continued, "I think it's time. He might not approve, but neither do I think he will end our understanding. We have known each other too long for that to be a concern any longer." She gave Rachel a sidelong glance. "If you will let me, I would like to do a little for her."

"What do you mean?" Aunt Rachel asked.

"Her clothes and personal appearance are modest, as befitting a clergyman's niece. But I would like to see her wear some clothes that are more fashionable. I have the money. Would Reginald disapprove of that?"

"You know he would. He'd say you were encouraging her to have airs and think herself above her station," Aunt Rachel said.

Celeste looked at Poppy. "I don't care. I have waited too long for this. I never thought I would actually meet Poppy. And now that I have, I don't wish to give up the connection. Mr. Greene wouldn't deny me that chance, would he?"

"I won't let him," Aunt Rachel said.

"Thank you," Poppy whispered, her throat tight.

Beatrice re-entered the room and retook her seat. "Have I missed anything?"

Poppy shook her head as Aunt Rachel said, "But now what are we to do about this letter writer? And stalker? Why have you not gone to the authorities?"

Beatrice spoke up. "We tried but because of our station and situation, the men wouldn't listen. Tom—Mr. Harris, I mean, he spoke up and tried to help, but even then… We haven't been able to stop this person or figure out who he is. We had thought it was the wife of one of the girls' gentlemen, or maybe the gentlemen themselves."

"That makes no sense. Why would a gentleman want to kill his own mistress?" Aunt Rachel asked.

"Maybe she wasn't very appealing." Celeste joked. Seeing the others' faces she added, "It is a concern. As a woman grows older, if she does not stay looking young, attractive, witty, or charming, she can lose her benefactor to another. Sometimes men return to their wives. Others can no longer afford a woman's charms, especially those they keep in a situation on the side. Some tire of the same woman all the time and look for someone new."

"What of these women, Miss Hayes? Could any of them have turned their benefactors away?" Aunt Rachel asked.

Beatrice thought for a moment. "Marie, not at all. She was scrupulously clean. And kind, and nice. She didn't have any enemies. Harriet is smart and clever. Her gentleman isn't so rich, but he is loyal to her and her to him, I think. Penelope... has gambling debts and a fiery temper. She argues a lot, with everyone. I can't imagine she is any different with her gentleman. But I don't know what's happened to her."

"She's also a thief. We caught her stealing on the night we met her," Poppy said.

Aunt Rachel's eyebrows rose.

"Don't forget Mollie," Poppy said.

"Oh yes. Mollie's the worst of them." Beatrice reddened. "I mean, she's, well... She has very strong opinions and dislikes it when people disagree with her. Her gentleman is also the wealthiest of our social circle, and she..." Beatrice shrugged.

"Tends to rule the roost, as if you were a bunch of hens in a henhouse," Celeste said with an amused sniff. "I know the sort. An insecure woman who bullies others to feel powerful."

Aunt Rachel shifted in her seat. "I do not like the sound of these women." She fanned herself. "I could use some fresh air. Shall we walk a little in the park nearby? I could use a chance to stretch my legs."

"Of course," Beatrice said, rising.

The ladies abandoned their tea and donned their hats, gloves, and coats and walked outside. Aunt Rachel walked beside Beatrice, as Celeste strode beside Poppy, a small huddle together.

"I say, is that Mollie?" Poppy pointed.

There near the entrance to the park, stood Mollie amongst a group of people, looking as if she were waiting for someone. But she stood too close to the street, and Poppy watched as the young woman took little heed of this.

"That Mollie, she's never concerned with the carriages in the road," Beatrice said.

"That girl has got a death wish if she's not careful," Celeste muttered.

Poppy walked toward her, steering their group in Mollie's direction. Something was odd. She couldn't put her finger on it.

Then as Mollie turned and waved, a carriage flew by, and Mollie disappeared into the crowd. A scream cut the air.

Poppy ran quickly toward the group and pushed her way through.

At the side of the road lay Mollie, dead.

"Mollie!" Poppy moved people aside.

Gasps and cries sounded as people asked, "Is she dead?"

"That poor girl. Did you see the carriage?"

Poppy ignored the voices as she touched Mollie's limp form. Her red hair had tumbled free of its fashionable arrangement and her head rolled to one side. Her light pink walking dress lay crumpled and dirty with mud from her fall, the hem and sleeves now stained. Poppy gently touched her shoulder. "Mollie, can you hear me?"

Poppy was shuffled aside by Tom, who said, "Mollie, what have you done?" just as Constable Dyngley appeared at Poppy's side.

"What happened?" he asked.

"This doesn't concern you, Constable," Tom said rudely. "Mollie, are you all right?"

"Hmmm…. Tom?" Mollie murmured, her eyes fluttering.

"Was the girl attacked?" Henry asked.

Mollie's eyes flew open and she uttered, "Oh!" she breathed hard and clutched her chest. "It hurts!"

"Where? Where are you hurt?" Tom asked.

"My chest. My ribs. And my arms. Oh…" Mollie uttered. She took a few deep breaths and said, "Please, help me up."

Tom held a hand, supporting her as she did so.

"Did you see him?" she asked.

"Who?" Tom asked.

"Whoever it was that pushed me," Mollie said.

"What?"

"I was walking along and thought I saw a friend. I waved and then as the carriage came by, I felt someone push me from behind."

"Could it have been an accident?" Constable Dyngley asked.

Mollie shook her head, her red curls shaking. Her arms were covered with scratches and her pretty light pink dress was ruined. "I didn't see who it was, but I felt it. Someone shoved me into the path of that carriage. And before I could turn around to see who, it hit me, and I couldn't remember nothing until you." She looked coyly at Henry. "What did you say your name was?"

"Never mind him," Tom said, annoyed. "Let me help you stand."

"Oh thank you, Tom," she said, eyeing Henry's athletic form. As she stood, she took a step forward and stumbled, as Tom caught her. "Oh my."

"You didn't see who did this?" Constable Dyngley said.

"No. But I know it was directed at me," Mollie said.

"Why do you think that?" Poppy asked.

Mollie pierced her with a gaze as if she might quell an insect. "Because of the letter."

"What letter?" Tom asked.

"This one." Mollie reached into her sleeve and pulled out a folded-up letter. She handed it to Henry. "What do you think of this?"

He took it and read:

Meet me in the park at midday. Watch yor stepp.

Henry surveyed it with a frown and held it out to Poppy.

"Look at this."

She read it. "How strange. Look at the cheap paper and handwriting. This is different than the other letters."

"I agree." To Mollie, he asked, "May I keep this?"

"Certainly," Mollie said, then touched her forehead. "Oh, I am feeling weary. Please, could you see me back to my rooms? I don't feel strong enough to make the journey alone."

"Mollie, who would have done this?" Tom asked, offering her his arm.

"I don't know. I haven't an enemy in the world," she said, watching the constable.

"There's no one who would have wanted to hurt you?" Poppy asked.

That earned her a dirty look from Mollie, who leaned heavily on Tom's arm. "No. Not a soul. But it's clear that it's whoever is coming after the girls." She gave a mighty sigh. "Now they've decided to come after me."

"You seem remarkably well composed," Poppy said dryly.

"I am doing the best I can, considering. But then you wouldn't understand. No one has tried to kill you."

"Actually they have," Henry said. "I am of the constabulary in Hertfordshire, and we have worked together on many crimes. Miss Morton has been in danger before."

Mollie gave a little shrug. "I feel tired. Sir, would you escort me home? I think I could remember more about what happened if we talked about it."

"I can take you back to your lodgings," Tom said.

"That's all right, Tom. I know you mean well, but I would rather discuss this terrible business with the constable. It's so horrid, I don't know what to do," Mollie said, disengaging her arm from Tom's and linking it through Henry's. "Call a carriage, will you?"

Henry looked, surprised to see his arm taken by Mollie. "Um, yes. Of course."

Tom and Poppy watched as Henry escorted Mollie away.

The crowd quickly dispersed, and they were joined by Celeste, Aunt Rachel, Beatrice, and Mr. Greene.

"What has happened?" Aunt Rachel asked. "Is that girl all right?"

"She's fine," Poppy said sourly, watching them go. She walked beside Celeste as Tom and Beatrice led the way back to Beatrice's townhouse.

"You say that girl was a victim of an attack, like the others?" Celeste asked.

"It seems that way. But it's strange. Who was she waiting for and where did the man run to? They were in a crowd of people, so why did no one see him?" Poppy said.

"It's possible that in the crowd the man pretended he was one of the onlookers. He could have blended in, and no one would be the wiser, especially if he acted as if he was concerned about her safety."

Poppy grew alarmed. "You think he is still here now?"

"No. The crowd has gone. Any chance we had of finding him has disappeared. What of these other gentlemen? The benefactors of the dead girls. What of them? Has anyone looked into their motives?" Celeste asked.

"I do not think so. When Marie died, Harriet and Beatrice went to her gentleman and told him, and by their accounts, he was distraught at the news."

"He could have been faking a reaction. What of the missing girl and Justine? Or Mollie, for that matter," Celeste said. "She seems very taken by your constable."

Poppy blushed and shot her mother a look. "He is not *my* constable."

"So you say."

Poppy frowned. "Penelope is the one who has gone missing and no, we haven't spoken to her gentleman. I don't even know who he is."

"I can find out," Celeste said with a smile.

"How?"

"I'll let it be known that Penelope borrowed a trinket from me, and I want it back. It shouldn't be too hard to find her, especially when I say it's worth something." Celeste smirked. "She's sure to come out of hiding then."

"I hope you are right. Let's see, we know that Mr. Dyngley was Justine's gentleman. But he was with his wife during the performance."

"Mr. Dyngley?" Celeste's face darkened. "You mean the constable? He was seeing the actress?"

"No. Not Constable Dyngley, his brother, John."

"Ah. I see. Then we shall look into these other gentlemen," Celeste said.

"I'll help." Beatrice came up to them.

"So will I," Aunt Rachel added.

"Rachel, you have no business involving yourself in this sordid business." Mr. Greene said.

"Yes, yes, I know. But this is the third murder investigation your niece has been stuck in, and if she's to come home any time soon, she'll need our help."

Mr. Greene stared at his wife.

"I want her home as much as you do, but it's clear to me that she's in the middle of this, whether we like it or not. I mean to assist her and help these women." Rachel took a deep breath. "I will stay with Poppy so there is no question about her situation or any sense of impropriety."

"Nonsense. You'll do no such thing. I will take a room in Town," Mr. Greene said.

"Forgive me, Mrs. Greene," Beatrice piped up, "but aside from my bedchamber and Miss Morton's, the only rooms left are the servants'."

"You can have my room," Poppy said, "I can sleep on the sofa in the parlor, I don't mind."

"Stop this, you're overlooking the obvious," Celeste said. "Rachel will stay with me. As my sister, it's only right."

Mr. Greene stiffened and looked at her with a scandalized

expression. He uttered, "There is no need. I will take a room immediately for us nearby. Rachel?"

Aunt Rachel looked from her husband to her sister and saw the embarrassment, anger, and pain in his eyes. "Thank you, sister. I'll stay with Reginald, but we'll visit." Seeing his mutinous reaction she added, "Every day. Until our business in London is complete."

Celeste smiled. Reginald winced. Poppy grinned.

CHAPTER TWENTY-SIX

THAT EVENING BEATRICE, Poppy, and her aunt and uncle held a council of war over dinner. Meaning that Beatrice entertained the Greenes at her home with Poppy's help, and over a meal of roast pork with crackling, boiled herb potatoes, and peas, they spoke of topics other than the murders. Once plied with wine, the company became more comfortable with their surroundings and their hosts, and once the Greenes had been served a raspberry trifle to enjoy for dessert, Poppy settled back in her chair and observed the others.

Her aunt had been warmth itself, cordial and polite. She had praised the decoration of the rooms and declared it a most comfortable place to live, while her husband ate his dinner, drank his wine, and spoke to Poppy about Hertford.

It was a sorry place without her, he said. "The chickens have run amok since you've gone, and the flower beds need tending. You know that we are no gardeners, we haven't your touch."

Aunt Rachel shot her husband a look and then agreed, "Yes. You will come back and see the sorry state of our gardens and laugh, I am sure." She offered Beatrice a smile, "You are welcome to come too, Miss Hayes." She ignored her husband's choking on his wine. "For any friend of Poppy's is most welcome at our home."

"Rachel, I do not think—" he started.

But Beatrice said, "That is very kind of you, thank you, Mrs. Greene. But I would not wish to disturb the peace and quiet of your home. Besides, I do not know if Mr. Farrars will agree to my leaving Town."

Mr. Greene's eyebrows rose. "That is your father?"

"My gentleman, sir. It is to him I owe everything."

"What do you mean?"

Her smile was kind as she said quietly, "I grew up in Bristol. Happy enough, I had a mother and a younger sister. But when my pa died, my mother had to remarry to support us, and the man, Mr. Piggot..." Her face fell, and Poppy caught traces of anger in her.

"He was the local butcher. He brought food to the table and a roof over our heads, but he did not treat my mum well. And once I got my courses, he began to look at me." Beatrice bowed her head. "The first time he came to my room at night I pretended I was still sick with my courses and that deterred him. The second time he did it, I had a knife and told him if he lay a finger on me again, or my sister, I'd cut his throat." She swallowed. "I don't know if I'd ever actually hurt him, but I was so scared. I was only fourteen."

"The next day he threw me out of the house, claimed I was a troublemaker. My mum begged him not to but then he told her that I had tried to seduce him, and she wasn't having that. Not a harridan in her house." Beatrice took up her glass of red wine and drank deeply. "I had nowhere to go. I stole some money and took a carriage to London, where I met a bawd who had me working in her house for a time. Tom met me and got me out of there, it was a bad situation. Then he let me a room in his quarters while I worked as a barmaid in the tavern, and it was there that Stephen and I met. I thought nothing of it until he kept coming back and eventually made me an offer. Never again would I have to sell myself on the streets."

"You could have stayed as a barmaid," Mr. Greene pointed out.

Beatrice offered him a wan smile. "It was only ever temporary. I attracted too many men's glances and without a protector, many men at the tavern thought I was easy prey. When Mr. Farrars made me an offer, I took it."

"But why? You could have returned to Bristol and turned in your stepfather as a sexual predator," he said.

"Who would listen to me? When my own mother disowned me and would say I'm speaking falsehoods?" She shook her head. "When I myself would have to declare how I have survived since leaving her home, that alone would condemn me in the eyes of the constabulary. No one believes a whore, no matter how many rings or pretty dresses she wears."

"I am sorry for the hand life has dealt you, Miss Hayes," Mr. Greene said.

Her smile was bittersweet. "Thank you, vicar, but I do not mean to complain about my situation. It is how I have survived, and it is why I am so thankful that you have allowed Miss Morton to stay on as my companion. I am grateful you both have come, for I can think of no greater compliment to my home than to have a clergyman present." She met his eyes.

Mr. Greene blushed then, but it might have been the wine. He cleared his throat. "Yes, well. Now that we are here, we should all be able to help you with your predicament. I confess I have little experience or knowledge in murder investigations, but I am a good judge of character. How can we be of service?"

Beatrice beamed at him. "Oh, thank you. Um, to be honest, your guess is as good as mine. I don't know. Miss Morton?" she asked.

Poppy wondered aloud, "Where is Mr. Parks these days, Miss Hayes? I haven't seen him for some time now."

Beatrice shrugged. "If he is not in the vicinity, then he is likely reporting to Mr. Farrars." She explained to the Greenes, "My gentleman cares for me and has assigned a man to care for my safety. Mr. Parks escorts me to most places and keeps a watchful eye over me most of the time. Although in truth, I do not know where he is."

"A good and thoughtful man, your gentleman," Aunt Rachel said. "But what of this Mr. Parks? Is he capable of looking after you?"

"Oh yes. He's ever so fierce when he wants to be," Beatrice said. "Stephen is always doing good work. Mr. Parks had just lately come out of a bad situation when Stephen hired him."

"What do you mean?" Mr. Greene asked, "What sort of situation?"

"I do not know the particulars, but from what Stephen said, Mr. Parks was a good man in a dire situation who needed help, so Stephen took him on as a minder for me. So you see, Stephen has helped two of us now." She smiled fondly.

"Let us think. Of the young women who have been targeted, who are the men connected to them?" Aunt Rachel asked.

Beatrice thought aloud. "There's my gentleman, Mr. Stephen Farrars. You know of course that Justine was connected to Mr. Dyngley."

"The older brother, not the constable we know," Poppy quickly pointed out.

"Then there's Mr. Hollingsworth, he was seeing Marie but now that she's gone, I don't know what's happened. He seemed very put out that she was dead."

"But not enough to give a penny for her funeral," Poppy muttered.

"There's Harriet's gentleman, Mr. Farthing. He's young and handsome. I guess they met in a shop? They seem very happy together. Although... She does hide herself away when his wife comes to visit. His wife, Mrs. Farthing, sounds ever so fierce, to hear Harriet mention her."

"So many names..." Aunt Rachel said.

"And you never met Penelope, but her gentleman is Mr. Nutt. He's quite young and loves to gamble. Makes sense that he and Penelope would pair up. And then of course there's Mollie, she's kept up by Lord Aylesbury, and very proud she is, of that too."

Mr. Greene choked on his wine.

"My dear, are you all right?" Aunt Rachel asked.

"Yes, yes." He coughed and dabbed at his face with a napkin. "Miss Hayes, did you say that girl's patron was Lord Aylesbury, of Essex?"

"Yes, why?"

He tugged at the prim white cravat around his neck. "I am sorry to say that the living near his estate became vacant last year when the local rector moved away. The old gentleman passed away in November and in his will, the parish parsonage was to be passed to his son, but the boy had no interest in taking orders, so the clergy was deciding who to recommend to him to take it up."

"My dear, you never told me this," Aunt Rachel said.

"There was little need to mention it. It is still in contention, even now. But you see, Lord Aylesbury could not be your friend's patron. He's been dead these past eleven months."

Beatrice's eyes widened.

"Could she not have known? Perhaps she wasn't aware and has been waiting to hear of him," Aunt Rachel suggested.

"Could she have been lying?" Poppy asked, "Would she?"

"To stay the center of attention and appear to be the best of us? Absolutely," Beatrice said with a frown.

THE NEXT DAY the group made inquiries. Beatrice learned through Mr. Parks that Stephen and his wife were still in town, so it would be unlikely Mr. Farrars would call on her anytime soon. Beatrice and Harriet learned that since Marie's death, her patron had shut up the house and left for the country. The word at the tavern and corroborated by Tom was that Marie's patron, Mr. Hollingsworth, left the very day they told him of her death, and hadn't returned to London since.

In a conversation at a walk around the park, Harriet laughed at their questions. "My gentleman have a wife? You're joking. There is no Mrs. Farthing, or Mrs. F, as you say. My gentleman is not yet thirty. As he made clear to me upon our first meeting, he is enjoying all that London has to offer and has no wish to chain himself to a wife until he is forced to. Sure, he is being forced into courting a girl, but this woman can have designs on becoming Mrs. Farthing all she likes. He won't do it. Loves his freedom too much."

The Dyngleys stayed incommunicative, although Henry did call on them later, seemingly out of sorts. He sat down in the parlor. "The sooner we solve this mystery the better. I do not like the players in this game."

Poppy and Beatrice looked at each other. "What do you mean?"

"You recall I escorted the young woman, Miss Mollie Jones, to a carriage to take her home." He removed his hat and ran a hand through his hair. "She begged me to see her home and then take refreshment, for she feared for her safety. I agreed." He raised his eyes to Poppy's, then looked away. "She tried to…"

"Flirt with you?" Beatrice asked.

"More like seduce. In the carriage. She thought it would be amusing." A blush crept up his cheeks.

"Oh," Poppy said, "and you…"

"I did not accept her invitation if that is what you are thinking." He stood, dropped his hat on the sofa, and paced around the room. "I had thought her a young lady in need of some help. She had just nearly been run over by that carriage. I had thought that she had vital insights to tell me about her attack. Instead, I find she is nothing but a wanton, thoughtless…"

"Whore?" Beatrice supplied.

Henry stopped pacing. "She had hoped to win me over with her story about being attacked. When I rejected her advances, she turned nasty and began remarking how I was the one who had lost out, for she had many young squires to attend to her needs."

Poppy's cheeks grew warm. "Goodness."

Beatrice waved a hand. "She talks a good game, but she would never turn on her patron. It's the one thing the women of our society don't do. But then if what your uncle says is true, then…"

Henry shook his head. "By that time we had arrived at her lodgings. I got out immediately and left, then from a short distance away, spied her welcoming a young man into her home."

Beatrice frowned. "This supports what your uncle told us, Miss Morton, about her patron being dead. Could she have taken another?"

"I don't know. But I overheard two women talking about the deaths and the letters, and it sounded like they were both involved. I don't think it has to do with the men at all," Poppy said.

"So who could have delivered the letters? How would one of these women have gotten into the homes of all these mistresses without being seen?" Henry asked.

"They would have had help. They could have sent a servant to each of the mistresses' homes with a note. Any servant would take it and leave it for their mistress to find," Poppy said.

"But how would the women even know where the mistresses lived? That requires knowledge. Are you certain it is just two women and not more?" Henry asked.

"Yes, there were just two. And of them called the other 'Mrs. F,'" Poppy said. "I think there were just the two women involved. It sounded like one had tricked the other into writing the letters, and she didn't think there would be murder involved. I think one might be innocent."

"They are most definitely not innocent. An innocent person would have gone straight to the magistrate," Henry said.

"What if they couldn't?" Beatrice asked.

"Why not?" Henry asked.

"Anytime a woman chooses to speak in public, she risks being laughed at and dismissed as a fool, a bluestocking, or a harlot. What if these women had their reputation to lose?" Beatrice said.

"It seems unlikely that there would be an entire group of

women behind this. And besides, the letters to the mistresses were all on the same sort of paper and in the same hand," Poppy said.

"Except for the one addressed to Miss Jones. Hers was different," Henry pointed out.

"It's a collemdrum," Beatrice said.

Poppy and Henry looked at her. "What?" Poppy said.

"A puzzle. It's like a riddle," Beatrice said.

"A conundrum," Henry said.

"Yes, of course. That is what I meant." Beatrice blushed.

They were interrupted at that moment by Fanny, who stomped into the room and announced, "You've got a visitor." She shut the door after the new arrival.

"Mother." Poppy stood.

"Hello, Poppy." Celeste walked in and gave her daughter a sunny smile.

"Hello Miss Grey," Beatrice said. "Please do sit down."

"Miss Hayes." Celeste nodded a greeting and her mouth quirked in a wry grin at Henry. "Constable. I would say it's a surprise to find you here, but it isn't."

"Miss Grey," Henry bowed.

"I have come to take Miss Morton away with me for the afternoon. If that is acceptable to you, Miss Hayes?"

Beatrice's face lifted and then settled into a gentle smile. "Of course."

"Most kind. And how is your detecting going? Have you narrowed down your list of suspects?" Celeste asked.

Henry frowned and crossed his arms.

Beatrice said, "It is odd. We think it is likely two women, one of whom is called 'Mrs. F.' But... not all the gentlemen of my friends are married, and not all of them have surnames beginning with the letter 'F.'"

Henry stiffened.

"Surely that makes your search easier," Celeste said.

"Or harder," Henry said irritably, "If you will excuse me, I have just recalled an errand I forgot. Good day." He took his hat, bowed, and quit the room.

"How odd." Celeste wondered. "Never mind. Come, Poppy, we have our own errand to run." She turned to Beatrice. "Don't worry, I shall return her in time for dinner."

Poppy just had time to don her bonnet, walking coat, and boots when Celeste pulled her outside to a waiting carriage. It looked smart, with a sleek shiny black body and a light cushioned interior. A driver sat on an upraised seat, managing two horses. Poppy's eyes widened. Not overly ostentatious, yet it struck her that this was a fashionable mode of transport.

"We'll take my barouche. It's Blackwood's really, but he lets me use it whenever I please." She stood by and helped Poppy into the carriage. "You'll have to excuse the fact that it's a year out of style. It threw a wheel last year and Blackwood's wife refused to ride in it again, so he had it fixed and gifted it to me. You don't mind riding in it?"

Poppy shook her head, tracing her gloved hand across the smooth cushions. It was very comfortable, and from her height, she felt at once on display and yet above, as though she could look down upon others. She felt very fashionable indeed. "Where are we going?"

"To a modiste. It's time I took you in hand. If I'm going to properly recognize you as my daughter, I need to have you look the part."

Poppy's eyes widened. She had thought so long and hard about how much she wanted to meet her mother, she had never thought about the situation of her mother's life, or how it might impact her own reputation, to be seen as the daughter of a mistress. Would a man still want her then, or assume she was of low morals due to her parentage?

"Unless you do not wish to come?" Celeste paused, seeing Poppy's expression.

"I do." Poppy looked her mother in the eye. "Very much."

"Good. Drive on," Celeste instructed the driver.

They took off. Poppy saw Ann crossing the road and raised her hand to wave. Ann stood by and watched them go, her face in shadow.

"Who was that?"

"An acquaintance of mine. We met at the races when she helped save Penelope from being trampled by horses."

"What?"

Poppy told her mother the tale.

"My, my. I'd never have expected such heroism from a woman so tiny. She looked like a little bird."

It was at a cheerful pace that the driver put the pair of chestnut horses through their paces, their hooves striking the ground with a clatter as the barouche drove down the city streets. They positively sped along, causing more than a few people to watch and admire them drive by.

In short order, they had arrived at 59 St James Street, outside a shop that bore many beautiful dresses on models in the window. The sign overhead read "Milliner and Dressmaker."

Poppy said, "It seemed like we traveled for no time at all. Couldn't we have walked?"

Celeste snorted. "And ruin our fine shoes? I will move in parks, ballrooms, and fine houses. But dragging my hem through the muck and whatever else lies on London's streets is not something I would willingly submit to."

Poppy answered that with a snort of her own, and Celeste opened the door. "Mrs. Lanchester?"

A woman of middle age, in a fine cloth patterned dress that enveloped her form well, peeked around a corner. "Hello. Ah, Miss Grey. And who is this?"

"My daughter, Poppy. She will need a new wardrobe. She has been living in the country where life is decidedly less...formal." She looked at Poppy's plain cloak and sturdy, thick boots, well suited for walking but less so for gracing the dancefloors of London assemblies.

The woman looked Poppy up and down, taking note of her

plain brown hair, pinned back into a messy bun, her tall height, and narrow shoulders, down to her small bosom and skinny waist. Poppy smoothed down the folds of her dress under the woman's gaze and wore a polite smile.

"Yes, I see. Just a moment and I will bring out the latest fabrics I have in stock." The woman disappeared around a corner as Celeste grandly took a chair and waited while Poppy stood, looking around.

"Poppy, I have been thinking."

"Yes?"

"I should like it if you called me Mama. Would that suit you?"

Poppy felt a small glow in her chest. "I should like that."

They spent an hour at the modiste, having Poppy measured for day dresses, walking dresses, evening dresses, and gowns, as well as hats, coats, spencers, pelisses, and cloaks. Then a trip to the glovemaker, shoemaker, and shop for ladies' undergarments, including stays, corsets, and stockings. After Celeste dragged her to a shop for ribbons, Poppy was ready to scream. "Please, Mama, no ribbons. I'm tired."

Celeste grinned. "Tired of shopping? Don't let anyone hear you say that. It is what some women live for."

"I'd rather pass."

Celeste looked at her. "What I don't understand is, where did the money go?"

"What do you mean?"

"For years, since you were born and I left you to be raised by your aunt and uncle, our agreement was that I would pay them regular installments for your upkeep. I assumed this meant you would be clothed, fed, and taken care of."

"I was. I am." Poppy felt a flutter of indignation in her chest.

"Then why are you dressed so simply? There is no art to your movements, your complexion is ordinary, and I detect no beauty in your dress. It's as if you were wearing second-hand clothes."

Poppy blushed. "The living for Hertford parish, as I understand it, is not worth much. Your kindness kept us in candles, meat, fresh vegetables, and food for the animals we keep. Your generosity kept us all in comfort."

Celeste frowned at the state of Poppy's dress, which had once been in fashion some five years previous, was secondhand from a neighbor, and had been washed so often it was a dingy gray. "You have lived plainly for far too long. That money was for you to be raised properly, not to give Mr. Greene more candles to read his sermons by. Have you any books?"

"Some. I can read, if that is what you're asking."

"A life without books is not worth living. Have you any books of your own?"

Poppy shook her head. "Very few. But I read my uncle's newspaper every week when he has finished it."

"Good God. Come, you are in dire need of fiction."

After dining together on a light luncheon at a cafe in town, Celeste took Poppy to a lending library in town, where she set up an account in Poppy's name and quickly loaned her copies of the latest poetry by Walter Scott, including *Lay of the Last Minstrel*, Alexander Pope's *Rape of the Lock* (Celeste's choice) and Voltaire's *Candide*, translated from the French.

Overwhelmed with books, the stockings and stays and so many boxes and bags of purchases, it was a tired but happy Poppy who returned to Beatrice's lodgings that evening, shortly before dinner with Beatrice and her aunt and uncle. If her relations disapproved of Celeste's lavishing gifts upon Poppy, they did not say so. Instead, her uncle advised her to put aside the poetry and instead read the classic histories, like Homer's *Iliad* and Dante's *Divine Comedy*. Poppy was less certain she would enjoy these, but the stories sounded interesting.

THE NEXT DAY, Poppy sat in the parlor drinking tea with Beatrice when Fanny handed Beatrice a letter and held out a parcel for Poppy, then let it fall to the floor. "This came for you."

Poppy stood. "You could be a bit more careful. What if it was glass?"

"What do I care? I've got better things to do than run around fetching your things all day." She walked off.

"That maid is very rude," Poppy said, picking up the small brown parcel from the floor. "Why don't you dismiss her?"

"I can't," Beatrice said, opening her letter. "Stephen hired her. Apparently, she is a charity case he took on, out of the goodness of his heart. Isn't that kind of him?"

"Very, but he cannot know how rude she is. And not just to me, she's rude to everyone," Poppy pointed out.

Beatrice gave a little shake of her head. "I know. But there's nothing I can do about it. I don't choose the servants, he did. Well, he and that wife of his."

"She chose your servants?"

"No, God no. Stephen's wife doesn't know I exist. Well, I hope not anyway. No, I mean together they choose the servants, and she was in a bad situation, so Stephen hired her. Apparently, she was in a spot of trouble, and being a scullery maid was the only work she could get, on account of her face."

"The pox scars, you mean?"

"Yes. She won't talk of them and I don't dare ask, but I'd guess she was pretty once. She won't meet anyone's eyes." She read the letter. "I've heard from Harriet. She told her gentleman about the murders happening and showed him the nasty letters she received. He's taken her out of the city for a few days to escape it all."

"That explains why we haven't seen her for a few days." Poppy opened up the brown paper. Inside was a pretty box and a note.

"Ooh, what's that? Is it from an admirer?"

"I don't know." Poppy opened the box. Inside was a hair comb with pink pearls on the top, and a dainty pink pearl necklace. Poppy held up the necklace.

"Oh, how pretty…" Beatrice said, "Who's it from?"

Poppy set down the necklace and read the note.

There is to be a ball tonight at Mr. Macallister's residence. I

*hope to see you there wearing this little gift when I introduce
you to your father.*

Love,

–C

"It's from my mother," Poppy said with a smile. She instantly
felt nervous. Her father. She had never thought of that. She had
always thought her father was dead, like her mum. Now she
would meet him in a few hours. What if he didn't like her?

Beatrice cut into her thoughts. "That's so nice. My mum
never did anything like that for me."

Poppy held out the box. "Want to try them on?"

Beatrice's eyes gleamed at the sight. "Oh yes."

THAT EVENING, POPPY wore a new dress that had arrived from the
modiste. Normally it would take some time for a dress to be
made, but this one had been hanging on a model in the shop
window and it required only a little alteration to be made to fit
Poppy perfectly.

As she slipped on the light pink gown of airy muslin, trimmed
with gold around the scoop bodice, sleeves, and high waist,
Poppy reflected it was a pleasure to wear a dress that had been
made for her and her alone. The dress matched her new necklace
perfectly, and with Beatrice's kind maid's help, her hair was
arranged in a pretty updo, with the pearl comb stuck at the
bottom of a clever bun. The effect was charming, and as Poppy
swirled in her new gown, she could not wait to show it off. This
wasn't a secondhand dress received from a neighbor or one that
her Aunt Rachel had altered to fit her growing height, this was
light, airy, delicate. Fashionable.

She couldn't get to the dance fast enough. It seemed that
parties, balls, dinners, and evenings at cards or the theater were
the common entertainments, and she and Beatrice were accepted
inside without a word, although Beatrice was pouting.

"What is wrong?" Poppy asked.

"Stephen was supposed to escort me. It was to be the first night we would spend together in days."

"Where is he?"

"How should I know?" Beatrice snapped, then shot her a look of apology. "I don't know. He sent a note saying he was detained and would meet me here. But now I don't see him anywhere."

Poppy looked around.

"Are you looking for your mum?"

"Yes, but I don't see her anywhere either."

The girls walked around the fine house, staying close together.

Poppy wished she had a fan. The room was getting warm with so many people inside.

Then Beatrice was asked to dance, and Poppy stood by watching the dancing when Tom came up beside her. "Hullo, Miss Morton."

"Tom, hello."

"Might I have the next dance?" He extended a hand.

She took it without a word, and he led her onto the dance floor. "Have you learned anything new about the girls and their gentlemen?"

"Not much. Only that Harriet and her gentleman are out of town, Penelope is still missing, and we have far too many suspects."

"Tell me about them."

"We know that whoever is doing it is targeting the circle of mistresses: Marie, Penelope, Justine, and now Mollie. We thought it was perhaps their gentlemen, but these men would have no reason to wish harm upon the women."

"My thoughts exactly. If a man wants to dispose of his mistress, all he has to do is let her go. Tell her it's over or have a servant do it. They'll get the message clear enough," he said.

She disliked the emotionless, factual way he spoke about it. As if ending a relationship built on affection—however physical— was something to be tossed away like a day-old newspaper.

However disapproved of by society, even mistresses deserved to be treated better than that.

"So who could have done it?" he asked.

"I think it was someone known to them. But I overheard two women talking and I'm convinced they are behind these crimes. One seemed to be blackmailing the other into it."

"Women? I should have known." He grinned. "That would explain the tone of the messages, telling the girls to leave their gentlemen."

She frowned at him. "Their voices were familiar, but I could not see who spoke. But it's odd."

"What is?"

"I too received a note. But it was not on fine paper or in a sealed letter, it was on my pillow when I returned from the Thorpes' a few days ago."

"You were threatened?" His smile disappeared.

"I had forgotten about it until now."

"You must take more care." He squeezed her hand.

"I will. But I wonder how the notes were delivered."

"By a servant, no doubt," he said.

"But how? And to all of the girls? How is that possible?"

"It bears thinking about, surely. But Poppy, there is something I must ask you. Will you come out for a bit of air?" he asked.

She nodded and allowed him to lead her out of the dance and to the balcony.

His plain clothes were gone. In place, he wore tight-fitting breeches, a light waistcoat, a dark overcoat, and a fussy white cravat. He'd raked his fingers through his hair and the result was rumpled curls that looked overly boyish and handsome. His brown eyes sought hers.

Poppy lifted her head up to the sky, feeling relief at the cool night air on her skin.

"You look beautiful," Tom said. "Are you cold? Here, let me." He rubbed his hands up and down her bare arms, trying to warm them. But his movements were too brisk and instead had the effect of moving her.

She stepped back. "Thank you, I am fine."

"I am not."

"What is wrong?" she asked.

"I am sick."

"You are? What's wrong, Tom?"

"You. You plague my every thought. At first, I thought that I was only doing this out of concern for the girls, but then I realized that I investigated so as to spend time with you."

"Tom," Poppy started.

"Poppy. Miss Morton. You are different than the other girls."

"I'm taller," she joked.

He smiled. "You are. But more than that. You are genteel, you have breeding, you are… a woman I would like to court."

"Court?"

"Yes. You like me, don't you?" he asked.

"Yes, of course, but…"

"I would like to pay my addresses to your uncle. Or your mother. Whoever I need to speak to, I will. I want to see you again. Formally. Not within the means of a murder investigation."

"Tom, I…"

"You think I am too lowly to be worthy of you. That I understand. But what if I told you that I wasn't low, not at all? That it was just an act, a persona I put on to make my way in the world?"

"As a pimp?" she asked.

He stopped as if she'd struck him.

"You procure women for men and sell them to the highest bidder. You offered me the same within days of our meeting."

"I am not what you think. I am the son of…" he mumbled.

Beatrice entered the balcony, out of breath. "Poppy, there you are. I've been looking for you everywhere. Come, come at once. I need you this instant."

"What is it?"

"Stephen is here, with his wife. She has seen me. She knows who I am. We must go at once," Beatrice said.

"Oh." Poppy realized she'd left her friend and employer alone during the dance. She felt slightly guilty.

They were soon joined on the balcony by Constable Dyngley, looking dark and handsome in a trim dark suit and snowy white cravat. "Poppy? I came to find you." His eyes landed on Tom holding Poppy's hand. "Is he bothering you?"

Tom said, "Oh, it's you. You're like a boil that won't go away."

"You would know, of course. A consequence of your profession, I imagine."

Tom shot Henry a nasty smile.

"Never mind that. Poppy we must leave. Now," Beatrice said.

"But I haven't seen my mother…"

"Blast your mother! She's already gone. You can see her tomorrow. I need you, now. As my companion." Beatrice's voice trembled and she clasped and unclasped her gloved hands, fretting.

"Okay. I'm here," Poppy said, tugging her hand free of Tom. "We can go."

"Thank you," Beatrice said, exiting the balcony.

"Poppy, will you stay?" Tom asked.

"I can't. She's my employer."

"You can say no to her," Tom said.

She shot him a smile. "She's also my friend and needs me." With a blink of surprise, she realized it was true. She did value Beatrice as a friend.

Tom stayed while Henry followed her out of the balcony and back into the ballroom. "Miss Morton, wait." He put a hand on her arm.

"What is it, Constable?" she asked, looking after Beatrice.

"Won't you call me Henry?" he asked.

"Is that really what you stopped me to ask?" She faced him.

"No." He reddened. "That man, Mr. Harris… I do not like

him."

"He asked if he might court me."

Henry laughed. "Court you? Be serious."

She stiffened, her face turning red as a tomato. "What is so funny about that? An honest man wishes to court me. Is that so wrong?"

Henry's laughs stopped. "You cannot accept him. He is beneath you. He is lower than dirt. He isn't honest at all, he is—"

"A pimp?"

"Exactly. You are above him in station, situation, manner, and intelligence. Don't throw yourself away on a miscreant like Mr. Tom Harris. He is nothing but a man of poor taste and obscure birth who makes a living preying on the innocence of others and ruining girls' reputations." He snickered cruelly. "As if you could accept him."

Poppy froze him with a stare. "You forget sir, my mother is a mistress. Tom is a pimp. He may be of obscure birth, but then so am I. We are not so different."

"You cannot mean to accept him."

She sniffed, almost shaking with anger. "I don't see why not. I imagine we will be very happy together."

"Poppy," he said, his hand tracing up her arm. "Don't lie to yourself."

She left, batting at her eyes before he could see her tears. As she hurried, she bumped into Beatrice's gentleman, Stephen. He stopped and bowed to her. "Miss Morton."

"Sir." She curtsied.

"Stephen, you know Miss Morton?" Stephen's companion turned around. It was Ann.

Stephen smiled thinly and said, "Are you acquainted with my wife, Mrs. Farrars?"

Poppy returned the smile. "Yes, we met at church."

Ann said, "Hello Miss Morton. You look very nice."

Poppy felt Stephen's eyes glance over her, taking in her fine dress and evening gloves, her pink pearl necklace, and matching hair comb. She blushed at the scrutiny and said, "My mother is in Town and wanted to treat me to some dresses more suited to a London assembly."

Ann and Stephen laughed politely. Ann asked, "But you are not leaving?"

Poppy looked from Stephen to his wife, feeling all too aware of her precarious position. "Yes, my good friend is unwell. I am seeing her home."

"That is very good of you. Who is it?" Ann asked.

"Oh, she's already stepped outside. I'm sorry, I shouldn't keep her waiting. Excuse me," Poppy said, curtsying and leaving. She looked back and saw Ann watching her, her arm linked through her husband's.

As Poppy stepped outside the main room, she realized she'd been clueless for a very long time. Beatrice's benefactor and gentleman, Stephen, was also the husband of her acquaintance Ann.

Ann Farrars, with an F.

"There you are, Poppy," Beatrice said in the main foyer, taking her arm. "Let's leave. I want to go home."

"Of course. I got waylaid by Mr. Farrars."

"Did you see that nasty wife of his? Such dark beady eyes. It's no wonder he looked elsewhere," Beatrice said.

"You said my mother had gone. Did you see her?"

"No. But while I was dancing I asked a couple if they had seen her, or Lord Blackwood, and they said we had just missed them. Apparently, they got into an argument and left. Lord Blackwood was most angry."

"Oh." Poppy bit the inside of her cheek as she climbed into a hackney coach after Beatrice and Mr. Parks. "I see."

Mr. Parks sat grimly inside the coach beside her, ignoring their conversation.

Poppy reflected that at times like this, she didn't mind the surly fellow, even if he came across as a bit rude and disapproving sometimes. As she observed Mr. Parks, she spied him watching

Beatrice steadily, his eyes never leaving her. It was good of the man to be so attentive to his employer's mistress, she thought. But the way his gaze raked along her body as if he were picturing her without her clothes, disquieted her. Could his attention be due to admiration rather than duty?

CHAPTER TWENTY-SEVEN

T HE NEXT MORNING a note was delivered to Poppy, shortly after she had risen and dressed for the day. It was in her mother's hand.

My dear girl,

Something came up tonight and I wasn't able to see you. I hope you'll give me another opportunity in the future. Do call on me tomorrow morning, we can break our fast together.

-C

Poppy folded the note back and shared its message with Beatrice, who said, "She must have sent this last night. What am I to do about Stephen's wife? Their surname is Farrars. Do you think she could be behind it?"

Poppy shook her head. "I doubt it. I've met her before at church and she seems like a good, kind woman. What business would she have in tormenting a bunch of women she's never met?"

"When you put it like that, it does seem farfetched," Beatrice admitted. "Are you leaving now?"

"Yes, I'll go. If that is all right with you?"

Beatrice nodded. "Yes. I... I hope you didn't think me too demanding last night. I didn't know what to do and I was so nervous she'd seen me. You understand."

Poppy nodded. "I do. I'll be back soon."

Beatrice smiled as she received a parcel from a servant. "What's this?"

She opened it and her face fell. "What do I want with pencils and paper?"

Poppy looked over them. "They're sketching materials. Is there a note?"

Beatrice picked it up. "There is. It's from Stephen. 'My sweet, I wish I could be with you. Sunday morning I will visit you. Draw me a pretty picture to look at while we are apart, Stephen.'"

"That's sweet of him," Poppy said.

"Is it?" Beatrice's expression was chagrined.

"What's wrong?"

"I…I can't draw. I never learned."

"Me neither. It can't be that hard, can it?" Poppy asked.

"I don't know." Beatrice's shoulders slumped. "At least I'll see him soon. Sunday morning is tomorrow. Will you go to church?"

Poppy nodded. Poppy took her leave and dressed in a new walking coat and hat with a dark purple ribbon and light gloves. She had no calling cards of her own but didn't think she'd need them as she was expected. To her surprise, Celeste lived only a few streets away, and so decided to walk.

She was hungry and so walked quickly. She knocked on the fine door and was admitted into a stiff, formal-looking townhouse with tall, creamy stone outside, facing the street.

Inside a clean foyer with smooth polished floors and attending footmen walking around, she stood quietly and shared how she had been invited to join Miss Grey that morning for breakfast and was shown into the parlor, where she sat on a comfortable sofa. The room had a lived-in look as if the occupants had decided to make the room pleasant and cozy, rather than opt for the latest styles and fashions. The result was that some of the chairs and furniture were mismatched, but the scuffed carpets looked worn with use, the fireplace was well tended and the room itself was clean, bright, and airy, with large windows letting the morning sunlight in.

She waited until a scream rent the air. She ran, stumbled out of the room, and bumped into a footman. "Did you hear that?" she asked.

She followed him up a set of stairs, holding her skirts above her feet as she hurried to avoid tripping, and dashed after him. She turned right at the top of the stairs and headed down a corridor, where a maid backed away from an open doorway and fell back to the floor. The footman and Poppy reached her at the same time as he asked, "What's happened?"

The maid was speechless and pointed, her mouth opening and closing like a fish. Poppy hurried through the door to find herself inside a bedchamber.

Inside was a man, half-dressed, leaning over a woman's body. "Wake up, my God, wake up. Please," he begged.

"What has happened?" Poppy demanded.

He turned around. "Who are you?"

Poppy gaped at seeing him bare-chested, and a stranger at that. He looked to be about fifty, with hair on his upper chest and a middle that had turned to fat. His nose was long, and he had a head full of silver hair that was going white at the temples.

"I say again, who are you? Are you a nurse?"

"No."

The bedclothes were strewn around as if its occupants had tussled or had recently engaged in very energetic lovemaking, and clothes lay discarded on the floor. But as Poppy's eyes took in the room, her gaze traveled up from the floor to the bed, where the half-nude body of Celeste lay, staring up at her.

"Mama!" Poppy ran to her, ignoring the fact that her mother lay bare-chested. Her skin was cold, too cold for a person to be healthy and well. Poppy pressed her gloved hands against her mother's head, but Celeste's eyes stared straight ahead. They were bulging and bloodshot, and her mouth was open in a silent scream.

Poppy stepped back and called, "Someone help!" She ran out of the room to the footman and maid. "Call a doctor. Get help, please!" she cried and ran back into the room.

The man sat on the bed, trying to shake her by the shoulders. "Celeste, please, wake up. Wake up. Don't leave me." His voice shook.

Poppy stood by and stepped into a puddle. She looked down. There on the floor at her feet lay an overturned wine bottle and a glass. The bottle rolled at her foot's touch and spilled a few drops of red wine on the floor. Poppy stepped back. "Is she…?"

"I don't know. God help me." The man stiffened. "What is that?"

Poppy looked closer. A silken neck scarf was tied tight around her neck. Poppy gasped at the sight. She tore the neck scarf away from Celeste's neck, but the marks of strangulation were unavoidable. Dark angry red and purple marks marred the pale delicate skin of Celeste's neck, and her jeweled necklace tugged against Poppy's gloves as she pulled the scarf out completely from where it was wound tightly around her mother's neck.

"Was this….?" she asked.

"It wasn't me. I don't know how that got there," he said. "Is a doctor coming?"

"I've called for one." She wrung her hands, unsure what to do. "Is she breathing?"

He touched her neck. "No. She's ice cold. I think she's…" His voice shook and he snatched his hand back. "I don't understand."

Poppy put a hand beneath Celeste's nose, but there was no breath. No warmth. She stood back and fretted. The way Celeste's eyes stared straight ahead, looking at nothing, chilled Poppy's blood.

The man leaned forward on his knees, uncaring about his state of semi-dress. He touched Celeste's cheek gently with his hand. "She's dead." His voice choked. His face screwed up and he clutched a pillow to his chest.

Poppy collapsed to the floor, landing near the puddle of wine.

She crab-walked backward, bumping into a side table.

"Girl, are you all right?" The man got up and walked around the bed, crossing to her. He held out a hand. "Who are you? What are you doing here?"

"My name is Poppy Morton." Her chin trembled and her eyes turned glassy. She accepted his hand as he helped her up, and they stood together looking down at Celeste's body.

Poppy moved forward and raised the bedding so it covered Celeste's bare chest. But even coming that close to her mother's body sent chills through her, and she shivered.

"We were going to break our fast together." The words sounded dull in her ears.

The man was silent. They did not wait long, but Poppy could not say how long she and the man stood there, looking at Celeste's body. The woman was icy cold to the touch. There was nothing either of them could do, and they both knew it. Hot tears rolled down Poppy's cheeks, and she wiped her face with her gloved hands. She sniffed and her throat felt tight.

She hardly noticed when the servants brought in a doctor, who came and pronounced her mother dead. The doctor quit the room, just as Constable Dyngley entered and bowed. "Miss Morton."

"Constable," she said, wiping her cheeks. "What are you doing here?"

"I was coming to call on Miss Grey when I heard the commotion and was brought up here." He surveyed Celeste's body. "I am sorry."

Poppy shook her head, unable to offer him a polite smile she usually reserved for him. "Thank you, I—"

"What is this?" Henry moved past her. He went to Celeste's body and held up the silken tie. "What is this doing here?"

"It was around her neck when I came in," Poppy said.

Henry looked closely at Celeste's neck. Angry red and purple lines still were present. "This woman was strangled. The marks on her neck and the state of her eyes, her expression, it is clear she died from lack of air." He turned toward the shirtless man standing there. "Who are you?"

The man looked affronted. "I am Blackwood. Celeste is my… was my…" He took a deep breath and look around for a chair. When he found one, he sank into it and looked at Celeste's body with bloodshot eyes. "I do not know what happened. We spent the night together and had a drink, then fell asleep. When I woke up she was cold to the touch, and then I saw her like that, with the tie around her neck." He shuddered. "You look familiar. Who are you?"

"Constable Dyngley. Miss Grey and I were acquainted."

"How?"

"Through her daughter, Miss Morton." Henry nodded to Poppy.

The man blinked at her. "You? You're her daughter?"

Poppy nodded.

The man raked his fingers through his hair. "I need to think." He stood up and sat down again. "I don't understand. How did the tie get around her neck?"

Henry cleared his throat. "Perhaps we might speak in private, Mr. Blackwood."

"Lord Blackwood. Everyone knows me." He glanced at Poppy. "I think that would be best."

"She was my mother. Why are you acting as if I am a stranger?" she asked.

"This is no place for a young woman," Blackwood said.

Henry coughed politely. "I need to ask Lord Blackwood some questions which are indelicate for feminine ears. Would you excuse us, Miss Morton?"

Poppy's face turned pink, and she felt her hands curl into fists. Celeste was her mother, why was she being asked to step aside? Why was Henry being so damned formal? But she knew he must have a reason behind his question, and so she shot him a hard look. "Very well. I shall wait outside."

She gave her mother a fleeting look, felt her eyes water and she stepped from the room.

But quietly she tiptoed back and hung just outside, leaning against the wall. She could hear the men well.

"I take it you and Miss Grey were lovers," Henry said.

"We had an understanding," Blackwood said. "What business of this is yours? You're a constable. Have you any say in this city? You don't sound like you're from London."

"I'm not. But I am investigating a series of murders in the city."

"Murder? What makes you think this was murder?"

Henry paused. "Were you and Miss Grey engaged in a love game? With ties?"

"No. Definitely not," Blackwood responded immediately, his voice hard.

"Then how did the tie get around her neck?"

"I don't know," Blackwood said. "You can't think I had something to do with this."

"I find it odd that you went to bed with your mistress and woke up with a corpse. Did your love game take a wrong turn?"

"I beg your pardon." Blackwood sputtered. "We played no such game. I would never—"

"Then how do you explain it?"

"You can hardly think I had anything to do with her death when I am here. If I had killed her, wouldn't I have left, to avoid suspicion?"

"Not necessarily. How do you think she died?" Henry asked.

"She must have wound it around herself and... Maybe it was tied too tight. I don't know." Blackwood sounded exasperated.

"How do you think it got there? Why would she have put it on herself? Did she often wear ties to bed?"

"No. She didn't. We didn't... She wasn't that sort of woman."

"How long have you two known each other?" Henry asked.

"Some twenty years past. Why?"

"It seems odd that a man who knew a woman for twenty years would suddenly wake up and find her dead with a tie around her neck, and have no knowledge of it."

"And yet that is the case. I do not know how it ended up there, or what she was doing."

"Tell me what you did last night," Henry said.

The man coughed. "We went to the ball. We came back home—"

"I heard you had an argument there. People were talking about it. What was that about?"

"Nothing to concern you," Blackwood said.

"I wish to know."

"Damn your impudence." Blackwood called out, "Servant!"

A footman hurried past Poppy and stood at the door.

"Fetch me a magistrate. This man is an upstart."

"The magistrate has given me license to investigate this matter," Henry said.

"There is no matter. My mistress is dead. Cannot you see that?"

"I can, and it seems she died in a most suspicious manner. What did you argue about at the ball?"

Poppy breathed in and listened as the footman hurried away down the hall.

"She told me some unexpected news, and we left."

"You were angry with her," Henry pressed.

"I was. We argued and decided to leave rather than cause a scene. There, are you satisfied?" Blackwood asked.

"Not quite. What was the news?"

"It is none of your business. It was a private matter. We left and returned here, had dinner, shared a bottle of wine, and fell asleep, then I woke up as you see."

"You have no idea how this happened?"

"None."

Poppy heard footsteps as Henry walked around the room. She heard the clink of a bottle against the floor as Henry said, "This was the wine you drank?"

"Yes."

There was a pause, when Henry said, "Did you notice that this wine is off?"

"What do you mean? It tasted fine to me."

Henry's footsteps came closer. "Can you smell this?"

"It smells like red wine. Maybe a bit sweet. Celeste commented it was."

"Who was the servant who brought it up?"

"There was no servant, it was already on her dresser when we walked in, with the two glasses."

"You just drank wine without questioning where it came from?"

"I own this house. Why shouldn't I assume the wine is fine?" Blackwood retorted.

"You don't think it odd there was a bottle of wine just waiting for you?"

"No. Some servants wait for orders and others are thoughtful. The best ones know when we will be hungry and have food prepared. When we are tired, and the bed is turned down and hot bricks put between the sheets. I assumed that this was a servant being intuitive. That's no crime."

"No, it is not," Henry said.

"What are you doing?"

"I'm smelling her breath. It smells like wine. Too sweet."

At that moment Poppy saw two footmen leading the magistrate down the corridor. He looked stern but took note of his surroundings. He peered at Poppy as if trying to place her but could not recall her. He followed the footmen into the room. "What's all this, then?"

"Ah. You are the magistrate?"

"Yes, and I don't like being called away early in the morning."

"Magistrate Tomlinson, I was calling on Miss Grey when I encountered this," Henry said.

"Tell me what's happened."

Poppy listened as Blackwood repeated his story.

The magistrate hemmed and harrumphed as Dyngley pointed

out the silken tie, the strangulation marks, and the sweetened wine. "What think you, constable?" Magistrate Tomlinson asked.

"I suspect this wine was drugged," Henry said.

Poppy breathed in. Drugged?

"For what purpose?" the magistrate asked.

"If Lord Blackwood is telling the truth, then it would appear that the wine was drugged to incapacitate them both."

"But why?"

"This is quite a wealthy neighborhood. Was it robbery?" Magistrate Tomlinson asked.

"Nothing appears to be disturbed," Henry said. "There on the dresser are Miss Grey's personal effects, but nothing appears to have been touched aside from the bedding and her person. Lord Blackwood, can you identify if anything seems amiss?"

"Aside from Celeste? No. It is as he says, magistrate. Nothing has been tampered with."

"Hmmm. a nasty crime. My condolences, your lordship. Nothing for it now. Poor lady. She's a pretty one," Magistrate Tomlinson said.

"Magistrate, I believe this to be the latest in the series of murders we have seen."

"What? Oh yes. Those. Mistresses, weren't they? Actresses?"

"Celeste was no actress," Blackwood said.

"I thought all mistresses were. Part of their job, eh?" the magistrate said.

"Sir," Henry started.

"Aye, I know. Pardon, your lordship. You have no idea who might have done this, do you? Anyone who wanted to hurt her? Or yourself?" the magistrate asked.

"No. No one. That we had an understanding was fairly common knowledge."

"What about your wife?" Henry asked.

"My wife has not shared my bed in years. I think to her Celeste was a blessing. She never wanted children." Blackwood said with a trace of bitterness. "You say someone is going around killing women?"

"We think so. Many young girls have been receiving nasty letters and shortly after, have been attacked. Did Miss Grey receive any such letters?" Henry asked.

"No, none. She would have told me if she had."

"May I look through her belongings to see?"

"You don't believe me?" Blackwood asked.

"It's not that. Many of the women felt it necessary to keep the letters secret, rather than ask for help."

"Be my guest."

Henry rifled through some drawers and boxes and said a minute later, "Nothing. No letters."

"I wouldn't think so." To the magistrate, Blackwood asked, "What do I do now? I'll need to arrange a funeral, and..." He sounded haggard.

"Your steward will help you with that, I'm certain," Henry said.

"Yes. of course. Forgive me gentlemen, but I must go, I have a lot to do. You will excuse me. Unless you suspect me of doing this?"

"No, course not. Wouldn't dream of it, your lordship," Magistrate Tomlinson said.

The men walked out, right past Poppy standing outside the door, not looking back. As Poppy held her breath and tried not to make a sound, she waited quietly for them to leave her sight. Once they disappeared and headed down the stairs, her shoulders slumped. Her mother was dead, and the killer had struck again, robbing her of the mother she'd never known. She would find this killer if it was the last thing she did. Even if it endangered her own life. After the kindness her mother had shown her in their brief time together, Poppy owed her that.

CHAPTER TWENTY-EIGHT

POPPY DIDN'T REMEMBER how she got back to Beatrice's apartment. She recalled vaguely that she stood in Beatrice's parlor, tears running down her face, and servants asking her what was wrong. She told Beatrice everything, vaguely aware of a few servants standing around watching, listening, taking down every detail of her story to repeat to others. Her awareness was forgotten as Beatrice embraced her in a hug, ordered a cup of tea, and sent someone out immediately for her aunt and uncle. Poppy didn't remember much of that day, only that she sat and received callers, and told her aunt and uncle when they came.

THAT EVENING IN the London gazette there was a notice:

> *This editor regrets to share the news that a patron of London society, Miss Celeste Grey, died this last Sunday. She will be fondly remembered as "the Grace" who charmed us all with her wit, laughter, and subtle digs at society's buffoons. Our little Town has lost a jewel and she will be greatly missed. Mourners may pay their respects at her address on Orchard Street on Tuesday at twelve noon, to be followed by a procession to St Botolph's church.*

On Tuesday, Poppy donned her drabbest, darkest frock, a deep purple dress that was a bit faded and worn, but looked suitably dull, pulled on her gray walking coat, bonnet, and gloves, and was joined by Beatrice and Mr. Parks, and made her way to her mother's apartment. To her surprise, there was a queue that led out the main door and down the walk. Poppy blinked.

"Was your mother very popular?" Beatrice asked. "There are a lot of people here."

"I don't know," Poppy admitted, looking around. "I don't recognize anyone."

They waited in the queue until they were allowed inside, and Poppy was hailed by her Aunt Rachel at the front.

"Go on, we'll see you afterward," Beatrice told her.

Poppy nodded and walked up and joined her aunt and uncle. Her uncle wasn't in his clerical suit, but she didn't mind. They were both dressed somberly, and her aunt looked her over. "Oh Poppy, you should be in mourning clothes." She shot a look at Poppy's uncle and said, "This will do for now, but we'll have to purchase you some black bombazine or at least some crepe. As her daughter, you'll have to wear mourning attire for at least six months."

Poppy looked around. The room they stood in was large, like a large banquet room, except the table and chairs had been removed. An elm coffin sat in the center of the room draped with black cloth, and all the windows and mirrors in the place had been covered with black. The effect was somber and slightly chilling, but the room was warm from so many people and the air was stuffy with the strong scent of flowers.

Poppy observed many people in fine clothes, talking and milling about, accepting small glasses of wine, and biscuits. Poppy wandered beside her aunt and uncle, listening to other people's conversations.

"Such a tragedy," said one, "and she was not yet fifty."

"She looked so young," said another. "How did it happen?"

"I heard she was in debt to her creditors and took her own life."

"You wouldn't think so from the service here," a lady responded. "Could Blackwood have left her, and she died from heartbreak?"

"With this funeral? Not a chance. A man doesn't put on all this for a woman he stopped loving."

Poppy turned away and couldn't listen anymore. The air felt stifling, and she felt tight in her stays. As she stood nearer the coffin, the scent of the flowers was overpowering but didn't quite mask the sickeningly sweet, putrid odor that leaked from Celeste's resting place.

The coffin was closed, for which Poppy was grateful, but she needed air. She moved through the crowd and down the hall, into another room, for quiet. It was dark and in shadow, and she moved toward one of the few windows where the black drape had fallen, and she drank in the sunlight. She pushed open the window slightly and stood, breathing and taking in gulps of air, when a voice said, "They're peacocks, all of them."

Poppy whirled around. It was Lord Blackwood.

He came toward her, dressed in a black suit that fitted him well, down to the dark breeches and fine shoes that gleamed with polish. He stood beside her and opened the window wide, letting in some fresh air. He closed his eyes and breathed in, as did Poppy.

When she opened her eyes, he was looking at her. "I didn't expect to see you again, after the other morning. I rather suspect you didn't expect to see me again either."

"Not fully clothed," she quipped.

He threw his head back and laughed, a warm sound. "That's like something Celeste would say." His smile fell as he took in the sight of her. "God, it's like looking right at her." His shoulders slumped. He gave his head a little shake, as if at war with himself, and then he straightened his shoulders, raised his head, and met her eyes. "I don't believe we've been formally introduced. I am Blackwood."

"Poppy Morton." She curtsied, and he bowed.

"You knew Miss Grey," he said.

"She is…" Poppy looked down. "She was my mother."

"How do you know this?"

Poppy began to tell him of her life, growing up in Hertford with her aunt and uncle. She spoke of never having met her mother, but of finding their family tree and her name crossed out, and of her journey to London to find her. Of finally meeting her, and looking for her at the ball, then at breakfast.

"Where you found me in a state of undress and her dead." He paled. "I am sorry you had to see that. That is no sight for a young lady."

It wasn't the first dead body she'd seen. It just hurt the most.

"What will happen now?" she asked.

"You mean today?"

"I guess so. Who are all those people?" she asked.

"Vultures, magpies, and peacocks, mostly. People love to come and gawk at a death. Especially of a woman so popular as Celeste. She had many acquaintances but few real friends."

"But there are so many people here. The queue to get in was out the door."

He smiled. "That's not surprising. Celeste held certain notoriety in society, due to our relationship." He looked at her. "What has your mother told you about our connection?"

She looked him in the eyes. His expression looked harried, tired, weary but kind. She spoke honestly. "I learned that your relationship was romantic but transactional a few months ago."

He had the grace to blush.

"I didn't care."

He looked at her, taking in the tilt of her angular face, her narrow waist, and her skinny form. "She was my mistress."

"I know."

"I loved her, in my way. As much as I could. As much as any man could." He walked away from her then and turned, eyeing her clothes with an air of suspicion. "What is it you want? Money?"

"No. I came to London to find her. I had no idea you even

existed until she told me a few days ago."

He breathed in and pinched the bridge of his nose.

"I know she was going to tell you of my existence, soon. Before she died. I'd hoped to see her at the McAllisters' the other night, but I heard you two quarreled and left early." She dug her shoe into a sore spot on the aged rug that covered the floor. "Was it about me? Did you not…" Her throat felt tight. She could hardly speak. "I don't want anything. I just wanted to know her. To get to know her. My aunt and uncle kept her a secret from me for so long, I just wanted to meet her."

"Miss Morton," he began, when a servant entered the room.

"Lord Blackwood, there are guests wishing to speak to you in the parlor."

"Damn." He muttered. "Forgive me, Miss Morton, but I must see to my guests. Excuse me." He bowed and left the room.

Poppy returned to her aunt and uncle in the parlor and met with Beatrice and Mr. Parks. Then the funeral furnisher announced the procession to the church was about to begin, and Poppy, along with her aunt and uncle, joined the queue. Everyone stood outside as Lord Blackwood and a series of black-suited gentlemen hoisted the coffin, draped in black, and carried it on their shoulders out of the house.

Poppy joined the crowd of onlookers outside as the men loaded the coffin into a black hearse with a black-suited driver on top, who held the reins of two pitch black horses with startling, large black plumed headdresses. "My word," Aunt Rachel said in her ear, "he spared no expense, did he?"

"He loved her, I think," she replied. They watched as the men, led by Lord Blackwood, began a slow but steady walk behind the hearse, down the road to the church. It was only but some three streets away, but the procession was stately and formal. It was the grandest funeral procession Poppy had ever seen, and she felt warmth in her heart to see her mother treated so well. She swallowed and wiped at her eyes.

The walk to the church was relatively brief, and while they

did not go inside, they followed the black plumed horses and hearse to the churchyard, where the coffin was unloaded and gently laid in a large hole in the back of the yard. There was no headstone, not yet. The clergyman looked very formal in his robes and stole, and said a few words.

"That'll cost a pretty penny," Aunt Rachel said, "but then this is no ordinary funeral."

"What do you mean?"

"My dear, every aspect of today's event comes at a cost. That little fussy man in clerical garb saying a few words over your mother's grave? He'll have cost at least one pound. The hearse, the horses, the coffin, the procession, it all costs money. The black drapery inside the house must have cost a few shillings, not to mention the funeral furnisher. And all this, for a mistress. Lord Blackwood must have cared for her very much." She wiped away a tear and sniffed, "It is what Celeste would have wanted."

"I'm glad we'll be going home soon," her uncle said, "I don't like being away from the parish for so long."

"Home?" Poppy echoed.

"Yes. Now that your mother has passed away, there is no more reason for you to stay."

"Reginald. That's my sister you're talking about. Have a care," Aunt Rachel said, her voice tight.

Poppy's uncle tugged at his collar. "What I mean to say is, it's very sad of course, but Poppy, you must understand. You have no more connections here. I understood that Celeste would look after you while you were in Town, but with her gone, there is no one here for that purpose."

"I mean to stay here, Uncle," Poppy said.

"You may stay another day or two to conclude your dealings with Miss Hayes," he said generously, "but then you must come home. The garden needs tending and so do the chickens, as well as—"

"I am a companion," Poppy snapped, "And my mother has just died. So please forgive me if I am rude. But, Uncle, I mean to stay. I did not wish to leave Hertfordshire to escape feeding the chickens. I came to find my mother and I did, but do not ask me to return to a situation where I had no worth at all and expect me to blindly go along with it."

"You are helping no one here. At least in Hertford—" he started.

"That is your plan. Not mine," Poppy said, her voice low.

They went head-to-head and faced each other. Poppy stared into her uncle's eyes, never more feeling distant from him than at that moment. He didn't understand, she could see that now. He would never understand. He had never had to depend on the kindness and generosity of others to survive. He had always had the option to work and make his way in the world, so why was it so difficult to comprehend that she might wish to do the same?

"We will talk later when you are less emotional," her uncle declared and crossed his arms.

Poppy wanted to kick him. Being emotional had nothing to do with her logic or reasoning. She turned and walked away, mixing in the crowd.

A few minutes later her aunt found her. "I love your uncle, but he does say the wrong thing sometimes. Don't take what he said to heart. He's trying to find a way to reconcile what he thinks a young lady should do with what he knows of you."

"That I am reckless, willful, and show an alarming degree of independence, which he finds hard to forgive?" Poppy's words were bitter.

"All of that and more. It is why he loves you so."

Poppy glanced at her aunt.

"He would not have you any other way, Poppy. We Morton women never were meek misses, and I think he would find life decidedly more dull if we were. You go your own way, and he'll follow."

"He thinks of me as a little girl."

"He always will. He will always remember you as the blonde-haired babe that wanted to catch frogs in the pond near town."

She smiled and gave a little breath. "I do not know this Lord Blackwood, but I'm mighty grateful he went to all this trouble. If Celeste were alive and well, she would be pleased."

Poppy and her aunt were silent when Petunia and John Dyngley walked by and stopped. "Miss Morton, Mrs. Greene. So sorry for your loss."

The ladies nodded as they walked by, leaving the churchyard. "I never thought they would show up," Poppy said.

"I agree. I would've thought this would be too low for them to condescend. But they do you a great honor in attending, Poppy. Especially as they knew of Celeste's occupation. They came here to show you the respect they have for you. You should take that as a compliment, I say," Aunt Rachel said.

But Poppy felt angry. She felt cheated that her mother had been taken away from her so soon. She felt annoyed that she had spent more time wondering about Henry and whether he fancied her than solving this mystery and looking for her own mother. But most of all, she felt angry with herself, for not looking sooner for the woman she'd barely known.

Her thinly gloved hands curled into fists. She had to find this killer. She'd let them get away with too much. Every moment she spent trying on pretty dresses and escorting Beatrice around London was a minute wasted when she could be finding a killer.

"I recognize that look," her aunt said.

"What look?" Poppy asked.

"You look like you need something useful to do. Some useful employment. Is your life as a companion not challenging?" Aunt Rachel asked.

Poppy shrugged. "It can be very diverting at times."

"Are you trying to convince yourself or me?" Her aunt asked.

"Is it so obvious?"

"A little. But only because I know you. Poppy, there's no shame in coming home. You've proven your independence."

"I like being out in the world. Making a wage. Beatrice depends on me and we're friends."

"I know you are. But… Well." She paused. "Just because we are away from the parish does not mean we stop our Christian charity. I don't suppose you could help me tomorrow? I'm heading to the Newgate prison to visit the prisoners."

"You are?" Poppy inwardly shuddered at the idea.

"Yes, there's good work to be had at all walks of life. Those poor souls could use some spiritual comfort," her aunt said.

"Will it be safe?"

"With the guards watching my every move? Of course. Reginald will accompany me anyway, but… You could come with me as well. It would be good to have you along."

"All right. I will."

With the funeral ended and her mother laid to rest, Beatrice was happy to see Poppy given a task, even if it was to visit a prison. Beatrice had wrinkled her nose at the invitation to join them but wished them well.

THE FOLLOWING DAY, Poppy, still dressed in her drab dark gown, joined her aunt and uncle at their lodgings and then took a hackney together to the prison. Upon explaining their purpose, they were admitted and accompanied by prison guards.

The walls were dark, and the ground was damp. The air smelled of urine, shit, and the overwhelming odor of unwashed bodies and rotten straw. Poppy could barely breathe in the dirty air. She coughed and tried not to gag.

While Aunt Rachel went to the first cell they passed, Poppy struck up a conversation with the guard watching over them. An older man surveyed them and said, "This your first time?"

Poppy nodded.

"It's good of your parents to bring you along. I wouldn't myself, but seeing the unfortunates is a good lesson for any girl."

Poppy swallowed, wondering how he could tolerate the smell. "Do you see many people coming to visit the prisoners?"

"Aye, we get some society types coming in, aside from the families when they can afford it. It's no place to be."

"We get some like you." A prisoner spat on the ground. "Looking to save our souls when all we want is some gin or bread. Got any gin?"

"No."

"We get some pretty girls in here, but they don't stay pretty long. Not once the men have their way," an older woman croaked.

An idea came to Poppy. "I say, do you have a Frances in here?"

"I'll be your Frances if you want." The woman gave her a toothy grin.

"No, I mean a person. A prostitute."

"There's a lot of whores here, love. No virgins in prison," the prisoner said.

"She was a mistress who cheated on her benefactor, and he threw her out on the street. Frances Landry," Poppy said.

The old woman scratched her head. "I dunno."

"I heard she was here."

"She was here," the guard said.

Poppy turned around. "She was? Is she still?"

"No. Left with that man of hers."

"Who was that?

"Harris."

Poppy stopped. Not Tom. Had she been wrong about him from the start?

"Frances met Harris and they were a pair. Looked after each other. Even when the pox took away her looks, he didn't let anyone touch her. He always did look after the ladies. Just as well, she'd have given all the men the clap otherwise." He grinned. "Though some 'round here wouldn't care about that."

Poppy repressed a shudder. "Is she here? Could I speak with her?"

He shook his head. "She's long gone. Got out not six weeks ago."

"Do you know what happened to her?" Poppy asked.

"Well, I heard that as soon as she gets out, Frances finds work for some lady, and then once she's out, she gets him a job too. Think she works as a charwoman or scullery maid. It's all she's good for now."

"Pray, do you happen to know what she looks like?"

"Frances? Shorter than you, blonde hair. She was always frowning, but no woman ever liked being here. She was real pretty when she first come, but the disease took care of that, she's not fit to be seen now. Her face is all scarred."

"And Mr. Harris? What about him?"

The jailkeeper scratched his chin. "He's a nobody. What do you want with him?"

"Who does he work for?"

The man shrugged. "I don't know. Could be anyone. You ask a lot of questions."

Poppy gave him a sweet smile.

"Never mind. It's good of you and your parents to come by. We used to get genteel women come 'round, but not anymore." He paused. "Matter of fact, Frances used to get a visitor now and then. Real often now that I think of it. But then once Frances got out, she stopped coming. Funny thing, that."

"Who was the visitor?"

"Some genteel lady. Dark hair. I think her name was Merars. Meerars? Beerars? No wait, that's not it. We always called her Mrs. F."

Poppy's blood ran cold.

CHAPTER TWENTY-NINE

POPPY PAID A visit to Mollie the following day, to offer her an invitation to tea. Mollie said, "I may be busy, I may not. We'll see."

"We would love to have you join us."

Mollie fanned herself and looked bored. "Was there anything else?"

"I think I know who is behind this. You haven't received any more notes, have you?"

"No. My dear Aylesbury is worried sick since the vicious attack on me. He won't let me out of his sight, the dear thing," Mollie said with pride. "Actually, you're friends with that constable, aren't you? Dingme?"

"Dyngley, you mean. Constable Dyngley," Poppy said.

"Yes, that's him. He looks posh. Would he happen to know Lord Ernest Carr?"

"I don't know. Who is he?"

"Just the gentleman of an old friend of mine. I've tried calling on him in Wimpole Street but whenever I call, he's not in. Do you think that constable could speak to him?"

Poppy shrugged. "I will ask, but if he does not know the man, there's little I can do."

"That's all right. I reckon one good word in his ear will do," Mollie said, shutting the door in her face.

THE FOLLOWING DAY, Beatrice and Poppy hosted an afternoon tea party. It was to be a large gathering. She had invited her aunt and uncle, Constable Dyngley, his brother John and Petunia, as well as Mollie, Harriet, and Magistrate Tomlinson, in addition to Tom, Mr. Parks, Stephen Farrars, and his wife, Ann. Poppy had also sent an invitation to Penelope's address, in the hopes she might return, and one to a certain gentleman.

Beatrice had dressed in a light-yellow muslin dress, suitable for the afternoon. She and Poppy had sent a servant out to buy many cakes and sweet tarts for the group, along with tea. Beatrice fussed around the parlor, straightening cushions and moving chairs. But by the early afternoon, the sun disappeared, and the skies grew dark and gray.

"Oh no, it's going to rain. Do you think they'll still come?"

"I hope so." Poppy smoothed down the folds of her dull black dress as she stood by the window. Then the sour-faced maid held open the door and let in the first guest.

Poppy's Aunt Rachel and her uncle entered the room. "My, you've gone to some trouble. And so many chairs. Tell me, Poppy, are you expecting a large party?"

"Something like that."

Beatrice swiftly curtsied hello and pulled the bell pull for a servant. She ordered tea and gestured to the sofa, encouraging them to sit.

One by one they came. Stephen came with Ann on his arm, looking around. He pointedly did not look at Beatrice but nodded hello to Poppy and Mr. Parks, who stood like a quiet sentinel behind her. The Dyngleys also came, and Mollie was the final addition, who took a seat by Beatrice. Once everyone was sitting with tea and a plate holding a plum tart or sweet biscuit, Poppy looked up. One by one, the guests quieted and looked at her.

"I expect you're all wondering why we've called you all here. The reason is that the murders which have happened involve everyone here, and I mean to reveal who did it."

The magistrate shot to his feet. "What are you saying, girl?"

"This is nonsense. Utter nonsense. I'm leaving." John Dyngley shot to his feet.

"Don't be a fool, John. You don't want to miss the entertainment, do you? This is better than a play," Petunia said.

Ann looked at Poppy. "I've heard about these attacks. Do you really know who is behind them?"

"Better than that, I can show you. Look around. The killer is in this room."

People looked around askance as if the murderer was hiding behind some curtains.

"You are joking. You are after a bit of drama and mean to poke fun at us," Stephen said.

"The killer is one of us, and I mean to show it. If you'll forgive me, I'd like to tell you a story," Poppy said.

The two maids, Nancy, and sour-faced Fanny, moved to leave when Poppy held up a hand. "Oh, please stay. We'll need your help in a minute." She turned to the group. "It starts with mistresses. Two, in fact. Mollie and Frances got into an awful argument. When Mollie teased Frances about her gentleman, Frances revealed she'd broken one of the vows of mistresses, to never cheat on their patron. What started with an insult ended with Frances being thrown out by her gentleman, into the street. For all we know, she was never heard from again."

"That's right," Mollie said. "I heard she caught the pox."

"She landed in Newgate Prison."

"Charming story, but what has this to do with us?" Stephen asked.

"I'm getting there," Poppy said, "I had only recently joined Miss Hayes as her companion when I met her circle of acquaintances in the same trade and began to learn of their situation."

"What is that?" Petunia asked.

"The letters. Someone has been writing nasty letters to them, one by one, and killing them."

People looked around the room.

"It started with Marie, but in my first few days here I learned that not only Marie, but also Harriet, Justine, Penelope, and Beatrice all received the notes. Each of them held nasty messages telling them to leave their gentlemen, or else face the consequences."

"Don't forget me," Mollie said, sitting up straight in her chair. "I got one too."

"Yes, you did. But yours was different." Poppy went to a drawer and pulled out a small valise, which she opened and removed letters, passing them around. The people took them and read them. Poppy said, "You'll see that all the letters are in the same hand, on the same sort of paper. These were all written by one person."

Mollie took one and looked it over. "How is my letter any different?" She tossed the letter on the table, where it fell to the floor.

"The paper is different," Petunia picked up Mollie's letter. "Any fool can see it. This paper is fine, and the handwriting is neat. Your letter is on cheap paper and the writing, well…" She looked at it dismissively.

Mollie glared at her. "Are you saying I'm cheap?"

"Your note certainly is. Did you write it yourself?" Petunia snapped.

Mollie's face bloomed red.

Petunia's eyebrows rose. "You did, didn't you? What a horrid thing to do."

There were snickers and quiet smiles around the room. "You wrote your own letter. Why?" Poppy asked.

Mollie crossed her arms beneath her chest. "I don't have to say."

"You might as well, otherwise we'll think you're behind this. Did you kill those mistresses?" Henry asked.

"No!"

"Then why write yourself a letter?" he asked.

"Because," Mollie said.

"Because what?"

"Because..." She glared at Beatrice. "You girls all got letters, but I didn't get one. Not a single one. I checked the post every day, twice a day, and no letters. No invitations, no nothing."

"Some might say that's because you wrote the letters. It's a little obvious, isn't it?" Petunia asked.

"But I didn't. I didn't write any letters. You've got to believe me."

A snicker was heard in the room. Mollie looked around at the disapproving faces. "I didn't do it."

"I believe you," Poppy said.

"You do?" Mollie said.

"Yes. It's too obvious. All you wanted was to be part of the drama, but someone had overlooked you. The other girls have been receiving letters for weeks now, but you have none, until just the other day. Whoever wrote the letters purposely left you out, I suspect to torment you."

"But why? Why would anyone do that?"

Poppy shrugged. "Because Frances wanted to have her revenge on you."

"You're missing something," Mollie said, "Frances is in jail, she couldn't have done this. And she couldn't read or write. She never learned."

Poppy stood from her seat and walked around behind it, resting her hands on the back of the chair. "I visited Newgate prison yesterday and learned that Frances got out of jail some weeks ago."

Mollie paled. "So she's back and out for revenge."

"It does seem that way. One by one, the girls were sent messages to meet the letter writer, and then they met their deaths."

"Poor Penelope," said Beatrice, "she died next."

"But we never found her body," Tom pointed out. "She might still be alive."

"It's true. But she was attacked too. On the day of the races, we found her stumbling toward the racecourse as if she were drunk."

"That's right, we thought her drink was spoiled with some substance," Beatrice said and looked at Mrs. Farrars. "Thank goodness you were there to save her."

All eyes looked to Ann, who blushed.

"You saved a young woman?" Stephen turned to her.

"It was nothing, truly." She looked embarrassed. "She looked unwell, so I happened to help her, that was all."

"I believe you gave her your card and an invitation to tea, is that right?" Poppy asked.

Ann swallowed. "Yes. But she never came. I thought it was rather unappreciative, but then I suppose these young girls are." She folded her hands in her lap and looked demure.

"Hmmm, and then she disappeared. We still don't know what happened to her," Poppy said.

Tom added, "It's true. I met you and Beatrice at her lodgings, but they were disturbed. Her servants didn't know what happened to her. We found a nasty note in her belongings, but don't know if she met the letter writer or not."

"Then there was Justine," Beatrice said sadly.

"She is a sad case. And that's what was so strange. During the interval between acts one and two, Tom, Beatrice, and I went to her dressing room. Justine was frightened, for she had received a letter," Poppy said.

Beatrice looked at John. "You were there."

"No, I wasn't. I was in my family's box," he retorted.

Poppy said, "I didn't see him."

"I did. He's lying. He was gone during the interval. He could have gone and…" Petunia stopped and set her teacup aside, resting her hands on her knees.

"Petunia, how could you say such a thing?" John asked.

"How could I not, when you've been making me a laughingstock all this time? You hardly spent a moment by my side at home and then at dinners and assemblies people ask where you are, and then exchanged pointed looks behind my back when they think I don't see. And then, then of all things, I find a letter addressed to Henry, begging you to come back to London."

"Well, that was…"

"Never meant for Henry. Everyone knows *he's* the honorable Dyngley. He would never do something so untoward as engaging a mistress," Petunia almost spat. "I knew there must be some mistake and that it was meant for you, so I came to London. I knew that's where you must have gone. And then I find her in your arms at the races. How much more can a woman take? So no, John, I bear you no ill will as my husband, but I bear you little loyalty since you would rather take up with a harlot than be with me." Her chin trembled and she blinked hard.

"You cannot think that I went during the interval to harm her?" he said.

"Then what of the letter in your breast pocket? I saw you looking at it that evening. Did you mean to invite her to a private tryst somewhere?" Petunia wiped away a tear.

"No." He looked at Dyngley, then at Petunia. "No. I did leave briefly, I wished to give her this, but I spied the others in her room, and did not wish to be seen." He removed a somewhat wrinkled letter from his jacket pocket and handed it to her. "Read it if you like; she never got to."

Petunia stared at the offending letter for a few seconds and snatched it from him. She ripped it open with shaking hands and read it. She lowered the letter and passed it back to him. "You were ending your relationship."

"Yes."

"You write to say you thank her for the favors she bestowed upon you, but your duty is to your family, and you wish her the best of luck." The breath went out of her in a small sound.

He nodded. "I returned to our box then."

"Whoever tampered with the makeshift guillotine had to be strong, and know about carpentry and how the device worked," the magistrate said.

"Could a woman have done it?" Stephen asked, looking at Beatrice.

"It's possible," the magistrate said. "When a woman is involved, anything is possible."

Poppy smiled. "I think someone else was involved. Someone who could slip in and out backstage, unnoticed. But I was sloppy. I ignored the signs. I was too busy thinking about my mother to notice what was right under my nose."

"Like what?"

"Like the fact that the person who is behind these murders was here in our very house. They were able to slip in unnoticed because, like Mrs. Dyngley once said, 'A good servant is like furniture, silent and available.'"

Heads turned to Petunia, who shrugged. "She's not wrong."

"But my mother…" Poppy's throat grew tight. "Those of you who know me knew my sole purpose in coming here was to find her. If you don't already know, she is—she was a mistress, to Lord Blackwood. We had met and spent time together when I found her strangled to death in her bed."

"My God," Uncle Reginald said. Aunt Rachel beside him gripped his hand.

Poppy blinked back tears. The pain was still raw. "But her death didn't make sense. She had never received any threatening letters or had a rude word from anyone. Even her death notice in the paper said she was beloved and a jewel in society. Who then, would want to hurt her?"

"Lord Blackwood?" Mollie asked.

Poppy shook her head. "He was distraught on the day, for he had woken up next to her corpse." She looked around the room. "I think her death was a mistake. She was murdered, we know that much. But I think the killer mistook her for someone else. That's the only reason I can think of for someone wanting to kill my mother."

"Unless you did it," Mollie said. People looked at her. "What? I'm just saying, it's not unheard of," she said.

"I didn't kill her. And I don't think someone would have wanted to hurt me by killing her. It's too great a step to take to achieve that," Poppy said.

"So what do you think?" Henry asked.

"I think there was more than one person involved in this. There was the letter writer, the brains behind the attacks, and the person who committed the crimes."

"You think three people were involved?" Magistrate Tomlinson asked.

"But who?" Petunia asked.

"When I visited the prison, I learned something interesting. The prison guard said that Frances took up with a man who protected her from others, and in return when she got out and got work, she got him a position too, to a gentleman. But more so, I learned that she had a regular visitor during her time in prison, a society lady, and once Frances got out of jail, the lady's visits stopped."

"Who?" Mollie asked.

"Yes, who? Tell us," Magistrate Tomlinson said.

"Someone who had suffered her own embarrassment from her husband cheating on her. Someone who had stuck up a friendship with a former mistress, and together they hatched a plan to take out the mistresses, one by one. It would be easy. Isn't that right, Mrs. Farrars?"

"Me?" Ann squeaked. "You think I did it?"

"Miss Morton, you overstep yourself," Stephen said. "Apologize to my wife, this instant."

"No. I'm positive you're behind this. The prison guard identified you as the visitor to Frances. He said everyone called you 'Mrs. F,'" Poppy said.

Ann blanched and squirmed in her seat.

"You knew that your husband was cheating on you and had taken up a mistress, but you didn't know who. Perhaps your visits to the prison began with good intentions, but then they took a different turn."

"You have no proof," Ann declared, a dark light in her eyes.

"All I need do is match the paper purchased and compare that to the letters written to the mistresses."

"Anyone could buy paper."

"But this paper is expensive. It's not cheap like what Mollie has." Poppy turned to Tom, who pulled out a sachet of paper from his jacket.

"Found this in her writing desk not an hour ago."

"You were in our home?" Mr. Farrars asked.

"I know a lot of people in service. Everybody knows me."

"I'm going to speak to our staff. Whoever let you in will be fired," Stephen said.

"First, can I just see that paper, son," the magistrate said, standing and reaching for it.

"Quit that! Stop that at once. Can't you see this is all one big misunderstanding?" Stephen said, stepping between them. "This girl, this companion, is only out to cause trouble with her accusations."

"How do you explain it?" Dyngley asked.

"Anyone could purchase that paper. Her accusations have no bearing, they are circumstantial," Stephen said.

"I want to hear the girl out. Go on," the magistrate said.

"I will not stand here and hear my wife's good name be besmirched by a common companion. You cannot prove anything."

"Sit down, Stephen. Let Miss Morton talk," Ann said.

"But Ann…"

"I want to hear what she has to say. Let the girl dig her own grave," Ann said coldly.

"I say, madam," Poppy's uncle said.

Poppy said, "I think that Frances teamed up with her visitor in prison, and hatched a plan to exact her revenge on her former friends once she was released. And she's been working in various households to dispatch her messages. She even got her partner a job in her benefactor's household, once he was released from prison. Isn't that right, Mr. Parks?"

Mr. Parks gaped at her. "What?"

"You were in prison recently. But you changed your name

when you got out. When the prison guard told me your name was Harris, I thought it was my friend Tom. But he was never in prison. Then it dawned on me. You were hired recently by Mr. Farrars, were you not?"

"That is none of your business," he muttered.

"It's true," Stephen said and cleared his throat. "But we always do good works here, one man is as good as the next. What does it matter?"

"It matters. He kept a watchful eye over Mr. Farrars's property. He never let Beatrice out of his sight."

"What are you saying, Miss Morton?" Ann asked.

"That you teamed up with Frances in prison. You wrote the letters, and under her guiding hand, you sent these mistresses to their deaths."

"That's a lie!" Stephen shot to his feet. "You have no proof, and yet you go around pointing your finger at good, God-fearing citizens. Magistrate, you should arrest this girl for disturbing the peace."

"He won't arrest her," a feminine voice said, "Not when you hear what's happened to me."

Heads turned toward the sound. There in the entryway stood Penelope, on the arm of a well-dressed gentleman.

Chapter Thirty

"**P**ENELOPE, YOU'RE ALIVE!" Beatrice said.

"I am, no thanks to some people. When a random woman accuses me of stealing her trinket, I had to respond. I had a note from a Celeste Grey to go speak with you, and then I return to my lodgings and find an invitation for today. So here we are." She glared at the maid. "I overheard what you were saying. What Miss Morton says is true, Mrs. Farrars is behind this, and so is her maid, Fanny. Or should I say Frances?"

Fanny laughed, a sour sound. "Me? I don't have time to do anything. Spend my time cleaning up after the lot of you."

Mollie approached Penelope. "You, on the arm of Lord Carr? I don't believe it. What are you two doing together? He was Frances's old patron." To him, she said, "I've been looking everywhere for you. I have some very important information to tell you. Perhaps we could go somewhere private?"

Penelope smiled as Lord Carr ignored Mollie. She said, "I expect you're wondering where I've been."

"We went looking for you. We worried something had happened to you," Harriet said.

"Something did. I went to visit Mrs. Farrars for tea like she invited me, but when the maid served the tea, I thought I recognized Frances. At the first sip, I thought it tasted funny, and I saw Mrs. Farrars watching me closely, along with the maid. I pretended to faint and then I heard them talking. Mrs. Farrars shrieked and asked if the maid had poisoned me. I acted as if I was dead, and recognized Frances's voice. She said yes, and dragged me behind the sofa. Said she'd call for her friend to dispose of me later." She shuddered. "As soon as I heard them leave, I got up and made my way to the door, then Mrs. Farrars found me and hid me in a closet. I slipped out a ground floor window. I knew it wouldn't be long before people started looking for me, and I couldn't go home. So I went to Frances's gentleman."

The man gazed down at her fondly. He said to the group, "I am Lord Carr," as if that was enough. He added, "Miss Smythe came to me and told me everything. I would not have believed her, except that when I ended my relationship with Frances, she threatened me. She told me she would get back at me for what I did. I never thought she would stoop to poisoning."

All eyes fell on the maid. "I didn't do it. Dunno what you lot are talking about."

Mollie turned to her and looked her up and down. "My God, it *is* you. Prison hasn't been kind, I see. So the rumors are true. You did get the pox after all. Shame it took away your pretty face. That was the only good thing about you."

The maid slapped her.

Mollie stepped back, a hand to her cheek.

"You scheming, sniveling whore," the maid said. "I work all hours to care for my mistress, and you all call me a murderer? That's it. I'm quitting. I'm going where I'm wanted." She turned to go.

"Stop her," Poppy said. "Don't let her leave."

The magistrate and Henry apprehended the maid, who tugged and pulled but could not release her arms from their grip. "This ain't fair, I done nothing wrong!"

"Oh, give it up already," Ann said. "Magistrate, I did it. I wrote those letters."

"What?" Stephen said.

"You?" Magistrate Tomlinson stared.

"Yes." To Poppy, Ann said, "You were right. I was the visitor to Frances in prison."

Stephen said, "Excuse my wife, she is not well."

Ann looked at her husband with mild disgust, then at Poppy. "I am perfectly well. But you give Frances too much credit. Taking revenge was her plan, but the means of delivery was all my idea."

"What?" Stephen said. "You? I don't believe it."

"You think me a meek, quiet little woman to look after your children and be ignored. You're wrong. Do you really think I would stay silent when I knew you had a mistress?"

"I… Ann, you don't understand," Stephen started.

"I understand completely. I've known for months you were seeing another woman. I just didn't know who. That's why when I met Frances in prison and learned she was a former mistress, she said she knew the girls and could find out who you were seeing."

Stephen stared at his wife as if seeing a stranger for the first time.

"We agreed that once Frances served her time, I would take her on as a maid, as a charitable gesture. You hardly notice the servants, you wouldn't notice one more. Then when her partner was released, I would recommend him to you as a good man of all trades. You were so trusting, of course, you agreed."

Stephen's mouth opened and closed. "You used me."

"I needed to know who you were seeing. I had found letters of yours, exchanges here and there, but I couldn't figure out who. In a few weeks, Frances said she knew and would tell me. All I had to do was write her a letter and she would deliver it and enable us to meet in person, so I did."

"She's lying," Fanny growled.

"She's talking about Marie," Beatrice said.

Ann nodded. "Yes. Little did I know that when we did meet on the riverbank, the girl had no idea who Stephen or I was. She was clueless. But it was too late. Frances was hiding behind a corner and pushed her into the river. By the time I tried to reach her, she had drowned."

"I think she blackmailed you. I think she forced you to write those letters," Poppy said.

"The first one I wrote because I thought it was a good idea. Why not ask the mistress to see reason? If they took my advice and left Stephen, then we could call it even and I would have my husband back. But Marie wasn't the one I was looking for, and by then it was too late," Ann said.

"You were an accomplice at that point," Henry said.

"Yes, exactly. I wanted to go to the watch and confess that very instant, but Frances wouldn't let me. She said no court of justice would let me go, once they knew I'd written the girl a letter and was present at her death. They would convict me and send me to prison. I knew that much." She shook her head. "I've seen the conditions women have to live in there. The noise is appalling. The floor crunches beneath your feet as you walk from the bugs. And the men…I don't want…I don't think I would do well there."

"Nothing will happen to you," Stephen said.

"I'll be the judge of that," the magistrate said, "You say she forced you?"

"Yes. At the races I saw Frances speaking to that girl and giving her a drink, then I spotted the girl stumbling toward the racetrack as if she was drunk. I ran to stop her, which is where I met you all. Inviting her to tea seemed the perfect way to find out if she was my husband's mistress. But when we met the next day, she didn't know about my husband either." She looked at Penelope. "I'm so sorry. I had no idea she was going to doctor your drink."

"If you hadn't found me and shown me to that window, I never would have gotten away," Penelope said, clutching the arm of her gentleman tighter. He patted her hand.

"So all this time, Mrs. Farrars, you've been writing to random women, inviting them to meet you, and then standing by as Frances kills them," Constable Dyngley said.

Ann looked down at her hands folded demurely in her lap. "Yes. I've been miserable for weeks. Each time I thought I could speak with the girl, reason with her to get her to leave my husband. But each time Frances got involved, they died." She looked at the magistrate. "I wrote the letters. I was complicit in these women's deaths. I won't deny it."

"Ann! How could you say such a thing?" Petunia said.

"Because it is true, Petunia, and you have been too blind to notice anything beyond your own troubles," Ann said.

Petunia recoiled and sniffed loudly. "Well, I never."

"I don't understand. You thought all of these women were sleeping with me?" Stephen said.

"Not all of them, dear, just one. But I didn't know which," Ann said.

"But why go to all this trouble? Just because you thought a woman was sleeping with me?" he said.

"It's more than that. You recall that my sister, Eleanor, died last year?" Ann said.

He nodded.

"Her entire life she had been a good God-fearing woman, with never an unkind word to anyone. But on her deathbed, she told me that her husband had taken a mistress in their town and was seeing her on the side. She had done her conjugal duty and slept with her husband, even though she knew she was sleeping with an adulterer."

She took a breath. "What I never told you is that her husband's mistress contracted the pox and gave it to her husband, and he then to his wife, my sister. Except that while he purchased medicine for him and his mistress, he left my sister to suffer. Her condition was diagnosed too late, so he didn't bother wasting any medicine on a lost cause. She died in bed, alone. Disfigured and her body ruined, all thanks to her husband and his whore." Her upper lip twitched in a sneer, and she glared at Stephen. "When I found the letters between you and your mistress, I could see it was happening again. I refused to let that happen to me. I love you, but I don't love your choices or the women you sleep with. I thought I could reason with her if I could only meet her face to face. That's where Frances came in."

"My God. I would never..." Stephen began.

"Don't lie, it doesn't suit you," Ann told him. "As I said, I knew you were cheating on me with a woman, but I couldn't figure out who. I had to trust Frances." She looked at the maid, who gave her a toothy scowl. "That poor actress, I don't know what happened there. We were at the theater that night, but Frances didn't take the letter, someone else did."

"Who?"

"The man who was Frances's protector in prison. The man who looked after her, and in return, looks after her plans now," Poppy said, turning to Mr. Parks.

"You're daft. You've had too much wine," he said.

"You were to accompany Beatrice and me to the theater that night, but you were late. Where were you?"

"None of your business."

"I think you took Ann's letter and left it for Justine. I bumped into you backstage and thought nothing of it when you said you were looking for the privy. I think you read Ann's letter and once you had delivered the note to Justine's dressing room, you stayed backstage. During the interval, you acted as though you were one of the members of the crew, and tinkered with the guillotine. You removed the guard so the blade fell. You are the one who killed Justine." Poppy gripped the back of her chair so hard her fingers hurt.

Mr. Parks laughed. "You should stop reading so many novels. You're seeing villains everywhere."

"It's true. I saw you backstage as we left Justine's dressing room," Tom said. "I thought you were there to escort the ladies back to their box, but you disappeared."

Mr. Parks shot him a dirty look.

"All right, all right, I can see this is a muddle. Could someone please tell me what happened to Miss Grey, the Grace?" the magistrate asked. He looked hard at Beatrice. "You seem to know a lot about these deaths. Perhaps you had something to do with killing Miss Grey. Didn't want her getting in the way, eh?"

"Stop it," Mr. Parks said.

"Oh, I think I'm on to something. You look all sweet and innocent, but you're just as blackhearted as the rest of 'em, I bet."

Mr. Parks's face grew grim. Beatrice quailed.

The magistrate started toward Beatrice. "What say you and I have a little chat down at my office? I'm sure we can come to some arrangement." He reached for Beatrice's arm when Mr. Parks shoved him back and planted himself in front of her.

"She's not going anywhere with you."

"Mr. Parks!" Stephen said. "You forget yourself."

"She looks guilty to me. I say she done it. She's a mistress. She knows everyone who died. Who's to say any different?"

"I did it. I killed Miss Grey. Miss Hayes had nothing to do with it." He looked hard at the magistrate, willing him to come any closer.

Poppy's shoulders slumped. "You?"

His head dropped to his chest. "I was there in the park and saw Miss Morton talking with Beatrice and then her mother. Ann wondered if Miss Hayes was the mistress of her husband. I could hear her plotting with Frances and told her they were wrong, Miss Grey was Mr. Farrars's mistress, not Miss Hayes. They believed me and I killed her that same night. I did it."

"How?" Henry asked.

"Frances and I did it. She slipped into the household as a maid and set up a bottle of drugged wine and two glasses by the bedstand. Once she was certain they were out cold, I crept in and strangled her with a silk tie." He pushed up his shirt sleeves to reveal angry red claw marks on his arms. "If you don't believe me, the evidence is here."

Poppy fell to her knees.

"Oh Poppy!" Aunt Rachel flew out of her seat when Tom caught Poppy and helped her up.

"You did it. You killed my mother," Poppy said, not bothering to wipe away the tears that coursed down her face.

"I did and I'd do it again," Mr. Parks growled.

"But why?" Poppy's voice was raw. "She never hurt anyone."

Ann scoffed. "A mistress hurts everyone in their way. The husband, the wife, and the children. This all started because of a silly girl, and a man too dumb to refuse her."

Poppy stood, vaguely conscious of Tom's hands about the small of her back and at her elbow, propping her up.

Beatrice faced Mr. Parks and demanded, "Why did you do it? How could you?"

Mr. Parks looked down at her. "Is it not obvious?"

"What?" Beatrice asked.

"I love you," he said.

Beatrice's mouth dropped open.

"I would not have you go to jail for something you didn't do," he told her.

"But I did. My word, if only I'd known. This was all because of me." Beatrice turned to Ann. "I'm the one you want. I'm your husband's mistress."

Ann looked at her with curiosity.

Frances snarled, "I should have known you were weak, Parks. Who falls in love with a prostitute? We would have gotten away with it if you hadn't opened your stupid mouth."

Mr. Parks looked at her, then the magistrate. "That woman is Frances Landry. She's a whore. Send her to jail. She fooled Mrs. Farrars into playing a part in these murders. She's behind it all." He turned to Beatrice. "I did it all for you. I won't let anything happen to you."

"Mr. Parks, she is none of your concern," Stephen said, his voice sharp.

"I quit your service, Mr. Farrars," Mr. Parks said, looking only at Beatrice.

Ann turned. "You deceived me. You both lied to me. You told me Miss Grey was sleeping with my husband this entire time."

Her voice became cutting and cruel.

Frances offered her a nasty smile. "And you believed my every word. How does it feel to be duped by a whore?"

Ann ran at her and before the men could stop her, she clawed at Frances's pockmarked face with her nails, leaving bloody lines down her cheeks.

Tom abandoned Poppy and restrained Ann, pulling her back as she kicked and elbowed him in the face.

"Tom!" Poppy said.

Tom fell back, blood gushing from his nose. He landed on the floor as Poppy ran to him. Henry dropped Frances's arm and moved to stop Ann, catching her as she screamed.

Ann turned to Beatrice and cried, "You were seducing my husband all this time. How could you do it? Don't you know the pain you've caused?"

Beatrice fretted, her hands darting to her mouth. "I never, I mean…"

"You deserve to die!" Frances howled. "You all do for leaving me to rot in jail. But you most of all, Mollie dearest. You deserve to be forgotten."

"Hah!" Mollie cried. "I should have known you'd stoop so low as to trick a genteel woman to do your dirty work. You couldn't write to me yourself, so you had someone else do it. What a coward you are, Frances."

"You're the one who started it."

Mollie laughed. "You are obsessed with me, aren't you? I should have known you'd make it all about me. Really, Frances, get over it already."

"You are so proud of your patron, so high and mighty, giving yourself airs, when you're just a whore like the rest of us," Frances sneered. "I wanted you to feel like me. You're so proud of having a better patron than the rest of us."

"I *am* better than you," Mollie told her.

"You're a liar. I told you my secret in confidence and you used it to ruin me. Do you know what happens to ladies in prison? You deserve to know what it's like at the bottom. This is all your fault."

Frances twisted and kneed the magistrate in the groin. He doubled over and she cried with triumph, turned, and ran.

She would have escaped had not Penelope's gentleman, quiet until now, stuck his leg out and tripped her. As Frances landed face-first on the floor, the gentleman pinned her to the carpet with the skill of a wrestler. She howled and cried, beating her hands on the floor, but she couldn't move. "You have caused enough trouble for one day," he said.

Penelope looked on with a smile. Meanwhile, Henry and Mr. Farrars grasped the struggling Mrs. Farrars, her arms held fast between them.

The magistrate slowly got up from the floor. "You are coming with me to jail. All three of you."

"Not my wife, surely. She's done no harm," Stephen said.

"She's a part of this mess, so she's coming too," the magistrate grunted.

"My wife is from a well-respected family. You wouldn't dare," Stephen said.

"I would and I will. Bring her along," the magistrate told him.

Mrs. Farrars, Frances, and Mr. Parks were all escorted away with the help of some footmen, Tom, and Mr. Farrars. Mr. Parks gave Beatrice a fleeting look as he was led away, followed by Mollie, Harriet, Penelope, and Lord Carr.

Poppy stood by watching them go. Beatrice said beside her, "What will happen to me?"

"I don't know."

"Well I am glad the culprits are found, but one thing puzzles me," John said.

"What is that?" Petunia asked.

"You, my dear. During the interval at the theater that night, you left, didn't you?"

"Me?" she said.

"Yes. Where did you go?" he asked.

"I…" She blushed. "I don't wish to say."

"Why not?" Beatrice asked.

"It's not something a *lady* talks about." Petunia gave her a hard look and sniffed.

"I think you had better tell us, to avoid suspicion, Mrs. Dyngley," Constable Dyngley said.

She glared at him. "Very well. I needed to use the necessary."

"You never do. You have a bladder like a horse," John said.

Petunia laughed. "Just because ladies do things in private does not mean that we are not human, John."

"You haven't touched your cakes. Are you feeling all right?" Dyngley asked.

"I am perfectly well." She pushed the plate away.

"You're not. You're pale. Petunia?" John asked.

She fanned herself with her hand and said, "I did not want to say this here, but…"

Poppy's mouth dropped open at the same time as Aunt Rachel blurted, "You're with child."

"What?" John's eyes grew wide. "Petunia?"

She took a quick sip of her tea. "John?"

"Is it true?"

She nodded.

His mouth fell open. "I had no idea."

"Yes, well. This sort of thing does happen on occasion." She blushed.

"Petunia," John started. He ignored everyone else in the room and took her hand. "Come, let us go."

"But I wanted to hear who was behind all this."

"Henry will tell us later. We have preparations to make. We have a child coming!" He shot to his feet. "Drinks for all!"

The assembly clapped and raised their teacups. A servant was sent for and brought sherry and sparkling wine. Once congratulations were passed all around, John and Petunia left, arm in arm, smiling and looking very much in love.

Poppy stood beside Henry. "I hope they will be very happy,"

she said. "Your brother and sister-in-law, I mean."

"I expect they will be. John has long needed something stable to focus his attention on. Perhaps a wife and child will do the trick."

Aunt Rachel and Uncle Reginald approached Poppy. "This has been a dire afternoon. Positively dire turn of events. Will you not come home with us now?" Her uncle looked hopeful.

Poppy said, "I need to speak with Miss Hayes and conclude my affairs. I'll be a few days yet."

Her uncle nodded and left. Her aunt squeezed her hand. "I'm glad we finally know who killed Celeste. I'm just sorry you never got a real chance to know her."

"I'm glad I got to meet her, just a little," Poppy said as they left.

CHAPTER THIRTY-ONE

BEATRICE AND POPPY bid the rest of the guests farewell. Neither was in a mood to eat or drink much. Beatrice's face was drawn when later that evening there was a knock at the door, and Stephen arrived.

His face was firm and angry as he said, "Miss Morton, I would speak with Miss Hayes alone."

"Of course." Poppy left them but sat in her bedroom, looking out the window. She did not know what Stephen might say to Beatrice, but she had an idea. The muted shouts and slamming of doors confirmed her suspicions, as Beatrice ran to her room minutes later in tears. "He's left me. He's kicked me out. You too."

"Oh my God." Poppy took Beatrice in her arms and hugged her as Beatrice cried, loud wretched tears amidst gulps for shaky breaths.

"He said it's all because of me that this has happened. He says he is going to close the house and wants me out tomorrow. I've never seen him so angry. Can you believe it, he actually asked if I was sleeping with Mr. Parks the whole time?" She wept miserably, throwing herself on Poppy's bed. She hugged Poppy's pillow to her chest and cried, wetting it with her tears. "I've never felt so alone in all my life."

Poppy held her hand as Beatrice cried herself out, then raised her face from Poppy's pillow. "Oh! I've just realized. I can't afford you as a companion." Her red eyes teared up. "You'll go back to Hertford, and I'll never see you again." She stuffed her face in the pillow again.

Poppy sat by her as she shed a few tears of her own. It was almost the worst outcome she could think of, but not unexpected. She thought Stephen was better than that, but the entire experience had taught her that as much as literature bemoaned the fact that some women were flighty creatures, some men were equally as fickle.

"I'll have to sell myself again," came Beatrice's small voice.

There was a knock on the door and Nancy, the sweet maid entered. "There's a visitor for you in the parlor. It's Mr. Harris."

"Tom, you mean?" Beatrice asked.

The maid nodded. "Is it true we're to be turned out?"

Beatrice shook her head. "No, just me. You all still have a place here, as far as I know."

The maid curtsied and left.

Beatrice rose and wiped her eyes. "Come, we'd best see Tom and tell him the news."

Poppy brushed a tear away and followed her out, as Beatrice said, "Oh, I can't see Tom now. I'm a mess. Could you talk to him instead? Tell him I'm indisposed."

"Of course."

Tom greeted Poppy and offered her a bow as she received him. "Hello, Tom. Please, sit."

He sat beside her on the sofa and said, "Well that was an entertaining afternoon, wasn't it?"

"Not for all," she said gravely.

"No. But all's well that ends well. Didn't Shakespeare say that?"

"I don't know." She met his eyes. "Tom, you should know that we're being asked to leave."

"What? What do you mean?"

"Mr. Farrars has decided to end his relationship with Miss

Hayes, and no longer needs me to act as a companion for her."

His eyes grew wide. "What a bastard. I never liked him. I always thought he'd turn on Beatrice."

Poppy nodded. "We are given until the end of tomorrow to leave."

"Tomorrow? But that's no time at all. Where will she go? Where will you go?"

"I will go home. My aunt and uncle are waiting for me to pack up my affairs and return to Hertford with them." She paused. "But I worry about Miss Hayes. Could you find a place for her in your tavern? Look after her, until she finds another gentleman or lands on her feet? I would offer to take her to Hertford with me, but I fear my uncle would object."

"He'd have apoplexy, more like," Tom said with a dark laugh and ran a hand through his light brown curls. "She can stay with me. I've no idea where we'll put all her clothes and nice shoes, but we'll sell a lot for some quick coin, and she can work in the tavern. I'll keep an eye on her. Maybe she'll meet a nice gentleman to keep her company."

"Thank you."

"Miss Morton?" he asked, edging closer to her on the sofa.

"Yes, Mr. Harris?"

He pulled her to her feet, gripping her hands. "For weeks now, I've watched you. Fancied you. I didn't realize it at first, not until I saw how you threw yourself into helping the girls. You didn't care that they are called whores, you cared about helping them. There's many a genteel person who would turn their noses up at that, I know. I came here to call on you, to ask…"

Poppy looked down. "Tom, I don't…"

"I'm not proposing to you," he said, causing her head to shoot up. "But I think I'd like to get to know you. You'll be returning to Hertford, but I wonder, may I write to you?"

She blinked. "I…I don't know. I—"

He kissed her, lightly on the lips. Her eyes widened as she felt the brush of his lips against hers, and she tensed as his hand caressed her hair and cupped the back of her head, slightly pulling her toward him.

"Ahem."

Poppy jumped. "Constable Dyngley."

"Miss Morton." He looked hard at her and stood there, his hands curling into fists. "Mr. Harris. I didn't realize I was interrupting."

"You are," Tom said.

She tugged her hand back and stepped around him.

"Miss Morton, is he harassing you?" Dyngley looked at her with concern.

"It's not harassment if the lady says yes." Tom smiled lazily.

Poppy blushed. "Mr. Harris was just leaving."

Henry's eyebrows rose.

"As the lady says, I was just paying my respects. I do hope to call on you again soon." He grinned at Poppy, who turned pink up to her ears.

Beatrice entered the room. "Oh, hello, constable. Tom, what are you doing here?"

"Hello Miss Hayes," Tom said with a smile and straightened his suit jacket. "I was just calling to see how you girls were."

"He was just leaving," Dyngley said.

"Oh, well, that's thoughtful. I'll walk you out," Beatrice said, waiting for Tom to offer her his arm.

Poppy watched them go. Once they left, Dyngley said, "That young man is impertinent."

"He has a good heart," Poppy said.

"Does he? He seems to pay his attention in irritating ways." Dyngley frowned.

Poppy stood and curtsied to him. "Forgive me for not receiving you properly, I—"

He stepped close to her, so close they stood barely a foot apart. "For months now we have been apart. I must know. Did you come to London to escape me?" he asked.

"No. I came to find my mother, as I have told you before. We are friends, Constable. I would not run from a friend."

"Is that all we are? I seem to remember that the last time we were alone in the parsonage, I kissed you. Have you forgotten?" He stepped closer, removing the distance between them.

She could smell the trace of tobacco on his skin, the light cologne he wore, and the clean scent of his hair. She closed her eyes and breathed him in for a second.

"Poppy?" He took her chin in his hand, slowly raising her head up to his. "Am I so forgettable?"

Her eyes flew open and her breath caught. "No you are not," she whispered.

"I have missed you, Poppy. Since we parted that night in Hertford, I have thought of little else. I have missed you each minute of every day. Have you missed me?"

She could not deny it, not without lying to herself. She nodded.

He took her face in his hands and kissed her, with a force that sent waves of heat through her body.

Her skin burned at his touch. "You take liberties, sir." She blushed, stepping away, but he snatched her left hand and pulled her to him with a smile.

"My name is Henry."

Her heart beat madly in her chest.

His dark eyes were like deep pools that threatened to overwhelm her. They stood chest to chest. He smelled intoxicating, and even if they were frozen into statues at that moment, she never wanted to leave.

"Henry, I want you to know I—"

He kissed her again.

Her heart beat as fast as a hummingbird's wings. His lips traced hers and her knees began to tremble. She could melt in his arms. She felt she might swoon. Yet if she were to fall, she knew he would catch her.

"Say anything you wish, but do not deny me this," he murmured into her left ear. "What is it you wished to tell me?" He traced kisses down her neck. "Talk and I will listen."

Poppy's breathing came out staggered and she pulled away. "Henry."

"Yes?" He eyed her openly, taking pleasure at the sight of her flushed cheeks, her bright eyes, and mussed hair.

"Behave yourself, sir. I cannot allow such liberties. I am nineteen. You are…"

"Twenty-five. Does that matter?"

"No, but we are not courting. What would my uncle say?"

"I do not know, and that is why I have come. I came here with the express purpose of asking your permission before I asked his. I respect you, Poppy. I would not force you into something you did not agree to, nor would I willingly set myself up for disappointment. But I have acted no better than a rake and have stolen kisses from you." He gripped her hands as if he would never let them go. "Miss Morton, would you do me the honor?"

"You wish to court me?"

"Yes. May I have your permission? Unless you do not wish to?" His face held a seriousness she had rarely seen before. His fair skin looked flawless in the light, yet with a word, she felt she could break his heart. He had never looked so vulnerable.

She paused and took the measure of him. She was nothing but the daughter of a mistress, the niece of a clergyman with no dowry and nothing to offer. He was the second son of a baronet who wanted to court her. This was the man who had encouraged her, inspired her, and had not dismissed her when she began to solve murders with him. He had stood by her.

No matter what answer she gave, it would change their relationship irrevocably. She might remain an acquaintance but lose a friend. Or gain so much more.

In the end, it took no time at all for her to give her answer.

"Yes, I do. I would like that very much."

Henry's smile could have outshone the sun at that moment. He picked her up and twirled her in the air, laughing as he set her down. He clasped her tightly and wrapped his arms around her, crushing her against his chest.

The breath whooshed out of her as she tensed, then relaxed against him and closed her eyes. She felt warm and safe, and then he kissed her again. He released her and stepped back. "I must mind myself around you. Forgive me. I have wanted to kiss you again for a very long time." The intensity in his gaze made her shiver. His dark brown eyes shone as his hands curled around her waist and pressed her to him, hip to hip, nose to nose. A stray noise escaped her, and his smile widened as his eyes danced and promised mischief to come.

Beatrice's voice could be heard from outside the room, so he dropped her hands, stepped back, and aimed for a semblance of normalcy. "You have made me very happy, Miss Morton."

Her smile was answer enough for him.

"I still have affairs to attend to in Town. Will you stay in London, now that your business is done?" he asked.

She shook her head and licked her lips. "We are asked to leave here tomorrow. Tom will take in Beatrice, and I will return home, to Hertford."

"Then I hope we shall have occasion to meet again, Miss Morton. I would like to court you properly." Henry kissed her left hand.

She nodded, unable to find the words.

He traced a finger down her cheek and tucked a stray hair behind her ear. "I shall look forward to it. I shall speak with your uncle as soon as I am able." His dark eyes were laughing as he left her with a formal bow.

Poppy waited for him to leave, then sank onto the sofa and felt her overly warm cheeks. A moment later Beatrice entered the room. "What was that about?"

Poppy laughed. Her heart was pounding so strongly it felt as if it might burst out of her chest. She rose, crossed the room, and poured herself a glass of brandy. "I could use this."

"Pour me one too," Beatrice said. "If this is to be our last night here, we might as well enjoy it."

THE NEXT DAY was spent packing. Poppy had little to attend to—except the gowns her mother had ordered from the modiste arrived, along with shoes, ribbons, gloves, and underthings. So many boxes, Poppy observed, and all were paid for already.

She wondered if she should send them all back.

"Don't you dare," her aunt said.

Beatrice agreed. "Your mother wanted you to have these things. It would be a shame if you did not keep them."

Poppy opened one box and looked at a fair white gown trimmed with ornate thread that shone in the light. She closed the box and nodded. "I'll keep them."

Once Beatrice's effects were packed and sent on via a hackney to Tom's lodgings, Beatrice and Poppy made their goodbyes. Beatrice was slightly tearful. "I don't know when I will see you again, or if I ever will."

"I'm sure we will. You must write to me and tell me of your adventures in London," Poppy said.

"And you must come to Hertford for a visit," Aunt Rachel said. "We have plenty of room at the parsonage."

Beatrice embraced Poppy warmly and pressed an envelope into her palm.

"What is this?" Poppy asked.

"Your wages. I know Stephen hasn't paid you for some time and it's the least I could do, to say thank you for all you've done for me."

"Are you sure? Won't you need it?"

Beatrice shook her head. "I want no memory of Stephen. I'm selling all the jewelry he gave me, although I might keep some of the dresses. I'm not so sure we would have lasted for very long, either. Do you know he farts in bed?" She rolled her eyes.

Aunt Rachel's eyebrows rose, and Poppy laughed. "No, I didn't."

"Well, he does. I'll be glad to be rid of him."

"And what of the three in prison? What will become of them, I wonder?" Aunt Rachel asked.

"Will you visit them?" Poppy asked Beatrice.

"I didn't know Frances very well, but I might check on her. And… I might meet Mr. Parks. I've never had a man love me before. When he said those words it felt… nice." Beatrice blushed and straightened her hat. "Thank you, Miss Morton. I hope we will meet again soon."

"And I, Miss Hayes."

The girls hugged one more time and left.

IN THE FEW days that took Poppy and her relatives back to Hertford, she felt a small sense of relief at being back in her old home, and at the prospect of sleeping in her old bed. Everything seemed slightly smaller than it did when she had left, but she didn't mind. Perhaps she had grown taller, or rather her perspective on the world had increased, and so ordinary creature comforts now seemed small in comparison.

A week later, Poppy sat with her aunt in the blue sitting room, mending one of her uncle's shirts, when her uncle came in with a paper. "Look at this," he said, passing it to Poppy. "Read it, just there." He pointed.

Poppy read:

An editorial note—A case of mistresses gone awry

As some may know, men will oft seek pleasures outside the marital bed, and in some rather indiscreet corners of society. What happens when the doting wife learns of these escapades is unknown, but in the case of a certain gentleman, whose wife had lately learned of his tastes and of his mistress in London, this led to the very worst outcome.

Aware of his indiscretion but uncertain with whom, the wife struck a deal with a prostitute in prison and agreed to write threats to a series of ladies about Town, in the hope she might convince one and all to abandon their gentlemen and let these love-addled men return to their wives.

But what began with one death, led to another, and unbeknownst to the watch, three mistresses lost their lives, including the promising actress Justine Vane, who lost her head in an ill-fated production of Marie Antoinette, and our beloved Grace, Miss Celeste Grey.

This editor has learned that through the discerning investigative skills of Constable Henry Dyngley of Hertfordshire, and his comrades including a Miss Morton of Hertford, not one but three criminals were brought to justice and currently reside in Newgate awaiting trial. One can only imagine that had a certain gentleman been more discreet in his affairs or more keen to fulfill his marital duties, this might all have been avoided.

Poppy handed it back to him. "So it is over. They will stand trial."

"I doubt Mrs. Farrars will."

"Why is that?"

"You see how they are not mentioned in the paper? She is a lady of fortune and good family. Her husband may have driven her to crime, but they are linked. For him to throw her over now would show a lack of concern for his wife, who carries his name and reputation. For the good of himself and his family, he'll have to pay very much to have her removed from the proceedings."

"She was blackmailed into it," Poppy said.

"Exactly. Enough guineas in the right pockets, and it will be that horrid maid and Parks fellow who face a judge."

Poppy shuddered. "I cannot think how horrible it must be."

"Don't waste time thinking about them, dear, they deserve it," Aunt Rachel said as Betsey approached with a packet of letters. "Oh, what's this, not another letter? That's the third one today, and all for you, Poppy."

"Who is writing to you, girl?" her uncle asked.

"I hardly know." Poppy received the letters and said, "May I be excused?"

"Of course."

Poppy left her sewing and went out into the back garden. There, on a bit of green grass, she sat near the chickens that wandered around the yard and pulled open the first.

Dear Poppy,

I hope you don't mind my writing to you. I am sorry I never got a chance to properly say farewell before you left London. Miss Hayes and I are working together at the Shakespeare's Head by Covent Garden. You should come here, or I shall have to visit Hertfordshire and encourage you to return. I am keen to renew those addresses which were so pleasurable, I hope, to us both.

Yours faithfully,
Tom Harris

Poppy let out a breath and felt her warm cheeks. She had wondered if she would hear from Tom again. What would she write to him? She didn't know how she felt about it, not since their kiss. Feeling curious, she opened the second letter.

Dear Miss Morton,

Forgive me for not writing sooner. I expect you are wondering about the outcome of the case involving your former employer and the three criminals we apprehended in your parlor that afternoon. The former prostitute turned maid, Frances, is now back in Newgate and is expected to hang for murder. I took the trouble of visiting the prison and conditions are very bad, particularly for women. But Frances seems resigned to her fate and has taken to wearing rags, sleeping with whoever will have her, and throwing her droppings at anyone who comes near. I hope you do not waste any time worrying about her, for I know you have a gentle heart toward others, even those who do not deserve your attention.

Mr. Parks admitted his involvement in Justine's and your mother's deaths, and will also be hanged for murder. Miss Hayes has visited him, and I gather they have struck up a friendship, even if it is to be short-lived. I know she is a friend, but I wonder, can you forgive a girl who befriends a murderer? I cannot.

Mrs. Ann Farrars, or Mrs. F, as she is known, did not see trial. Her husband pleaded with the magistrate and from what I understand, paid him a sizeable amount to overlook her involvement in this sorry business. She and her husband have returned home. I can only guess what will come of their marriage now.

Forgive me for calling on you so rudely, and for forcing you to accept my attentions in such an ungentlemanlike manner. When I next call on you, I will be the perfect gentleman, you have my word. Also, you might have noticed we were mentioned in the paper. As a result of this attention and thanks to the generosity of the magistrate, I have received a promotion for this case and expect to receive your congratulations when next we meet.

Your obedient servant,
Sergeant Henry Dyngley

Poppy felt a flutter in her chest she had not known before. She was happy for Henry, truly. But what to make of his letter? Did he regret kissing her? She didn't know, and desperately wished she had Beatrice around to discuss it with. She turned to the last letter and turned it over. She didn't recognize the handwriting, or the ornate wax seal on the back, which bore a fine design of an initial B. She opened it and read:

Dear Miss Morton,

I have long debated what to say when I contacted you, or whether to write at all. But for too many years now, an injustice has occurred which I cannot let lie. The night that Celeste and I quarreled, we did leave early and it was due to my anger, but not with you. I grew angry with her for hiding your existence from me so completely, and for nearly twenty years. I felt rage inside, that the woman whom I knew so intimately could hide a secret so important from me.

When we first met, I thought you were some charitable case that Celeste had taken on as a distraction. Had I known you were my daughter, I would never have treated you so coldly.

You may or may not have heard, but I have a title and an

estate in Somerset. Out of love and civility for my wife and family, I cannot recognize you as my legitimate child. However, I should like to support you in any way I can. I have heard of your exploits and your skills in investigation and would like to learn more about your life. Even illegitimate, you are my blood, and I do not wish to ignore you. May I have your permission to write to you?

Upon the loss of Celeste, I feel like my heart is cleaved in two. Broken and sick for the women I loved and lost, and joyful for the girl I've just come to learn exists. I hope you will do me the honor of allowing me to find a place in your life as your father, as I will endeavor to find a place for you in mine.

Lord Hugh Blackwood

P.S. It is not much, but I hope the enclosed amount can act as a start for the many birthdays and holidays I have missed. I have set up an account for you at my bank in London to establish an annual income for your dowry and living, and I took the liberty of arranging a credit account for you at that modiste Celeste likes. I hope when you are in London you will make use of it.

Poppy stared at the banknotes that were primly folded in the envelope, along with the letter. It was more than one hundred pound notes, more than she had ever seen in her life. She gathered up the notes, and the letters, and ran inside the house, almost breathless as she came into the blue sitting room.

"My goodness, Poppy, whatever is the matter? You look like you're about to faint," Aunt Rachel said.

"I..." She swallowed. "My father has written me. He asks leave to write to me."

"Your father?" Uncle Reginald dropped his pipe.

"Yes. Lord Blackwood, of Somerset." She held out his letter and the envelope full of banknotes. "I think I'm an heiress."

The End

Historical Note

The stories of the "bawds" and "girls" in Harris's List were major inspirations for this story, and I relied on Hallie Rubenhold's book, *The Covent Garden Ladies,* for details of the time period, and was inspired by the TV program *Harlots*. The characters of Beatrice Hayes and Tom Harris are inspired by the infamous 18th-century pair Charlotte Hayes and Jack Harris, but I have done little real comparison beyond borrowing their names.

I have also breathed life into a real person: the modiste Mrs. Ann Lanchester, dressmaker and milliner, who designed many fine gowns for members of the *ton*. She is recorded as having a shop at 59 St James Street in 1806. Three years before this novel is set, she produced her own fashionable pamphlet, which only lasted a year in print. She later wrote fashionable samples for a magazine and went bankrupt by 1810. It has been suggested this is largely because her well-dressed customers did not pay their bills.

While the term "poison pen letters" originates from 1913, I am positive the idea of people writing nasty letters to each other predates that. The first nasty note demanding a ransom or a "ransom note" dates from 1874 (if we discount medieval demands for ransom), so while I couldn't use these terms in my novel, they aren't too far off, historically speaking.

On the subject of mistresses, prostitution, and sex work discussed in this novel, in some instances I have painted the men who kept mistresses as sometimes fickle creatures, sometimes saviors who at least in one case helped a starving girl off the streets. I do not condone the keeping of mistresses, nor do I believe in the whole "boys will be boys" mentality as a way to justify adultery. People, regardless of their gender, will cheat on their partners. I think the question is, what do you do if it happens to you? That was where I came up with the character of Ann.

Prostitution has always been a part of society, no matter how disapproved of and disliked. I wondered how it was for women who were of a small subset of that society, who had no other social acquaintances but each other, aside from the people of their sphere that they relied on for survival. What would a mistress's social circle be like? Who would her friends be? Then what if someone started to kill them off, one by one? That was the idea behind this story.

Sources

Primary sources

Cary's book of transportation

Harris's List, 1793. Ex-Classics.com

Secondary sources

Hailee Rubenfeld's *The Covent Garden Ladies*

MAPPING *HARRIS'S LIST OF COVENT-GARDEN LADIES* (1788)

The British Museum, "Mrs. Lanchester"

Acknowledgments

As ever, I am grateful to my family for their constant support, and for showing great interest in the historical sources I found.

I am also grateful to have the constant support of my critique partner Melanie Savransky, encouragement from Rachel Ann Smith, Emily E.K. Murdoch, Melanie Rose Clarke, and my stalwart champions Theresa Green, Sarah Perchikoff, and S.E. Reed, as well as my exceptional editor Amelia and the team at Dragonblade Publishing, in addition to my colleagues at BITC, who regularly make me smile by cheering me on as an author. Thank you.

About the Author

E. L. Johnson writes historical mysteries. A Boston native, she gave up clam chowder and lobster rolls for tea and scones when she moved across the pond to London, where she studied medieval magic at UCL and medieval remedies at Birkbeck College. Now based in Hertfordshire, she is a member of the Hertford Writers' Circle and the founder of the London Seasonal Book Club.

When not writing, Erin spends her days working as a press officer for a royal charity and her evenings as the lead singer of the gothic progressive metal band, Orpheum. She is also an avid Jane Austen fan and has a growing collection of period drama films.

Connect with her on Twitter at twitter.com/ELJohnson888 or on Instagram at instagram.com/ejgoth.